# What People Are Saying About

# Coldwater Revival

Coldwater Revival *introduces a new author, Nancy Jo Jenkins, who writes with a lyrical style that makes my heart sing. Her characters take enough twists and turns to keep the reader totally involved, but make sure you keep a box of tissue handy.*

—LAURAINE SNELLING
AUTHOR OF *SATURDAY MORNING, AMETHYST,*
AND ALL THE RED RIVER NOVELS

*An astonishing debut!* Coldwater Revival *is a hauntingly beautiful story made doubly so by Nancy Jo Jenkins' stunning, lyrical writing. I was mesmerized from cover to cover.*

—DEBORAH RANEY
AUTHOR OF *A NEST OF SPARROWS* AND *A VOW TO CHERISH*

*Nancy Jo Jenkins has stepped into the world of publishing with superbly written ... fiction that ushers you down an unforgettable path strewn with the flowers of forgiveness.*

—DIANN MILLS
AUTHOR OF *WHEN THE LION ROARS*

*With* Coldwater Revival, *Nancy Jo Jenkins joins a small cadre of southern writers who manage to weave a subtly nuanced story with words so evocative that we savor the images long after the story ends. And Jenkins introduces us to flesh-and-blood characters we remember even longer. What a stunning debut novel.*

—WENDY LAWTON
AUTHOR OF *IMPRESSIONS IN CLAY*

D1051241

# Coldwater Revival

A NOVEL

# NANCY JO JENKINS

Good News in Fiction

COOK COMMUNICATIONS MINISTRIES
Colorado Springs, Colorado • Paris, Ontario
KINGSWAY COMMUNICATIONS LTD
Eastbourne, England

RiverOak® is an imprint of
Cook Communications Ministries, Colorado Springs, CO 80918
Cook Communications, Paris, Ontario
Kingsway Communications, Eastbourne, England

Coldwater Revival
© 2006 by Nancy Jo Jenkins

This story is a work of fiction. All characters and events are the product of the author's imagination. Any resemblance to any person, living or dead, is coincidental.

Cover Design: Greg Jackson, Thinkpen Design, llc
Cover Photo: ©2006 BigStockPhoto

First printing, 2006
Printed in the United States of America

3 4 5 6 7 8 9 10 Printing/Year 10 09 08 07 06

Unless otherwise noted, Scripture quotations are taken from the *Holy Bible, New International Version®*. *NIV®*. Copyright © 1973, 1978, 1984 by International Bible Society. Used by permission of Zondervan. All rights reserved.

Library of Congress Cataloging-in-Publication Data

Jenkins, Nancy Jo
  Coldwater revival / Nancy Jo Jenkins.
    p. cm.
  ISBN-13: 978-1-58919-061-0
  ISBN-10: 1-58919-061-0
  I. Title.

PS3610.E545C65 2006
813'.6--dc22
                                                    2005033524

# In Memory of

Mary Wagner Collins,
Mildred and Mac Collins,
Clint Weigl

## Acknowledgments

Tom Weigl, who patiently taught me about the craft of ironworking.

Jeannie Weigl, who shared her knowledge of horses, livestock, and ranching.

Michael Manigold, who enlightened me about hunting, fishing, and the ways of sportsmen.

## Thank You

To my Creator, who dropped Emma Grace's story into my heart and taught me how to write it.

To David, for lifting me up with love, and for never doubting my call to write.

To our children—Lori and Steve, Tamara and Clark, Mike and Melinda, Terri and Kevin, Rene and Cliff, and our wonderful grandchildren—Jordan, Chelsea, Bailey, Madison, Avery, Sheridan, Michael Zachary (MZ), Colton and Justin.

To my sisters—Marilyn, Jeannie and Terry—and their families.

To longtime, and new friends who supported me with prayer: Bob, Bobbie, and Naomi. The Snoopy Dancers—Paddy, Eileen, Kathleen, Ceil, Mona and Diana. Myrtle Coe, Kay Ball, Butch and Karen, Carolyn, Donna and John "Olboot." Brenda Blanchard who was there when I began the journey. Lauraine Snelling who let me sit at her feet and learn. Cindy Woodsmall, for her "vision" and friendship.

To Jeff Dunn—for believing in my story. And to Jon Woodhams, Ingrid Beck, and Phyllis Williams for their "repair" work.

To Steve Laube, my agent, for creative ideas and support.

To the Mount Hermon Christian Writers Conference, for years of inspiration, learning, and lasting friendships.

To my ACFW family, for laughter, sharing, and of course, Brandilyn's theatrics.

To Lyle Blackwood and the Prayer Ministry Team at Hyde Park Baptist Church. Your prayers carried me though.

To Ruth and the library staff, and Billie and Lewis' Sunday school classes.

# Prologue

Some miracles pour down on us like a mighty river. Some fall with the gentleness of raindrops.

To hear my papa tell it, I was the tiniest miracle ever dropped from the heavens. At least from the cloudy firmament hovering over Coldwater, Texas.

Seems my bent toward stubbornness first evidenced itself while I was ripening in the fountainhead of my beginnings, and it persists until this day. Culling out the hottest day of 1915, I arrived two-and-a-half months ahead of schedule, on a day so hot the Devil himself must have been riding the wind. Anyway ... that's what Papa claimed.

"Should've stayed put in your swimming pool," he used to tease. "Been a heck of a lot cooler."

But, of course, I hadn't. My willful foot had reared back and mule-kicked Mama in the stomach, commencing her birthing pains. Thus I was born, smack in the middle of Mr. Oswalt Peavy's dry, dusty cotton patch.

# One

**COLDWATER, TEXAS**
**1933**

Three weeks before I was to marry Gavin O'Donnell, I set my feet upon the beaten path leading to Two-Toe Creek. What I had to offer Gavin in marriage—my whole heart, or just a part—depended on the decision I would make today.

As my feet tracked the dusty pathway they stirred loose soil to the air. My heart stirred as well, for the guilt I had buried in its depths smoldered as though my brother had just died, and not five years earlier. In the shadowed days following the tragedy, my disgrace had glared like a packet of shiny new buttons. I'd not thought to hide it at the time. In truth, I'd thought of little, other than how to survive. But at some point during that time of sorrowful existence, when my days and nights strung together like endless telegraph wires, I dug a trench around my heart and buried my shame.

From that day until this, I deeded myself the actor's role, closing the curtain on my stain of bitter memories, hiding my sorrow behind a veil of pretense. But that old deceiver, Time, had neither softened my guilt nor put it to rest; only allowed it ample pause to fester like deadly gangrene. Now, as the day of my wedding drew near, my heart cried out for healing. It was, you see, far wiser than my head. My heart understood its need for restoration—before I exchanged wedding vows with Gavin. For this reason, I now walked the trail to Two-Toe Creek. To revisit my failures of yesteryear and reclaim the peace that had slipped past the portals of my childhood. Perhaps then I could give Gavin the entirety of my heart.

# Two

The trail to the creek was strewn with autumn clutter and the fragrance of days gone by. I longed to pluck a memory or two from this path of ripe remembrances. Maybe chew on them a while. But then I recalled that life was a sea of tangled memories—both good and bad. Barren was the possibility of unraveling one from the other. And so I prompted my feet down the path, not halting until I reached Two-Toe Creek.

The creek tumbled along at a spirited pace, seeming ever in a hurry to inhabit new quarters. I'd been but a bare-toed sprite, no taller than a stump, the first time the creek crooked a liquid finger and beckoned me to take a closer look at its seamless movement. Despite Elo's warnings, I'd chased after it.

"You pea-brained idiot," my older brother had berated. I can see it still, that fire streaking Elo's eyes. "You only got one good leg. You couldn't swim out if your life depended on it."

Elo's scruffy paw had yanked me from the stream that day, but only because of Papa's hands. They held persuasive sway, and had captured my brother's liveliest respect. Left to himself, Elo would have let the water carry me away.

I swept the memory aside with a smile and turned my feet to a lesser trail, rendered grassless by deer and small game. The footpath ascended a knoll and ended at a slab of granite, sandpapered smooth by centuries of east Texas winds. An ancient oak grew nearby, shading the ledge like a tombstone. I had used the shelf as a stage in years past, spewing legions of homespun tales from its center. After dusting it with my handkerchief, I sat down.

Audiences had been difficult to snare back then, so I entertained the occasional sparrow or springboard cricket that wandered near, though they poked the earth and bounded from sight without once uncorking deaf ears. When Elo, or my younger brother, Nathan, strayed within shouting distance, I recited my stories for them. They never tarried long. While I spouted my heart sentiments across the narrows, Elo hooted and howled like the wild coyote he was. But his rudeness had backfired, for it served only to flex the muscles of my stubborn pride.

I shifted position on the ledge, viewing the sky through chiseled treetops. Gray overcast of an hour ago had given way to a shellacking of sunlight and flocks of portly clouds. As the sun began its descent into western sky, a chill filled the air. Even so, my palms dampened with perspiration. Would this journey into the past heal my heart? I wondered. Or splinter it into a thousand pieces? Uncertainty crowded my mind, yet here I sat, poised on the moment. Did I have the courage to cross over the bridge? To return to the place where grief had cast its first shadow?

*Father, I'm afraid. I don't know if I can go through it again.* I swiped at my tears with shaky fingers. *You said the truth would set me free. Free me from the past, Lord …*

*Trust me, child.*

My heart quickened, for surely I heard the Father's voice; not aloud, for the woods to witness, but deep within where I lacked boldness and strength.

*Lord, heal me … please.*

For a moment, the universe stood still. Then a rush of wind blew past, setting The Wheel of Time in motion. As it drew me to its wake, I gathered my cloak of faith more tightly about my shoulders and prayed for a gentle journey.

*Please, God. Let me see sunshine and sparkles first.*

We sat around the kitchen table—all ten members of the Falin clan—our Irish laughter lifting the ceiling in celebration of my twelfth birthday. As the jubilance wound down, my three older sisters, whom I called The Ollys, cleared dirty dishes from the plank-board table, even as Mama scoured it to death.

"Tell us stories, Papa," Caleb pleaded. Micah—his matching book-end—gave his head a vigorous nod, setting brown curls to bobbing. Rare were the times my five-year-old brothers disagreed on anything.

"Seems like only yesterday I was telling Emma Grace's story," Papa said, his deep voice hiding a smile. "Has it been a year already?"

Pride being a sin, it grieves me to admit the self-importance I felt when Papa told my story. While he packed his pipe, I sat tall in my chair and stretched my troublesome leg a mite straighter. Most likely, even the man in the moon could detect the grin on my face.

Papa cleared his throat, spilling a hush over the room. As the twins permuted into pillars of salt, I caught a whiff of Papa's pipe and shifted my gaze upward. Wobbly smoke rings sputtered near the ceiling, and then thinned to nothingness, clearing a way for Papa's story.

"Twelve years ago, it was," Papa began. "Mama and the little ones were picking cotton in Mr. Peavy's north section while I tramped down a wagonload across the field. When I heard your mama scream, I jumped off the wagon and vaulted those cotton rows like I had ol' Pegasus's wings growing out of my back. You remember the story I told you about the flying horse?" Heads around the table nodded. "'Twas one of my papa's favorite tales. He read it to me on the trip over from Ireland when I was just a lad." Papa turned his gaze on The Ollys, who sat at the table like ducks in a row. Love fairly flowed from his bluebonnet eyes as he studied Holly, seventeen, Molly, sixteen, and Polly, fifteen. "Papa sure liked to read stories to his children." He pointed his finger toward the parlor. "A lot of those books are from his collection."

I grinned and nodded at Papa, proud that Nathan and I had inherited his love of reading.

Papa's cheeks dented as he took a lengthy draw, sparking life into his pipe bowl. "But—back to Emma Grace's story. When I finally got to your mama, she was lying on her cotton sack, but with all the cater-wauling going on, I couldn't hear a word she said. I feared she'd been snakebit or hit with heatstroke."

"Tell the part about me," Elo commanded, proving true Mama's claim that Impatience was my fourteen-year-old brother's middle name.

"Well, Son, you sat atop your mama's skirts, bawling your eyes out. Though how you managed with a fat thumb rooted to your mouth, I'll never know."

We laughed at this familiar part of the story.

As Papa painted word pictures on the parchments of our memories, he pointed his pipe toward his eldest son. "Mama pinned a cord to your overalls so you wouldn't crawl off and find some nasty worms to chew on."

While The Ollys squirmed with squeamishness, I asked, "What happened then?" mostly because I cherished this part of the story.

"My heart almost stopped when your mama told me the baby was coming. I knew it was too early. Way too early. I handed Elo to Holly and sent you all to Mr. Peavy's house for help.

"Ten minutes later little Emma Grace slid into my hands. She was the tiniest thing I'd ever seen. But I couldn't get her to breathe. Tried everything. My big ol' thumb would've crushed her chest if I'd pushed on it, so I just stroked her back like you'd rub a puppy behind the ears. Massaged her little arms and legs … held her close. Wasn't much else I could do but pray. Mama was wailing for Emma Grace, so I cleaned her up with my handkerchief, best I could, delaying the time I had to hand her over. Out of the corner of my eye, I saw her little finger twitch, and then she hiccupped. I tell you, that little gasp she took swelled my heart up like Mr. Johannson's bellows." Papa turned his gaze on Mama, grilling her with a questioning look. "Didn't believe me when I told you our baby was breathing, did you, sweetheart?"

"Of course I believed you. I knew my baby girl would make it."

Eight heads pivoted toward Mama. This was a new twist. Her eyes usually misted over about now, recalling how she had almost lost me.

Papa gave us a broad grin. "Why, sure you did, honey. Sure you did." He shared his conspirator's wink and resumed the story. "I wrapped Emma Grace in my shirt and handed her to Mama. You wouldn't believe how tiny she was ... could hold her in one hand with room to spare." Papa formed his fingers into a tight circle and looked at me. "Your face was no bigger than this, 'bout the size of a silver dollar. Hate to tell you, sweetie, but with your face all scrunched up like that, you looked like a little shriveled-up monkey. 'Course, we thought you were the prettiest thing God ever created.

"Mr. Peavy took us back to our farm in his truck. Your mama cried all the way 'cause she thought every breath would be your last. We lined an old boot box with a blanket, but the second we laid Emma Grace down, she started turning blue. Seems she needed a human heart to keep her own heart ticking, so Mama made a sling and carried our baby next to her heart all day long. I'll tell you one thing," Papa said, zeroing his gaze in on me again, "you kept us on our toes night and day."

"Mama used to let me hold you, Emma Grace, and I was only six years old." Holly tilted her head as she talked, her eyes casting radiance about the room. "I rocked you like a dolly and cried when Mama took you away."

I looked into Holly's startling blue eyes and something scrambled my heart. The Ollys were like second mamas to me, and I loved them with fierceness. But love hadn't hindered me from coveting their corn-silk hair and rare beauty.

"We kept the boot box between us on the bed at night," Papa said. "Took turns keeping a hand on Emma Grace's chest so we'd know if she stopped breathing. Many's the time my hand fell asleep from hanging over the edge of the box." He laughed. "She was too weak to nurse, so we fed her with an eyedropper. Every couple of hours we gave her milk from Mr. Peavy's goats."

"Guess that explains the pack of wool you've got growing out of your scalp," Elo snickered.

Ten-year-old Nathan cleared his throat. My ears perked up, being that I was bright enough to pay attention when the genius of our family rationed out a portion of his knowledge. "Actually," Nathan began, "goat hair is quite distinct from lamb's wool. The wool fat in sheep fleece produces lanolin—"

"We get the picture, professor," Elo interrupted, jostling Nathan in the ribs.

Nathan retaliated with a Herculean jab to Elo's shoulder, grins splitting both lads' faces. Papa stayed the match with one stern look.

"Couldn't afford a doctor," Papa said, "but we got one anyway. Scrounged up some canned goods so ol' Doc Horton would come out. He took one look at Emma Grace and said she'd be gone in a week. Didn't give us a bit of hope or a single idea about caring for such a tiny baby. That roused my anger just a tad. I grabbed him up by the belt loops and shoved him out the door. Told him I'd greet him with a shotgun if he ever showed his ugly face at my house again. Had Holly run some beets and tomatoes out to his buggy. Didn't trust myself to go near the doddering old fool again."

Papa's countenance grew angry in the telling, Irish blood pounding his temples, blotching his face to the redness of our ancestors. We watched like walleyed perch as his ire climbed to the boiling point, and we spoke not a word until it simmered down to fine bubbles. A grin reshaped his features, his chest rumbling a bit as laughter spewed forth like a belching volcano. We joined in. Even Mama had happy tears flowing into the wrinkles on her face.

"Guess I did get a mite carried away," Papa admitted, his countenance reverting from warm red to sandy brown. "Emma Grace's first year was a scary one, let me tell you. She stopped breathing a number of times … flickered and sputtered like a candle in the wind." Papa sent me a long, narrow-eyed look, as though peering into the days of my infancy. "We watched you like hawks, sweetie, but one night I startled awake and saw that you weren't breathing. 'Lord, help us,' I cried. Your mama went to pieces, beating the bed with her fists … near hysterical. Didn't know if it would do any good, but I told her to share some of her breath with you."

"I stood in the doorway and saw Mama crying and kissing Emma Grace good-bye." Softness feathered Holly's voice as she spoke. "I ran to the bed and begged Papa not to let my dolly go away. Mama shushed me, said she wasn't telling Emma Grace good-bye, she was helping her find her breath."

Papa's voice softened to a whisper. "I pushed on Emmy's chest, trying to jump-start her heart, but she just laid there like a stillborn calf … her lips as blue as Nathan's eyes. Didn't move so much as an eyelash. I thought she was … gone. But I couldn't let her go. Just couldn't. Loved her too much."

It seemed like a quagmire sucked Papa's words right out his throat and swallowed them whole. Elo and I exchanged glances as Papa dragged a handkerchief across his eyes. Like a finely wound clock, Papa had welled up right on schedule.

He blew his nose into his handkerchief and said, "It felt like an hour passed before I had any hope Emma Grace would make it. Finally, one little eyelid fluttered, soft as a moth's wing. Then she opened her mouth and sucked in a breath, letting out the weakest, most pitiful cry we'd ever heard. It sounded like angels singing to Mama and me. We grabbed up Holly and danced around, laughing and thanking God for our miracle. Didn't sleep a wink the rest of the night." Papa beamed a steady look on Molly and Polly. "You two beauties slept through the whole thing. As did Elo."

All gazes converged on my being then, once-overs inspecting my face, my bramble-brown hair, the shirtwaist Mama had stitched from store-bought fabric. I squirmed in my chair as the twins darted glances at the quilted cusp of my crutch, lying against the table. Being the center of attention was a thing I often sought with unflinching immodesty. But seeing the perplexed looks on my family's faces now, as though questioning why God had bothered with so ordinary a child, was another matter, indeed. Perhaps, like me, they simply were in awe of the miracle our family received on that extraordinary night, almost twelve years earlier.

# *Three*

"Well, I'll be. Says here that ash wood is real light, but strong and springy, too." Papa shoved the advertisement under Mama's nose. "I'm gonna write this Minnesota company tonight and order a box load."

"But, sweetheart, do we have enough money?"

"I don't care how much it costs. If I have to—I'll sell the mule. Emma Grace is gonna have the best crutch her papa can whittle out."

"Oh, Roan, you know we don't own a mule."

Of course, I wasn't there to hear this conversation firsthand, but learned of it through a story bantered about our house. The tale pricked my attention and stilled my busyness the first time it rolled over my ears. With a bum leg like mine, I'd often wondered how I'd become such a gadabout at the early age of fourteen months.

From the mind's eyes of my childhood, I recalled a tiny wooden crutch—one of many Papa carved in my growing-up years. When I parted company with crawling and attempted to walk at twelve months of age, my leg—which appeared normal in every way but length—toppled me over every time I took a step. After declaring I needed a "second leg," Papa squirreled away the necessary coinage, ordered a box load of wood, and whittled a crutch to fit my runt-sized body. Mama padded the arm basin with soft cotton and bound my arm and leg to the crutch with cloth strips. As the story goes, from that point on the wee colleen with a less-than-perfect leg scooted about the house like the queen of pixie land.

Nathan, born two years after me, busied Mama's days, so when I turned three, she charged Elo to keep a good eye on me. Overnight, I became his least favorite person in the world. He blamed me for stifling his wicked boyhood adventures and fled my outstretched arms with the swiftest of feet. But I followed in scampish pursuit, extending leg and crutch over logs, rocks, and varmint holes. His usual path of evasion led to the woods, where he bonked the noggins of jackrabbits and squirrels with his slingshot. His aim held true, even while I clumped about the woods and chattered like a magpie. Between his steady hand and my wagging tongue, we scattered the wild critters on our farm from hither to yon.

By the time I was five, Elo had accepted our twosome. Our choicest adventures occurred at Two-Toe Creek, a beauty of rushing water that traipsed the south edge of our property. After picking summer days away in Mr. Peavy's cotton fields, Elo headed for water. I was never far behind. We held no secrets between us, Elo and I, as we stripped to our underwear and dived into hollowed-out water holes along the creek bed. After weeks of flailing and thrashing, in poor imitation of Elo's powerful strokes, a wondrous thing happened: I learned to swim. I must have painted a frantic picture, lurching after my brother, struggling to match him stroke for stroke. But all that lurching and struggling prompted a second miracle of the season: Muscles in my stunted leg strengthened and grew.

During the next two years, Elo and I swam, fished, hunted, and scoured the woods for hidden treasures. Cold weather found us with overalls rolled to our knees, our feet tiptoeing over stone pathways washed smooth by eons of rushing water. While tiny waterfalls tickled our toes and wrinkled our skin like old turtle leather, we flitted about the stream like sprites in a water fairyland, our feet as sure-footed as the deer that sipped from its depths.

"Quiet!" Papa said in hushed voice. "I know you're excited, but you've got to calm down. Mama needs her rest."

His red-rimmed eyes settled a gaze on The Ollys. "Watch the little ones while Elo and I do the chores. Polly, why don't you cook up some of that vegetable soup Mama likes?"

By "little ones," I knew Papa was referring to me, as Nathan never required looking after. His blond head, forever snuggled in a book or angled over a writing tablet, seemed incapable of thinking up ways to displease Mama and Papa. Though our parentage was identical, Nathan and I were as disparate from one another as pigs and woolly worms. My seven-year-old head was more akin to the daring young man on the flying trapeze. Willful thoughts soared through its density with the greatest of ease. Or perhaps I just lacked ordinary sense.

As Papa and Elo made their way to the barn, The Ollys flicked a glance in my direction, then headed for the kitchen. They whispered secrets, most likely about Flynn Aarsgard, the latest boy to fall under Holly's enchanting spells.

Had it been but an hour ago I heard that first mystical sound—the tandem wailing of babes sucking in the breath of life? The wails had shifted to bleating cries of hungry lambs, the crescendo heightening when Papa opened the door and rejoined his surplus flock. He gathered us near, inspecting us with good-shepherd eyes as he warned us of the behavior he expected at the first viewing of the new lambs. Springy fingers and shuffling feet garnered his shushing twice more before he led us into the birthing room. My heart soared as we crowded the bed, snatching peeks at our little brothers. But all too soon Papa ushered us from the room. Now my fingers twitched with the need to hold the newest members of the Falin clan.

I tiptoed to the door of Mama's bedroom, bracing myself for the dressing-down I was sure to receive from The Ollys. But they were distracted, their chitchat buzzing the air like hungry mosquitoes. Turning the doorknob with cautious hands, I padded into Mama's presence on gentle feet. When her eyelids shot open, I withdrew a step, thinking to be shooed from the room. She reached out a hand, consigning it to the handle of my crutch.

"Hi, sweet-pea. Come up here and take a look at your brothers. They're quite a sight."

I flew to Papa's side of the bed, casting my crutch aside as I scrambled to the twins, tucked in close to Mama. My brothers looked like duplicate dolls. Mama must have oiled their shiny curls that coiled up like corkscrews all over their heads. As I studied my brothers, I decided they were a pair of scrappers. Why else would their fingers be curled into tight little fighting fists?

"This is Micah, firstborn. And this is Caleb. What do you think, punkin?"

What did I think? That my heart might flutter away like a butterfly on wing. As I stroked brown curls, the same color as my own, my fingers shook like windy-day leaves.

"They look just alike, Mama. How can you tell them apart?"

"Well, if you look real close, you'll see a birthmark behind Caleb's right knee. Papa and I examined them from head to toe and that's the only difference we found."

"Can I hold them, Mama?"

"Soon, sweetheart. But for now let's let them sleep. I'm kind of sleepy too."

"If I'm real quiet, can I stay? I won't wake them up."

"Honey, they're your babies too. Of course you can stay."

Mama's eyelids closed and I knew she slept. My chest lifted with the scent of newborn babes. My skin prickled with love and excitement. I tried to slow my runaway heart, but it hammered along as though a rabid dog gave chase. *The babies are mine—Mama said so.* As my heart bobbled and skipped about, it delved into a new world of promises, devotion, and overwhelming love for my baby brothers. Somehow, in their first hour of life, they'd managed to reach out, grab a great chunk of my heart, and claim it as their own.

As I lay beside them on the bed, my gaze lifted to the high, yellowed ceiling. The weight of many timbers had cracked the plaster, and now it forked and branched-off like the river of veins in Granny Falin's hands. That set me to worrying. Would Granny come visiting, sparing Mama a bit of the workload? A stay from Granny suited me fine, so long as she confined her busyness to cooking and helping Mama clean. But she needn't worry herself over the twins. That was my job.

Lazy quietness settled over the darkening room, flour-sack curtains blotting late afternoon sun. I yawned and slid my gaze back to the babes. Wild heartbeats hoisted my chest as I vowed to fight for my brothers as Mama and Papa had fought for me. How else would they survive? I leaned in close and whispered secret promises to my babes: I would be the best sister in the world; I would protect them from harm; I would keep them safe. Before I slipped off to the Land of Nod that afternoon, I checked and rechecked the twins, convincing myself they were healthy and strong. *Surely, I won't have to fight so hard to keep my brothers alive. Not like Mama and Papa had to fight for me.*

At the time, I didn't understand the swarm of restless thoughts and fears that circled my head that day. Many years passed before I understood the truth: 'Twas God's hand that reached down and touched me on that late afternoon—preparing me for what was to come.

# Four

After the twins' births, I scheduled my creek excursions around their naptimes and feedings, though I continued to shadow Elo's trail whenever the babes weren't in need of my mothering care. The parcel of adoration I heaped upon Micah and Caleb must have relieved Elo greatly since it often kept me from stubbing my toes on his heels.

There arose in me a possessive nature of which Mama and Papa felt the need to address. Seems I didn't tolerate gawking neighbors and church busybodies as well as I should. How could I not defend the babes with my crutch, when necessary, from visitors who swooped down, grabbing and fondling my brothers in ways I thought careless?

I recalled the afternoon of Mrs. Fenster's visit. She and Mama sat at the kitchen table while I lurked in the hallway. Mrs. Fenster clasped Caleb to her overgrown bosom, the gleam in her eyes of particular grievance to me. As she cooed and pounded on Caleb's back, he strained for release. She held him with force, it seemed, and he wanted down. He wanted me. Mrs. Fenster's possessive nature and greedy behavior churned my insides into a boiling frenzy. Before I knew what I was about, I stomped into the kitchen and snatched Caleb from her monstrous paws.

"It's past time for you to go home and feed your family," I blurted in a stern voice, surprising myself, and from the look on Mama's face, surprising her, as well. I gripped the corner of the table, having not yet mastered a steady stance while clutching a babe. My crutch spread wide, stretching me to a near split. I would have toppled both Caleb and myself to the floor had Mama not jerked him from my grasp. My bottom smacked the floor, but not one bit harder than my heart pounded in my chest.

"Emma Grace Falin," Mama sputtered, her face darkening like the skin of a threatened chameleon. "You apologize to Mrs. Fenster this instant!"

Oh, the glare Mama hurled my way! I looked up at Mrs. Fenster's walruslike face, with its sprinkling of chin whiskers, but couldn't dredge up an apology I wouldn't have to later confess as a lie. Mrs. Fenster's cheeks puffed in and out like sheets on the line as she squirmed in her chair and heaved coffee-scented breath to the floor. I sat wide-legged and wild-eyed until, with great suddenness for a woman of her girth, Mrs. Fenster bent over and scooped me onto her pillow-soft lap.

"I know just how you feel, Emma Grace," she said, roaring with laughter. "I didn't want anyone holding my babies, either. You just keep on watching over them, little princess. These angels are fortunate that you love 'em as you do."

She beamed down at me, her grasp leakproof, but reassuring. As the eyes behind her spectacles misted over, her greedy nature upped and disappeared. I hurried a smile back to her, which she accepted with another head-locking embrace.

When Papa was present at such visitations, he hauled me to his lap and tightened his grip if I sought post near the twins' crib. Or when I approached a visitor with murder in my eyes.

On the night of Mrs. Fenster's visit, Nathan and I sat at the kitchen table, wolfing down cold biscuits. It remains a mystery how my bottom tolerated such an unyielding stool after the three hard wallops it received from Mama's untiring hand. But there I sat, my backside warm and stinging as I jabbered to Nathan about the babes. I spoke as though he hadn't the wherewithal to notice the twins' uniqueness.

"Micah's the quiet one," I said, happily assigning myself the teacher's role while biscuit crumbs rained from my mouth. "He's the follower." Knowing my brothers as well as I knew the names of the seven dwarfs, I continued blissfully on. "Micah's heart is as tender as a steamed turnip. But Caleb … well, he's the leader of the twosome. Micah will tag behind Caleb like I run after Elo."

"Yeah. Well … together they're a perpetual motion machine," Nathan said. With a jerk of his wrist, he wrenched a biscuit in two, flooding both halves with pear-blossom honey.

I returned his grin as though I knew what he was talking about.

As is the way with coincidences, a few weeks after my twelfth birthday our family received startling good news—on the exact day I survived my first, and only, lesson in chewing tobacco.

After swiping a wad of tobacco from Papa's pouch, Elo hauled himself to the creek, stationed his slimness behind a curtain of trees, and packed his cheeks full. Before he dived into deep water, I begged him to share with me, but he refused. Being the stubborn Irish girl I was, I snitched a handful from his pants pocket while he splashed fish from the depths.

What wafted sweet and aromatic from Papa's pipe proved no such thing once I champed down on it. My mouth filled with wretched vileness that lurched in my stomach, forcing me to gulp down the putrid mess. Sickness hit, spinning my head, roiling my insides as though I had turned cartwheels in the air. I lay on the creek bank, clutching my belly and blubbering for Mama like a two-year-old.

"Told you to leave it be."

I rolled a watery gaze upward, viewing Lord Elo through a haze of nausea. To this hour, I stand amazed at how Elo maintained that awful sneer while laughing his dunderpated head off.

"I'm sick, Elo. Take me home. I need Mama."

"You crazy? Papa would string me up to a sycamore if he found out you'd been chewing tobaccy."

"I won't tell. Promise!"

The brother I adored laughed and dive-bombed into the creek. I prayed he would drown in his own spittle on the way down. As I lay there dying, I thought about The Ollys, wishing I had hound-dogged them instead of Elo. Perhaps I'd have turned out prim and proper-like, instead of the brier-bush ragamuffin I was.

The sickness lasted past noon.

To make up for his nastiness, Elo shared his secluded spot on the Brazos River with me, though Papa had warned me against swimming the river. Too unpredictable, he'd cautioned. After following Elo through a mile or more of sticky-fingered thicket, we spied the river. I reconciled myself to this truth: Before eventide, Mama would have me sitting with a needle and thread, mending all the damage done by those black-hearted thorns in the bushes.

A tall cypress slouched over the water, its gigantic roots rising from the muddy banks like prehistoric claws. After Elo secured a rope to the loftiest branch, we swung ourselves into high arcs and plummeted into the rolling river for hours.

In late afternoon we dragged ourselves out of the water. If I looked half the mess Elo did, I was in a heap of trouble. I examined my sorry condition, knowing Mama would soon do the same with her twenty-twenty eyesight. My eyes felt as though they'd been used as pincushions, and the other parts of me, those I could view through puffy, slatted lids, appeared to have been hurled down the rocky side of a cliff.

Hands on her hips. That's how Mama greeted us when we tried to sneak into the house later that afternoon. Before my bare toes touched cool linoleum, Mama had commenced with the third degree.

"Where in the world have you been, Emma Grace? You look like a grizzly's been chewing on you." Relief danced in her soft brown eyes and a hint of smile played on her lips, but gathered brows let me know her scolding held meaning. Though used to my wanderings, she maintained a high fear that something evil would someday overtake me.

Mama threw her arm across my shoulder, tucking me in close. "Honey, you're a young lady now. It's time you start behaving like one. Just look at your hair!"

"Told you that brillo pad was a dead giveaway," Elo said with a snort.

"Which was it, Emma Grace—the stock tank or the river? Must've been the river. You've got twigs and leafstalks sticking out all over your head."

Since both were forbidden swimming holes, and I couldn't conjure up an excuse, I plastered a hangdog look on my face and said not a word.

"It's time for a haircut, young lady," Mama said as she stuffed straggly curls behind my ears. I recognized her stalling tactic. Punishment would come, but not until she could ponder a bit over what it would be.

"This is the thickest head of hair God ever created. I can't believe he graced one of my children with it."

I had heard all this before. When Mama felt badly about the short-change I received in the leg department, she heaped that bit of praise on me. The compliment didn't sit true. Tuning her out, I detoured my thoughts to The Ollys' pale-gold, satin-smooth hair. My tumbleweed hair had proved a bother to me, nothing more. Though I'd inspected it in the mirror a hundred times, I'd not once identified the lambent luster of which Mama spoke. It had certainly not attracted the boys' admiration at school. Their interest lay in pulling it by the roots, not ogling it as they did Olly hair. A hankering to snip golden tresses had me scanning the cabinet for Mama's scissors.

As Mama tweaked sprigs and offshoots from my hair, Papa's wide shoulders burst through the back door, his stature crowding the kitchen.

"Gather round ... got some exciting news."

Exulting in my temporary reprieve, I scuttled off to gather The Ollys. With Mama's elephantlike memory, I knew my obstinate feet would soon reconnect with the path of discipline. Mama seemed compelled by some unspoken maternal law to see that I walked the straight and narrow.

I sat on the kitchen floor with Micah in my lap and Caleb tucked beneath my arm. The Ollys sat at the table, looking wide-eyed and expectant. A furrow riddled Nathan's brow as he stood beside Papa, but Elo appeared unfazed as he slouched himself in a chair and stretched his gangly legs halfway across the floor. Mama stood at the sink with a worried look in her eyes.

"You remember that ol' Clive Huggins—Mr. Peavy's foreman— died a few weeks back?" Papa asked his brood. We nodded our heads. "Well, Mr. Peavy has asked me to be his new foreman ... that is, for the cotton season. He knows I've got this farm to run and have no interest in a permanent position. He wants me to oversee his next year's cotton production from planting to harvesting. If I accept, we'll move to the foreman's house and live there from March through September. Somehow, we'll keep this place going too."

"Oh, sweetheart, won't the load be too much? Tending our farm and managing the workers at Mr. Peavy's place?"

"I'm not saying it'll be easy, but I can manage for a few months."

My gaze rode the family. Thoughts of living in a larger, grander house sounded alluring—tantalizing. How did the others feel? The Ollys twittered and squawked like a gaggle of geese while Mama stood open mouthed, looking a bit shaken. Nathan cleared his throat. He spoke infrequently, but when he talked, we listened.

"It'd require some adjustments, Papa, and a timetable to keep the farm operating at peak efficiency. I'd be happy to work up a schedule for you."

Papa clasped his big hand over Nathan's shoulder. "That'd be most helpful, Son, most helpful."

Nathan's smile flashed bright as he dashed off to fetch his tablet. Mama collapsed on a nearby chair. Papa lowered his weight to the one beside her and spoke with quiet persuasiveness.

"We'll get a hefty salary those six months, and with Elo and Nathan already doing grown-man labor, they could keep this place going while I work Peavy's fields. We'll be able to pay our taxes, buy supplies, and put something aside so Nathan can go to college someday. Heck, we could even buy you and the girls something new to wear. What do you say, honey?"

Mama swiped dewdrops from her eyes. "I won't give up my garden, Roan. You know I've got to work my garden."

"You will, Henri, you will."

I felt the furious blinking of my eyelids. For a moment, I'd forgotten that Mama's given name was Henrietta Annaleen. Papa never called Mama by her first name, which proved the seriousness of their conversation now. With a label like Henrietta, 'twas no surprise that Papa reserved sweet endearments for our mama. And no surprise that Mama had assigned soft, lyrical names to her children.

From that point on, our thoughts centered on springtime and the welcome upheaval soon to alter our lives. As giddy excitement replaced the humdrum motion of my life, I packed our future full of rose petals and set my daydreams adrift on the high pinnacles of prosperity. I assumed my family did the same.

But now, as I gazed back in time, I wondered how we had overlooked the dark bank of clouds that had poised nearby—right over the horizon of our tomorrows.

# Five

After Papa accepted Mr. Peavy's offer, we abode winter on the farm, dreaming of the hour we'd relocate to the foreman's house. Mama alone dragged her feet at the prospect of leaving.

I recalled the day we left our home, having not the slightest suspicion that our lives were about to change forever. When winter had bid its final adieu, we packed the wagon and loaded our belongings to the hilt. Spring hovered at the gateway, prodding tiny buds into yawning blossoms, and gentle breezes kissed our faces as we plodded down the road to new beginnings. How were we to know that the indulgent gusts ruffling our hair that day would evolve into howling gales of pitch-black sorrow?

As we traversed the rutted artery leading to Mr. Peavy's property, Mama glanced back at the old homestead—more than once. Years later, she confided that vacating her birthplace, even for a few months, had been a heart-wrenching decision she hoped never to make again. While the wagon jostled us like dice in the hands of a desperate gambler, I clenched a firm stare on Mama. My instincts shouted she might "jump ship" and swim back to port any minute.

We were a ragged sight, our bounty spiking the air like a gigantic pile of pickup sticks. As Lily and Old Jack strained the harness and snorted crisp March air, I sat atop our worldly possessions, my mind fastened on the future and grand adventures waiting ahead. As I rode in my high carriage of creaking springs and groaning sideboards, I felt like a princess who was about to enter her kingdom.

Through the discord of clanking metal, shambling hooves, and rattling sideboards, I heard the gentle whisper of spring's arrival. I saw it in the swooping dive of a blue jay, and in the trackless winds that stirred field grasses to life. I smelled its arrival in the wild honeysuckle that grew beside the road, and in a host of other scents that anointed this newborn season.

"Doesn't the breeze feel good, Mama?" Polly Pauline asked as she smoothed her skirt with dainty fingers.

Mama glanced at trees rooted along the roadside; branches of elms and weeping willows spiked with tightfisted buds.

"Yes, dear, but don't get too used to them. Remember—March comes in like a lamb, but it goes out like a lion."

As our wagon wheels trundled over the outlying portion of Mr. Oswalt Peavy's grand estate, I watched a slow-turning windmill siphon water from the earth and deposit it in a trestle-supported tank. Cattle loitered nearby, prospecting for food, young calves abiding in the shadows of their mothers.

At midmorning, Lily and Old Jack pulled to a halt in the drive of our new home. As Papa hauled me down from my roost in the furniture tree, I set my gaze upon the two-story house with the alfalfa-green roof. It appeared recently painted and had more windows on the front side than our old weather-beaten house had altogether. With shivers telegraphing up my arms, I leaned against my crutch and sighed with anticipation. I could hardly wait to explore the house.

We unloaded the wagon, much to the horses' delight, I'm sure, and padded through the front door in stocking feet. Mama's orders. As we entered light, airy rooms, whose floors were burnished to a high sheen, it felt as though we were crossing the portals of a glass castle.

In typical gauche fashion, Elo whistled through his teeth. "If this ain't the cat's meeooww."

"Boys," Papa said to Elo and Nathan, "heft your beds up to the loft. You and the twins will be sleeping up there. I'll get things settled down here. Micah and Caleb, come help your papa."

"We'll stock the pantry and kitchen first," Mama said, motioning for The Ollys and me to follow. "Then we'll tackle the root cellar." Mama viewed the kitchen range with what looked like suspicion. She groaned and chewed on her lip, as was her habit back then. "How in heaven's name will I ever learn to cook on a gas stove?"

"Don't worry, sweetheart. You could fry our food in boar grease and pack it with swamp mud and this bunch would still eat it," Papa said. He laughed and tucked a box beneath each arm, banking his head, grazing Mama's cheek with his lips. I supposed the boxes curtailed further smooching, for he turned and walked to the hallway, speaking over his shoulder. "It's for sure the boys and I won't miss having to fill the wood box for a while."

After stocking the kitchen and cellar, Mama and The Ollys unpacked our belongings, hanging clothes in real closets, not on hooks. They made beds, stored linens, and dusted furniture Papa and the boys had situated about the house.

While Papa worked in the barn, sorting implements and storing saddles, harnesses, and feed, Elo secured Old Jack and Lily in the corral and released our milk cow, Rumple, and her calf, Itsy Bitsy, to the pasture. Nathan and I made sandwiches and poured glasses of milk for everyone.

"Caleb and Micah! Quit flipping those light switches," I scolded. "You're going to wear them out." I hated fussing at the boys about something I would love to be doing, the wonders of electricity being truly fascinating.

On-off, off-on, the light switches traveled. Screwing my face into what I hoped was a feral glare, I marched to the twins and perched my head inches from their bright eyes. "I told you not to turn the lights on and off. Papa's gonna get you good."

The twins peered into the depths of my eyes, Caleb gauging the gravity of my warning. He glanced at Micah and passed him a silent message, then outdoors they scampered, seeking a new road of mischief to travel.

Though I knew of the existence of the mysterious, mute language the twins shared, I had not yet glimpsed its interpretation. Inaudible signals coursed the air, linking the twins' eyes in a sharing of thoughts.

This uncanny communication, almost mystical in nature, kept me hopping all the time.

I sank to the window seat in the bay area of the kitchen, restlessness spurring my heart until I spied my brothers dangling from a tire swing in the front yard. *Emma Grace,* I warned myself, *you can't let them out of your sight for a minute.*

A feeling of estrangement crept across the first evening in our new home. In place of soft lantern glow, overhead fixtures reflected brightness off paperless walls, revealing the plight of our condition. "Worthwhile weariness," Mama had called it. Having brought order to our domicile in a single day, we were too dog-tired to prepare a hearty supper. We filled our stomachs with cold potato soup, cold cuts, and cold biscuits. Afterward, we gathered in the fancy parlor, our furniture appearing rough-hewn when compared to the polished floor and high-beamed ceiling. I feared to blink an eyelash, lest the magical scene disappear before my eyes and I awaken in my bed at home.

"What're you ladies sewing on?" Papa asked. "Making some fancy pillowcases for Widow Lindstrom?" He stilled his hands on the whittling stick and set a gaze on Mama and The Ollys. Had not a mischievous grin twitched his sandy-gray mustache, one might have trusted his sincerity.

"Now, Roan …" Mama began.

"I heard she's having an awful time of it. Down to threadbare sheets—linens you could poke your fingers through."

"And from whom, *exactly*, did you hear that?"

"Well … I'm thinking it was Henry Lee. Yep, her nephew Henry Lee told me how bad off she was. Poor thing can't tell a doorknob from a cucumber. Take care when you hand over all that fine stitchery. The excitement might up and kill her."

Being well acquainted with Papa's teasing, The Ollys spewed batches of giggles at his outrageousness.

"Don't pay him a bit of mind, girls. He knows quite well what we're working on—and *why*."

Seems the ladies in our household were intent on stocking Holly

Heleen's hope chest, but Papa wasn't about to let them work without a little grievance. Mama penciled trailing designs on a flour sack, her flair for curlicues and wispy vines taking shape before our eyes. Less-gifted ladies in the community had shown signs of envy from time to time, drooling over sackcloth Mama had turned into flower gardens. Not quite on the scale of Jesus turning water into wine, but a miracle just the same—especially to inept stitchers like myself. Mama wasn't stingy with her talent. She'd passed it on to her oldest daughters.

Flynn Aarsgard had courted Holly for most of a year. In six weeks, when she turned eighteen, we anticipated he would propose to her.

I liked Flynn. He never gawked at my leg, and I never laughed at his Norwegian accent.

I glanced at Nathan, buried in a book at the kitchen table, and then I cringed when I heard the twins in a rear bedroom, flipping light switches.

"Micah and Caleb … in here, right now," Papa roared.

Within seconds, two moppy heads popped around the parlor entrance, followed more slowly by the rest of their bodies.

"Yes, Papa?" they said in unison.

"What did I tell you about the light switches?"

The twins lowered their heads and ambled to separate corners of the parlor. Facing the wall, they sat crossed-legged, backs to the room.

My heart went out to them, though I dared not say a word. I knew exactly how they felt. In my days of hard-fought discipline, hadn't I passed an inordinate amount of time sitting thusly? After a time, I raised my gaze above the pages of the book I pretended to read. Papa seemed quite pleased with the boys' repentant behavior, but I wasn't fooled for a minute. Papa didn't recognize the secret code racing from one twin's fingers to the other twin's lowered eyes. Nor did he realize their head hanging stemmed from remorseless scheming, not regret. I smiled behind my book, wishing I'd had a co-conspirator during my corner-sitting days.

Perhaps it was because they were childless, or because Micah's and Caleb's allure proved too compelling to resist. Whatever the cause,

Mr. and Mrs. Peavy took to the twins something awful, their affectionate doting on my brothers more dominant than that of blood kin. Mrs. Peavy invited them to her house daily; bribing them with bubblegum, store-bought toys, and peppermint sticks. She asked Mama if they could spend the night, to which Mama explained they were too young for such outings. Mr. Peavy told them stories. Perching one of the boys atop his knee, he wrapped his arm around the other, reciting tales that captured their imaginations and rendered them spellbound. The boys gawked openly, eyes widening like a cellar door in a windstorm whenever Mr. Peavy's bushy eyebrows rose up like the tufted horns of a great owl.

This kidnapping of my brothers by the Peavys left me frustrated and angry, for I possessed no ransom worthy of securing their release.

Mr. Peavy gave the boys a puppy, a furry ball of indistinct pedigree. We all fell under the puppy's spell, but none harder than Micah and Caleb. They named him Whisper. I thought the name ironic since the twins never spoke below a shout. Whisper followed my brothers everywhere, and they followed Whisper everywhere.

The puppy played with the boys, slept with the boys—even tried to eat with the boys. Micah and Caleb loved the puppy with every bit of their beings. At the time, I didn't know that their strong attachment to Whisper would change the course of our lives for all time.

# Six

"Molly Marie Falin, quit spying on those two lovebirds and come cut the cakes." Mama's voice droned low as she tugged Molly from the parlor window.

My gaze darted from my book to Mama. Cakes? Quick as a doe, I followed Molly's heels to the kitchen, feeling my eyelids widen at the tribute set forth on our table. While I'd been tumbling with the twins at the creek this afternoon, Mama's hands had not been idle. Apple strudel, cinnamon coffeecake, sweet potato and buttermilk pies, peach cobbler, and a chocolate layer cake filled our fanciest serving dishes. I couldn't remember a time when Mama had baked with such abundance, though I wonder now why her exuberance had stunned me so that night. It was, after all, a most notable occasion—Holly Heleen's eighteenth birthday. Before the evening ended, I believed Mama and Papa's firstborn would have another, even more hallowed rite of passage to celebrate.

As I returned to the parlor, I envisioned the front-porch scene. Within the stirring of nocturnal breezes, but out of range of the night bird's call, Holly and Flynn would be sitting on the swing, heads together in whispered secrets. No doubt, their breaths interlocked with vows of eternal love. Love not measured in mere days and years … but in forever. Holly and Flynn would be holding hands in the moon's full glow, their promises signaling a beginning with no end. An unbroken circle in the curve of time, like the ring Holly would soon wear. As my fanciful mind conjured up romantic pictures that titillated my senses and sped the beat of my heart, my eyes filled with moisture. I'd been fighting back tears the entire day.

Papa smoked his pipe and Elo scanned the newspaper, both looking uncomfortably rigid in their starched shirts. Polly thumbed the Sears catalog, the toe of her slipper compelling the rocker back and forth. She had spruced herself up, wearing her Sunday-best bodice and the flowered skirt that flowed in a multitude of tiers. Even I had donned a dress for the affair.

Earlier in the evening, as I had studied my reflection in Mama's freestanding mirror, I considered marked changes in my almost thirteen-year-old body. It had sprouted in places, extended in others, narrowing my face and middle. Even my gimpy leg seemed to be feeling the effects of the growth spurt Mama claimed had overtaken me.

A few weeks earlier, I used Mama's tape measure to mark the breach between my right and left legs. The difference: a trifling inch-and-a-half. Thus began my feverish pleas for God to narrow the gap even more. Not allowing my excitement to take center stage, I continued putting on airs for the family, as though a waltz around the house on one good leg and a crutch suited me fine. Nevertheless, my heart held the hope that someday my leg would grow to its rightful length. Oh, to run across a meadow, free of crutch; slide into home plate; attract the attention of whisker-sprouting young men who worked the fields.

Though I had packed my heart with love for Mama and Papa, I wearied at the thought of living my entire life with them. Discontent filled my soul, knowing there'd be no handsome stranger to sweep me off my feet. No one to plunge head over heels for me as Flynn had fallen for Holly. Who would want to marry a three-legged lass when pretty girls were in such abundance?

When I was in Holly's presence, the joyous expressions on my countenance seemed artificially valiant, for her elation reminded me of my own impossible dreams. At the oddest moments, murky playscapes wiggled to the forefront of my mind, granting me glimpses of secret places I had yet to visit. They whispered tales about the true nature of romantic love, filling my head with puzzling questions. I felt defenseless to parry the emptiness they left behind, when, invariably, they faded from view.

I sat beside Nathan on the settee and waited with the rest of the family for Holly and Flynn to vacate their love nest. I lowered my voice, choosing Nathan alone to witness the lonely outburst of my heart. I dared not speak of romance, or lack thereof, as I felt certain that romance remained as great a mystery to Nathan as it did to me.

"It's like I've got this vacuum in my heart that needs filling, Nathan. I can tell the hurt isn't going away anytime soon." A whisper of irritation rose in my voice as I talked, along with a scrapping of tears.

Nathan scooted a few inches away, granting me more space on the love seat. Or, perhaps he sought distance between himself and the gloomy cloud perched over my head.

"It won't be the same without Holly here," I drawled on. Nathan gave me his skeptical look, the one suggesting I'd been reading too many tragic tales.

Now a foot taller than I, having shot up like Jack's beanstalk these past months, Nathan peered down at me over the rim of his spectacles. Using his pointer finger, he shoved his glasses a bit higher on his nose.

"You know, Sis, it's only 6.3 miles to the Aarsgard place. Old Jack could get you there in … one hour and twenty-three minutes."

"I know," I sputtered, somewhere between a sob and giggle. Nathan's seriousness always unmuzzled a case of the sniggers in me. "Guess I'm just feeling a little blue tonight." Then a true batch of melancholy hit me between the eyes. "First Holly will leave, then it'll be Molly, then Polly. I'm afraid every time one of The Ollys leaves, they'll take a piece of my heart with them."

Nathan's eyebrows closed rank. I knew the gears of his rapier-sharp mind were grinding away in search of comfort words.

We heard the creak of the porch swing and watched with unconfined interest as Holly and Flynn entered the house, ill-disguised blushes firing their cheeks. Holly unfurled her left hand, displaying a small stone of exquisite beauty, embedded in gold.

"Holly … it's lovely," Mama stammered. "Just … beautiful."

Falin clutches entangled the couple, squeals and laughter flying unfettered about the room. The twins, however, fled grasping arms and cheek kisses as though the family had contracted a deadly disease.

"Hey, Flynn, old boy—pretty shrewd—getting engaged on Holly's birthday. That way you just had to buy one gift. Right?" Elo smirked as he shook Flynn's hand, but his eyes gleamed with what looked like the stamp of approval.

The April night hummed with laughter and claps on the back. Soon we perceived the sound of the Aarsgard wagon, winding its way up our drive. We rushed outdoors in greeting as Aarsgard offspring spilled onto yard and porch. As our family welcomed family-to-be, I was torn between wanting to discuss wedding plans with the adults and the desire to linger a while longer in the realm of my childhood. After a moment's deliberation, I scampered off to the barn, joining those oblivious to the ways of love.

On June 30, 1928, the belfry chimes of Christ's Chapel pealed across the township of Coldwater, announcing Holly's marriage to Flynn Aarsgard. From high noon until one o'clock, a chime tolled every sixty seconds, symbolizing the townspeople's wish for sixty years of wedded bliss. Such was the tradition of our small community.

Two weeks after Holly's wedding, my thirteenth birthday arrived, at the peak time of cotton season we called, "working from can-see to can't."

Like popcorn in Mama's kettle, seedpods burst open, each boll releasing five locks of pure-white cotton. Overnight, Mr. Peavy's green fields turned as white as the snow-capped mountains I'd viewed in Papa's periodicals. To maintain high market value, Mr. Peavy harvested his cotton crop with haste, prompting a flood of pickers into his over-ripe fields. 'Twas a season in which we talked, breathed, and lived cotton.

Images of my family during cotton season remained engraved on my mind. They never changed.

At twilight, the twins and I habitually gathered at the kitchen window, making a game out of who could spy the family first. I thought of Papa and his brood as a troop of weary cotton soldiers, trudging home at dusk after a long day's battle with the hot Texas sun. While the family made their way across washboard fields of ebony loam, I reheated supper and poured tall glasses of cool milk. And while my family tended swollen fingers, lacerated by razor-sharp cotton tines, I tamped down my guilt, for I was the sole adult in our family who didn't sweat out each summer in Mr. Peavy's cotton furnace.

# Seven

Papa always kept his family entertained and informed, seldom reining in his witticisms or teasing tongue when we were in audience. The twins had learned to prick up their ears and listen well when Papa read stories to us.

But Papa made a grave mistake the night he shared the story of Robert Peary's daring 1909 expedition to the North Pole. As he narrated the true tale about Peary's trek across the frozen tundra, we could almost feel the ice between our toes. This adventure, above all others, tickled the twins' insatiable curiosity. Question upon question popped from their mouths at the story's end. They were fascinated by blizzards, boreal winds, and—because they'd never seen, felt, or tasted it—snow. The questions continued to erupt like faithful geysers, though the well of Papa's patience had already dried up. When he refused to answer another question, the twins turned on me. Like the blizzards in Papa's story, they bombarded me with queries about the mystery called *snow*. For a week or more I answered every bubbling question they spit at me.

"What does snow taste like, Emma Grace?"

"Where does it come from?"

"Mama said that when the angels cry, it rains. Does it snow when the Devil goes to bawling?"

"Why don't it snow in Coldwater, Sis?"

"Tell me about them bluzzards, Emma Grace."

"Have you ever seen snow, Emma Grace?"

Having seen snow at age six, I drew pictures for them: sketches of a snowman wearing Mama's frayed hat; snowflakes, falling from the sky like raindrops. I penciled in snow blankets on rooftops and stick figures in a snowball fight. I assured the twins that if they waited long enough, they were sure to see snow in Coldwater ... someday. Someday wasn't soon enough for my stouthearted brothers. They persevered, pounding me with a profusion of questions that left dents in my hide.

The idea struck me on a hot August afternoon. I believed it came to me out of desperation, as the twins had driven me to near madness with their bottomless bucket of snow questions. I grabbed their grubby little hands and dragged them to Mama's cedar closet. Digging through the trunk of winter clothes, I retrieved mittens, scarves, hats, and jackets.

The boys and I soon crossed over the bridge, entering the land of pretense with thumping hearts and feet rooted to the pathway of perilous adventure. Micah and Caleb had few tokens of courage and valor to their credit, so they were anxious to join my expedition to the cold north. It wasn't far—just a few steps inside the door to our imaginations.

"Ooooh, that bored wind is mighty cold, Emma Grace. Think we'll make it to the North Pole, or d'ya think we're gonna freeze to death on this ithberg?"

I pinched my lips together, biting back a giggle at Caleb's playacting. He was quite the performer, pretending to be cold when our outdoor thermometer read 103 degrees. Sweat rolled down his face and neck, dampening the earflaps and brim of his wool cap.

Micah pulled his jacket closed and rubbed his arms with vigor. His body shook with a tremendous shudder. "My ears are plumb frozed off, Emma Grace. Don't think I can take 'nother step on this frozen 'tandruff." Micah wagged his head as though filled with great disappointment and regret. "Think we ough'ta turn back? That sky don't look good, a'tall."

I glanced at the bright cloudless sky and turned a grin on my brother. Caleb stepped close to Micah, his right hand grasping his brother's shoulder as a comrade might. "We're not turning back, Micah. Brave s'plorers don't give up and they don't turn back, even if they get kill't."

We walked past the horse corral, our trek to the North Pole having taken us but a few yards from the back door of our house. Caleb stopped and studied the barn. He ran into its interior, returning moments later with Papa's pickax. The ax was almost as long as Caleb was tall. He tried to heft it to his shoulder, but ended up dragging it by the handle.

"We'll need this to break through the ice," he said. His stern demeanor reminded me of Pastor Emery's face when he stormily reminded his congregation about our multitudinous iniquities.

Inwardly, I groaned, for I knew I'd be carting the heavy pickax home at the end of our outing. Sometimes my ideas—deemed as inspired and ingenious at the time—ended up tottering on the realm of insanity.

We trudged closer to the North Pole, that magical, invisible place where all of earth's longitudinal lines meet together at a single point. The wool jacket I wore scratched my neck and arms. Sweat pooled in my armpits, behind my knees, and in the hollows of my collarbone. It slid into my belly button and down my back. I wished to throw my coat, hat, and mittens into the burning bin, but I couldn't, for the boys were true explorers now, bravely fighting the elements and any polar bears that might try to eat us. They spoke in the lowered, deepened voices of men on a mission as we staggered on, battling boreal winds, storms, blizzards, and snowdrifts up to our knees. How valiantly they surged forth, fearless of frostbite and subzero temperatures. We plunged on in our quest to reach the North Pole, and felt we had accomplished the task when, at last, we reached the ridge overlooking Mr. Peavy's farthermost field.

The twins turned their beet-red faces downward and gazed at the white world below us. Cotton covered the land—white ruling the world as it had in the time of Robert Peary's expedition. As our gazes soaked in the blinding whiteness, for a brief moment in time hot Texas cotton became cold arctic snow. It was a winter of cotton.

"We did it, men!" I shouted. "We reached the North Pole, and just in the nick of time. See that black cloud, way over there on the horizon? It's heading this way, and it looks like trouble."

The boys' gazes followed my extended finger. A single white cloud appeared in the distant sky. Though tiny and far away, it sufficiently fueled the twins' excitement.

"We'd better ... uh, what's that word, Emma Grace?"

"Stake our claim."

"Oh, yeah. We'd better stake our claim right now, 'fore that bluzzard hits us," Micah said. He withdrew a swatch of cloth and a small stick from his pocket.

Caleb glanced at Micah and nodded. Micah smoothed the scrap of cloth—his American flag—and together my brothers raced down the ridge.

I stayed my position at the top, watching with wonder as Caleb lifted the pickax with wobbly arms. I cringed as he rammed it into the first row of cotton. I sighed with relief when Micah jabbed his flagpole into the hole and planted the flag of the United States of America into a winter world of snow.

Micah and Caleb stood like little tin soldiers, straight and tall as they looked across the glacial field they had just conquered. In their mystical, unspoken way, they raised right arms at the exact same moment, saluting the starchless flag that hung limply in the breezeless afternoon. Then they turned as one and marched up the ridge. We linked arms—we, the conquering heroes—honorable patriots of our country. We, the hot, weary wanderers who were more than ready to shuck our winter uniforms.

"Men," I proclaimed in the manliest voice I could muster, "you've vanquished the wilderness and triumphed over the elements. You completed your mission despite dangerous storms, boreal winds, and record-breaking snowfalls. Now it's time for you to go home and tell the world about your victory."

"Don't forget about them cold, cold bluzzards we had to fight off, Emma Grace," Micah reminded me.

Off the twins ran; peeling outer garments as though the cloth crawled with vermin. I stooped and retrieved discarded articles, lest Mama give me a good skinning when I got back to the house. Then I hefted the weighty pickax to my shoulder and followed my brothers home.

# Eight

Tragedy struck our family at the end of cotton season, when the ground lay cracked and parched beneath a ruthless sun and the few remaining pickers worked an entire day to fill a single sack.

Mama and the older boys left early that morning to work the crops on our farm. Molly and Polly would be toiling alongside Papa today, yanking the last scruffy bolls from the stiff, withered stems of Mr. Peavy's cotton plants.

The morn began as any other: purple light dancing on the horizon, the sky aquiver with lavender hues. I recalled thinking that those first streaks of daylight were truly beautiful. I watched as the dawn swapped shades, blushing to peach as stars paled in the sky and the night skittered away. At the time, I had no way of knowing that the glorious dawn would end in the most sorrowful twilight of my life.

I scrunched kinks from my back and gazed through the bedroom window, my thoughts sailing across the fields to where my family waited for daylight and another day of picking cotton. My mind idled in laziness for a time, until I remembered the chores Mama had ordained for my day. It seemed another Falin would also be hard at work this day. Because of the long hours Mama spent at the home place, or in Mr. Peavy's fields, most of her chores had fallen upon me. I'm uncertain when it happened, but at some point in that interminable cotton season, I came upon a fine appreciation for my mama.

I lay in bed, running a mental finger down my work list. *Sort the dirty clothes; set them soaking in tubs of cold water. Drain the water and sprinkle soap powder over clothes in late afternoon. Peel and chop vegetables. Cube and brown the meat; set it to stewing. Mix a triple batch of cornbread. Cover it with oilcloth to prevent drying. Wash dishes, clean the house, feed the animals, and corral the twins. Or did the list say to feed the twins and corral the animals?* I shoved the entire roster to the flip side of my brain, desiring only to lie abed like a princess. For a few moments, I forgot all responsibilities required of me this day.

"What'cha got for breakfast, Emma Grace?" Micah floundered down the stairs, briefs riding helter-skelter on his narrow hips as his fist rubbed sleep from his eyes.

I giggled at his early morning presentation. A thatch of light brown curls jutted from his scalp, as tangled and disheveled as Whisper's furry pelt. I leaned over, wrapping my arms around him.

"Mornin', precious. Where's Caleb?"

"Comin'," Caleb called, his voice thick with sleep-hoarseness.

Caleb cuddled Whisper in his arms and stepped into my morning hug. Both smelled of puppy. Hard-pressed to distinguish Whisper-fur from Caleb's mane, I stroked all hair in sight.

"You two—go wash up and slip on some overalls while I dish up your oatmeal. Have you visited the bathroom yet?"

"Don't Whisper haf'ta wash up too?" Micah asked. The flow of love from his eyes to the puppy was palpable. I felt my heart swell as it absorbed a bit of love's power.

"Guess it wouldn't hurt to run a cloth over his face," I said, hiding my smile between pursed lips. "Don't forget to take him outside to pee."

"Why can't he pee in the …" Caleb's whiney tone was predictable. 'Twas the one he used to wear me down. I straight-eyed him and slipped into the no-nonsense voice of my mama.

"We've been over this before, Caleb." I bent my elbow, placing a fist against my left hip, as Mama was prone to do. "Take him outside like I said. That's why God made such a big outdoors. So all the animals would have a place to do their business."

The boys dressed and stomped to the front door, their bare feet pounding the hardwood floors like yoked oxen.

I turned the gas jet low and stirred the oatmeal, scraping glutinous bits from the bottom of the pan. As my thoughts drifted to the book on my bedside table, I wondered if I'd have an opportunity to read today.

In late afternoon, I studied Mama's overlong list, checking completed chores with a stubbed-off pencil. As I recited my accomplishments aloud to Micah and Caleb, they yanked on my pants legs as though they were bell ropes at Christ's Chapel.

"Hold on, you two. Let's see now, stew's in the warming bin. Three pans of cornbread ready to bake. I've laid the table, tidied the house."

"We wanna play som'more hide-and-seek," Caleb demanded, jerking on the legs of my overalls in singsong with his words.

"No more hide-and-seek today. And you can bet I'll be keeping a hard eye on you two—stowing away in the root cellar like that when you knew it was off-limits. 'Bout scared me to death. Best you abide by the rules if you want me to bake any more sugar cookies...." My voice trailed off, the boys having forsaken my company. As my nagging drifted to the far side of nowhere, I grabbed my book and followed the twins outdoors.

The boys and Whisper ran free. But for the lack of war paint, they looked like a couple of want-to-be braves, running and hollering as though they were part of a raiding party. I propped my crutch against a pecan tree and plopped to the grassy slope, my fingers a' twirl as they parted the pages of *Gulliver's Travels*. A duel of sorts interrupted my reading, the boys' impish squeals contending with Whisper's sharp, persistent barks. As they tossed sticks for the puppy to fetch, their high jingling laughter proved heady to my ears. They ran without care, their brown curls jouncing the air as they leapfrogged the tall grasses. A familiar wave of love unfurled in my chest as I watched them scamper about. Sometimes even my eyes ached with love for Caleb and Micah.

Engraved on my heart was this picture of the twins at play in the high-grass field. Other visions were there as well. Visions I feared to call to the light. I found no pleasure in them at all, for they hung about my heart like an albatross; a harbinger preceding a brewing storm. For five years, I had separated my memories, knowing some held the power to toss me back into the pit of despair I had but narrowly escaped. Now I had no choice. I had to let my memories play out, for they were a barricade on the timeline of my life, and I could straddle them no more. Fear slapped a padlock around my chest, trapping my breath as I stretched to retrieve my most dreaded memory: the hour I had so miserably failed my little brothers.

I heard the high, keening wail, but held no thought that it seeped from the recesses of my heart. 'Twas not until I felt the flow of tears that I realized the keening was my own. It lifted to the highest branches, stirring treetops on my behalf. It swayed the evergreen pavilion over my head with a crush of mournful waves. The trees alone knew I could not face the swell. Just as I knew it was not yet in me to set my memories free.

I bolted from the granite ledge and stumbled down the slope, sinking my knees into damp creek sand. My gut-wrenching wails erupted upon the solitude of dusk, startling tree birds into a squawking frenzy. As my tears splattered into Two-Toe Creek, I prayed my pain would wash away, as well. The wailing quieted after a time, leaving dried tears and salt tracks that pinched my face. I leaned forward, splashing icy water onto my overheated cheeks. Then I sat on the sand.

I wondered about my resolve to visit the past, questioning if the trip was necessary, after all. Why did I have to face my demons? Couldn't I exist as before? I had grown used to the baggage of guilt I carted around, and life *had* been somewhat peaceful, hadn't it? My head ached with questions for which there were no answers. The truth was that I had known but half-a-heart's pleasure since the day of the tragedy.

Truth and I tangled in a battle of wills that afternoon. In the end, I won the fight, for I had not the courage to nudge my memories from their womb of shame. They had been sheathed against the world far too long for me to take comfort in the parting.

Turning my back on all I had dreamed of accomplishing, I rose from the sand and walked down the path that led home. I'd come within a hair's breadth of reliving the horror of five years past. I shook with the thought. *You're not ready yet,* my heart cried. *You're not ready to go through it again.*

The woods quieted. Subtle were the sounds that accompanied twilight's descent: birds twittering in the roosts above my head; the age-old hum of creek chatter. Exhausted, and depleted of anything resembling stoutheartedness, I walked away, postponing my date with grief until another day.

A stronger day.

# Nine

I arrived home from the creek in time to help Mama prepare supper. The boys seemed not to notice my stagnant listlessness, but Mama's keenness detected it at once.

"Do you feel all right?" she asked. "Are you tired, Emma Grace? Is something worrying you, sweetie?"

I mumbled answers, most insufficient, I'm sure, as they failed to soothe the worrisome look from Mama's face.

I helped her clean the kitchen, and then I hurried to the bathroom. After filling the tub with hot water, I washed myself from head to toe, cleansing away everything but the cowardice in my soul. Trying to put the afternoon behind me, I thought about the dress I would slip on in a few minutes. Holly's wedding dress. Mama would hem the skirt to proper length and alter the dress to fit my shape; just one more item to check off the final list of wedding preparations.

But later, as I stood on Papa's footstool, turning a slow circle while Mama tucked and pinned the white cotton skirt, I knew I had pushed the cart before the horse. Again. Seemed the bad habit had been showing up a lot lately. Shouldn't I have ventured into the past and dealt with my guilt before completing my wedding plans?

As Gavin and I strolled hand in hand down familiar pathways near my home, I lifted my gaze and studied his face. His was a striking face; finely chiseled features cutting a strong, masculine silhouette against the moon-lit sky. Darkness lent its own measure of mystery to the man I would call husband. A bit of panic sashayed across my heart when he swept me into his arms, his embrace more fervent than tender. I knew a moment of dread, as though a stranger had purchased my affection, leaving me no choice in the matter. The thought knotted my heart. As quivers shot up my spine—the kind not born of romantic notions, but of fear—I blamed my irrational reaction on jumbled nerves, and on my afternoon of emotional upheaval. Still, I wondered if my fear centered on today's failure at the creek. Or was my heart speaking to me of other matters, entirely?

"What's wrong, sweetling? You're trembling."

I stretched on tiptoes and met Gavin's gaze, steadying my voice to prove him wrong about the trembling. "I was just wondering why your dancing feet stopped when they did. Traveling all the way from Ireland, but choosing to halt right here at me."

"Why, Emma Grace Falin. 'Tis fishing fer a compliment. That's what ye're up to."

Gavin's quick grin drew a breath from my chest. His smile had always affected me so.

"No, not really. Just considering the facts. You know that half the girls in Coldwater are in love with you. When you walk by, their eyes go all mopey and their tongues hang out like a passel of starving puppies. I've seen the way you look back at them, Gavin. Don't deny it."

Gavin laughed his rascal laugh; the laugh that could entice Finnian's rainbow to drop its pot of gold at his feet.

"'Tis a man I am, lovey. Ye'd not be wanting me blind now, would ye? Of course I notice the pretty lasses, but 'tis you who owns me heart. No one else, darlin' girl."

I detested the feeling of unrest in my heart. The feeling that something wasn't right between Gavin and me. I decided that my unease had more to do with unfinished creek business than a problem with our relationship. Most likely.

"I tried on the wedding dress tonight."

"You mean … *your* wedding dress?"

The look on Gavin's face gave me pause. I felt my cheeks burn beneath his keen glare. I stammered out an explanation. "Well, of course it's mine. I just meant that Mama hemmed Holly's dress to fit me. It was perfect for Molly and Polly, but I'm a lot shorter, and—"

"And 'tis nicely packaged ye are, little one." His lips met mine in another firm joining, his body sheathing me like an overgrown vine. "Emma Grace … Emma Grace. Do ye feel how me heart's near to bursting from wanting ye? I'm needing yer love, sweet girl. The love a woman has for her man. 'Tis all I can think about. Are ye feeling it too?"

Though my head bobbed "yes" against Gavin's broad chest, my heart shook its head "no." A cloud of foreboding rolled over my soul. I had almost convinced myself that failure to face my past was the reason for my apprehension. Now, as I swayed in Gavin's embrace, I wondered if it were true. I loved him as I had never hoped to love a man. But was I deeply in love with Gavin, or with the thought of being married? When he and my cousin Robert Falin first arrived from Ireland, I believed God had sent Gavin to be my husband. Now I wasn't sure. A wave of heartsickness pressed my ribs, lolling my uncertainty first one way, then the other.

"Jesus, bless this food we're about to eat. Amen."

The brevity of Papa's prayer spoke more of the lateness of the hour than his relationship to the Almighty.

Sunday lunches at our house were habitually tardy, due to Pastor Emery's long-windedness and the extra care Mama took in preparing the Sabbath feast. Today the plank-board table groaned beneath the plates of twelve hungry adults who packed its borders. At a smaller table, situated behind Mama's chair, were Holly's three-year-old son, Kade, his sister, eighteen-month-old Karen, and Josey, Molly's two-year-old daughter. They squirmed, giggled, and banged the midget-size table with pewter spoons that had been pocked and dented by past generations of Falins. With all Mama had to do, she still insisted on having her grandbabies within arm's reach. Her selfless attention to the children provided Holly and Polly the rare blessing of an uninterrupted meal.

My motive was not so selfless. As I sat at the table, dwarfed by Elo on my left and Gavin on my right, I luxuriated in maternal fulfillment. Baby Abigail, Molly's seven-week-old daughter, lay stomach-down across my knees. Her diminutive body and light brown curls quickened my pulse, for they called to memory a picture I held dear: Micah and Caleb when they were tiny babes.

Elo seemed unusually quiet today, but the same could not be said for our cousin Robert or my fiancé, Gavin O'Donnell. I only half-listened to Robert's tale concerning Gavin's decision to cross the sea.

"... And the young ladies, though ye'd never guess they were twins, followed this poor fellow aroun' like himself was the Pied Piper. Everywhere Gavin turned, one or the other would be tossin' her pretty head, or lifting her skirt a wee bit so's he could take a peek."

The conversation had a familiar ring. Strange. Hadn't I been speaking to Gavin about his beguiling charm, just three days prior? The magnetism with which he had snagged the female population of Coldwater and held it spellbound? My hand stilled on Abby's back as I glanced up at Gavin's face. *Is the whole world crammed full of lasses just pining to be in your arms?* Gavin's face held no answer to my silent question; just the Devil's own roguish smile. No doubt, the same smile that had enticed the girls from Ireland in the first place. I made one of Elo's snorting sounds, which drew a puckered squint to Gavin's face. Then his grin broadened. Evidently, it pleasured him to be the center of attention, for he turned a slow gaze on his audience of eleven, one eye twitching into a mischievous wink as it paused on Mama and The Ollys. What a flirt!

"Well, anyways, he must've feared the law'd be after himself, or something, 'cause he ups and orders me to purchase our tickets to America two months ahead of schedule. Sure enough, here he comes, running to me house in the wee hours o' a morning, telling me to pack me things and meet him at the wharf in Limerick in two days' time."

As I waited for Robert's garrulous tale to wind down, I prayed I'd hear at least one redeeming factor to prove Gavin's virtue true.

Robert lifted his chin and laughed at the ceiling. I studied the faces of my family, perceiving looks of astonishment on the women's countenances, a variety of expressions splattering the men's: concern, disbelief, disgust, anticipation. Caleb's mouth turned up in a naughty grin. At eleven years of age, he rode the edge of adulthood, while basking in the shade of childhood. Anything implying impishness or disobedience snagged his attention like a widemouthed bass clamping down on a night crawler.

"What'd you do? Get some girl in trouble, then run away like the yellow-bellied polecat you are?"

I almost dropped Baby Abby to the floor when Elo's growl shot past my ear, scorching the air with the stench of hostility.

Time slowed, actions occurring simultaneously as I looked on in bewilderment. Papa ripped the napkin from his shirt collar and slammed his fist to the table. Elo and Gavin rose in parallel motion, teeth and fists clenched as their chairs pummeled the floor behind them. I heard a piti-ful squeal fly out of Mama's mouth, right before she pressed fingertips to stop its advance. My body instinctively curled around Abby, trying to protect her from blows I thought were coming.

"Say what ye mean, boy-o, lest ye want me to sever that fat head from yer shoulders." The voice of a sinister stranger rang across the room; Gavin's laughing eyes now deadlier than a viper's. Pulses of fire flamed his face, while the maze of blood vessels in his neck burgeoned like thick purple ropes.

I surmised that Elo chose not to fight in front of Mama and Papa, because he did two things I had not witnessed before: He turned from his enemy, and he left a half-full plate of food on the table. Neither action spoke of Elo, the fearless brother I had adored and parroted since childhood. I knew it wasn't cowardice that compelled him from the room.

Without thought for Molly, I lifted Abby to my shoulder and cov-ered her with the blanket on my lap. She and I followed the path to the barn Elo had taken. I knew he would be waiting there, should Gavin choose to end the duel. I suspected Molly would march her body out the door any minute, demanding I return her baby to its rightful place next to her heart. But Molly didn't appear, and neither did Gavin.

Elo stood where he invariably stood, outside the stall that housed his most prized possession: Samson, a sleek, piebald stallion. Elo stroked Samson between the eyes, tracing the snowy blaze inscribed on his face.

I stared at the two of them, the horse that had cost Elo two hard summers of picking cotton, and the man who loved him. Elo squirreled away his affection like King Midas hoarded gold, but he lavished it abundantly upon the horse in the stable; the white horse whose hide appeared to have been splashed with a bucket of black paint.

I loved Samson too.

Elo turned his back on me. I knew he needed time. Enough time to shut off the valve that was about to blow a gasket under his collar.

"Elo? Why'd you say those hurtful things to Gavin? Don't you like him? I thought you liked …" Tears sprang to my eyes. I swiped them away with the corner of Abby's baby blanket. Elo didn't abide tears well.

He turned to me, lids narrowed to slits. As he spoke, his mouth jerked as though palsied with a tic. "What do you know about this so-called *man* you're about to marry? Huh? Oh, I know he collects females like they hadn't the worth of a copper penny, but what else do you know about him?"

"Elo …" I whispered his name for lack of a better reply.

"I'll be answering fer meself, Emma Grace."

I swung around and faced Gavin. He leaned nonchalantly against a barn post, his stance belying the vials of wrath mottling his face to angry red. As he spoke, his piercing eyes stayed fixed on Elo.

I stepped back, removing Abby and myself from a path the two snorting bulls would take, should either one charge.

"What's this all about, Elo?" I despised the way my body cringed, as though I wanted to know; yet feared hearing my brother's answer.

"He don't know what the word *respect* means when it comes to a lady, that's what!" Elo roared.

Gavin straightened from his slouch and set a slow stalk toward Elo. A lion on the attack. During the past weeks, I'd witnessed Gavin packing his cotton sack twice over while other men ran out of steam before filling a single bag. His strength had come with him from Ireland, where he'd done a man's work since his days in primary school. Workman muscles knotted his arms now, an unruly power barely contained beneath the faded seams of his chambray shirt. A hurricane whipped up in his eyes, tainting their blueness to stormy gray. As he prowled closer to Elo, I squelched his advance with a hysterical screech that would have put a witch to shame.

"Stop it, you two. Stop it this instant!" Baby Abby whimpered and writhed in my arms, readying herself for a full-blown yowl. "Now, see what you've done, you two dimwits? You woke Abby." Knowing 'twas my own shrillness that had roused Abby from her baby dreams, I ceased my shrieking. I patted her tiny body with powder-soft strokes until she quieted and snuggled into my neck as though I were her mama. "Please, Elo," I whispered. "Just tell me what you're talking about."

Elo glared at Gavin, his mouth clamped as tightly as the lid on Mama's pressure cooker.

Whiffs of barn air wormed their way into my nostrils. Though saturated with danger, the pleasurable rankness of musty hay and horse droppings calmed my nerves. Stillness settled between the two men I loved, not a twitch disturbing the raised hair on their arms. Elo's anger remained a mystery to me. But, because Gavin's behavior lay in the path of my brother's displeasure, I had to seek it out.

I heard Gavin emit a soft chuckle. I whipped my head in his direction. How dared he laugh, as though the victor, while my heart shuddered with the dread of truth.

"I'm thinking I know what's got yer brother's tail in a twist," Gavin half-laughed, half-spoke. "'Twas because he saw his sweet Coralee and meself passing the time of day together over at Kerner's Drugs."

Elo jerked his fist to the air and took a step toward Gavin. Gavin thrust his shoulders forward, his smile abandoned for a lip-curling snarl.

I glanced at Elo, not previously aware of his affection for Coldwater's most beautiful maiden. That is, if the contest didn't include The Ollys.

"Elo, are you and Coralee seeing each other … I mean, are you sweet on her?" If my voice sounded incredulous, it was because of the absurdity that rich, snooty Coralee Kerner would have anything to do with a poor farmer like Elo, handsome though he was.

While I waited for Elo's answer, the two men glared holes into each other, their bodies coiled and ready to spring into action. Ruggedly handsome they were, with their blond hair and blue eyes that could stir a woman's heart to palpitations. Elo's height held no advantage over Gavin, and Gavin's strength, mighty though it was, could do no more than equal that of my brother's. Who would be the victor in this senseless war? I wondered.

With a suddenness that shocked me, Gavin retracted his claws and slumped into a friendly, buddylike posture. His grin reappeared, melting the anger from his face, altering his expression from foe to ally.

"Listen, man. I know where ye're coming from. Tell ye what. Why don't I put in a good word fer ye … speak to the lass about the feelings ye have for her? You know—sort o' build ye up a bit. What'a ye say?"

"I ain't no Cyrano de Bergerac, and Coralee ain't no Roxanne. I don't need no dumb foreigner speaking on my behalf." Elo's words expelled from his mouth in a roar that made Abby jump in my arms again. With feverous rocking motion, I held her close to my heart and soothed her back to sleep. I needed the comfort of her in my arms. She felt right in a world gone awry.

My mind couldn't believe what I'd just heard. All the years Papa read stories to us, Elo hadn't paid the least attention, or so I'd thought at the time. Too involved, he'd been; rubbing beeswax into a catcher's mitt, honing a frog gig to piercing deadliness, burnishing his rifle until it glistened like fire-spitting sparklers. Not once had he asked a question, or quirked a brow to advise us that he'd heard what Papa said. But my brother had been listening! He'd heard the story of Cyrano de Bergerac and his beloved Roxanne. My heart thumped with pride for Elo.

"I've not had the pleasure of making this Cyrano fellow's acquaintance," Gavin said on a grin. "And, as far as the lass Roxanne is concerned, 'tis God's truth I've never laid a hand on her. But the offer stands. I'm thinking Coralee might sweeten up to ye a bit if I was to—"

"If I ever … *EVER* … hear your filthy mouth speak Coralee's name again, there'll not be enough left of your body for Emma Grace to marry. Do you understand what I'm saying, *Boy-O?*"

It seemed as though the sun proceeded through its daytime courses before I saw Gavin nod his head, almost imperceptibly. He clenched and unclenched fists that, I'm quite sure, itched to take a crack at Elo's jaw. He kept them glued to his side as he turned his dazzling eyes in my direction, sharing a sliver of rascal smile with me. I nodded at Gavin before turning away on the pretext of tending Abby's needs. I knew the truce had cost Gavin dearly. Like Elo, he wasn't one to back down from a fight.

# Ten

The single light bulb above our kitchen table cast vague shadows over Gavin's features. I thought it a somber pall, fitting the occasion. I rose from my chair and lowered the window above the sink, paring off all but a small draft of October air. Soft breezes ducked beneath the window, stirring Mama's gingham curtains to life, and raising chills along my forearms. I sensed that not all my goose bumps related to the weather.

I reseated myself at the table, across from Gavin, and with reluctance lifted my gaze to his face. His eyes held a pleading presence with which I felt most uncomfortable. Had I coveted power and control, the look on his face would have been one to relish. But I desired neither. I simply wanted to hear Gavin speak the truth.

The house droned with quietness. Mama and Papa had retired with the chickens, and rightly so, since they rose with them also. A beam of light shone beneath Nathan's bedroom door, his attention fastened on a math formula book, I presumed, or another of equal interest. Where Elo and Caleb were I couldn't say. Probably puffing Elo's pipe out beyond the trees, their bodies catapulting moon shadows across the ground. Caleb's words would be stinging the air by now, but

Elo's thoughts would remain stockpiled in his heart. Stockpiled or not, I knew they'd eventually circle back to the lovely Coralee.

"Ye've got to believe me, sweetling."

Gavin's voice fell like softly plodding raindrops, hauntingly clear, yet filled with unfamiliar angst. Like the supplications of a raw, green, wet-behind-the-ears youth.

"When I set sail for America, I left no Irish lass behind carryin' me babe in her belly."

*Yes … but was it because of your Irish luck or because of your abstinence?*

"Yer cousin gets carried away sometimes, adding sparks to his tales till they're so far-flung he knows no one will believe them. 'Tis his way of grabbing for the attention. In me homeland we call it the blarney.

"There were two sisters, 'tis true. And they were twins. That much is fact. Somehow, the girls got it in their heads that I'd be making a fine husband. So they started fighting over me. But, outside of enjoying the fuss and the flattery, I never encouraged them—not them or their fanciful dreams."

"And what about Coralee?" I recognized the same stab of jealousy that had pierced Elo earlier today. Though mine was more of a prick, it hurt just the same.

"That bit of English snobbery? She don't begin to compare to you, Emma Grace. Ye're more beautiful by ten, and yer softness … yer tender heart … she don't know what that's all about, little one."

The tears in Gavin's eyes rattled my concentration, alien as they were to his handsome features. They tracked ruddy cheeks, drawing my gaze to the mouth that had first claimed my lips for its own. Now I asked myself the question: *Had Gavin's heart claimed ownership of another, before me?*

"How many women have you loved, Gavin?" Pride pinched my breath as I awaited his answer. The long moment held a lonely feeling.

"I've loved others, sweet darlin'. But I've never been *in* love with anyone … until you."

I sat without moving, as tight-lipped and stubborn as Elo. I would not allow Gavin to draw from his reservoir of blarney just to quench my thirst for soothing answers.

*If I put a torch to your vows, Gavin, would they burn with the truth, or blow away like ashes in the wind?*

Shifting my gaze, I stared at the pegboard hanging on the wall above Gavin's chair. Papa's sweat-rimmed hat hung from the first peg, along with a wire-mesh flyswatter, curled and frayed at the ends. Mama's flowered apron hitched the middle peg, and Elo's railroad cap draped the last. Elo loved that pinstriped cap. He had yanked it from the brakeman's head one foggy night when the poor man leaned out the caboose to swing his signal lantern. A reminiscent smile curled my lips, Elo's naughty antics a perpetual remedy for the blues. Returning my gaze to Gavin, I sought an end to the turmoil in my heart.

My breath caught when I peered into his eyes. Openness and honesty had replaced earlier tears, mirroring the exact traits I'd longed to witness in his eyes. My lips parted, setting free the clutch of air I'd been hoarding in my throat. Gavin had to have detected its noisy departure, for he squared his shoulders and stared a blue hole into the depths of my being. Since the near fight between Elo and Gavin earlier today, I'd yearned for Gavin's honesty. Now I needed more than honesty to assuage my hurt. I needed promises fulfilled. Gavin's words meant nothing if they'd been declared countless times, to countless others.

I recalled Gavin's vows to me. Like a record on the phonograph player, I played them over and over in my mind. Played them until they settled into the grooves of my confusion and disillusionment. Played them until they stroked the furrows in my heart and eroded my fears to nothingness.

"America's a new beginning fer me, Emma Grace. One look at you, and I knew me heart had found its home. I want to marry ye, sweetheart. Have a dozen kids, and—"

"And, Ireland?" I interrupted on a whisper. "Are you thinking of going back to Ireland? Taking me and the twelve kids with you?" I smiled, letting Gavin know my soul had survived. I'd not send him packing, after all.

A long, slow breath stole from Gavin's chest. His shoulders relaxed, as did the tension in his jaw. Had I not been sitting across from him the entire evening, I would have thought he had imbibed a calming tonic. Gradually, his countenance reverted to its old flirtatiousness, a rascal grin broadening his face like Rumple's pregnant belly. Shaking my head, I prayed I'd never again have cause to question Gavin's honor.

Despite my resolve to trust Gavin implicitly, I slept fitfully that night. Nightmares taunted my sleep. While my body lay bound to the mattress by the weight of a single blanket, my inner being roamed territorial waters of the past and beyond to the future. I startled awake from each dream, damp with perspiration. The future called to me, asking me to verify that Gavin was my one true love: the man with whom I wanted to spend the rest of my life. The past called upon me, also, reminding me I had unfinished business within its borders. Reminding me that a future overwhelmed by yesterday's sorrows was no future at all.

The most disturbing dream was about me. I floated in water more vast than river or lake. The water eddied, sucking me under. I fought to stay afloat, quaffing air, spitting wetness back into the swelling sea. Peering beyond a ruffle of whitecaps, I caught sight of a man on the beach, nebulously screened between two sand dunes. A benevolent man it seemed. I lost sight of him when my attention turned to raucous laughter on shore. A pack of barefooted revelers tracked the sand, the leader aiming her derisive laughter at me like a deadly sword. Her hideous shrieks rose above the ocean's roar, bruising my heart. Before she faded from sight, I gained clear sight of her hate-filled face. 'Twas Coralee Kerner—large with child.

I awoke in the predawn, erratic heartbeats thrumming my eardrums, wisps of damp hair clinging to my face. The sound of silence filled our old wooden farmhouse, or so I thought until I detected Caleb's adenoidal wheezes rattling through a bedroom door. Nathan must be sleeping the sleep of Rip Van Winkle, I determined, or he would have already flipped Caleb like a pancake: stomach-down, staunching his snores.

Crawling from twisted covers, I sat on the side of my bed, sleep and I parting company for the night. I dressed with quietness, not wishing to disturb the family, especially Mama, who would have tortured me with questions about my insomnia. Snagging a jacket from the hook, I opened the back door and stepped onto our wooden porch.

The late-hour moon had strayed to the far side of heaven, buttercup beams shadowing the farm in a lambent glow. A habit from childhood had me searching for the elusive man in the moon, but finding him not. Smooth gravel formed a footpath from porch to barn. I tread it with lopsided gait, having left my platform shoes tucked beneath the bed. My bare toes tingled as they pressed the cool, mist-covered stones Papa had evacuated from the river. I reached the barn, but didn't venture inside, electing to sit beneath the stars instead. Slipping into my jacket, I leaned my back against the barn door while worry careened across my mind like tumbleweed in a dust storm.

Last week I journeyed into the past, but had not had the fortitude to face my foes. Had I greeted guilt and sorrow head-on, wouldn't I have severed their stranglehold on me? How pleasant it would be to bid them both a sound farewell.

Now my heart carried new doubts; questions I had to answer with haste, for in two weeks it would be too late. Was my love for Gavin true? Did I trust his fidelity? If I had it to do over, would I choose Gavin as my forever husband?

Compelled by an undeniable force, I raised my blurred gaze to heaven. Somewhere in the starry vastness, God was listening to my cries. He heard my thundering heart and saw my fear. Since his fingers had etched the pathway of my tomorrows before the existence of time, surely he would provide the answers I sought. As my gaze traveled over murky patches of the Milky Way, I agonized about which path God would have me follow. Moreover—where that path might lead.

*Be still and know …*

"Oh, Lord, I'm in so much trouble. I tried to face my guilt … and my grief … but it hurt too much to go back. And what about Gavin, Lord? I thought you brought him to America, just for me. Now I'm not sure. Was I wrong, Father? I have to know—the wedding's in two weeks."

For an hour or more my pleas rose to heaven like wisps of trail dust. Up, past the firmament they climbed, into the realm of God. Answers would come in his dear time. That much I had learned during the last five years. But I wanted more than answers. I wanted healing.

# *Eleven*

"Careful with that lamp, Emma Grace! It was your grandmother's."

I nodded my head and turned my back on Mama, wishing she'd go find something to bake in the kitchen. As I polished Mama's fragile keepsake and installed the glass chimney in its four-pronged base, I heard the creek calling to me. I knew I'd best answer the summons, before I backed out altogether. But calling even louder were Mama's speculating eyes. They'd been pondering me since breakfast, fastening a glare on my person she'd not yet chosen to unhook. What better way to shift her gaze elsewhere than to complete my chores and make tracks for the creek? Before she cornered me with kindly concern and yanked the truth right out of my heart.

Breezes lifted dust from our gravel drive, winnowing it through a sieve of window screens. From there it floated on silent wings, shrouding our living room with powdery dirt. Each morning my oilcloth and broom stripped it away, but by evenfall I could write my name in its reappearance. Though I could tidy the house with my eyes closed, today I bumbled about the room like a disjointed beetle, displacing heirlooms, rattling lamps, tripping over rocker legs. No wonder Mama's gaze followed me like a pickpocket tracking a plump wallet.

Screeching brakes snagged my attention as Molly's Packard—an extravagance in these days of Depression—halted on the front drive. I flitted from window to window like a honeybee, releasing tethered sashes from wooden frames, trying to outpace the mounting swarm of dust headed our way.

Holly and Molly debarked from the auto with three toddlers and a babe in tow. I thought it peculiar, this weekday visit; Monday being woman's busiest workday. Then I recalled the conversation at our dinner table the day before, and knew I should have anticipated their coming. Fortunate I was that Polly lived in Arkansas. Otherwise, female philosophizing might suck all the oxygen from the air, and I would suffocate like a landlocked gill-breather. I'd grown up under The Ollys' tutelage and understood them well. They were here for the scuttlebutt. They'd not depart until their ears were packed with every titillating bit of palaver they could unearth. That alone would have driven me to the creek, but for the children.

While the women drank coffee and devoured Mama's banana fritters, I gathered Kade, Karen, and Josey to the porch, having already collected Baby Abigail from Molly's arms. We headed out to visit the newest litter of barn kittens. I determined to lose myself in the children until their mothers had feasted sufficiently on the morsels of my present-day predicament. Unwilling to reveal the promises Gavin maneuvered into my heart the night before, I stomped my way out to the barn. Three little stomperettes followed close behind. Some things between a man and a woman were too private to share.

My sisters seemed sluggish on departure that afternoon, the grapevine of gossip having weighed them down, I supposed. Who knew? Perhaps Mama and the girls had straightened out my life appropriately, and the lonely trip to the creek was unnecessary, after all. Had I a more agreeable spirit, I would soak up every dollop of counsel my family had to offer. But I was too stubborn by far. When their advice came—as it surely would—I knew I would wave it a hasty good-bye as it sailed over my head. Papa claimed my head was harder than teakwood. But my heart wasn't. For that reason, I planned to revisit my childhood this very afternoon. I needed sweet release from the past. And … I needed direction.

A stiff breeze hustled me down the path to the creek. I had scratched Mama a note, explaining my need to be alone and think things through. I might have told her face-to-face before she lay down to rest, but for the coward's trait marking my existence of late. Treetops circled in the wind, a sure indication that a thunderstorm was brewing. Even so, I knew the time had come to follow my childhood to its conclusion.

I scurried to find shelter as autumn chill filtered into my bones and the wind kicked me in the backside, spiking my skin with the scent of rain. I followed the stream to an outcropping of rock that slanted over the water, forming a protective shelf. Sculpted beneath the shelf was a small dwelling with craggy ceiling and sandy floor. Elo and I had tromped this cave in our rough and tumble days, when downpours caught us unaware, and winter days beckoned us to explore its chiseled cavity. During rare hiatuses from picking cotton, my family had used the cave as a bathhouse; men changing into swimsuits on one side of a strung quilt; ladies on the other.

I flung myself into the cave just as a downpour of fat raindrops riddled the creek like Tommy-gun bullets. I yanked the privacy quilt from the wire, spread it on the sand, and sat down Indian-style. Though the quilt smelled of mildew and timeworn stitches, I wrapped it around my shoulders, for the wind had shifted its chill in my direction. I would wait out the storm in this dry, safe grotto. The storm in my heart was another matter entirely.

I untied my shoelaces, running appreciative fingers over platform shoes designed by Nathan's ingeniousness and manifested by the cobbler's prowess. Nathan had presented me my first pair of platform shoes on my sixteenth birthday. In a moment's time, my feet experienced the unbridled flight of fairy wings. For the first time since birth, my untrammeled steps lifted me over field and meadow, as unencumbered as the wind. I danced on our porch like a maiden possessed. Raced along paths I'd merely hobbled over before. My treasured gift, the first of many shoes to come, had rubbed my feet raw, but I disallowed whelks and blisters to slow their unfettered stampede. Bulky and unladylike, some called them. But I recognized my shoes as an answer to my prayers of a decade, or more. Without hesitation, I banished my crutch to a berth beneath the bed, rousing it only in emergencies. Silly or not, I now raised the shoe, whose heightened heel and sole evened out my legs, and caressed it like a newborn babe. Then I placed both shoes on the quilt's edge and turned my gaze on the weather.

Rain splatters dug tiny volcanoes into the sand, like the doodlebug holes I had poked with a stick and chanted over as a child. I shifted to my stomach, tucked my faded skirt around my legs, and watched the storm's fury. Water cascaded over the limestone ledge and meshed with a tangle of rivulets that emptied into Two-Toe Creek. Beyond the falls, giant cedars twisted and curtsied in the wind like green-haired maidens at a highland fling. I flinched when a bolt of lightning blanched the sky and clapped another round of thunder over my head. The way the storm crawled across the sky like a furry black caterpillar, it looked to be a long time ending. So I rolled to my back and studied the bedrock ceiling. In my stowaway cocoon, there would be no interruptions. No distractions. It seemed a safe place to make peace with the past. Though I dreaded the journey I was about to take, I felt an eagerness to begin the trip. I closed my eyes, blocking damp chill and howling winds from my mind.

While the storm raged outside, I struggled for inward calm.

*Remember—you're not alone.*

Images from yesteryear crept into view: images of the tragedy that had knocked me from my moorings on a hot August day in 1928. The memories approached more boldly now, sidling into full view. They drifted across my heart like a vapor in the wind, curling beneath my lids, whisking my breath away.

The day's chores completed, I followed the twins outdoors. As they scampered off to play, I settled beneath a pecan tree and watched while they tossed sticks for Whisper to fetch. I had lain my book on the ground. Now whiffs of wind flipped the pages about like playful cat paws. I looked down, seeing that my copy of *Gulliver's Travels* had opened to the enchanting land of Lilliput: my choicest place to visit in the entire book.

Sometime later, I forced my thoughts from Lemuel Gulliver's travels and swept my gaze over the horizon. I finally spied my rambunctious brothers, loping behind Whisper, crossing unfamiliar fields at too great a distance for me to find comfort. High genuflecting grasses hid all but the boys' shoulders and heads. I screamed their names, but they didn't answer. Nor did they seem inclined to obey my rule about staying in my sight. Tossing my book aside, I braced my hand against the tree trunk, grabbed my crutch, and surged after Micah and Caleb. It became increasingly difficult to pinpoint their bobbing heads, their images dwindling in the widening gulf. My high-pitched shrieks went unheeded, but I gained ground when they stopped and bent their heads down. Wheeling on in a frenzy of crutch and leg, I watched in horror as first one head disappeared, then the other. Grievous hands clutched my chest, squeezing breath from my lungs as I raced on, parting grasses like the Red Sea. Stitches seized my side, twisting me into a boomerang while angry words mounted in my heart. As I ran, I tailored scathing lectures in my head. Lectures my brothers would not soon forget. How dared they disregard the rules I'd so carefully seared into their mischievous little heads? Where could they be? *They must've found an anthill … or a gopher hole. Please, God, don't let it be a snake pit.*

I reached the spot where I last saw the boys, but no one was there. It was then I heard the whimpers. *Oh, God, let it be the puppy I hear.* Throwing my crutch aside, I fell to the ground, crawling on hands and knees, trembling fingers plowing the tall grass. Surely, the boys were playing a trick—hiding from me as they had earlier in the day. But the whimpers persisted, and I knew instinctively the utterances I heard were of human pain. I followed the sounds, swiping hands across the ground like a scythe. *Please let them be all right, Jesus … please.* Suddenly, my right hand sank into a hole. I placed an ear over the opening, hearing low moans. Shudders racked my body. "Micah … Caleb? Are you all right?" I pleaded for my brothers to answer, my fear so intense I felt I would die from it. The whimpers ceased, plunging my heart into even greater anguish. Shudders racked my body as I knelt over the hole and heaved for air. Dark clouds inhabited my vision. I collapsed and spilled to the ground, for my arms and knees would hold me no longer. While an undertow of fear siphoned hope from my heart, I rolled to my back and stretched my hands toward the hole. I tried to scream my brothers' names, but found no breath with which to cry. Silent screams pulsated through my head until darkness sloped over my being, covering even the pounding of my heart.

I awoke, hearing the far-off sound of Elo calling my name. As I lay curled on my side, memories returned, slapping me in the face like a blast of furnace fire. How much time had passed since I fainted? Were my brothers alive? Elo's voice grew more frantic—closer now. My heart swelled with regret; because of my carelessness the earth had swallowed my brothers. I lifted on an elbow, calling Elo's name, not knowing if I cried it aloud or in the silence of my heart. Feet thundered the ground nearby. I thought I heard Elo call to me. My head spun again—as it did when Papa twirled me in his arms.

"Emma Grace, what's wrong? Wake up! Tell me what happened!"

The most active part of my body wouldn't utter a word. I burst into sobs, Elo lifting me from the ground, hugging me, telling me everything was all right. But everything wasn't all right, and I knew it never would be again. I scrambled from his arms, crawling on hands and knees to the grassy weeds that covered the hideous hole. Though I pointed and sputtered, my words remained trapped within, unable to breach the barricade of terror in my heart.

Elo yanked grass from the mouth of the hole. 'Twas then I saw the abyss into which my brothers had fallen. About the width of my shoulders, the opening was a circle of rocks. A few smaller stones broke loose when Elo shoved his arm inside.

"Looks like an abandoned well. Probably an old water well." He cupped his mouth and yelled into the darkness. "Caleb, Micah—can you hear me? Are you okay?"

Silence joined space with darkness.

Elo wrenched me from the ground and cradled me to his chest. I pointed to my crutch, but he shook his head. "We'll leave it here as a marker," he said, and then rammed it into the ground. He wheeled around, setting his feet to running as though the hounds were after us. I felt secure in his arms. Secure in the thought that he and Papa would deliver my brothers from the monster that had snatched them away.

I must have swooned again. When I awoke, I was in bed; Mama by my side with a wet cloth aimed at my forehead. I opened my mouth to speak, concentration fierce and determined. But my words stayed locked inside. The only things escaping my throat were garbled sobs and pitiful moans that filled the room with echoes of condemnation for the poor attention I had shown my little brothers.

"Are you hurt, sweet-pea?"

Mama's concern, after the way I let her down, slashed a deeper gash across my heart. I tried to speak, but salty tears flooded my throat, clogging it like a beaver dam. When I tried to tell Mama the fault was mine, all that exited my mouth was an explosion of incoherent babbling. The room blurred as I rose to a sitting position. Mama pushed my shoulders back, wilting me into the pillow. A galloping pulse pounded my eardrums, joining chorus with whispers and sobs from my sisters. I closed my eyes against the clamor, darkness carrying me away.

# Twelve

My voice returned with Papa. He slipped into my bedroom and knelt on the floor, cradling me to his broad chest. His eyes were puffy and streaked with red, and his hands shook when he smoothed hair from my face. It didn't matter that calloused fingers snagged my curls or that grimy overalls rubbed the stench of kerosene and smoke into my skin. Papa was there. That was all that mattered. He would free my brothers from their earthy prison.

"How're you feeling, sweetheart?"

I nodded, clenching teeth together, staving off another crying siege.

"Papa, it's my fault ... my fault." The dam burst open then, my tears flowing like a river out of its banks. Nothing could hold back the onslaught; that portion of penance I was able to slide past the broken pieces of my heart. Wanting to spill out the pain bottled within, I bawled, for what seemed like hours.

Papa planted kisses on my hair and stroked my back until the sobs subsided into hiccups.

"This here wasn't anybody's fault, Emma Grace. Mr. Peavy didn't even know there was a well on his property. The only person to blame is the coldhearted cur who dug the well but was too stupid and lazy to cap it off."

Fire sparked Papa's eyes. Then he sighed, extinguishing the flames. He ran trembling fingers over his face, looking as tired—as beaten—as I'd ever seen him. "We need your help, Emma Grace. It'll take no small amount of courage. But I believe you can do it."

I knew it! Papa had a plan! My head bobbed and I felt my eyes widen with determination. I'd do anything to help my brothers. If it were possible, I'd switch places with them, even if it meant I'd never see my family again.

"Mama's going to bring you some milk. I want you to drink all of it. You're going to need your strength. Can you do that, little-bit?"

Holding my crutch aloft, Papa carried me papoose-style on his broad back. Out to the high-grass field where torches burned holes in the darkness and a horde of neighbors circled an area cleared of grass and stone. Men carried shovels and lanterns. Some wore rope loops over their shoulders. All stood in solemn quiet, wary glances darting from beneath the brims of their hats.

Papa sat me on a toolbox and squatted beside me. "The well's deep, Emma Grace, and it's narrow. We've done our best to reach the boys, but we're too big to make it down the hole. You're the only one small enough. Think you can go down and tie ropes to Micah and Caleb, so we can pull 'em out?" Tears glistened in Papa's eyes, and his Adam's apple wobbled when he swallowed.

I nodded my head.

Papa smiled.

In a flurry of motion, Elo tied a rope around my chest while another man strung a flashlight through the loops of my overalls. Someone placed an old miner's cap on my head, a carbide lamp attached to the top. Hands stuffed handkerchiefs beneath my headband to take up slack, the cap too large even for my bushy head. The light beam pierced the darkness, bobbing over the frowning faces of Elo, Nathan, Mr. Peavy, Flynn Aarsgard, and others, unrecognizable in my shaken condition. I tried to steady my head, but the lamp's heaviness made it awkward and unwieldy. I feared it would fall off and shatter into a thousand pieces. Nathan rested a hand on the doddering lamp, stabilizing it while another man prepared me for the ordeal ahead.

"Best I can figure," Nathan said, "the well's about twenty-five to thirty feet deep. Looks like whoever dug the well hollowed out a wider hole, then lined it with limestone. You'll need to take care, Emma Grace. Calcium carbonate in the rock may have softened over the years. It could crumble on you."

The tremors in my body were so mighty, they shook even the tips of my curls. Elo knelt down, wrapping his strength around me.

"You'll do fine," he said.

He lifted me before the gaping dent of earth, and there I stood, as wobbly and frightened as a sacrifice about to be offered to the gods. Without my crutch, I listed to the right—like a broken ship ... or a broken heart.

My heart thudded while I waited for the men to hasten me into the hole. Didn't they understand I needed to hurry and rescue my brothers?

Papa's voice rose in prayer, catching me by surprise. He had two children in the ground. I supposed he didn't want another slipping away without first petitioning his Father. During the prayer, I held the dark clouds of fear at bay.

"Father, God ... take Emma Grace safely to my boys. Return them to us in your loving care. Amen."

Unanchored and dangling now, the taut rope gouged my chest as Papa lowered me into the hole. My head remained above ground while he plied me with last-minute instructions.

"Slip this loop under the boys' arms—whoever you come to first— and cinch it tight. We'll pull both of you to the top. Then you'll have to go down again for the other one. Tilt your head down and the lamp will light your way. You've got a flashlight, too, if you need it. Thank you, sweetheart, for being so brave. Do you know how much I love you?"

I wagged my head, flinching at the persistence of my muted condition.

My descent was slow, torturous. The well narrowed as I wiggled past jagged rocks into a veil of darkness. My heart picked up speed,

Elo's words fainter now, echoing with the sound of good-bye. Dank earth smells curled my stomach, threatening an upheaval of milk. I dipped my head, the spotlight beaming on my pinioned arms, now nicked and bleeding. Something moved across a blood trail on my arm. I swiveled my head, spotlighting hundreds of spiders that skulked from crevices and soft pockets of stone. Spiders crept onto my body, beneath my pant legs, below my shirt collar. Screams tore from my throat, prompting an immediate halt to my descent. The rope tugged me upward, but I wedged my feet against the wall and hollered for Papa to sink me lower. As I shouted, I kicked at spiders and tossed my head to knock them from my face. The miner's cap toppled forward. When the rope finally slackened, I pushed the lamp against stone and straightened it. I moved downward, hastening the descent by nudging my fingers to walk down the wall. Aware that spiders crawled inside my clothes, under the cap, and across my face, I forced back screams and braced for a fatal sting. I was certain the spiders were deadly black widows.

I descended deeper into the black hole; arms scraping chalky stone, feet dangling like a broken marionette. The smell of decay surrounded me, clogging my pores and filling my head with the putrefying reality of how deeply I was embedded in the ground. When the light tumbled over rocks that marked the well's foundation, I knew I was near the bottom. With infinite care, I steadied the beam on a small, still form. *Whisper.* I gasped aloud when I recognized his bloody body. Inching past the last jagged stones and chinking, I veered my light beam to the right. There, in a pile, lay the ghostly bodies of my brothers.

Caleb lay crumpled against the wall, Whisper beneath him. One hand clutched fur; the other hand fisted the hem of Micah's shirt. Micah lay atop Caleb, his head bent at a sharp angle. God blurred my vision then, tears sparing me the grief of viewing my brothers' broken bodies.

I fought dark shadows, the same darkness I had yielded to earlier in the day. I half-squatted, which freed my arms to slip a rope over Micah's head. I cinched it as instructed and cradled his head to my chest. Then I yanked the rope, my heart drumming toward rupture as I rode to the top in blind fear for Micah. I gave no thought to spider nests, praying only that I'd not pass out and cause Micah further harm.

When we cleared the entry hole, shouts of rejoicing filled the air, the ground rumbling as excited feet drew near. But there was no rejoicing in my heart.

"Get that tarp over here!" Papa's words were sharp, raspy, as his arms waved wide circles in the night.

After someone plucked Micah from my arms, I sat on the ground, feeling witless and dazed, as though I'd been slathered with a coat of numbing ointment. Had poisonous bites paralyzed me so quickly? I wondered. I discarded the thought, seeing that my hands roved freely in the riddance of spiders.

No one needed to explain the deep, wailing heaves that broke from Papa's chest. Elo and Nathan joined the mourning; inconsolable howls hoisting the night air like a pack of sorrowing wolves. My own howling found no such release. It swelled within—broken and keening: the cries of a protector who had failed to protect.

Papa laid my brother on the tarp, his body covering Micah like a quilt. "My boy ... my boy," Papa cried, his fractured voice sobbing into Micah's tiny body. "Oh, God in heaven, have mercy ..."

"His neck's broken," someone whispered.

Unable to fight it any longer, I succumbed to the darkness.

"Emma Grace ... Emma Grace, wake up!"

Never before had I seen Elo cry. Not even the time Mama threaded eleven stitches into the underbelly of his seven-year-old foot. Tears streamed from his eyes now, and his hands trembled as he shook my shoulder. "You've got to go down again. You've got to get Caleb out. Do you understand what I'm saying?"

The chronic nod of my head resumed its twitching jerk. "Yes, Elo."

"That'a girl."

A broken heart guided me down the shaft a second time. I feared nothing—darkness, the well caving in, silent spider legs converging on my body. In a trancelike state, I slipped the rope beneath Caleb's arms, my gaze focusing on a gash that lay bare his skull from forehead to ear. I ruffled his curls, now dry with blood, half-expecting him to brush my hand away as was his habit. A picture formed in my mind as I swiped at the blood with my shirttail: a higher world where my brothers ran hand in hand, faster than the wild stallions they so admired. With fervency heretofore unknown to me, I pleaded with God to let me join my brothers on the other side. I lifted Whisper with my left hand and postured myself defensively around Caleb's lifeless body, then yanked the rope.

No shouts of joy welcomed us above ground this time. Nathan gathered Whisper from my arm as Papa released my deathlike grip on Caleb. I slipped the rope over my head and turned away. I cared not to witness Papa fight another round with grief.

"Roan, this one's alive!" Mr. Peavy's shout thundered the air.

I spun around, losing balance, falling to my knees. "Papa … what?" I implored, furious tears streaming down my face. How could Mr. Peavy play such a cruel joke on our family? Hadn't we suffered enough?

"Yes! Yes!" Papa shouted, his fingers outstretched as they punctuated the night sky. "Caleb's alive! Thank you, Lord … thank you."

I clasped my crutch, staggered to my feet, and hurled myself on the tarp. I fell in a heap at Caleb's feet, disbelief filling my soul. It must have filled my eyes as well.

"Put your finger right here, girl," Mr. Peavy said, shoving my hand against Caleb's blood-soaked collar. "There ain't a whole lot of punch to it, but it's a pulse, all right."

Commotion followed. Papa shouted at Mr. Peavy, charging him to get that fancy new Buick of his and hightail it to town.

"Get Doc Landers out here on the double."

No one, especially Mr. Peavy, seemed concerned that the hired man had ordered the boss around like an admiral commanding his fleet. "We're not moving Caleb an inch until the doctor says to. Nathan, go fetch your mama and sisters."

"We're here, Roan."

Four shadowy figures stepped into the circle of light; The Ollys girding Mama like battle armor.

"We couldn't stay home, Roan … not without knowing. I heard shouting … what …?" Mama's voice strangled as Papa snagged her in his arms.

"It's all right, sweetheart. Just wait here a minute … before you see our boys."

"I can't bear it, Roan ... tell me they're alive ... please, dear God ..."

Mama's pain-wracked voice twisted my heart into a knot, squeezing the last drop of hope from it. I layered her sorrow atop my own, compounding my own soul's wretchedness. It seemed a rightful torture, and deservedly befitting the wickedness I had done.

But Mama's sorrow—heaped upon my own—proved an impossible burden to carry. Easing from the light, I stumbled away, into a night far removed from the family I had betrayed.

# Thirteen

Intent on separating myself from the bleakness in Mama's eyes, I hurled through the black night, falling down, picking myself up countless times. Escape led me over uneven, uncharitable terrain whose foliage tugged on my hair and ripped my clothes to snippets.

As deep night settled in, I scoured the horizon for a pocket of security. I spied a moonlit copse of trees beyond the farthermost field. Aiming my crutch toward the thicket, I gave no thought as to whether or not my actions caused the family additional angst.

As I struggled to reach the shelter of timbers, fresh waves of sorrow reminded me that Micah was gone forever. *And Caleb? Will he die too?* Blood-chilling fear evoked both the longing to know Caleb's fate—and the desire to never know.

Live oak and cedar inhabited the leafy boscage into which I delved: my hideaway from varmints and humans, alike. I collapsed at the foot of an oak, arms bloodied and bruised, head throbbing from incessant crying. The physical pain seemed inconsequential when compared to the ache in my heart.

When the rushing in my heart quieted, I curled to the ground, pillowing my head with my hands. Moonlight filtered into the grove, illuminating bare patches of earth, spotlighting leafy shadows that swayed with the wind. All else was stillness and quiet, as though my friend, the woods, had turned its back in shame. I had separated myself from the family I loved and the little brother I would never hold again. Now I sensed the forest withdrawing from me also. Treetops rustled overhead, dropping whispers into my ears. *If you had kept stricter watch over the boys, Micah would still be alive.* I stiffened at the trees' reprimands, but then nodded my head, for I stood in wholehearted agreement with their condemnation.

Crunching leaves roused me from sleep. Though torchlight shone through the trees at some distance, I knew who hoisted the flame. I could identify Elo's angry footfall no matter the span.

"Emma Grace! Answer me, girl! Are you in here? You'd better pray I don't find you, 'cause when I do I'm gonna wring your scrawny neck."

Elo's bark hastened my wakefulness. I should have known he'd track me down, despite the care I'd taken in hiding. I held my breathing steady, relying on silence to conceal my position. But Elo's sixth sense charged ahead, his circle of fire lighting my space, striking me full-face with the flame of disgrace.

"You selfish little twit! Do you have any idea the pain you've caused Mama and Papa tonight?"

I knew Elo spoke of my negligence in tending the twins, causing Micah's death. Yes, I knew the pain I'd caused my parents. But what Elo didn't understand was that I would gladly trade my life for Micah's. If only I could.

Elo snatched me from my cleft in the tree and slung me atop his shoulder like a sack of cornmeal. Holding my legs and crutch with one hand, his torch with the other, he cleared the trees and set off at a brisk trot. I presumed we headed for the foreman's house. But had he galloped to the river and dumped me into its flow, it would not have bothered me a pinch. I cared not where Elo carted me, so long as sleep and I traveled there together. Sleep was the only place sorrow could not find me.

My jostling ride ceased some time later. I raised my head from Elo's shoulder and glanced around, noting a sky gone pink. As Elo dumped me onto the lifeless grass of our front yard, I saw Mama, rushing to my side.

"Emma Grace … how could you do this to us? Didn't you know we'd be …?"

A fogbank rolled in, obscuring Mama and the sound of her pain-wracked words. I felt her pursuing arms reach out and try to envelop me, but I turned my back on her and scrambled away. Having no suitable apology or explanation for failing my brothers, I hobbled to the house as fast as my crutchless legs would take me. A drone of incoherent words accompanied me like a swarm of bombinating bees, whirring over and around, but not into the world of my understanding. The droning followed me into the house and into my room, where I slipped beneath the covers of my bed. There, under a tent of blackness, I keened in silence until the humming went away.

Gentle hands massaged my body, but I resisted the attempt to rouse me.

"Emma Grace, you must wake up. Mama says you have to eat something. She'd be here herself, but she's … Come on, little sister, wake up."

Sniffles wobbled Holly's voice, but I hardened my heart against her entreaties. My thoughts turned to Mama. Was her grief such that she had taken to her bed? What was she doing? Preparing Micah's body for burial? Cooking for the hordes that would descend upon us soon enough?

Though Holly's voice sounded most forgiving, I feigned sleep and didn't budge from my quilted refuge. I wished to talk to no one, especially Holly. What could I say to a sister who had been straight on perfect for as long as I could remember?

"C'mon, sweetie. No one blames you for the accident. Don't you understand? It could've happened no matter who watched the boys."

*But I'm their protector, Holly. Don't you understand? I should have kept them out of that field. Please, just go away and leave me alone.*

"Come on, Emmy, eat some food. You've not eaten in … goodness knows how long. Give Mama a little peace of mind, okay?"

Holly hummed as she patted the lump of me. I spent all my energy in remaining motionless; nevertheless I treasured Holly's caress, for it restored to life a portion of my soul I had thought dead. Too soon, the patting ceased and I heard Holly's footfall tread to the doorway. She paused for long moments, perhaps to verify whether there was breath left in my body. Then she walked away.

I left my bed well after nightfall. The house was dark, doused of light save the moon's pale glow and a flickering lantern in the hallway. During my long hibernation, Mama, or one of The Ollys, had cleaned me up and dressed me in a nightgown. I rolled back the covers and sat up, feeling a moment of light-headedness. Securing my crutch, I walked from the room with but a brief glance at the tray of food on my bedside table.

Holly was right. I should have eaten. At the entrance to Caleb's bedroom, a wave of tremors buckled my legs. I grabbed the doorpost, telling myself that sickroom odors had set my legs to trembling. The air reeked of carbolic acid and liniment: fetors that packed the punch of a fish, three days dead. I gagged and clutched my stomach, though nothing abode in its depths worth the heaving up.

Mama dozed in a chair near Caleb's bed. White bandages swathed my brother's head, reminding me of crypt mummies in comic books we used to laugh over. His dormant state fretted my nerves, for he slept as one who would never awaken. For a boy of constant motion, he appeared more than unnatural.

I gazed at Mama's fingers, entwined with Caleb's as though she might prevent his departure from this present world. My heart ached for her. And it ached for the son who appeared more dead than alive. Most of all, it ached for the loss of Mama's less rowdy son. The one so gentle natured that even the bluebells of springtime held no fear his grimy hands would snatch them from the earth. How would our family go on without Micah? How would I go on?

Though Mama slept the sleep of exhaustion, her face wore a pained expression. One I'd not forget in a hundred lifetimes. I was responsible for her pain. For the stain of blood on her apron, and the hole in her heart that could never be filled. Tears blurred my sight as I slipped from the room and felt my way down the hall.

Someone had stopped the mantle clock in our parlor at 5:37, the assigned time of Micah's death yesterday. The unmoving pendulum wreaked havoc on my heart. I wanted to force it to action, charge its momentum until the hands of time swung back to the days when Micah romped and laughed and played. But the pendent remained fixed in time, as did my heart. Every mirror and picture in the room was draped with black cloth—even the family portrait, taken by an itinerant photographer last summer. In happier times, I would have laughed at remembrances of the day: Elo lurching for the woods when Mama called us to gather for picture taking; Papa threatening to hang him from the baling hooks if he didn't join us on the front porch. On any other day, my heart would have smiled. But not today. Death had come to our house. Its evidence was not just in my heart. It was everywhere.

Most likely Elo's hands had fashioned the cedar coffin resting on the table in our front room. Single candles, at either end of the box, provided scant light for the darkened parlor. I tore my gaze from Micah's burying box, smaller and more heartbreaking than other coffins at which I had brazenly gawked. Someone had cleared the room of furniture, but for a few straight-back chairs. Papa sat hunched in one of them, chin propped on his chest. I hoped his eyes closed in sleep, not prayer, this being his second night without rest. Elo eyed me from across the room where he sat slump-shouldered, his narrowed gaze trained on my awkward approach. Without words, my big brother upped and left the room. 'Twas the displeasure of seeing me again, I feared.

As I walked to the table, an urgency to pray rushed over me. I could think of no part of my body or mind that wasn't in dire need of shoring up. But I swayed my stubborn will from seeking even a morsel of God's strength and courage. He had chosen not to spare Micah—the most prized of his beloved. I felt certain he wouldn't bother to bend an ear to the likes of me. In that sharp moment of acuity, I understood I was turning my back on God. Perhaps out of anger, for failing Micah—for failing me. Perhaps because I no longer believed in his love. The thought was so disheartening, so foreign to all I had believed since infancy that I knelt on the floor and bawled.

"Come here, Emma Grace."

I shook my head, not allowing Papa's storehouse of love to ooze even a mite of warmth onto my ice-packed heart. However, I hadn't reckoned that Papa's stubbornness might be as weighty as my own, for suddenly I was in the air, swung into his burly arms as though I bore the weight of a newspaper. For a while we just sat in his chair. As he cradled me against his chest like the baby I wished I were, the pungency of freshly hewn cedar and Mama's tallow candles joined force, stamping a memory scent on my heart I knew I would never forget. After a time of coddling, Papa set my feet on the floor, retrieving my crutch as he gripped my hand with firmness.

The awful finality of Micah's death struck me anew when I leaned over the coffin to tell him good-bye. *This is the last time I'll ever see you, sweet Micah. I'm so sorry, little brother. So very, very sorry.* A gully wash of sadness and guilt flooded my eyes. If only my tears could wash away the suffering in my heart. The suffering of my family.

How could I live in a world that no longer claimed Micah's bare feet on its paths? His bright gaze darting to nature's wonders? His silly, snuffling laugh that put me in mind of a snorting piglet? I wanted to shake him awake. Tell him to be up and about the business of following after his brother. A beautiful world awaited his exploration and a pile of mischief lay neatly stacked, ready for him to claim.

Not a scratch marred Micah's perfection. Nor did a bruise fade purple into his skin. Yet, he was dead. *Why, God?* I wanted to scream. But God and I no longer acknowledged each other. The thought mangled my heart even more. Micah wore his Sunday best: the muslin shirt with buttons from the tinker-man's wagon; the shirt that bore the embroidery stitches of Molly's pearl-white buttonholes. Micah had been scrubbed speckless, the faint scent of Mama's lavender soap tarrying on his pale skin. And his unruly locks now lay in shiny array, for they'd been plastered down with Papa's hair balm. His appearance gave me pause, for I'd never before seen his free-flying curls subdued in such manner. I could almost imagine it was someone else's little brother lying in the casket.

I stood close to Micah, even after Papa returned to his chair. It discomfited me to no end that his body felt cold. And it troubled me that he slept alone. He'd never slept alone in his life, even in the womb. I turned, watching Papa through bleary vision. When I determined that he dozed, I did what needed doing.

"Roan … come look at this."

I awoke at the sound of Mama's voice, but stayed my lids from opening, though they betrayed me with a bit of fluttering as the moments passed. A quick peek revealed the night's persistent darkness. Its slow passage had frittered away a portion of candle near the head of the coffin, puddling it into a saucer of melted wax.

"What in the world?" Papa whispered.

Mama and Papa circled the table, Papa hefting me from my nesting spot beside Micah's casket. I had tried to cram myself into his burying box, but hadn't fit. At least I'd gotten an arm inside, to comfort him and let him know he wasn't alone. And I'd pleated the yards of my nightgown over his chilled body, warming him best I could.

"We know you're awake, Emma Grace. Come on, child, open up and talk to us." Much weeping had deepened Papa's voice, coating it with the gravelly hoarseness of a sore throat.

As Papa steadied my stance on the floor, I blurted out the question I'd been most fearful of asking. "Is Caleb going to live?" I sought Mama's face, my reluctant eyes finally agreeing to meet the penetrating sorrow in hers.

"He's not awake yet, but he's—"

"He's gonna die too," I exploded, detonated by the anguish in my heart. Turning my back on Mama, I grasped the table's polished edge, battening myself against more of grief's savage attacks.

"It's too early to know, honey, but Doctor Landers says Caleb's got more than a fighting chance." Mama's hands rested on my shoulders with heaviness, her magnetic fingers exerting force as they persuaded me to turn and face her.

Micah's death had robbed Mama of her usual vivacity. She seemed older, depleted. Gone from her face was the youthful laughter that could tease the pout out of me with the wink of an eye. Staring into Mama's face was like looking into the mirror of my soul and discovering nothing but impoverishment. It was then that the shakes streaked up my legs in a fearful rush. As tears washed Mama's semblance into a watery mirage, she wrapped me in her arms, swaddling my twitches and spasms as only she could. The quavers were a long time leaving.

At noon the next day, we gathered on a knoll above Two-Toe Creek, more people bending the grass there than I had energy to count.

It was on this hilltop that my grandparents lay buried, along with a baby Mama had birthed three years after the twins were born. Though my little sister had never drawn breath, Mama had reverenced her life with a name: Elena Dawn Falin. It was beside her that Micah would forever rest.

"Friends, we gather today for the saddest of life's occasions—the burial of our little brother, Micah Roan Falin. He departed this world on August 25, 1928, at the tender age of six."

I closed my ears to the remainder of Pastor Emery's remarks and kept them closed until Polly sang a hymn that ended the service. Leaning on my crutch a few feet from the casket, my mind gnawed on thoughts more palatable to my soul: Micah as a babe and as a toddler. For all the gladness in his heart, I'd often imagined he would grow up to be a preacher, or a song-and-dance man. He had a smile that ignited sparks. Not in my eyes, alone, but in all who got caught up in his bright burst of sunlight. In his brief six years on earth, he'd lavished more love and affection on my heart than a girl could expect from a lifetime of loving.

*I'll never kiss him good night again.* The thought ripped through me like a spring twister. All I could see in the whirlwind was a lifetime without Micah. A lifetime of heartache. I heaved the scene from my mind, knowing my survival depended on keeping Micah alive in my heart. Not in accepting his death. But how could I deny the truth when he lay before me—bundled in Mama's favorite quilt—and packaged in a box carved by Elo's masterstroke? The answer? His death could not be denied.

Micah's coffin leaked a familiar, intimate scent into the air; a scent that spoke of happier times and places. It smelled like the siding boards Papa used to erect our tree house in the backyard. It brought to mind cedar shanks Elo peeled and scraped to frame our chicken coop. And it reminded me of Mama's cedar-lined closet. Though moths fled its fulsomeness, I had acquired a liking for the sharp fragrance; inhaling it during stowaway times, when I crept into the dark closet and dreamed up wild, hard-to-swallow tales.

I turned my eyes from the coffin and gazed at my family. Outwardly, they showed me no contempt, but I wondered if my failure to protect the boys would someday sift into their considerations. Would they eventually place the blame where it belonged? I glanced up at the bulwark of our family. Papa would never speak of blame. Not aloud. Nor would he allow my negligence addressed in our home. But over the course of time, would my carelessness eat its way into his secret thoughts? Would it gnaw away his love for me?

Mama stood straight, her chin maintaining a high tilt, perhaps to contain the flow of tears. Papa clenched his arm around Mama's shoulder, keeping her vertical. Flynn had enveloped Holly in his arms, and Polly and Molly embraced each other like twins joined at the hip. Nathan stood hunched beneath a tree, standing brave against the pain while gentle breezes set his overlong hair adrift. Elo had distanced himself from the crowd, his solitary gaze fastened on the ground, but then rising to the clouds. Did he think to spy Micah amidst the snow-white pillows of heaven? I wished Elo and I could share our sorrow, as we'd shared the woods and creek in our youth. But it seemed Elo was inclined to fight his battle alone.

Overnight my proud family had turned into a stoop-shouldered bunch, wide Falin shoulders not squaring the air this day. Nor did our laughter fill the void with an Irish flair. We had shrunk and aged in a day's time. Would we ever walk tall again? Would the sparkle in Papa's eye ever reappear?

Friends withdrew, granting us privacy while we said good-bye to Micah. As Papa wedged a sturdy wooden cross in the mound of earth, Elo dug a second burial hole, this one near the foot of Micah's grave. Nathan placed Whisper's body in the narrow pit and covered him with rich, crumbly soil. The puppy had saved Caleb's life, buffering his fall against a caved-in foundation of deadly stones. I thought my family had no more tears to cry, but I was wrong. Joining hands, we formed a circle of broken hearts around the two graves.

"Show us your mercy, Lord. We're broken and afraid. We can't bear this sorrow alone," Papa whispered. "Spare Caleb. Heal him, Father. And please, Lord ... hold our beloved Micah in your arms ... until we can all be together again."

"Oh, Roan ... I want my baby ... I just want to hold my baby again," Mama wailed, her despair collapsing her to a near faint.

Papa lifted Mama off her feet, sheltering her in his able arms. He carried her down the rolling hill that cradled Micah within its folds, his flock following his lead like dull-witted sheep. Our descent to the valley floor was as silent as a deerstalker, words meaningless in sight of our loss.

# Fourteen

"She's wasting away before our eyes, Doctor ... grieving herself to death, and we can't do a thing to stop it."

Mama's weepiness plucked a mournful chord in my heart, joining the dirge that had echoed across my days and nights for most of a month. I shifted my stance in the hall, leaning against the wall as tears plopped from my chin to my nightgown. A fitting baptism, it seemed, for my new life of constant sorrow.

"I want her well, Doc! She's been on this downhill slide too long ... you hear me?" Papa's words sounded fierce, demanding. I welcomed them as though they were the bells of Christmas morn. I, too, wanted healing, though I merited nothing of the sort.

I sneaked a peek into the kitchen from my vantage point in the hallway. Mama and Papa sat across the table from Doctor Landers, who drank from a mug as though in a weary daze. Elbows resting on the table, his haggard appearance suggested he wasn't immune to the high toll imposed upon our family. A satchel rested on the floor by his feet, old leather collapsing into the cavity like a canister vacuumed of air. A man of middle years, Doc Landers looked as crumpled and worn out as his ancient medical bag.

I had halted my steps to the bathroom minutes ago when I heard Mama's voice. Wary of being detected, I listened now with ears that had been useless of late, except for eavesdropping.

"Depression is sometimes difficult to diagnose, Mr. Falin. But not in Emma Grace's case. Based on studies I've read, she exhibits all the classic symptoms: pervasive sadness, lethargy, excessive sleep, loss of appetite, and the inability to function in normal circumstances." As Doctor Landers cleared his throat, I detected the soft sound of his mug settling onto the table. "I believe she's sleeping through her pain instead of facing it … instead of accepting it. Guilt just adds another dimension to depression. I'm afraid it's not going to go away overnight. It could last for months—even years. But that's rare in one so young."

"It could last for years?" Mama parroted the doctor's words, her voice raised in a raspy squawk.

"There's got to be a way to reach her, Doc. We can't lose another child. This blackness is *not* going to take our Emma Grace!" I jumped when Papa's fist pounded the table, rattling Mama's teacup in its saucer.

Papa understood! My pain *was* blackness, darker than the blackness of midnight. The somber gluttony had feasted on my heart for weeks now, sparing little, save a few hollow crumbs.

"I have a suggestion that wouldn't require hospitalization," Doctor Landers said. "If you were to move her elsewhere, it might speed up the healing process."

"I'm moving the family back to the farm this week. My work's done here." Papa's words were hushed, almost imperceptible. I leaned forward to hear them better. "I never should have taken this job in the first place."

*Please, Papa … don't …*

"Oh, Roan—don't you go blaming yourself for what happened." Most likely, Mama clasped Papa's hand as she spoke, trying to stroke the hurt away.

*It wasn't your fault, Papa … it was mine … mine …*

"Do you think she'll get better when we move back to the farm?" Mama asked, notching her voice to a hopeful pitch.

"I doubt that will help, Mrs. Falin. No, I had something else in mind. A location far enough away so that people and places don't serve as constant reminders of her loss."

Mama's keen vision spied me as I stumbled down the hallway. She called for me to join them in the kitchen, but I plowed on, locking myself behind the bathroom door. Visions of my family packing me off to some faraway hospital or home for wayward girls clamored my head. I gathered tissue, wiping perspiration from my brow and upper lip, then opened the faucet full force, drowning out the pitiful whimpers that shinnied up my throat.

I blew my nose, wiped my eyes, and lifted my gaze to the medicine cabinet mirror. A stranger peered back at me. The girl's brown hair bounded far beyond the allowed limits of Mama's scissors. Could she be me? Her windblown effect looked similar to the one that perpetually marked my appearance, yet her face looked unfamiliar. She had overlarge eyes, a tight face, and prominent cheekbones that cast shadows onto her sunken cheeks. There was a look about her: a look of hopelessness.

I sank to the rim of the tub, sitting on the edge while my knees thwacked each other beneath my gown. As I agonized over what Mama and Papa's decision would be, I pined for the earth to split in two and swallow me whole. I knew I would obey their wishes, no matter what.

Suddenly, a chunk of awareness smacked me with the truth. I had no choice but to leave. How could Mama's heart mend if the blackness and I hung around, waving our red flags before her eyes? She had worried herself to reed-thinness, her mother-hands tending Caleb's every need, even as she grieved for the son buried on the hilltop. A heart could endure only so much pain. Mama didn't need me under thumb, adding more misery to her life.

But—could I survive separation from my family? A more dangerous prospect I couldn't imagine, being that they stood in the gap for me. They were my safety net when blackness hurled me into the distant night, snatching away my every resolve to get well. Even Elo's churlish put-downs held restorative power.

As Mama banged on the bathroom door, a high wailing skirl buzzed my head. Had a banshee piped out the garish squall, or had it risen from within me? The door splintered from its hinges, Papa rushing through to halt my slow sinkage to the floor. Before my eyelids closed, a thought passed through my consciousness: *Any sacrifice I make will blanch pale when laid beside the tombstone of little Micah.*

# Fifteen

"My mother gave this to me the day I got married. It's yours now, sweetheart. I pray it will be a reminder of how much we love you and want you back home with us."

When Mama slipped the heart-shaped locket around my neck, I caught a glimpse of my reflection in her tears. I cherished the embrace she tugged me into, knowing it would be many days before I felt her arms around me again. Mama's hands trembled a bit, but oddly, mine were as calm as Passion Pond after the turtles have had their fill of dragonflies. At some point during the last week, I accepted my departure as inevitable, and the ensuing numbness that settled over me as my just reward.

I studied the teary group bidding me farewell. Elo, alone, stood as though indifferent to our parting, his eyes as clear as Mama's windows after a fine vinegar washing.

"I'll write you every week," Molly said, brushing my cheek with a kiss.

"So will I," Polly said as she hugged me to her side.

I nodded my thanks, but wondered if I would ever dare read anything again. The last time I opened a book, my world split apart at the seams, and I had gone tumbling into a fathomless abyss I couldn't climb out of.

Papa opened the door and motioned us onto the front porch. Autumn mist hovered over the yard, oozing its way into fissures along the treetops. And darkling fog obscured my view of borrowed car, gravel drive, and the road that would take me away from my family. A jolt of panic darted across my heart, for the mist evidenced itself to me as a last gasp of air, exhaled from some invisible force above. I turned my face from gray-shrouded vapors, frozen in time and space. I'd not let them seep into my heart. Nor would I allow them to be my last thoughts of home.

Nathan approached, his customary quietness blending with early morning stillness. As we latched together in awkward embrace, his height and my crutch set our bodies at odd angles to each other. No matter the fit, warmth and acceptance seeped through his faded overalls, brushing my cheek with love. He shoved us apart without speaking. *At least one of my brothers will miss me.*

I'd come to think of six-year-old Caleb as my sleepy brother. Worn out and tired—not grievously ill and unconscious. I'd whispered my good-bye to him earlier this morning, muffling sobs into his pillowcase during the darkness of predawn. I had begged his forgiveness for the hundredth time. What would life be like for Caleb when he awakened and discovered he had lost his playmate and best friend? Perhaps my prolonged absence was a good thing. I knew not if my heart could withstand Caleb's sorrow when he found out his birth partner was gone forever.

None too gently, my cardboard suitcase and crutch were shoved into the trunk of the car by Elo's broad hands. Papa, Elo, and I settled onto the front seat of the smoke-tinted Buick Mr. Peavy had lent us for the twenty-mile trip to Brenham. In Brenham, Papa and I would catch a bus to Galveston, and Elo would drive the car home.

Galveston was where Granny Falin lived. Papa's mother. I'd be spending time with her, my parents had explained. They had urged me to forget about the accident. Just get well, they counseled … over and over. Perhaps they thought advice, alone, would heal me. Had it been an option all along, and I was just too stubborn to obey them?

I sat unmoving between two giant pillars—Elo wedging me on the right, Papa sitting behind the wheel on my left. They spoke little, though an aura of excitement radiated from Elo. He'd driven a tractor many times, but never a car. During the past week, Mr. Peavy gave Elo driving instructions, and now he considered himself an expert. At least, that's what Molly had whispered to Polly from behind her slender fingers.

Despite the luxury status of Mr. Peavy's Buick, our ride to Brenham was rough and hazardous. As we traveled a route that consisted of more chug holes than level road, I gripped onto Papa's pants leg and bounced all over the seat. A glance at Elo revealed he had lost his sneer somewhere along the way and acquired a smile. Height had him hunching his shoulders, lest his noggin meet the rooftop and give it a dent. No need to fear for Elo if such a thing were to happen. The hardiest blow couldn't dimple Elo's thick skull. Hadn't Mama always claimed his head was the hardest of her hardheaded lot?

Papa parked the car in a cordoned-off area at the station. After retrieving my crutch and suitcase, he left to purchase our tickets. Elo sprang from the Buick as though he'd been accused of car theft. After several moments, I scooted across the seat, opened the door, and reclaimed my crutch from the front fender. I shuffled to Elo, who stood with hands braced against a wooden fence, face averted. He had donned his corduroy trousers for our unprecedented jaunt out of Coldwater, and hobbled himself into a pair of fancy boots with tooled stitching. But he was still the same stoic Elo: silent as a goldfish in a pond. As I lifted my gaze to his face, I tried to conjure up words of parting that wouldn't cause rancor between us.

Nearing sixteen, Elo had reached Papa's lofty height, and had the lean, stringy look of a green bean climbing a pole. Tall and lanky, that was Elo. And probably the most handsome young man in Coldwater. He appeared oblivious to the young women who brazenly pursued him. Deceptively unaware. But I believed he had received and posted for future reference every flirtatious signal that had come his way.

I stood beside him now as I had a thousand times in the deep woods near our home: quiet as a sunset and immobile as a tree trunk. I had learned those traits from Elo, along with the skills of shooting, gutting, bleeding-out, and skinning a kill. Being silent had always been the toughest part of hunting with my brother, but as quietness engulfed me now, a core of contentment reconciled my emotions with a meas-ure of peace, and I was grateful. I lifted my gaze to a flat-winged hawk, soaring effortlessly over Brenham's rolling plains. Wing tips curled, it plunged toward earth in a fluid dive, most likely in search of prey. My gaze was so intent, I jerked near out of my skin when Elo muttered in my ear.

"I want you to get yourself well, Emma Grace, and get back home. Do you hear what I'm saying?" The way his teeth gnashed together, I couldn't fathom how he managed to shoot spittle and snarl at the same time.

*What's this?* Elo desired my speediest return? Had I misjudged the molten lava I'd spied in his eyes earlier? My befuddlement grew in sync with his narrowing gaze. Additional words spewed from his mouth, booting to kingdom come all the naïve nonsense I'd been coddling. After a glance at the ticket office, he leaned in close, voice dulled to a roaring whisper. "Mama ain't gonna have a bit of rest till you're back home in Coldwater, all cheered up and healthy. After what she's been through … don't you think she deserves that much from you?"

I squared my shoulders as any respectable Falin would and spewed out a hot-tempered retort. "Don't you lecture me on how to respect our mama. I'm not going to Galveston because I want to. I'm going because it's the only way I know to help Mama."

From the corner of my eye, I glimpsed Papa's approach. Blinking away the wetness, I faced Papa square on, managing what I pictured to be a smile.

"Our bus doesn't leave for another forty minutes, but I want you to head on home, Elo. Get Mr. Peavy's car back to him straight way. Don't go driving it around town. You hear?"

A flicker of what looked like surprise darted from Elo's eyes. "Yes, sir."

"You'll be the man of the place till I get back." Papa cast his gaze heavenward and shifted his stance. It seemed he would fain stay planted there until a new batch of words drifted his way. He lowered his eyes after a moment, pinched the bridge of his nose, and routed a look straight into Elo. "Take extra care with your mama and sisters. They'll be looking to you for support ... and a bit of comfort."

Elo gave his head a slow nod.

Papa cleared his throat and swallowed hard, his gaze fixed on Elo's impassive face. "A man couldn't ask for a better son."

Though the description most appropriately fit the brother I had lost, I knew Papa spoke of Elo—not Micah.

*But a man sure could ask for a better daughter.* I turned my face from Papa and Elo's embrace, my heart laden with guilt. I understood that Mama's welfare had been at the heart of Elo's lambasting moments earlier, but that didn't explain the feverish glint in his eyes. Couldn't his thick skull absorb the truth? I wasn't withholding my wellness from the family. I would latch onto every bit of healing that came my way, were it not as elusive to grasp as the wind.

An attendant hefted my suitcase to the roof as Papa and I boarded the bus, securing my travel mates' luggage to my own with a long rope. The green boxlike bus had a painted border midway up, on which greyhound pups chased each other. A second border, near the rooftop, contained the names of hamlets and towns along the route to Galveston. The interior of the bus looked fancy to my eyes, each set of windows having its own pair of brocade curtains, either tied back or drawn against the sun. Black-and-brown checkered seat covers proved cushion-soft, more so than Mr. Peavy's leather ones. Pillowed headrests added a touch of extravagance.

When the uniformed driver revved the engine and yanked the door handle, it seemed the gateway to hope slammed shut in my face. Trapped and locked in a world of sadness I couldn't deal with, I pictured Mama—standing just beyond the louvered glass. Tears streamed her cheeks as she waved her hand and released a kiss of farewell to the wind. As her image faded from view, I whispered good-bye to her around the lump in my throat. 'Twas but an illusion, after all.

Our journey began. Hopefully, we'd be on Galveston Island in four hours. Papa removed his scratchy wool jacket and placed it next to my crutch on the floor. He stuffed the pillowcase containing our food and his clothes under his seat. I wadded my coat and wedged it into the niche between cushion and wall. Papa reached for me then, stroking the thick braids Mama had plaited at daybreak.

"You won't be gone long, sweetheart. I'll have you home before ice coats the roads."

I lay my head on Papa's leg and curled myself into a kitten ball. My eyes leaked onto his dungarees, and I couldn't hold back my whimpers. Tears squeezed through my lids like bubbles of soap. Papa's hand slid past my braids, onto shoulders that refused to be still.

"Shush, Emma Grace … don't cry so. You're gonna make it. I promise you, sweet girl … you're gonna make it."

Papa didn't lie. The thought should have massaged a little peace into my heart. But what if—this one time—Papa was just plain wrong?

Cool breezes fluttered past the curtains, shooing away the stink of stale perspiration that had gnawed its way through the bus like wild locusts. But with the fresh drafts came the dust, pricking my eyes and watering them with fresh tears.

While I abode in the murky land of near sleep, Papa's hand stayed fixed on my back. 'Twas a comfortable, reassuring hand. I could almost believe Papa and I were off on a splendid vacation, and not the one-way trip I found myself traveling. A trip that might divide me from my family forever.

Papa awakened me when we arrived at the depot in Galveston. I'd been nodding in and out of sleep most of the ride. Upon awakening, I knew but a solitary moment of joy and wonderment as to the reason I was lying on a bus seat with my legs curled beneath me like those of a newborn colt. All too soon, the old blackness pounded on the postern of my heart, demanding readmittance.

As we debarked and began the long trek to Granny's house, Papa slung the pillowcase over his right shoulder and shifted our scrappy suitcase to his left hand. He raised it like a pointer, aiming it in an easterly direction. "Mama's house is on the east end of the island, about eighteen blocks from here. Think you can make it, punkin?" Before I could answer him, a shrimp-tainted gust of wind whipped up my skirt and tried to tear Papa's hat from his head. He rammed his felt hat down to his ears and strode down the walkway at a brisk pace.

We stepped from Harborside Drive and progressed through the alphabet streets until we arrived at Avenue G. From there, we turned onto Winnie Street, passing a multitude of houses, each one a letdown because it wasn't Granny's. I had used my crutch very little the last three weeks, and now my underarm ached with untried soreness. Though Papa adjusted his stride to match my sluggish one, I knew I pushed the limits of my strength.

When eighteen blocks had turned into twenty-two, we reached Granny's place. I saw her atop her high front porch, all atwitter and flapping her arms in hello. The house's tattered appearance rendered me dumbfounded, for Granny's residence lingered in my memory as a grand old mansion, rising almost to the clouds. A magnificent castle with a winding staircase and pointed, chopped-up ceilings. Now I viewed it in all its dowdy truth: an old, dilapidated, and lonely house, much like the empty place inside me. My gaze hustled past busted shingles, blistering paint, and windswept gables. It came to rest on the stairs leading up to the porch. As I counted them twice, then again, I swallowed a boulder of despair, knowing my crutch and I would probably topple before the fifth step, splitting my head like an overripe melon.

"I thought ye'd never get here," Granny bellowed, her feet taking wings as they soared down the stairway. A gust of wind—or Granny's anxious fingers—had released wisps of gray hair from the bondage of her topknot. She stroked them back in place as she made her way to us, wearing her trademark laced-up shoes and rolled-to-the-knee stockings.

"Come here, child. Let's have a good look at you." It came back to me then—the remembrance that Granny's hearing had begun a slow expedition away from her ears a few years back. She reeled in close, peering at me with watery eyes. She removed her spectacles and dabbed her eyes with an apron hem. "How're ye doing, sweet-pie?"

Though I jumped a bit at her overloud voice, the ancient nickname she had conferred on me at birth danced in my head like fireflies at midnight. Sunrays must have sparked my eyes, for Granny noted it in a voice the neighbors could hear four blocks away.

"See there ... ye're feeling a mite better already, ain't ye, Emma Grace?"

My grandmother had the Irish about her, slipping into her native brogue when her heart felt light and airy, and at other times as well. She clutched me to her bosom, the two of us swaying to the silent music in her head. We stepped apart, Granny seeming to covet a more intimate look at her eldest son—her one remaining offspring.

"How are you, Mama?" Papa asked as he waltzed her into his arms and a solid Falin hug. Three years of separation kept them locked together for long moments.

"Doing real good, Son ... but ... how are you and my sweet Annaleen faring?" Granny narrowed her eyes, checking for telltale signs it seemed that sorrow hadn't robbed Papa of his robustness. She clutched her apron hem again and removed her glasses a second time, patting her eyes as Papa draped his arm across her shoulder. "Just can't believe little Micah is gone." Granny's voice tottered like Widow Lindstrom's walking stick, and bore unaccustomed weakness, as though speaking Micah's name placed undue pressure on her vocal cords.

Papa's lids pinched together in a plaintive squint, the merest shake of his head a signal, no doubt, for Granny to refrain from talking about my brother's passing. At least while in my presence. Micah's death was something we no longer mentioned. It was as though it had never happened. Perhaps someday, when the weight of time had pressed the last bit of sorrow from our hearts, we'd speak again about the precious light that had gone out of our lives.

Papa placed his hand beneath my elbow and we began the steep climb to the porch. Granny's chattering recommenced, but I heard little, for I'd already lost my grip on the here and now. The mention of my brother's death had set my feet plodding down the dark, solitary pathway I seemed unable to resist.

"We're okay, Mama. But we'll be doing a lot better when Caleb wakes up and Emma Grace gets well."

Papa's words tugged on my heart, causing it to quiver like the needle of a compass. His voice was magnetic—drawing me to him as

though he were True North—The Pole Star. While my gaze recon-
nected to his prominent height and loving face, my feet slid off the dark
trail they'd been tramping and ambled into the light. I felt the corners
of my mouth tweak the tiniest bit as Papa's smile stretched the space
between us and sank into the depths of my eyes. With his hand grasping my arm with firmness, we climbed the stairs together—one step at
a time.

# Sixteen

I realized at once from whom I had inherited my chatty nature. It had passed through the blue-green bloodlines of Granny's Irishness, directly into me. Her uninhibited tongue shoved more thoughts into a sentence than the natural world had ever before heard. Or so it seemed to me. During the week of Papa's stay, her words pounded the air and caulked the gaps begot by three years of lost communication with her son. As Irish yarns and feisty phrases drubbed the walls, I concluded they were as slathered and spiked with puffery as our tall Texas tales. I loved her spirited chin-wag, for it claimed most of her time, leaving little leftover energy to scrutinize me.

Panic rose in my heart more each day, for Papa's stay in Galveston was about to end. His departure on tomorrow's bus was but hours away. He'd spent the week scraping clean, then painting Granny's blistered, peeling house. He'd replaced rotted boards and tightened loose shingles. He'd accomplished all he would have done in previous years, had time and money allowed more frequent visits.

The night prior to Papa's departure, I was unable to sleep. In the hollow hours before dawn, I rose from bed and walked to the window. Silver and blue stars pulsed in the pitch-black heavens, splashing the sky with bits of fairy dust, it seemed. The moon had waned to paltry insignificance, a mere sliver of mellowness on a vast parchment of black. I melded my gaze on the moon's paleness, sensing camaraderie with the lesser orb. Our lights were the same: diminished and weak, and shrouded in darkness.

Three blocks of habitation separated Granny's house from the ocean. Though the sea was too far away to hear, I recalled its never-ending sounds: muted whooshes and sighs as it sloshed about in a basin of sand, and the rush of tide as it flowed into inland pockets on shore. Were I to walk an eastern route, I would bump into its wetness, and once there, I'd hear the roar of waves breaking off and washing ashore, only to return again to the depths. Such sounds had always been, and forever would be. All this I remembered from my last trip to Galveston, three years earlier.

My reluctant ears identified the cadence of Papa's footfall tracking the back hallway. Boards squeaked more loudly now as the worn, wooden planking directed him to my room. I had but a moment to compose my emotions before he appeared in the doorway, his gait slacking not until it halted near the window. In the pale gray of near dawn, I made out the outline of Papa's felt hat, his broad shoulders, and his arms reaching out to me.

"I'll be taking my leave now, Emma Grace," Papa said as he dragged me from the window and into his arms. How warm and secure I felt in those brief moments. He lowered his pillowcase bundle to the floor and held me with tightness. "We'll be expecting you to write … want to hear in your own words how you're faring. And you can believe we'll be keeping ol' Mr. Hefflin busy, collecting letters to send your way." Papa stiff-armed me, holding me at a distance as he peered into the darkness of my face. "Listen to your granny, Emma Grace. She knows what it is to grieve. She has suffered more than her fair share of sorrow. Listen to her with your heart. Maybe she can help you find your way back to the Light."

I muffled my sobs into Papa's jacket and clung to him as though welded by blue-hot flames.

"Know this, little one. You hold a place in my heart that no one else can fill. You always have … always will. It's tearing me apart to go off and leave you like this, but for now, it's the only way I know to help you. Your family loves you, Emma Grace. I love you. Don't ever forget that. Just try to get well … for all of us."

Papa kissed my head time and again, squeezing me against his chest with gentle strength. After a while, he peeled my fingers from his jacket, bent over, and retrieved his bundle from the floor. Then he was gone.

After Papa left, Granny settled down some. I believed she had worn herself out, concocting meals fit for a king, for in Granny's eyes her son was a king. Her voice grew softer, previously unfettered words now shackled by the pain of her child's departure. When Holly married Flynn, Mama told us that though Holly no longer slumbered beneath our roof, she'd forever remain Mama's little girl. I supposed Granny felt the same way about my papa.

Though Granny and I both knew pain, we shared it not, mainly because I couldn't share my anguish with anyone. How could I parcel out a thing that lay twisted and gnarled within me like knotted strands of rope? Saying good-bye to Papa had been a repeat of the day our bus hauled out of Brenham, the door of hope slamming shut in my face a second time. As loneliness seized my waking hours, I discovered a more sinister blackness than the one companioning me these last weeks. This blackness avowed kinship with a deeper, darker place than I had yet visited.

Granny's obvious answer to despondency was food. Her own stoutness attested to its importance in her life. I thought she'd grow weary of trying to force-feed me, but her dedication to my diet only burgeoned as days slipped into one week and then another. She outdid herself, preparing savory recipes and personal favorites I had salivated over in years past. But my throat felt as though it had been stitched closed, disallowing most everything to glide through the sutures. When I tried to swallow—be it gruel, pork chops, oatmeal, or potatoes—I choked and gagged like a baby gulping his milk too quickly. My body slimmed to frightening boniness, apparel draping my skeleton like soggy clothes on the line.

I experienced passion for two things only: sleep, and Granny's stories. Both afforded hours of forgetfulness. I doted on those hours, knowing I could make it through another day—if I slumbered, or pretended the day away.

# Seventeen

Caleb, Micah, and I lay on a pallet inside the makeshift tent we had constructed from Mama's moth-eaten bedcovers. Night had tiptoed across our backyard, and now the sun poked white-hot fingers through the blanket holes. We lay close together, our legs entwined, and our arms flung out like the blades of a windmill. I was about to wake the little scalawags when someone rudely yanked the roof off our frame, exposing me to bright sunlight. As I rubbed my sleepy eyes, I tried to pinpoint who the bad-mannered intruder might be.

"Time to get up, sweet-pie."

"Whaa ... where are Micah and Caleb?" I asked in a panicky voice, my heart tripping with dread as my gaze raced across the bedroom.

"Ye must've been dreaming, Emma Grace. 'Twas just a dream, sugar. That's all it was."

I jerked myself to a sitting position, looking askance at Granny. Having no choice in the matter, I gnawed her troubling words with the teeth of truth, eventually swallowing them like bitter medicine. Antagonism replaced the wild joy of my dream. Granny's presence, along with her hard-biting words, filled me with untoward resentment.

The silence between us lengthened.

Granny edged her wrinkled face close to mine, her farsighted gaze beading in on me like vermin to lantern flame. As her morning kiss grazed my cheek, I nudged my head toward the wall and closed my eyes. Perhaps—if I tried ever so hard—I could recapture the precious dream she had stolen from my heart.

Why couldn't it have been my rowdy brothers' hands that bothered me from sleep, demanding I haul my lazy bones out of bed and join them in play? Why did it have to be Granny, her director's hands fussing over me, her peppery voice ordering me this way and that? Why had she pilfered the bliss from my nighttime illusion?

"After ye use the toilet and brush your teeth, we're gonna tackle that hair of yours. Ye've not washed it once since you got here, young lady." Granny dragged my covers to the footboard, untangling sheets, remaking the bed as though I weren't still lying atop it.

I glared at Granny, her nagging voice setting my teeth on edge. The same teeth that needed brushing, all right, but who had energy for such an arduous task? I grabbed my crutch and aimed for the bathroom at the end of the hall. The small amount of vigor I summoned up dwindled with each step I took. As I rattled the tooth powder can and collected enough in my palm to coat the bristles, I bid resentment good-bye. My energy level was too trivial to maintain anger and hold a toothbrush at the same time. I swiped my teeth with the brush, rinsed it, and replaced it in the cup holder. Never being the master of good judgment, I steadied my gaze on the creature in the mirror above the sink. She was far too ugly and broken to dwell upon, requiring more courage and fortitude than I could muster. Dismissing her with a pity-filled shudder, I retrieved my overalls from the door hook and dressed myself before Granny could bound through the door and take over the job.

Granny goaded the stove's belly with an iron poker, sparking flames and setting coals aglow. While she plied the heater with scraps of wood, I huddled on a nearby chair, covering my gooseflesh with a blanket. A blue norther had nose-dived into the city during the night, shocking Galveston's balminess with wild windflaws and frigid blasts. Evidently,

Papa had not had time to seal off Granny's windowsills. Through them, my ears detected the wind's whistling approach, and my face felt its frosty breath, puffing through cracks in the weather stripping.

"Never known such nastiness to hit so early in October. We'll be knowing some hard times this winter. Ye can bet on it."

I grunted in agreement.

Granny poured heated water into the wooden tub she had placed on a chair near the stove. Motioning me to her, she commenced with the head washing, three weeks overdue. I was relieved to have my scalp swabbed, as the itching had become more than bothersome.

Granny dunked my head, repeating the immersion several times, for my thick hair was averse to sponging up water. I felt the strength of Granny's fingers, scrubbing, massaging, and raising tingles along the bony ridge of my skull. She scraped the rough bar of soap through folds of thick hair, washing away the filth. I was glad that Granny didn't abide weakness in herself or others. Frail hands could not wash away all the dirtiness I had accumulated.

As Granny talked, my mind wandered back to the day Mama scrubbed my mouth with a bar of soap. Not her lavender-scented soap of special occasions, but, rather, lye soap made from hog tallow and strained ashes. She had become angry with me for calling Ray-boy Hodges "a spawn of the Devil"—a term I'd fallen in love with at one of the tent revival meetings in Coldwater. It had happened two years past. At the time, I'd not understood what the word "spawn" meant. I'd only known that the word *devil* fit Ray-boy Hodges like a skintight leather glove.

"Hey ... Mesobet. What's the matter—are you lost or something? Can't find your way back to Mommy?"

I turned to the voice, not at all surprised from whom the words had sprung. They'd belched out of the blubbery lips of Ray-boy Hodges—better known as Whale-mouth, for the proportions of food he gulped in a single swallow.

"What did you call me, Whale-mouth?" I asked with innocence.

"You heard me, Mesobet."

I had continued walking up the grassy aisle of the tent,

determined to ignore the one person who could raise my ire quicker than a hummingbird could swat its wings.

"Hey, Mesobet—don't you get tired of looking like a freak? Walking like a freak? Hey, I've got an idea. You could join the circus ... be a star in the freak show."

I turned and walked back to Whale-mouth, my brain calling forth all sorts of torture to levy upon his corpulent body. He always occupied the end seats of a row. It helped disguise the fact that it took two seats to house his double-berth bottom.

"It would help a great deal, Whale-mouth, if you could pronounce the name you're attempting to call me—like, maybe you'd actually learned to read and speak correctly at some point in your life."

Ray-boy's mouth slackened, then puckered, his lids squinting and his eyes disappearing amongst the folds of his face. He rose from his seat and waddled toward me with clenched fists.

"You heard me all right. You know who I'm talking about." Whale-mouth raised his palm and shoved my shoulder hard. "You're just like that guy in the Bible—Mesobet. He was a dumb cripple too."

I strained to keep my balance, looking the fool, I'm sure, as I struggled to stand upright. Gaining purchase on the uneven ground, I smiled with politeness, artificial though it was. "Oh, you mean Mephibosheth—one of King David's favorite people. Of course! I see the resemblance now. He was quite intelligent and very likable. I understand how you could've thought us similar."

"I ain't talking about his intelligence, dimwit. I'm talking about his crippled feet—just like yours!"

"That's where you're mistaken, Whale-mouth. I only have one crippled leg. Mephibosheth had two."

Ray-boy gave me another solid push, his flinty eyes striking the sparks of a victorious warrior.

I toppled against a folding chair, twisting my ankle, hitting my elbow on a wooden stake. A chair leg stabbed me in the gut, knocking breath from me. I lay on the grass, wheezing in air, or attempting to. Both my pride and my body hurt. Tears sprang up. I squeezed my lids, pushing wetness from them as I regained my breath and rose from the ground. 'Twas then Whale-mouth received the well-stocked brunt of my anger.

My deftness with a crutch displayed itself artfully, swinging a full arc, the handle landing upside Ray-boy's shoulder. Words flew from my mouth as though mounted on the wings of a hawk. "You spawn of the Devil!" I screamed, thrashing away at my ample target. His face quickly changed expressions, from startled, to frightened, then panicky as my crutch hit its mark. My tirade mounted. "You're too stupid to know I'm not—"

"Mama, Mama!" Ray-boy's screams puffed the canvas roof.

Mrs. Hodges rescued Whale-mouth about the same time Mama arrived on the scene. She had heard me cast curses upon my enemy, and she wasn't the least bit pleased. Riding home in the wagon that night, she'd explained the word "spawn." Elo, alone, had laughed with roguish delight at my word choice, Ray-boy being the preacher's son, and all. The spawn of the Devil—Reverend Ray Thackborn Hodges' only son.

Ray-boy's comeuppance had been worth the scouring Mama gave my mouth, not to mention those foul-tasting bubbles that had burped from my mouth for hours.

"Okay, sweet-pie. That should do it for another week or so."

Granny nudged my head over the tub, twisting my shoulder-length hair into a rope, wringing it like a wet mop. She wrapped my head in thick toweling, roughly patting excess moisture that oozed down my face and neck. My fat head-bundle wobbled a bit, reminding me of our old pet goose, Quicksilver.

After putting a kettle on to boil, Granny secured the towel to my head with her Sunday-best headscarf, and tied it with a sturdy yeoman's knot. The same knot Papa had taught the boys and me to tie. When

Granny's teakettle blew its whistle, she hurried to hush its shrillness while I seated myself on a slatted chair near the round-tummy stove. Weariness filled my being, though the mantle clock had not yet struck 9:00 a.m.

Mrs. Beushaker bustled through the back door, releasing a fresh batch of autumn into the parlor. Granny's longtime neighbor waved and smiled as she wrestled the hem of her dress to proper length, and then patted her wild gray hair back into place. She ambled to the kitchen when she heard Granny's voice. Both women reappeared minutes later, Granny thrusting a tall glass of chocolate frothiness into my hands while Mrs. Beushaker shoved a straw into the mound of pale bubbles.

"Take a sip, sweet-pie. I think ye'll like it."

"Culp Foggarty down at the drugstore gave me the straw, Emma Grace. Said it would help your swallow-up go down a little easier." Mrs. Beushaker bent at the waist, angling in close as though I couldn't hear well. Her wide grin displayed a perfect set of pearly-white teeth. I'd have bet a five-penny pack of gum they were as artificial as the smile I returned to her.

*Guess by now all of Galveston knows about my problem.*

"This'll be good for you. Better'n pot roast with all the trimmings." Granny squared her shoulders, boosted her chin, and grinned at Mrs. Beushaker. Granny's beaming smile took me by surprise, being she wasn't prone to giving herself a pat on the back. "I filled it with a heap o' good things: eggs, condensed milk, sugar, cocoa, vanilla. Drink it up. See if ye don't feel a bit of strength pour into you."

Granny crouched over me as though she might evidence the strength when it came pouring down. She didn't move until I had drained the tumbler. My hands shook as I returned the empty glass to her, my tummy hard and feeling as bloated as a fish corpse washed ashore. I feared Granny's brew might somersault its way back up my throat, onto her waxed floor, but, surprisingly, it stayed down.

As drowsiness settled over me, I began to suspect that Granny had stirred a sleep potion into her brew. She made a pallet for me in front of the stove, and I lay down. She removed the scarf and towel and spread out my hair like an oriental fan. Despite her scheme to hurry up the drying process, I knew its thickness would remain damp until the twilight hour. My eyelids closed.

I came alert some time later, softly-spoken words slurred in my haze of wakefulness.

"Seeing Emma Grace hurtin' like she is just brings back all the pain," Granny said in whispery tones.

"It's been twenty-eight years, dearie. You must let it go."

I lifted my head, viewing Granny and Mrs. Beushaker at the parlor table, drinking coffee or tea. From across the room I recognized the obvious sign of Granny's weeping.

"It's the time o' year, Mrs. B. Fall always resurrects memories of those dreadful weeks following the storm. Bodies washing up on shore … the burying … the burning stacks—humans set aflame along with the trash, as though they had no more value than a pile of refuse. It haunts me still. Lucky ye are you weren't living in Galveston when that wicked hurricane hit. Ye can't imagine what it was like, searching through piles of carcasses, hoping and praying I wouldn't find me family. Then, the horror of discovering my three little ones and their papa—half-buried in the muddy silt of Offat's Bayou."

Granny's throat clogged. I heard the gasping and gurgling, as though her words were drowning in a great rush of tears. I squeezed my eyelids shut, desiring to hear everything, yet recoiling from the sound of Granny's desperate sadness.

"I still see their precious faces in me mind. Sometimes, in me dreams, too. It's then I'll be reaching out to them, trying to pluck them from the water so's I can take them to higher ground. But me legs and arms won't work. They're weighted down like stone pillars. I keep plowing through the ruck of bodies, but I can never reach me children. Then I wake up, my sad old arms as empty as when I climbed into bed the night before. Oh, God, why didn't ye take me, too?"

"Perhaps … because he knew your oldest son would be needing you. You've been such a blessing to Roan and Annaleen. Look at you. Didn't they turn to you when they needed help for Emma Grace?"

Granny scraped her chair back, rising erect as she retrieved a hanky from her apron pocket. She scrubbed at her eyes and speedily returned the kerchief to its lace pouch. Her hurried fingers gathered up spoons, cups, and saucers while Mrs. Beushaker tidied up the tablecloth.

"Reminiscing won't get the chores done, will it, Mrs. B.?" Granny lifted her chin and ramrodded her back. "And it's for sure I can't bring my family back, though God knows I would cut me heart out and give it away if that's what it took to be with 'em again."

Mrs. Beushaker nestled Granny to her bosom like a little, lost child, but Granny broke free, as she'd brook no such coddling. As her friend departed through the back door, Granny scurried to the kitchen, most likely to whip up a culinary delight of which she expected me to partake. I doubted that would happen.

I lay on the pallet, ruminating on the desperation I had heard in Granny's words. Were our lives so different then? I thought not, for sadness linked us together in a bond mightier than the blood of our heritage. *For the rest of my life, I'll suffer the same agony as Granny. Asleep or awake, I'll be reaching out, trying to reel in my brothers, but like Granny ... I'll never be able to snatch them from the death hole.* A dull, lifeless pall crept over my being like soupy fog. I'd never felt so broken or frail. I shifted on the blanket-bed, turning my back on Granny's sorrow—and my own.

I studied the room, my glance stumbling over mantle photographs, old and long-faded to the hues of a newborn fawn. My gaze fastened on a picture near the center: *Papa, when he was a young man.* Then it fell on the likeness of three children, happy faces in the springtime of youth; children Granny had lost in the storm. At one time or another, each had been one of Granny's baby fawns.

Lace doilies and embroidered scarves decorated the parlor: the mantle, couch, end tables, and shelves. White dishes with bright blue centers stood upright in a windowless cabinet. Paintings filled the dishes: birds, dragons, odd-looking sailboats, and squat people wearing domed hats. One plate bore the image of a palace with an upturned roof. It appeared ready for flight; as though a stiff wind might set it free to soar like a March kite. Granny told me Grandpa Falin had given her the dishes the year before he died. The dishes were my favorite things among Granny's collectibles, for each dish had painted its own story on my heart.

My thoughts returned to the hurricane of 1900. How had Granny escaped the wrath of that terrible September storm? Why had her children and husband perished, but not she? A week or so earlier, I had asked Granny to tell me about the storm, but she had replied that hearing about that horrible tragedy was the *very* last thing I needed right now. She would tell me someday, she promised.

Granny and I abode in the aftermaths of separate storms. But had we both survived? I didn't think so. My day-to-day life—my existence—felt nothing like survival. I endured with a broken heart and broken spirit, and the knowledge that my brother had died because of me. If life consisted of no more than that—I had just as soon be gone from this place of steadfast sorrow.

Where could I find peace in the world? I wondered. It seemed there was always a storm brewing somewhere—either in someone else's heart—or in my own.

# Eighteen

Granny dangled the carrot in front of my eyes, and I grabbed for it.

"Put this dress on and go to church with me, and I'll tell you the story ye've been pestering me to tell ye."

*I only asked you one time, Granny.*

I chewed on my lower lip, not enjoying the discomfort of lying to Granny again. "My head hurts, Granny. I don't feel much like going to church."

"Ye've had a headache the last three Sundays, Emma Grace. I don't believe ye anymore. Now ... tell me why you don't want to go to the Lord's house."

I shrugged my shoulders and turned my gaze to my hands, fixating on the pitiful set of fingernails I'd chewed down like a well-gnawed bone. I lifted my head, hoping Granny had forgotten her question, but it was still there in her eyes, boring away at my conscience like a posthole digger. I'd not considered the strength and perseverance of Granny's tired old eyes, being that she had to have more years than the front-yard oak. If I didn't lead her down a rabbit trail, those eyes would dig and poke and scratch until they'd uncovered the truth for which they searched.

"Can't you tell me the story when you get home, Granny? I can make us some lunch while you're gone and then—"

"So … ye're feeling well enough to make lunch, but not good enough to go to church. 'Tis an interesting condition ye have there, Emma Grace Falin. Ye'll be getting no more stories out of me, young lady. Nary a one until you tell me why ye're avoiding church. Surely, you don't think God's own family would be making fun of yer leg. Now do ye?" As Granny stared me down, she cocked her head to the side and ruffled her lips into a hundred valleys and hills. She put me in mind of a great white-crested bird, readying itself to peck the head off a defense-less worm. And Granny was no skinny bird.

I shook my head, tempering the shake with gentleness so dampness wouldn't spill over my lids. Bawling was on the bottom rung of things I wanted to do while Granny stood witness. She must never learn that I had turned my back on God. Hearing about my blasphemy would break her heart, as she was one of God's kindest creatures; one of his truest disciples. I vowed she'd not hear of it from my lips.

"What's the matter, then? Don't ye like the new dress I stitched you?"

I shrugged again, but nodded my head also, lest Granny consider me ungrateful. Truth was I seethed with displeasure because she had hidden all but one pair of my overalls. I wanted a new dress about as much as I wanted my teeth to fall out.

An hour later, after I'd consumed another of Granny's chocolate con-coctions, she and I set out for church. The insides of my chest felt loose and wiry, as though a flock of starlings tap-danced on my heart. The jit-terbugging commenced every time I drank one of the mixtures I had secretly dubbed "sugar poison"—being that a single glassful set my heart to clattering for an hour or more.

My head ached in truth, for Granny had insisted on tending my hair, but in the end had yanked a brush through the tangled mess with less than patient hands. Headache or not, I now walked to church by my grandmother's side. A painful knot tightened my chest as I recalled my vow to never again darken the door of the Lord's house. Never again be forced to deal with the owner of the house.

The blue norther had moved on down the coast. Having remained chummy with Galveston for three days and nights, it now sought renewal of friendships further south. A salt-flavored breeze churned the warm, moist air. I'd become accustomed to Galveston's sticky clime by now, no longer wiping its tackiness from my skin after a venture onto Granny's porch swing.

I tilted my face to a noisy bunch of seagulls parading overhead. Each pass lifted them to steeper levels and stronger currents on which to soar. Perhaps they needed to rest their wings. Perhaps they were as weary as I was.

I wore the brown cotton dress Granny had fashioned by hand and with which she seemed quite pleased. Pretty, it was, though I was too bullheaded and upset with Granny to fork over an admission. As we walked the grassless path paralleling Winnie Street, I kept furtive vigil on my naked legs, preferring the mantle of privacy my overalls would have afforded my shorter, toe-scraping leg. Still, I should have worn the dress with pride, for it contained a wealth of beauty: slender sleeves that puffed out like tulip bells at my elbows; and a narrow skirt with a pointed waist. I'd not worn such a dress before. There was a king's garden of elfin white flowers on the brown cloth. They reminded me of winter storms back home, when ice pellets filled the furrows of our hibernating fields.

My gaze winded upward as we crossed the street and angled south. A structure came into view. Painted in a coat of purest white, the massive dome reared above the treetops, high splendor parting the elements into blue sky above, green trees below. 'Twas an architectural delight. A bounty of round windows, lacy turrets, and fancy towers decorated the many-storied building. Though I knew it was a church by the small cross on the dome, I pretended it was a majestic white rook, sitting atop a chessboard of leafy green.

"That's Sacred Heart Church. Ain't it a beautiful thing?"

I stumbled over a curb, not desiring to alter the direction my eyes had taken.

"It's been here since forever, ye know?"

*Granny's church. The inside must be as grand at the outside. I'll be having myself something fine to look at while the preacher's up telling his tales about God's love and protection. What slippery tongues these preachers have. 'Bout anything will slide off them.*

"Why are we walking away from church, Granny?"

"'Cause our church is two blocks down the street."

As my heart sank into my stomach, moisture from an endless well of seepage refilled my eyes. I angrily brushed at the wetness with the hem of Granny's handiwork while she continued to rattle on about nothing. I should have known Granny wouldn't take to worshipping in such grandeur, her tastes leaning toward the more simple things of life.

"That's the Catholic church, Emma Grace. And looky there, 'crost the street. That's the bishop's palace. 'Tis as beautiful and impressive as the church, don't ye think? Tell you one thing—them Catholics sure know how to treat their ministers."

I counted eight chimney-high towers on the palace Granny had been admiring. There were probably more my eyes couldn't see. The mansion looked familiar, like pictures of castles in fairy tales from my childhood. This one looked like Sleeping Beauty's castle, except that columns of overgrown hedgerows didn't surround the foundation, nor did wild vines climb to rooftop peaks.

"There's our church, Emma Grace."

I looked in the direction of Granny's pointed finger, disappointment pooling over me like grease in a pan of cold dishwater. A white frame structure occupied the center of an almost-vacant lot. It had a peaked roof and sawed-off steeple, and needed painting as much as the lawn needed mowing. At the side of the church, a group of five or six children played keep-away amongst a throng of moldy-gray tombstones. A trifling number of stones remained upright, but the greatest number tilted to one side, as though tuckered out by the tugs of too many little fingers.

"It's nice, Granny." I could think of nothing else to say.

"Let's go inside. Want to show you off to my friends."

The trip back to Granny's house seemed short, mainly because Granny splattered the air with nonstop chatter, allowing my mind to wander at will. And, because the road home always seems faster than the one that takes you away.

I had indulged in a nap during the preacher's sermon, despite

Granny's bony knuckle that had persistently tried to nudge me awake. An embarrassment I had been to Granny, I'm sure. But I had grown weary of her friends' scrutiny, as though I was a sliver of meat on the butcher's rack, and they were there to find which parts needed chopping off. My odd looks seemed to bring out the sternness in some of the ladies, their lips plaited together like a weaver's wattle. The other ladies simply smiled wider when I ventured to return their gaze with one of my own. I was certain Granny's friends had won the stare stand-off. When I arrived home and examined myself, I knew I'd find a pack of holes gouged straight through me.

"Set the table, sweet-pie."

"Yes, ma'am."

"After lunch … I'll tell ye the story." Granny peeled potatoes at the kitchen sink, her back to me as she spoke. But I noticed the way her shoulders hunched forward and her head drooped a bit. Did it slump in resignation? Most likely. To Granny, a deal was a deal. You didn't renege on your promises, even if keeping them might bowl you over with a heart attack.

"I think maybe I'll wait a bit for the story, Granny. I'm kind of sleepy. I'll probably take a nap, or write Mama a letter. She's fussing 'cause I only wrote home that one time."

It wasn't my imagination—the prolonged lift of Granny's shoulders—the way they settled back into place. That must've been some sigh she let out. For Granny's sake I had changed my mind about the story, but also because my heart was overly sad today. She was right, of course. I didn't need more sorrow heaped atop the landfill I'd already packed in my heart.

I missed my home. Everything about it: reading to the twins and having to explain the big words; Nathan's brilliance, and Elo's snarls; Olly giggles, and the ridiculous way they fretted over clothes, hair, and *boys;* snuggling between Mama and Papa on the sofa in the evening hours before bedtime. Sundays at our house were nothing like Sundays with Granny.

Granny took the Bible to heart, resting on the Sabbath as it commanded her to do. Of course, Granny rested on the other six days of the week, as well. I heard her now, snores bumping out her throat, followed by high whistles that probably had the neighborhood dogs yelping in distress.

I lay on my bed, rereading Mama's last letter, my investigator eyes searching for clues as to the true state of our household in Coldwater. Every letter she wrote said the same thing: Caleb was improving, everybody was fine, and Papa's fall crops looked exceptional; they'd provide an abundant harvest as long as the weather held true. The letter in my hand spoke of Elo's evening hunts, after he'd worked the fields with Nathan and Papa. During the past week, Elo had killed one wild turkey, three geese, and a bounty of dove and quail. The Ollys cooked the plumpest goose and delivered it to Widow Lindstrom, along with canned okra, squash, and beets. No, Caleb hadn't awakened from his coma, but he was showing signs that he'd soon rouse from his deep sleep. Perhaps, Mama explained, her next letter would tell me about his great breakthrough. She ended every letter the same: "We love you, Emma Grace, and miss you more every day. Without your smile to warm our hearts, the house feels cold and drafty. Get well, sweetheart."

I searched the house for paper. Mama needed to know I was doing … *better?* Maybe she wouldn't worry so much if she received confirmation by my own hand. And what was one more lie added to the platter of untruths I'd already served Granny? I looked everywhere, disgruntled because the one time I felt inclined to write, I could find no paper. I recalled the tablet Granny kept in her purse. She used it to write letters, grocery lists, and memory-jogging notes she left on the toilet lid, icebox shelf, and other strange places about the house. Notes to cover her forgetfulness. And when she couldn't hide her memory loss, she spun it into wisecracks, such as: "Seems like every time I stand up, my memory decides to sit back down."

As I plowed through Granny's shoulder bag, my gaze faltered on familiar handwriting: a letter from Mama—stuffed into the folds of her catchall purse. Gripped by a sense of foreboding, I slipped the letter into the pocket of my overalls and scurried to my room. I closed the door and sat on the bed, knowing I was at a crossroad, of sorts. But was I ready to choose the road to truth? As I unfolded Mama's letter, dated five days earlier, my hands quivered like a divining rod over water, for I sensed that the gnarly knots of truth were about to be untangled.

*Dearest Mara,*

*As I lift my pen to write the latest news, I do so with trembling hand and heavy heart. My heart knows little else than weariness, these days. Though Doctor Landers tries to extend us hope, his eyes cannot hide the truth. The longer Caleb remains in a coma, the less chance there is for a full recovery ... or any recovery at all. We've been warned that he may have suffered injury to the brain, which could possibly result in retardation of some sort.*

*My precious boy swallows juices and broth I spoon down his throat. It is a reflexive habit, I believe, for the rest of his body remains lifeless as before. Oh, Mara. What am I to do? How can I help my Caleb fight for life when my own heart knows only the emptiness of sorrow and broken dreams? My poor child. How ashamed he would be to know he now wears diapers as he did when a babe.*

*How did you do it, Mara? How did you lose your husband and three children, yet today remain staunchly vital and alive? Where did you gain courage and strength to bear such pain? I truly feel I could not survive the loss of another child.*

*At night, after the family has gone to bed, I return to my beloved Micah. Lantern in hand, I find my way to his side on the darkest of nights. I must! For I hear him calling to me. What kind of mother would I be to leave him all alone? I kneel by his headstone, missing him more than I did the day he left us. With every breath I take, I long to see his sweetness ... just one more time. To touch his face and nestle him in my arms. Oh, if only the boys hadn't wandered off into that field of death ...*

*Please, Mara, tell no one of my lingering sadness. Or the lost condition I find myself in. I admit to you and you alone that my faith has faltered a time or two. But I know it is because of my own weakness—and not because God has deserted us, for his love is unfailing. I continue to put on a good front for the family, especially Roan. He has taken Micah's death the hardest. For a father to lose his son … I didn't know what suffering was until we lost our Micah, dear friend. At least I have the sweet release of tears. If Roan finds such release, it is never in my presence.*

*It saddens me that Emma Grace has not regained her will to live—that fighting spirit that kept her alive during infancy. Where has it gone? She seems not the same vibrant child that filled our home with unceasing chatter and wild, wild tales. If only I could breathe life back into her.*

*Please pray that I will find the strength to take care of my family—to help them walk through this valley of grief. They need my devoted care and unselfish attention. Not a mother destroyed by loss.*

*I continue to thank God for your help. How blessed I was the day I married Roan, and gained not only his undying love, but also a mother and a friend. Thank you for taking care of our Emma Grace.*

*I must close now and try to rest, if not sleep. It brings me comfort to share my deepest anguish with you, knowing that once you felt the same hopelessness and sorrow I now feel. I beg you—let no one know the faithless words I've written.*

> *I remain your loving daughter,*
> *Annaleen*

Mama's words echoed in my heart like a trumpet in the wind. If only the boys hadn't wandered off into that field of death.… If only Emma Grace had kept her brothers near her, where they belonged. That's what Mama's words were really saying. My eyes spilled over, teardrops bathing Mama's penmanship, puddling her words and mottling the paper with streaks of black ink. I wadded the letter into my pocket and rushed to the front porch.

At the top stair, I tossed my crutch to the ground and bottom-bumped my way down to the foundation step. Retrieving my crutch, I raced against the wind, into the unknown. Mind-boggling urgency drove me from Granny's house. Away from the prison of my own making.

# Nineteen

Flickers of fire spun down from the sun, setting the ocean ablaze with feverish light. Such intensity hurt my eyes. Turning my back on the water, I hooded my eyes and scoured East Beach for a niche in which to hide.

My reservoir of energy had run dry some time earlier, and now my legs spurned the thought of dragging through one more pile of loose sand. Like a hermit seeking solitude, I aimed my crutch toward a cluster of sand ridges. Glancing behind, I noted the trail I'd forged in the sand: round holes paired with single shoeprints. They were the tracks a peg-leg pirate might have made once upon a time. Sinking to a sand bed between two dunes, I kicked off my shoes and dug my toes into the cool sand. I rubbed my afflicted leg, repeating a longtime habit of persuasive massage that purportedly helped it grow. The heat of day had deserted this valley floor, leaving only cool shade behind. Concealed from the curious stares of Sunday onlookers, I sat in the shadows and thought about Mama's letter.

Mama's letter burned in my pocket like a bonfire: her pretense and my hope—gone up in smoke and reduced to ashes by her neatly written words. Caleb would die, most likely. Even if he lived, he would not be the child he once was. Whatever the outcome, I was responsible for my family's loss. How I wished I could erase the past and roll back time to that hot August day my brother died. I would hold onto the twins with the strength of a mountain man, and though they'd scorn my protectiveness, I would bind them with a rope, if need be, and never loose them to wander the field of death.

Bitter tears poured from my eyes as I lay in the sand, pleading for a fairy-tale ending to my sorrow. But wishes were like dreams. They never really came true. Deep within, where my heart lay open and bleeding to the truth, I knew there'd be no happily ever after for my family. No magic spells cast in the name of true love. Life was permanent. Micah was gone forever, and Mama's arms would never cease their yearning. Were I to offer my life for Micah's a thousand times over, I could never right the wrongs I had done. Oh, that I could put my thoughts aside—if but for a moment—and ease the pain in my heart.

The overhead call of seagulls roused my awareness. Scooting from the shadows, I watched as a quartet of birds dived to shore and battled over bits of food plunder. They raced in wild plunges, attacking and withdrawing, their shrill squawks a bother to my ears. A lopsided pelican swooped low over the water, looking the blunderbuss as it scooped in a mouthful of sea. Even his wide beak and awkward takeoff couldn't fetch a smile to my face.

I sat in secluded misery as minutes nibbled away the hours, and breakers heaved ashore, carrying parcels of sea floor with them. The waves mixed with lacy whitecaps, leaving dingy ruffles of foam to scallop the sand. As clouds sculpted the beach with bizarre shadows, the hazy sun sank closer to the sea. For a while it rested there, as though a colossal Titan had tossed a fiery ball onto the water. Then the sun scrunched lower yet, dipping to ocean floor, it seemed. Nightfall would soon follow. Granny would be worried and ready to blister my hide. But I couldn't go back to her house. Not yet.

I left the dune at twilight and shuffled to shore, sitting myself upon a drying pathway of retreating tide. A few feet away, a sandpiper pecked out a nest in the damp sand. Tiny as a robin's egg, the wee piper popped its head above the hole, revealing a feathery crest. I watched with heavy heart, knowing this little life was in danger, for creatures more powerful and cruel roamed the sky and sand, seeking the weakness of others.

While I sat in the mute numbness of lost and shredded thoughts, the wind tossed my hair and delivered a surfeit of scents to my doorstep: the odor of petroleum from ships anchored in the bay, a whiff of decaying seaweed, and a sweet fragrance I identified as jasmine. They blurred together like the mishmash of thoughts in my head. I licked brackish sea spray from my lips and turned my gaze upon a noisy group of revelers that stomped the boardwalk of Murdoch's Bathhouse. There was no likening of their boisterousness to the silent sorrow in my heart. Their joyful laughter confounded me, for I could not understand how it flowed with such abundance when my own heart lay smashed in unmendable pieces.

When more of the sun rested below the horizon than above it, a young boy ran past me on the beach, his brown curls flopping like the tail of a high-soaring kite. As his bare feet stomped the damp sand, giggles poured from his mouth. Micah's giggles.

"Micah!" I shouted, leaping to my feet. I grabbed my crutch and chased after my little brother. "Micah—wait for me." The wind puffed my words back in my face, but quick was my gait and thunderous my heart as I followed the wee tracks of my brother. His feet churned ever faster, laughter trailing behind him like a string of ducklings on the heels of their mother. My eyes filled with tears of joy. *Micah! Oh, Micah, wait for me!*

"Jonathan! Jonathan Theodore Davidson ... you get yourself back here this instant. If I have to come after you, I'm bringing a belt." A voice ranted behind me, drawing closer as I slowed my pursuit.

When the woman hurried by, her face in what seemed a twist of anger and frustration, I slumped to the ground in despair. She lunged after the boy, catching a bit of shirttail, halting his escape. The child's eyes burned with a look of youthful mischief, reminding me more of Caleb than Micah. He seemed delighted to have the woman scoop him into her arms. As she turned and walked the path she'd previously galloped, the boy's grin set my heart to trembling. I broke down and cried for the hopelessness of my loss. Micah was dead and buried. He couldn't run on the beach, as Jonathan Theodore Davidson did. Micah would never run on the beach again. 'Twas a terrible thing to have a beautiful dream come true before your eyes—and then have that dream ripped out of your heart in a moment's time.

As the sky drifted into inky shades of darkness, I sat on my sand cushion, numb to everything but sorrow. The sea flowed without interruption and the stars—pocketed in hidden valleys of the firmament—blinked with eternal consistency. I placed my hand over my heart, wondering why my brokenness hadn't caused its collapse. The dull cadence wore on, steadfast, if not honorable. A bird with a broken wing cannot fly. How was it possible that I, who possessed a dead, lifeless heart, detected its beat within?

Blurred images and shadows of movement melded together with the passage of time. Across the bobbing surf, a light floundered. A pin-prick of brightness that flickered like a candle teased by the wind. I spied it again, blinking its own rhythm as it streaked the darkness above the rolling sea. The light called to me.

I followed its beam across the pages of time—back to the night of my baptism six years earlier. At dusk, after the Sunday evening service, Dutch Welgren hoisted a lantern above my head while Pastor Emery guided me into the spirited water of Susquant Creek. As he asked God's blessings on the three children who had just given their hearts to Jesus, of whom I was the youngest, I kept vigilant watch on the creek banks where patches of prickly ash grew. We called the brush "devil's walking stick," for within its spiny sharpness a nest of water moccasins was known to abide. Being far less spirit-filled than the preacher, I begged God for one thing only: to keep the snakes asleep in their beds of shrub until the dunking was over and I had bolted from the creek.

The memory departed as quickly as it had arrived. I blinked and narrowed my gaze, searching anew for a signal from the sea.

Lights along the seawall came on as if by magic. Granny had informed me about Galveston's modern electrical lights. But by the crispness of her voice I knew she preferred the olden days when gas lamps were set aflame by the lamplighter's torch and pole. Murdoch's Bathhouse was illuminated as well, lantern light bathing the building with saffron glow. However, darkness abode in its depths, just thirty feet below the fancy railing. Stabilized in shoes of ocean floor, wooden piers stood firm as the tide raced irresistibly out to sea. Those with tender ears could hear the sighing and moaning of the sea as it surged through the maze of timbered beams. They could hear the haunting melody it crooned. 'Twas a melody intended for the brokenhearted.

Fortunate I was the sea knew only the story of my grief. Had it also known my guilt, it would not have bothered to sing for me at all.

In the choppy water of the bay, the light toiled on. Perhaps my eyes alone saw the flickering message it sent across the waves. *Forgetfulness is waiting for you. Come—find it within my depths.* I could no longer deny the obvious solution to my pain. Rising from the sand, I moved toward the light.

I had taken but a few steps when I halted and turned away. Retracing an earlier route, I tracked back to the dune of my afternoon respite. Once there, I unclasped Mama's locket and held it next to my bumping heart. With each tear that spattered the sand, I felt more at peace with the decision I had made. And more sorrowful for the grief I had caused. I kissed the locket and pigeonholed it in a pocket of dune. After sprinkling it with a thin coating of sand, I lay my crutch atop it.

*Perhaps Mama will chance upon the locket someday, and remember me with love.*

I limped back to the water, content my wanderings had gone undetected. As I shuffled across the doorstep of the sea, waves lapped my ankles and splashed the cuffs of my overalls. Ocean breezes pelted me with moistness that felt more like aloneness. My teeth chattered from the cold. And from fright, as well, for though my will to live occupied less space than a gnat in the universe of time, the path I had chosen was still a fearful one to travel. Through a chute of tears, I located the blinking light and aimed my feet toward it. As I pushed through waves that had their genesis on the far side of the sea, I stayed my vision on the light.

# Twenty

Wave after wave pummeled my body with a liquid mallet, but still I pressed toward the light, its unmistakable message pulsing in my heart. Progress was slow and tedious, rendered so by pugilistic currents that knocked me from my feet like a prizefighter. The ocean had a fickle mind, tugging me out to sea with one heave, yanking me back to the shore with another. Saltwater burned my eyes, and my legs wearied of trudging a channel whose density was like cottage cheese. I no longer sensed the water's coldness as it swirled atop my shoulders and lifted my feet from the ocean floor. Dead to all feeling, save the sorrow that had led me to this time and place, I longed for one thing: to abandon my guilt and sorrow in the tides of forgetfulness. Purge them as I had purged my sins in the baptismal waters of Susquant Creek. As I bobbed in the currents and waited for the ocean to swallow me, I hoped the sea would be gracious and proffer me its forgiveness, as well.

The ocean roared in my ears, more intensely now that the sea and I had become one. A rogue wave poured down on me like the floodgates of heaven, plunging me to the bottom of the sea, and then sailing me high above the breakers. Why I struggled to stay afloat remains a mystery. Perhaps it was an instinct for survival, though I wished not to survive at all. My arms paddled like ferocious oars as I fought to gain purchase of the light, but another wicked wave picked me up like a rag doll and pitched me toward shore. I choked and quaffed water, spitting back into the wetness all I coughed up. When I pushed to my feet, I was dismayed that I stood in a mere foot of sea. I waded to waist-high water and turned toward the light. But the sea swelled again, towering high, catapulting me through the blackness and onto the beach where it pounded me into the fast-shifting sand. Exhaustion bound me with invisible ropes as I lay on the shore, heaving for air.

Moonbeams rained down from the sky like spears, tattooing the beach with a pale, sickly glow. I stood after a time, tottering in shallow surf that licked my feet while my heart responded with maritime pulses. Water rolled from my clothes in salt-tainted sluices as I sank deeper into my fluid sandbox. I knew weariness as never before. I, who had boasted of swimming the seeable length of Two-Toe Creek with barely a hitch in my breath. *A weakling ... that's all I am.* When I most needed to reach the light, I couldn't navigate past the first big wave. I wept again, saddened by another failure—too soon come upon me.

A voice thundered through the night air, rising above the squall of the sea. For one frightening moment, I thought I had unknowingly entered a netherworld—one existing in the deepness of middle earth or beneath the origin of the sea. Then I reasoned I must have been dreaming, and even now lay on my bed in Coldwater, for the voice sounded very nearly like Elo's.

"... and the three stars in the middle are called belt stars. Sure as the sun rises each morning, the mighty hunter rears up in the eastern sky every autumn, ready to do battle."

My ears rang with the sound of the sea, yet I imagined I heard Elo's voice a second time ... saying something about a belt. Was he thinking to use his belt on me? He'd never dared such a thing before ... what was Elo doing in Galveston, anyway?

"See that cluster of stars—right up there? Just follow my finger. That's Orion's head, and there's his shoulder. The stars off to the right make up his bow. Crafty fellow, isn't he? You can bet his quiver carries nothing but the deadliest arrows."

The voice moved in my direction. I whirled my head toward the sound. A man approached, setting a slow but steady pace on the path leading to me. His hand stretched upward, but his gaze never tarried from my face. In the near darkness, he looked menacing and as deadly as the arrows of which he spoke. A scream tore from my throat—an unending scream that snatched all breath from my body. I dropped to my hands and knees, crawling like a baby, clawing the sand as I scrambled for the safety of the sea.

"Whoa ... whoa there ... I don't mean you any harm."

The man fell to his knees in the water, his hands reaching for me as I cried and gouged my way into deeper ocean. When I let loose with another yowl, he reared back his hands like a robber surrendering to the police. I crabbed through knee-high water, coughing and yelping as I made my escape from the stranger.

The man leaned toward me and again raised his hands. "Hey, look ... I'm sorry I frightened you. I was just talking to myself, the way I always do. Then I saw you wash up on shore. You looked like you needed a little help. See that pile of rocks over there?" the man said, directing his finger to a mound of broken slab. "I'll go over there, if you like. You can stay here. You don't need to be afraid of me, little girl. You're safe. I wouldn't hurt you for the world."

For the first time, I detected a slight quiver of adolescence in the stranger's voice.

As I wheezed and coughed up saltwater, I kept a fixed stare on the trespasser. He walked to a pile of riprap some distance away and sat down. While he kept his attention trained on the sky, I gathered my matted hair into a rope and slung it over my shoulder. With stiff, dirty fingers, I brushed straggly forelocks from my eyes and studied him. 'Twas true—though the youth stretched toward manhood, he'd not reached it altogether. After my nerves settled down, I determined he was not the malevolent-hearted beast I'd presumed him to be.

Though I hated the young man for his meddlesome interference, it proved difficult to turn my eyes from his presence. He appeared close in age to Elo, and had the same wide shoulders and tallness of my brother. But their similarities ended there, for the intruder's hair was as black as the burning end of midnight. Faded dungarees and denim shirt hid portions of his shape, but they couldn't disguise his lanky height and sturdy build.

I had no choice but to wait out the hours there on the beach. It wouldn't do to appear at Granny's house in drenched clothing. She would grow suspect of the mission I had failed to carry out this evening. She might unearth the truth in my heart and discover what I already knew: My future aimed in one direction only—the sea of forgetfulness.

A stiff breeze drove a smidgen of dampness from my clothes, but not enough to fool Granny. With eyes blindfolded, she would smell the sea on me and wonder what I'd been up to. I sat with the night wind to my back, scanning my brain for a way to hornswoggle myself out of the mess I'd made. As I waited for evaporation to do its work, exhaustion and cold combined into a mighty case of the shivers. I dared not move and call attention to myself, so I clenched my chattering teeth and huddled my shoulders against the cold, damp air. My gaze roamed lovingly over the water, searching for the beacon. For the hundredth time I wished I had made it to the light.

My eyes stared at the sea, lost in the journey I had been traveling for the last few weeks. I didn't see the man-boy evacuate his place on the rocks, nor did I spy him walking toward me. Suddenly I heard a voice behind me. I whirled at the sound and opened my mouth to scream, but his words stopped me short, for they were breathed out like a prayer.

"Thought you might need my jacket. I could see you shaking from clear over there on the rocks."

He laid his jacket across my shoulders and stepped back a pace, revealing empty palms, with nary a weapon in either hand.

I nodded my head in thanks, or perhaps it nodded on its own, as the shakes had taken over my body.

"Look … you need to get out of the wind. Let's find you some shelter in those dunes." He pointed to the sand ridges in which I'd hidden earlier today.

I tried to motion him away and tell him to leave me alone, but my chattering teeth wouldn't allow me to say a word. Though he seemed kind enough, I wouldn't follow him into the darkness. My trust didn't extend as far as the dunes. I shook my head and backed up a bit on the sand.

"Shhhh … it's okay. I'm not going to hurt you. Didn't mean to sneak up on you like that, but you'd have screamed your head off if I just walked over and handed you my jacket. You're liable to catch pneumonia out here in the wind. Keep the jacket. Just forget about the dunes. Maybe that wasn't such a good idea."

Like a mother soothing her infant back to sleep, the youth cooed his hushed whispers to me. "I'm going back to the rocks now."

His stride appeared purposeful and steadfast as he walked away with only one backward glance at me. He reseated himself upon the riprap before turning his gaze to the heavens.

I settled deeper into the thick jacket, grateful for its warmth.

# Twenty-one

I was somewhat wary of the squatter who sat atop the slabs. But that didn't keep the shakes at bay, nor did it stay my eyes from closing. I collapsed to the sand and rubbed salt and grit from my eyes. They stung as if they'd rubbed up against a stalk of bull nettle. Had I crossed the Sahara Desert on foot, I couldn't have been any wearier.

I awakened with a start, looking first to the rock pile for the stranger's whereabouts. He no longer sat atop the stones. My gaze swept the horizon, but spied him not. Sand covered half of my face and most of my body. As I stood on shaky legs and brushed stubborn grit from my hair and clothes, I scanned the beach for the stripling.

He appeared then, sauntering toward me, his arms laden with sea trash. I stood, mostly on my good leg, and watched his approach, but he walked directly to the pile of stones and dumped his clutter of driftwood, paper, and dried seaweed to the ground. After digging in his pocket, he squatted in the sand and set aflame his stack of flotsam. The fire looked inviting. But when he motioned me to its warmth, I shook my head and stayed where I was.

"The fire sure feels good," the lad said in a voice that presented itself well across the distance. He held his open palms above the burning

debris and continued the one-sided conversation. "Oh, by the way …
my name is Tate."

I debated for a time, and then slowly made my way to the opposite
side of the fire from the youth. His eyes narrowed as he studied my face,
and he seemed to be waiting for a reply, though he didn't press me for
my name. 'Twas a good thing he didn't, for as surely as stars filled the
heavens, I would not divulge my identity, nor the reason I swam the
nighttime sea.

Tate spoke of the sea, the weather, birds settling in for the night.
His voice soothed my ruffled feathers and softened the shell of fear
around my heart. While he eyed me with the intensity of a bird-
watcher, a smile settled over his features, granting his countenance a
gentleness I couldn't deny. Surely I could trust a smile that held Mama's
own good sweetness in it. Tate must have sensed the moment I began
to trust him, for his eyes took on a glint of utmost satisfaction.

I slipped the jacket from my shoulders and held it out to Tate from
across the fire pit—a silent substitute for something I was unwilling to
share with him. When he shook his head, I sighed in contentment, for
I had grown used to the coat's warmth.

We sat near the fire, he on one side and I on the other.

"Do you mind if I ask you something?"

I knew what was coming. I turned my gaze to the sea and said
nothing.

"Never mind … it can wait."

Tate stirred the fire with a stick, setting aglow the embers of a dying
flame. Earlier, the fire had popped and spit, its glory brief, but conse-
quential. Now all that remained was a smattering of charcoal embers
and a pile of pale ashes.

The fire reminded me of Micah. His life had been brief and glorious, but now he was gone. His ashes would eternally abide in the
burying box on our farm. There in front of the stranger my heart
squeezed with grief. I would have chosen the pain of a thousand beasts
stampeding across my body rather than knowing again the fresh hurt of
losing Micah. I lay my head in my hands. The stranger would see no
more tears tonight.

I'm unsure if Tate sensed my sorrow. He resumed his lecture about the
stars, perhaps to turn my attention from something he didn't understand.

"See that bright star … above Orion's head? That's the planet Saturn. If we had a telescope we could see Saturn's rings."

I didn't respond, except to glance at the sky space of which he spoke. It wasn't in me to explain that Papa had taught us about planets, star constellations, and galaxies. He had sketched our planetary system and made us draw its duplicate. Most likely Papa was a teacher at heart. I knew Saturn had two sets of rings. He told us that even a weak telescope could detect their visibility on a clear night. Papa would probably be willing to exchange his right arm—or his fifth child—for such a telescope.

Tate's concentration attached itself to the night sky with deep devotion, as was the way with true astronomers. I rose quietly to my feet and disappeared into the darkness. I left him there, gazing at his stars, unaware that his audience had made her way to the dunes, where she retrieved her crutch and aimed it toward Granny's house.

I knew my appointment with the sea was but a temporary postponement. I would come back. The light awaited my return.

# Twenty-two

Granny stood on her front lawn, huddled with half a dozen people. She had gathered a posse, it seemed. I knew I was in a heap of trouble because people milled about as though searching for a lost puppy and every porch light in the neighborhood beamed with brightness. A finger pointed in my direction, turning Granny's head toward me. Like the prodigal's father, she spied me from afar.

"Emma Grace … Emma Grace! Where have you been, child?"

There was power in Granny's lungs. A mighty breath of fear hurled her scream through the night air like a ball slammed by Elo's bat. I imagined Tate hearing it from two miles away on the beach. Worried about her safety, I hurried as best I could, but she rushed on with anxious feet, meeting me head-on, wrapping me in a bear hug.

Granny's sobs tore at my heart. I cringed at my selfishness, knowing I desired to escape my pain more than I cared about Granny's feelings. I had hurt her tonight, as I would hurt my family when the sea and I parted no more. Even so, I had pondered it thoroughly and knew the only way to rid myself of guilt and shame was for the three of us to walk the plank together—so to speak.

"Let's go tell these good people that you're safe, Emma Grace, so they can go back to their homes. They've been helping me look for you all evening. Where in the world have you been, child? It's almost nine o'clock."

Granny didn't stop to hear any answers I may have concocted. She spoke quietly to each bug-eyed person in the yard while they studied my slovenly person with huge question marks in their eyes. When the yard was empty, but for Granny and me, she wrapped her arm around my shoulder and we walked up the porch steps together.

Granny lit one kerosene lamp in the parlor and one in the kitchen. There were electrical outlets all over the house, but she preferred her lanterns. Granny cracked and scrambled two eggs, buttered a slice of bread for oven toast, and poured a glass of milk. White milk. She turned to me and pointed to a chair at the table. I sat down, surprised by long-absent sensations of hunger that now rumbled in my stomach.

"Now, young lady … after you eat supper and take a hot bath, you're gonna tell me what in the world's going on."

I floated in coolness, moving without resistance through calm, peaceful water. The water's stillness unsettled me, for in my mind I still locked horns with the fearless sea. I had struggled with my eyelids, keeping them open while I scrubbed sand from hair, ears, toes, and every crevice of my body. But the task had proved too heavy-lidded to continue. Now I drifted in near sleep, the water in Granny's claw-foot tub as cool as the air outside. But I was too tired and sleepy to pull the plug and crawl out. Neither did I wish to, for Granny's tongue awaited me on the other side of the door.

"Emma Grace … what're ye doing in there? Reading the Sears catalog from cover to cover?"

I startled awake at Granny's voice. She stood outside the bathroom door—like a dog on point, no doubt. Before she took a mind to rattle the doorknob and burst right in, I grabbed a towel from the rack and covered myself with haste. Granny's idea of privacy was as far away from my own as China was from South America.

"Just a second. I'll be right out."

I scuttled from the tub and dried off, knowing a bit of renewed strength as I determined not to let Granny's gaze ponder my skin-draped bones. 'Twas enough—the lecture she'd lay upon me in a few minutes. Would it be too much to hope she'd take pity and postpone the grilling until tomorrow?

Granny directed me to the parlor sofa where I sat clasping my bathrobe, fending off a chill in the room. Could a person die from fatigue, I wondered? It seemed possible, especially if that person fell asleep during one of Granny's inquisitions and hit the hardwood floor headfirst.

Granny wasted not a heartbeat. Her scathing tongue scorched stale-ness from the air as it spewed blasts of condemnation all over me. I smoldered with embarrassment and regret, for I had so frightened my grandmother's heart that it had acted up, palpitating in hurried spurts and jerks. According to Granny, her heart hadn't settled down yet, though the doctor had administered a calming tonic to her an hour ear-lier. And what about her neighbors, Granny wanted to know. They'd left their supper tables and combed the alleys and streets looking for her lost granddaughter.

She leaned in close, her shrewd little eyes peering through her rimmed spectacles as she spoke.

"How'd ye say you got so wet?"

"Sand got in my shoes. So I washed my feet in the water. Must've lost my balance, 'cause next thing I know I was at the bottom of the sea." It sounded plausible to me. So long as I didn't volunteer too much information and go cross-eyed trying to keep my story straight, I would probably come out all right. "I'm real tired, Granny. Think I'll turn in now. I'm awful sorry that I worried you ... and made your heart hurt. I love you, Granny." I stood and leaned over, giving her cheek a peck. But when I saw the sadness in her eyes, my heart lurched and wobbled as Granny's had earlier tonight.

She could be a real crank at times, but more often she was loving and kind, a person who truly obeyed the commandment to love your neighbor as yourself. How could I amble off to my room when Granny's face wore such a tired and desolate look? She had to know I was withholding something, yet I couldn't bring myself to utter another lie. And never ... never would I tell her the truth.

Though I'd been washed by the sea, and scorched by the heat of

Granny's blistering tongue, I still reeked of sadness and guilt. I walked from the room, leaving Granny to stew in her kettle of doubts and let-down feelings. I had to leave her—lest I pass my stench onto her.

Three days passed before I again ventured to the sea. Granny flitted about the house with renewed robustness, especially for someone of her maturity. Since guilt had not slackened its tirade against my heart, Granny's recovery thrilled me, for it eased the way for me to seek the light. It was my stricken heart, therefore, that suggested the time had come to complete the task I began on Sunday.

I'd been in a tiff most of the day because Granny refused to relinquish my one remaining pair of overalls. She'd washed seawater from them on Monday, pressed them on Tuesday, but they'd upped and gone missing on Wednesday. When I awakened this morning, no overalls draped the bedpost. Instead, I found a gray muslin skirt and a blue shirtwaist, neatly folded at the foot of the bed. Without asking, I knew Granny had either disposed of my last pair of overalls, or vanquished them to a secret hideaway where others of its kind were stashed.

Granny's afternoon nap sometimes stretched to near suppertime. At midafternoon, I left the house and walked to East Beach. November sun rained warmth upon my bare arms while a restless wind whipped at my hair and skirt. In a few hours the sun would retire and stars would spark the night sky. When darkness covered even the slight form of the heavyhearted girl entering the sea, I would again stroke toward the light.

I stood near a group of young children who ran along the beach, exclaiming with excitement each time they spied a seashell or shiny rock. A spindly woman with graying hair watched over them, her parchment face evident even from where I stood. One wee child attempted to place her hand in the woman's, but the woman shoved the child's fingers aside and then brushed her own hands as if to rid them of an unwanted touch. I didn't have to hear her words to know they were spoken without warmth or tenderness. She pointed to the other children, and off the wee girl went with her arms crossed over her chest and a sullen look on her face. Anger at the woman fired my heart.

When I saw a boy with blond curls, my gaze fixed on him like frost on a windowpane. Not because he had handsome features or because he reminded me of Micah. I watched him because he held absolute authority over the other children. Of such characteristics was my Caleb hewn. Though the boy's stature was less prominent than some, he discharged orders as though he'd attained the height of ten feet. The little rogue captured his playmates with the iron fist of authority, just as Caleb had captured my heart the day he was born. I smiled as a picture came to mind: Caleb leading this pygmy group into guerilla warfare. Even the general-boy with blond curls would have acquiesced to Caleb's rule.

Longing seized my heart, pilfering my breath, glutting my eyes with tears. Oh, to see Captain Caleb well again—healthy and whole. I would follow him anywhere.

I'm unsure what caused me to enter the sea; what delusional thoughts persuaded me to seek forgetfulness before the appointed hour. Looking back, I believed my heart was too heavy with pain to determine other consequences, such as small hatchlings following my lead. Perhaps my mind just deserted me for the moment. For whatever reason, I walked straight into the water, confusion and pain flowing through my heart like the waves that wrapped around my legs. My knees buckled and I stumbled. How shocked I was to see little bodies close behind, flailing arms slapping at the rushing water that swept over their shoulders, knocking them down like bowling pins. Some toppled headfirst; others grabbed onto my skirt, tugging the hem, not understanding the dangerous game they played. When reality finally filtered into my head, fear for the little ones sped me to action. I knelt in the water, gathering children into my arms, shushing them with gentleness so they could hear my words. "Hold onto my skirt and follow me. The water's too deep for us to play in." With pounding heart, I held onto shirt collars and arms, herding all of them back to shore like a shepherd guiding his sheep to the fold.

Giggles spurted from their mouths as we stepped from the sea. Even the faces of those who had been fully dunked wore looks of delight. Delight didn't slip from their faces until the woman approached and spewed upon me the severest tongue-lashing I had ever received.

My apology to the woman went unaccepted as she prepared to march her little charges from the beach. Though I had explained that the fault was entirely mine, she stormed up and down the line of children, fuming and barking orders at every child who had followed the Pied Piper into the sea. The puckish pack looked a mess, all right, their clothes dripping, their shoes waterlogged, and spikes of hair matted to their happy faces. Despite the bad-tempered mistress, the children smiled up at me, and one by one waved me a cautious good-bye.

# Twenty-three

I held my tongue in check as the stick-lady led the children away, lest my riptide of naughty taunts sweep the old scarecrow off her feet. She took her place at the head of the line, marching with shoulders squared and nose perched in the clouds. The wee ones followed as best they could, though a few dared another turn of head in my direction.

*Yes, little ones ... I'm still watching you.*

I wondered if they attended a nearby school. Too bad—if they shared the misfortune of having that woman for a teacher.

I spat out the taste of sea while gravity tugged gallons of saltwater from my skirt. Water dripped on the sand and oozed down my legs, spilling into my laced-up oxfords. Granny would have a conniption fit if she were to see me now, in the act of ruining a fine pair of high-polished shoes. I wrung the hem of my skirt and yanked the tail of my shirtwaist free, hoping it would take a notion to dry more quickly in the breeze.

"Hey ... what are you? A fish—or a mermaid? You're too graceful to be a fish, so you must be a sea nymph."

I spun around at the sound of Tate's voice, wondering if he'd seen me plucking those bobbing minnows from the sea.

139

A grin split Tate's face as he trekked across the pallet of sand. It widened even more as my gaze lengthened into an impolite stare. Tate teased as Papa did, holding his eyes steady until the blush made its way to soft places on my face and neck. I felt the heat now. His teasing brought back a familiar—even comfortable—feeling.

I knew at once that Tate and the sun were fast friends, for his face was as brown as Elo's tanned rabbit skins. He chuckled, most likely because he'd not met with such rude gawking before. As my first reliable look at him stretched into eternity, I noticed straight brows and dark curls that caught fire in the sun. How much more the sun revealed than the moonbeams and lamplight of Sunday evening. The truth couldn't be denied: Tate was more than handsome. I turned my face away. He'd seen enough of my rudeness for one day.

I fidgeted with my hair, attempting to arrange it into something other than the windblown mass of my creation. And all the while I wondered why Tate had referred to me as graceful. Was he someone who could be careless with his teases? If there was one thing a cripple could never be, it was graceful.

"You know, you had me fooled the other night. I thought you were just a kid. What are you … thirteen … fourteen?" I saw a flash of white behind his smile and believed he attempted to put me at ease with his nosiness. I nodded my head in answer to his question, for my tongue had not yet recouped its glibness.

"Been looking for you every day. Wanted to give you this." Tate opened his hand, baring the wooden carving of a whooping crane. It seemed a perfect replica of the startling white bird that had forever been my favorite. My fingers shook as I placed the delicate figure in my palm, noticing the deftness of each feather tip and stroke of the knife.

"Thank you … but it's much too beautiful to give away. I've never seen such delicate carving before." I held out my hand, thinking the wonderful crane needed to remain with its maker, not with the likes of me.

"No, you keep it. I made it for you. Shoot … I've got a whole shelf filled with my whittlings. Seems like I've been cutting on wood or rock or something most of my life. Nothing special about it … I just like to work with my hands."

Tate shifted his weight and slid his hand into his pants pocket.

"They nest around here, you know, along with blue heron and pelicans. But whooping cranes are my favorite, 'cause you don't see so many of them anymore. Seems there's fewer and fewer every year."

Having found its true purpose, my tongue rolled out a soliloquy. "They migrate from Canada to Texas every autumn. They're the tallest birds in North America," I said on a rush of whisper. Tate arched an eyebrow and stepped a bit closer to me, surprise registering on his face. Perhaps he had thought me an ignorant twit, or maybe my voice just sounded weird to him.

"What's your name? You've got to have a name."

"Emma."

"Emma what?"

"Emma ... uh ... Grace."

"Grace. Hmm, don't recall hearing of any families by that name before. You live around here?"

When I didn't answer, Tate rephrased the question.

"You live over at the—"

"What are you, the census-taker or something?" My heart thundered as red flares of warning exploded in front of my eyes. Tate asked too many questions. Why was he so interested in me, anyway? I turned away without thanking him for the exquisite figurine he had carved, and walked away, my dispirited heart prompting me to recall the mission to which I'd made a vow. The mission I would complete tonight. It frightened me that—for a moment—it had vanished from my thoughts like a wraith in the night.

Tate jogged to me, grasping the boniness of my elbow, skidding me to a stop. "Please don't go. I won't ask any more questions. Look ... I just want to be your friend. Thought you might need one as much as I do."

I looked into the depths of Tate's eyes. Papa said you could discover a lot about a man just by observing his eyes. Tate's were chocolate brown with a slight shading of green near the pupils. They looked to be honest eyes—trustworthy eyes.

"Look, why don't you go find a place for us to sit and talk while I run over to Murdoch's and buy some soda pop. What kind do you like?" Tate awaited my answer, but I had turned my gaze to the sea, and there it remained. He tarried a moment longer, then dashed off to the bathhouse.

Inside my head, opposing thoughts warred with one another, each vying for the podium. The loudest of the two shouted that I didn't deserve Tate's friendship, nor should I be seeking unmerited favors, such as laughter and companionship. The other questioned why I would even consider slipping my melancholy to the back burner when one brother lay buried in the ground, the other beneath a blanket of unconsciousness. I shivered at a wind suddenly gone cold, and knew the time had not yet come to shed my hair shirt of guilt. Until I had forfeited full penance to the sea, my shame was visible for the world to view; splayed out and naked like a filleted flounder. 'Twas only a matter of time before Tate spied it.

Tate returned in a flash and together we walked to a level stretch of sand, mere feet from the water. Shock must have chronicled itself in my eyes when Tate spread his jacket and motioned me to sit down.

"Don't look so surprised. I can be a gentleman if I've a mind to."

"Thanks," I murmured. I sat on the far edge of his coat, feeling tongue-tied and more than a mite self-conscious. My hands trembled as I lifted the bottle of Delaware Punch to my lips and sipped its sweetness. I thought the young man beside me must be a seer or gifted mind reader. How else could he have chosen the drink I loved most?

Tate sat on the sand, his gaze fastened on the sea as he guzzled his soda. "Someday I'm going to board a ship and sail around the world. Visit all the places I've read about. Italy, Japan, Africa. Every one of them." He turned a sideways glance at me and our eyes met briefly. "What about you? What would you like to do with the rest of your life?"

I shook my head, my tears welling as I remembered there'd be no "rest of my life." Not after tonight. For the extent of my remembrance, I had aspired to be a wife and mother, a mother who wrote stories in her head and told them to her children. But that was before the tragedy; before I realized a mother's child could be snatched from her arms as quickly as an eagle could whisk a field mouse from the ground.

An hour passed in which a bank of clouds paused before the sun, broadcasting patches of shade over the cooling sand. Tate did most of the talking, except for a few grunts I tossed into the conversation at appropriate and inappropriate times. By the latter, I'm sure he knew I was only half-listening to what he said. I did glean a few facts: He was a dockworker and he lived with a lady he called Mrs. K.

One thing became clear: Tate had no intention of leaving. I held no doubts he would pitch a tent, if necessary, and sleep the night away on the beach if I didn't take my departure first. Had Tate somehow stumbled upon the truth of my shame? Had he prowled into my personal territory and now thought himself a hero who would save me from the sea?

I rose from the ground and brushed sand from my skirt and hands. "Thank you for the soda pop."

"Do you have to go right now?" Tate's voice carried a bit of forlornness in it.

I picked up his jacket and shook off the sand before handing it to him. "July—I'll be fourteen in July."

Tate grinned as though he'd just retrieved a star from the sky. "Let's see … that makes me your elder by two years … and eight months. No wonder I'm so much wiser. I could teach a tadpole like you a lot of things." As Tate hefted himself from the ground, muscles in his bronzed arms flexed like those of a youth familiar with hard work.

In consideration of Tate's wisdom and ancient condition, I swept into a full curtsy, then turned and shambled toward the dunes to fetch my crutch. As I walked, something soft as goose down brushed across my lips, carrying with it the intimate sensation of a smile. With great suddenness, my heart lurched with yearnings I'd not experienced of late. I knew the reason for those wild palpitations in my heart. 'Twas the forgotten dreams of marriage and motherhood I'd dared recall earlier, and the longing to someday hold my own child in my arms. The idea clutched at my chest, leaving me breathless. Those impossible longings could be attributed to two things only: the wee children who'd followed me into the sea today and Tate's nosy questions.

# Twenty-four

"I believe your hike to the ocean has perked ye up a bit. Put some pink in your cheeks." Granny beamed as she ladled soup into the bowls I had arranged on the kitchen table. While she sliced cornbread, I poured two glasses of milk. We sat across the table from each other, Granny's eyes peering at me with speculative interest. I was the one with the shifty eyes.

I had changed out of my salt-stiff clothes and into a clean outfit when I returned home this afternoon. My clothes were soaking in the bathtub now. If Granny were to determine the real reason I had trekked to the sea, I feared she might be stricken with a severe case of apoplexy.

"Yer appetite's a mite better too."

The hot soup felt good going down my throat. And Granny *was* the best cook in Texas, according to Papa's calculations. "I'm thinking about going back tonight. Wanted to study some constellations from the seawall."

"No … ye'll not be going back tonight. There's a norther comin' in. I can feel it clear down to the marrow of my bones."

"I won't stay long, Granny. It's something I need … to do." My chest squeezed as Granny's eyes narrowed on me from across the table.

Her head moved forward ever so slowly, like an old arthritic turtle distending her neck from the shell. She uptilted her chin and glared at me through the bedrock of her spectacles. The frown on her face was one to scare little children on Halloween night.

"We'll not be speaking of you traipsing down to the sea tonight … or any other night, for that matter. What we'll be doing is sitting over there by the fire. Just you and me. It's high time we passed an evening together, just talking to one another."

As my stare probed Granny's aged eyes, the look of determination I found there surprised me not. What I didn't spy was one pinch of giving in.

"'Tis good to see you eating again, sweet-pie. Maybe all ye're needing is a little more exercise. A walk down to the beach every day will add a little strength to your muscles, and you can soak up some sunshine at the same time. But remember this—I won't have you walking the beach at night anymore. Ye understand me? It's too dangerous for a young woman to be out alone at night."

"Yes ma'am." I glanced at my empty bowl, unaware I'd eaten its fill. When had my appetite returned? I wondered. During the nighttime hours, when sleep-dreams stole sorrow from my heart? Or had its gentle pangs returned this afternoon, while my heart basked in newfound affection for a passel of tykes who reminded me of my brothers? Or had it reappeared as I sat in silence, sipping on the spicy tales from Tate's brewery?

"Now, help me clean up and then I'll be teaching you some fancy stitches no one else is privy to. Might even tell ye a story or two."

The spellbinding beacon in the waves seemed but a distant spark in a long-ago memory, as did my vow to pursue the sea's forgetfulness. Pushing aside what had lain heavily on my heart for countless days, I gathered up the supper dishes and set them soaking in an enamel dishpan at the sink.

Granny gawked at me. If it were possible, I would have gawked at myself, for my bottomless pit of lethargy now seemed to be filling with something akin to energy. "I'll wash the dishes, Granny, while you lay the fire."

Most likely, Granny assumed the daughter of Annaleen Falin would possess the polished gift of stitchery. But my ineptness with a needle rang clear as we huddled beneath the reading lamp, my fingers a-fumble as I botched stitch after stitch upon the practice cloth. Granny's patience must have worn down to a nubbin after a while, for she rose with haste, collecting needles, embroidery thread, hoops, and cloth, stashing them in her sewing basket.

I shuffled to the stove in wild relief, making a pretense of warming my hands next to the tin-wrapped smokestack. My senses—once blunted by sorrow—burgeoned with renewal as I sniffed traces of burning mesquite and cedar. As the fire hissed and crackled in the belly of the stove, it called to memory nights whiled away beside our hearth in Coldwater. I glanced at Granny. How many nights had she sat alone in this room, recalling her life before the big wind sucked life from her husband and children? I now understood why her mantel overflowed with a menagerie of keepsakes, photographs, and mementos. They were all she had left of her family. I gazed at the carved casing above Granny's fireplace, which bore the weight of her treasures. A large brass bell occupied center stage. When Granny lifted it from its doily cradle and gave it a good polishing, what memories did it summon forth? I lifted the cumbersome bell with care, turning it belly-up as I studied the long, heavy clapper.

"'Twas your grandpa's bell," Granny said. Though her voice sounded flat and lonely, her eyes glazed over with obvious love.

"Grandpa Johnny's?"

"He was a fisherman, ye know. The best in Galveston. Used to clang that bell when he'd return from a spell at sea. Three times he'd ring it; four times if he was bringing back an exceptional catch. Dobber would take off 'fore I could say yea or nay about the matter, running lickety-split to the wharf to help his papa unload the boat. Dobber thought he knew most everything about the deep there was to know. But the sea had all of us fooled." Granny sighed and shifted on the sofa, sinking more deeply into the broken-down cushions that carried the permanent imprint of her heaviness. She tugged on her shawl and chafed her arms against the chill—of body or heart, I knew not which. Granny removed her spectacles and rubbed the bridge of her nose, lantern light casting sheen on her faded eyes. I lowered my gaze out of respect for my grandmother's pain.

"Bring me that picture, sweet-pie." Granny pointed to the photograph of her children. She leaned her head against the back of the sofa and squeezed her eyes. I worried about her as I placed the picture in her hands, for I knew that memories could strangle the lifeblood from a heart.

Granny's gnarled finger pointed to the oldest boy, shaking a bit as she outlined the lad's handsome face. "His baptized name is Griffen Delane, but his papa nicknamed him Dobber when he was a toddler. Called him that 'cause he flitted about like a dirt dauber. Never seen a swifter pair of feet in me life. And boy, did that child love to fish … got that from his papa. He was soon to be thirteen …" Granny's finger stumbled as it moved to the middle child. "This boy … this overly bright child is Logan." Her voice hitched, but she continued on. "He was eleven. Craved the book learning as much as his papa did. Like your papa still does." Granny's eyes stayed fixed on the boy with whom my papa looked most similar.

"Why was Papa so much older than his brothers and sister?"

"I had a baby girl when Roan was three years old. But she was weakly from the start. Got the pneumonia when she was five and … just couldn't fight it. Guess my body wasn't ready to go through that sorrow again 'cause I didn't bear another child until your papa was ten years old." Granny placed her finger on the last child in the snapshot. I looked up, anxiousness for Granny's heart causing my own to act up a bit.

"That's Katie Ann," I blurted out, hoping to give Granny's emotions a bit of time to rebound. "You named her Katie after your mother, and Ann after the little girl you lost, didn't you, Granny? Mama said I reminded her of Katie Ann."

Granny nodded her head. I felt sure it was all she could manage at the time. We stared at the pretty girl with blonde pigtails. She looked much younger and smaller than her brothers. "How old was Katie Ann when … when the storm hit?"

"She was only nine years old. Your mama's right … Katie Ann was small and pretty, just like you. Maybe that's why I've been partial to you since the day ye were born, sweet-pie."

I reached for the photograph, thinking it past time to draw

Granny's attention elsewhere, but she tightened her clasp on the frame, exposing the iron will and unrelenting fingers I'd grown used to. I should have known Granny wasn't finished yet, for once retrieved, memories were most difficult to dislodge. Nor could you wipe them away like dusty chalk from a blackboard. They lingered on ... until that moment in time when putting them aside seemed the only pathway to survival.

Granny and I sat shoulder to shoulder on the sofa. Part of me regretted my earlier request to learn more about the storm, for I now sensed the need in my grandmother to share all of her sadness with me. I'd barely begun to feel an ebbing of my own sorrow. Why had I thought myself strong enough to hear of another's unbearable loss? For sure my unshakable curiosity was a troublemaker at times, dealing me more misery than I could handle.

"We knew a storm was brewing, but we'd survived so many that we gave this one no particular heed. The rain started on Friday. Just light rain with a little wind. And mugginess ... my, was it muggy. The surf was higher than usual, but there was nothing astir to cause us any great alarm. During the night, I heard the wind pick up and knew Johnny would be moving his boat to the lee side of the island come morning, just like he always did when a storm blew in. It was hot and humid again the next morning, and the wind was brisk. Johnny and I talked about the storm, how it would probably be a strong one. He mentioned the sky—the red tint of the sky. After a quick breakfast, he readied to leave. The kids begged to go with him. Katie Ann liked to steer the wheel, you see, and Dobber and Logan wanted to get in an hour or two of fishing at Offat's Bayou."

"It was called The Great Storm of 1900, wasn't it, Granny?"

"Yes, it was called that, along with a lot of other things. September 8, 1900—'twas a day the world will never forget."

Granny closed her eyes. I imagined the years rolling away in her mind.

"If only I had made the children stay home with me that day."

*If only I had kept the twins out of the death field that day.*

"Johnny said the kids could go with him. He teased it would get them out of my hair, but even as we laughed, something inside me sounded a warning bell. I paid it little mind. I was too busy thinking about the baking I had to do, and how good it would be to have a little peace and quiet. Besides, Johnny never paid a bit of mind to my worry words and neither did the children."

"Where was Papa when the storm hit?"

"Why ... Roan was a grown man by then, working on a farm near Coldwater. Let's see ... guess he was about twenty-two at the time ... and already in love with your mama."

I smiled at Granny, wishing she'd let the story slip away so we could turn our thoughts from what was sure to follow.

"Katie Ann was so excited. I remember looking at her right before she ran out the door, thinking someday she'd be the most beautiful belle in Galveston County. I ignored the sick feeling in my stomach, and after a while it went away. Johnny slipped on his slicker and stopped in the doorway, taking hold of my hand. 'Ye're the love of me life, ye know,' he said. The second he let go my hand, fear clutched my heart in a way it never had before. 'Wait, Johnny,' I pleaded. 'Why don't ye leave the boat at the dock? Surely 'tis safe enough there. This storm is no worse than the others we've been through.' But he just smiled and said they'd be home by noon.

"I left the house around eleven, determined to find me family and bring them home. The wind had picked up to gale force by then, and I had this terrible, sinking feeling inside me. It wasn't just raining—it was blowing sheets of rain the likes of which I'd never seen before. Earlier that morning, I'd watched kids floating in washtubs, playing in a foot of water in the street, but now the water was up to my knees and rising fast. I tried cutting across the island to get to Offat's Bayou, but made no headway a'tall. The wind was ferocious. I knew I'd not make it to the boat, so I turned back, thinking maybe my family was already home, safe and warm. Probably messing up my kitchen, fixing sandwiches and the likes. I got back to the house about two o'clock but they weren't there. I was beside myself ... didn't know what to do. Our house was low to the ground back then, not set up on stilts as it is now. The water kept rising all afternoon. It came in under the doors and through cracks. I opened everything I could—windows, doors—even chopped holes in the floor with Johnny's ax so the water would flow through and not lift the house off its foundation.

"The storm surge hit about six-thirty. I heard it coming ...

sounded like a freight train steaming down the tracks. Later, I learned that the sea rose four feet in four seconds, and out in the ocean, swells reached a hundred and twenty feet. A huge dome of water swept over the island, knocking trains off their tracks, uprooting trestles and trees, carrying streetcars, trucks, houses, slate roofs along its path of destruction. Outside—everything was pitch black, except when a bolt of lightning lit up the sky. Then you saw the horror of it all: the sea of mayhem; people screaming for loved ones, injured and drowning people begging for help; dead animals and human bodies, floating with furniture, houses, and every sort of debris imaginable. I saw mamas pleading for their babies, and daddies clinging to a piece of wood with one hand, trying to keep their children's heads above water with the other. And I couldn't do a thing to help them ... any more'n I could help my own family. I was so afraid for my family. My only hope was that they had holed up on Johnny's boat and were riding out the storm. Our roof had blown away and the house was swelling like it'd split apart any second. I took a lantern and the family Bible and climbed the stairs to the attic. The end had come for me. But oh, if only my family could survive. I spent the next hours praying for that very thing."

Breath pushed through Granny's lips in mewling whimpers. She paused, brushing tears from her cheeks. But I knew from experience that she'd never succeed at brushing them from her heart.

I sat on the couch like a waterlogged sponge, unable to soak up another teaspoon of Granny's pain. It seemed I was in the flood, along with the part of Granny's heart she left behind, and both of us were drowning. I had to do something to keep my head above water. 'Twas then my heart backed itself into a far corner of my mind, and from that point on, every moan and word Granny uttered came to my ears as though spoken by a stranger. Pretending was the only choice I had in the matter.

"There was no place to bury me family. The island was too saturated to dig graves, and I wouldn't allow those men—those horrible burying gangs—to touch my loved ones. To stack 'em on barges and cart 'em out to sea like a pile of stinky fish. I know I should have been kinder to the workers. Most had been commandeered at bayonet point, forced into the gruesome job of disposing of the dead. But I couldn't help meself. I got Johnny's shotgun and cocked it at anyone who came near me family. Guarded them day and night, but in the end I had to burn them after all. There was no other way. The newspaper reported that up to eight thousand souls died in the storm, but I believe the count went much higher. The burning went on for weeks and weeks."

Granny's eyes glazed over at a remembrance I couldn't see, her hands lying limp atop her apron. "There was a man, a kind man who lived down the street. His family died, also. Together we built a burial pyre for our loved ones over at Offat's Bayou. He paid to have his family carted over there, and together we set the fire. I guess I went a little crazy when the flames caught. How could I not, when the last sight of me children was through the smoke and flames of a roaring fire? I ran to the bier and tried to drag them from the pile, but my skirt caught fire. If not for Mr. Panduso, I would have burned up with Johnny and the children. He pulled me clear and rolled me in the sand. I remember screaming for him to let me go … let me go … but he paid not a bit of heed to my ranting. Just kept a firm hold on me and told me over and over that everything would be all right."

My eyes sought Granny's. She must have perceived the look on my face as shock or disbelief. But what knocked around in my head was something more revealing. Etched on my mind was a vision of Granny—doing in the fire what I had tried to do in the sea.

"'Tis true, Emma Grace." Granny reached for the hem of her skirt and raised it to midthigh, then rolled her stocking to the ankle. "'Tis true, child … I'll carry the scars for the rest of me life."

I grunted and heaved, my chest rummaging for air as I took in the sight of Granny's leg. With eyes that surely bugged like frog eyes, I stared at patches of hairless skin, shining like glazed pottery. I'd not been exposed to Granny's nakedness before, nor had I eavesdropped on the tale of her one brief flight from reality. I sat fixated, my heart cudgeling my breastbone as I viewed mahogany ropes of puckered skin, climbing the muscles of Granny's leg. Despite her disfigurement, I knew the wounds of my gawking were the sort that one could forget—if but for a moment. 'Twas the invisible ones that could not be shaken loose. They clung to the heart like viper fangs. Granny and I shared kindred bruises, so deeply embedded that even the gloaming couldn't fade them from our view. Our scars would never go away.

I reached out my hand and glided it across the soft fabric of

Granny's muslin skirt. I grappled for her hand, and then clutched it to my heart. A parcel of the wall I'd built around my heart crumpled in that moment. I felt the shift within, as though a mighty chunk had fallen away. Perhaps it was but a single stone, sliding loose from the mortar. However large, or small, I felt the separation and knew it signaled a new beginning for me. Tragedy had thrust Granny and me together weeks earlier, but it took another tragedy—one occurring fifteen years before my birth—to set the gears of my healing into motion.

I crawled into bed that night with a heavy heart, which in itself was not a departure from life as I knew it. What was oddly out of place, and what seemed most peculiar to my self-centeredness, was the cause of my sadness. I hurt for someone other than myself. Tonight I ached for my grandmother.

Perhaps I could learn to live with Granny after all ... despite her persnickety ways.

# Twenty-five

I tramped to the sea, not in search of Tate, but neither would I turn tail and run if he happened near. I strode with purpose, for in the early hours of sunrise, Granny's words had found the open door of my heart and walked right in. If she could learn to live in the wreckage of sorrow's despair—so could I. The truth bubbled in my heart like an underground spring, seeping into the deeper flow of my life, filling the dry creek beds of my heart. 'Twas true that sadness and I remained consummate companions, but I no longer yearned to slink off in the dead of night and drown my sorrow in the sea.

Learning to abide in pain might take a lifetime to perfect, but in time, perhaps the darkness would press less firmly upon my heart and my pain would lessen. Granny had one crucial advantage over me: She had the Almighty to shore up her heart when pain tilted it beyond the limits of endurance. I would have to find such strength within myself.

I made additional plans beyond the decision to live. And with the plans came the first pricking of hope since Micah's death. I would bury my shame; hide its ugliness from the world so I would never have to deal with it again. It might die a slow death, but it *would* die. I would entomb it so deeply in my heart that no one would suspect its existence.

And then I would shovel tons of smiles atop it and cement the seams with laughter. My family would stand in awe of its disappearance, and in time, forget to remember I was the one who had ushered that perpetual season of winter into their hearts. I believed the plan would work, for I was, above all else, an actress at heart.

As I angled toward shore, warm breezes brushed my skin like Old Jack's snorts during a good nuzzling. As was the way with gulf northers, the frigid winds of three days past had blasted off to other locales, leaving behind the mellowness of springtime. Two-Toe Creek had called to me on days such as this; toasty temperatures tempting me to spend some splash time in the water.

I thought of home more often these days, missing my family and the open meadows around our house. But I no longer listened for a whippoorwill's call at daybreak or the predatory hoots of a barn owl at night. Now my ears quickened at the yappy chortle of a seagull, or an egret's low-throated whistle.

I told myself the tin of cookies pressed against my ribs was for the wee children, should I be so fortunate as to happen upon them again. I supposed I could share a few with Tate, though I'd not baked them specifically for him. As I ambled past Murdoch's Bathhouse, I recalled Granny telling me that the storm of 1900 had demolished every structure on the beach, including all the bathhouses.

I saw him in the distance, standing atop a stunted dune. His body angled toward the sea, but even at such a span, I spied his sightliness. I had misplaced in my memory the height he had achieved, and had forgotten the slender profile he presented. He turned then, recognition registering on his face. Did I only imagine his smile as he stooped and picked up his jacket and loped down the dune toward me?

"Been looking for you for three days. Where've you been?"

"Waiting for the weather to warm up."

"Surely, you're not referring to that little bit of wind that blew in."

"No … I'm referring to the nasty siege of arctic air that dumped freezing temperatures on our bougainvilleas and impatiens, killing 'em dead."

The width of Tate's grin rivaled the Gulf Stream. He slouched a knee and rammed a hand into his pants pocket, his headshake implying a disbelieving spirit. "You must be a stay-at-home kind of girl. That little spell of weather wasn't cold enough to sneeze at. Come on, got something to show you." And away he went without saying another word about where we were going, or why. Tate didn't mention my crutch. If he noticed it, he kept the knowledge well hidden. He grabbed the tin of cookies from my left hand and adjusted his pace, perhaps an inch slower per hour. That is to say he strode about three feet ahead of me, his emboldened gait impossible to match. Giving the top half of his body a slight turn, he looked back at me.

"What's in the can?" Before I could answer, his proprietary hands pried off the lid. He grabbed a handful of snickerdoodles and wolfed them down as though he'd not eaten since Sunday. "Did you bake these? They're good. Real good. Want one?" His stride slowed not a bit as he stuffed his mouth full. When he turned his head to gather my reply, I noticed that cinnamon crumbs had sprinkled his black bristly chin—mere stubs of hair—and flecked his mouth with reddish-brown powder.

"Not right now," I said around a smile. Something about him reminded me of Elo. Perhaps it was the way he took what he wanted without first securing permission, and did so with great ease.

Tate slowed his pace until we walked side by side. I decided he was a reader, also, for he spewed facts and information as though he'd been born with an encyclopedia glued to his tongue.

We halted farther down the shore. Tate bent his knees, squatting over the sand, peering into a hole of irregular shape.

"I think I found a turtle clutch, but I can't be positive. Look … see those pieces of shell?" Tate cupped his hands, lifting a pocketful of sand with archeological prudence, as though sifting through the remnants of an ancient ruin. Sunlight fanned across the arch of his back, casting incendiary sparks onto his midnight mane. 'Twas a snapshot that would most likely stay fixed in my mind for a long and pleasant spell.

"Ridley turtles?" I asked, leaning over and viewing the soil with a gemologist's eye. As I studied tiny particles of shell mixed with sand, I felt Tate's gaze on my face. Warmth flooded my cheeks, for I knew my scrawniness was a pitiful sight to behold.

I looked at his face, inches from my own. His eyes narrowed and he pursed his lips to one side, as though his thoughts dwelled in a far-away place. "Yeah … if this is turtle shell, it's got to be Ridleys. Who knows, maybe it's a just a stupid old bird nest, or snake incubator." I breathed in Tate's closeness, a faint trace of hair balm reminding me of Papa and my brothers.

Tate turned from the hole and trained his gaze on the glistening sea. He sighed and shook his head. "I wonder if they made it … or did something get to them before they hatched?" We stood side by side, our gazes melded on millions of white diamonds, dancing across a tabletop of light. Did we think to catch a glimpse of baby turtles—tiny flippers stroking for safety in the choppy bay?

*He's got a tender side … and a good heart.*

"I imagine they made it to the sea." My voice rang with reassurance. "Maybe not all, but surely most of them made it. They didn't have to crawl very far … and they would've been almost invisible on a moonless night."

Tate turned to me and smiled, then nodded his head in affirmation. "My thoughts, exactly."

We passed Murdoch's Bathhouse on the walk back and found a ridge of sand on which to sit. Wind had carved the dune into wavy layers, but the weight of our feet ravaged the perfect patterns into volcano pits that caved in on themselves as we ascended the knoll. Tufts of sea grass sprouted at the sides and top of the peak. Tate claimed the thatches of green looked like the crest feathers of a cockatoo. I viewed them as sparse clumps of hair on a bald man's head. Both comparisons were so absurd they birthed within me my first genuine laugh in more weeks than I could remember.

"Hey, it's good to hear you laugh. For a while there, I thought maybe you'd never learned how … oh, look … there's Mr. Panduso." Tate nudged his head toward a solitary figure walking on the sand. The man appeared to be of significant age.

*Mr. Panduso … Mr. Panduso. Where did I hear that name? Oh … yeah … the man who helped Granny bury …*

"Comes here at the exact same time every day. Lays a flower on that dune, right over there." Tate pointed to a ridge of sand near the seawall. I watched as the stooped-shouldered man walked to the dune and removed his hat. He stood for several minutes, then bent over and placed a flower on the sand. "They say he lost his wife and four children in the big hurricane. I suppose his family is buried beneath all that sand."

"No ... they're not." I regretted speaking the careless words before they were through spilling out of my mouth.

"How do ..."

I picked up my crutch and hoisted myself to my feet, gathering the cookie tin to my chest like a battle shield.

"Who are you—Cinderella? Why do you just up and disappear like that? Will you turn into a pumpkin or something if you stick around for a while?"

"Cinderella didn't turn into a pumpkin. Her coach did."

"Come on back. Surely, you don't have to go right now."

I snatched a quick glimpse at the sun and knew I had hours to spare before Granny's curfew. Still—I didn't cotton to Tate's questions, innocent though they might be. I knew that one question could lead to another and I didn't want to make thoughtless remarks that might reveal secrets I wasn't ready to share. I'd snuggled within my shell of pain far too long to open myself to the likes of a near stranger.

"I had hoped you'd tell me a little about yourself. Like, for instance, why you're not in school."

Tate awaited my answer with seemingly inexhaustible patience. After a time I slumped down to my sand cushion, stewing over my predicament while my eyes tracked the retreating form of Mr. Panduso. I truly desired to be Tate's friend, unless being his friend required me to reveal confidences I kept under lock and key. I flicked my thick braid over my shoulder with as much nonchalance as I could muster. Moisture had popped out on my face, plastering annoying spit curls to my forehead. I probably looked like a Kewpie doll. I retucked my skirt beneath my knees, away from the wind's fickleness.

"So ... do you like the orphanage?" Tate twisted a blade of sea grass by the roots, wiped it clean on his trousers, and shoved the white stem between his teeth. "I mean—do you mind living there?"

I turned and glared at the young man beside me. Under other circumstances, he might have been the boy of my adolescent dreams. He was intelligent, strong, and breathtakingly handsome. But he was, nonetheless, a busybody of whom I knew little, and a stranger to boot. *Why do you want to know about me? Why do you even care?* As sunlight spun golden threads in his dark eyes, my insides took a deep breath and held tight. Did Tate think to play cat and mouse with me? Sneaking his nose in here and there until I had answered questions I had not planned to answer? Tate—whatever his name was—didn't know how stubborn I could be.

"I think it must be a very nice place," I said, tilting my head back to gaze at a clump of birds. Seagulls hung in threes; faces to the wind as they hovered on invisible currents that ruffled their wing tips and froze them in midair.

"What do you mean? Don't you live there? Don't you know for sure?"

"What makes you think I live there?"

"You were playing with those orphan kids the other day like you knew them. Don't you remember playing in the water with them?"

My heart jumped into my throat. *The children live in an orphanage. They have no mothers and fathers to care for them.* Why hadn't I realized it before? My heart felt near to bursting for the wee ones whose lives were in the hands of that willow-whip woman—that witch who seemed to possess not a morsel of compassion in her pecan-sized heart.

"Where is the orphanage?" Panicky and desperate, I demanded an answer. I had to do something for the children. Make amends, somehow, for the blow life had dealt them.

Tate studied me hard, the lines of his mouth taut and unbreachable. "If you don't live at the orphanage, where *do* you live?"

Looking into Tate's eyes was like trying to stare down Elo. If I thought myself stubborn ... what in the world would I call the look in Tate's eyes? The unflinching brute force of an unconquerable warrior?

"You didn't know they were orphans, did you?" Tate's brows constricted again, his dark eyes studying my face as though it was one of life's great mysteries. He flexed both hands into fists. I pictured an ax in one hand, a sword in the other. "Where do you live, Emma? Tell me about your family." Tate's gaze softened as he molded his hand to my shoulder, warmth sizzling beneath his fingertips. His was a chivalrous touch, as foreign to disrespect as joy was to my life. When he kneaded my flesh, I felt no alarm in the contact, insistent though it was.

"Right now ... I'm staying with my grandmother. She lives over there." I pointed my hand toward the eastern end of the island, aiming it in the vague direction of Granny's house, but away from her specific location.

"Well, go on. Tell me about yourself."

My thoughts tumbled along various pathways to the truth, pursuing a middling-of-the-road that would satisfy Tate's thirst and stopper shut his jug of many questions at the same time. Like a miser distributing coins, I chose my words with care. "I was somewhat sickly. My family thought sea air would be good for me." I darted my gaze to Tate's studious face. While he took his sweet time replying, I toyed with the ends of my braided hair and wondered if he'd accept my weaseled-down version of the truth.

"Sorry to hear about your illness. First time I saw you, I knew you had been sick. Either that—or something mighty bad had happened to you. But you're looking better now. Truth is … you're looking prettier than a girl has a right to be."

I hadn't recalled a look of embarrassment filing across Tate's features before. But I saw one now. I believed we both felt the awkwardness of the moment. Tate removed his hand from my shoulder and shifted farther away on the sand. I lowered my gaze, knowing without the aid of a mirror that my complexion was as rosy as Granny's rouge powder, probably all the way from my toes to the roots of my hair. Maybe Tate would think it was the work of the sun.

A cold draft swept across my arm where Tate's hand had rested. I would have preferred the warmth of his touch a moment longer.

# Twenty-six

Tate and I met at the dune every afternoon. And every afternoon I searched for Mama's locket, without his knowing it, of course. I didn't want to talk to Tate about the night I swam the sea. The ache in my heart was still too tender to return to that night. And so I kept my search a secret, along with all the other secrets in my heart.

The days were cooler now, as gunmetal skies of November often ushered in blustery winds and turbulent clouds that formed brief, but savage thunderstorms. At such times, Tate and I sought shelter beneath the overhang of Murdoch's Bathhouse. Upon occasion, we entered the building and Tate treated me to a soda pop. I had regained much of my lost weight, and my appetite had restored itself sufficiently—enough to placate Granny's persnickety observations. Jubilant over my physical improvement, Granny rarely forbade my daily walks to the beach; though she sometimes wrapped me in so many outer garments I resembled an Egyptian mummy.

Tate and I shared favors each time we met. As he approached, he would extend a fisted hand, demanding I guess what he'd brought me that day. My favorite gifts from Tate were his carvings, all as finely etched as the beautiful whooping crane. My gifts to Tate were mostly edible, as food maintained a high priority on his list of favorite things. Sometimes our presents were ridiculously silly, like the paper ring Tate slid on my finger one afternoon. By the time we parted that day, it had shredded to pieces. But I hid the precious scraps of ring in my cigar box anyway, just as I did every keepsake Tate gave me.

I no longer peeked at him from the corner of my eyes, thinking him a stranger I should fear. Nor did his behavior remind me of my brothers, as before. Unsure of my feelings for Tate, I puzzled over the way my heart picked up speed at first sight of his lanky form. I questioned if I had stumbled somewhere along the path to friendship; taken a wrong turn and lost my way. Or had I already fallen over the precipice of love and now drifted like a senseless feather in the wind? Whatever my feelings for Tate were, one thing was certain: For the few hours I was with him each day, I forgot to hurt as I did when I was alone.

The idea came to me in the nighttime hours, while clumps of sadness did push-ups against my chest and my wakeful eyes stared at a dark ceiling. Ironic, this plague of sleeplessness that had invaded me—a foe I'd not clashed with during months of druggedlike slumber. I thought about Granny and Mr. Panduso, still grieving after twenty-eight years. I'd be forty-one in twenty-eight years. Would sorrow stand by my side even then, faithfully escorting me through each chapter of my life?

I slipped from bed and hobbled to the window. Beyond the spread of curtains lay the stirring sea. I would return to it tomorrow. My heart jerked as I walked back to my bed. I lit the kerosene lantern and fished beneath the bed frame, retrieving my keepsake box from the floor.

I got to the beach an hour earlier than usual the next afternoon. What I planned to do had to be accomplished in privacy. Even Tate's eyes were off limits to my sacred chore. Inspired by Mr. Panduso's love offering to his family, I scoured the beach for the perfect dune: one within easy walking distance, but beyond the stretch of the sea's far-reaching fingers. I recognized Micah's dune the moment I spied it. Surrounded by higher, plumper ridges, it lay protected from wind and tide, like a baby elephant encircled by mother cows and long-tusked bulls.

I retrieved several keepsakes from the pocket of my skirt: a ribbon from Holly's wedding bouquet, the flattened penny Elo and I placed on the railroad tracks, the China key Tate found on the docks. I spread them on the sand, along with a sand dollar and the lifeless pocketwatch Papa had given me a few years back. Such bounty! And I had many more treasures in my box under the bed. I sat and debated over which item to place in the dented cookie tin I had sneaked from Granny's kitchen.

Like Mr. Panduso, I planned to visit Micah's dune every day and add another memento to his tin. I dug a hole at the edge of the dune, wedged the can in, and pressed it to a depth of several inches. I spread a swatch of red velvet in the bottom of the tin and placed Papa's pocketwatch atop the cloth. In my mind I saw Micah—grabbing my hand, his eyes curiously wide as he gazed at the watch. While his smile flashed bright across my memory, I extended my pinky, readying it to poke the dimple in his cheek. 'Twas then he reared back his head, daring me to give chase. How the boys loved the chase, and once caught, they couldn't get enough tickling. I'd tickle them until laughter swallowed all the air in their lungs. But before I could walk from the room, they'd be begging me for more.

To halt more mind pictures, I turned my face toward the sea. But the sea held its own gamut of memories. After tightening the lid, I scooped sand over the hole and jabbed a stick into the sand, marking its location. Tears poured from my eyes as I stood and buttoned my jacket, for I ached with a hurt that had not diminished at all.

Most likely Tate was already at our dune. After blotting my eyes with my jacket cuff, I gathered my crutch and gave Micah's dune one last look. His treasure hole blended in perfectly with the sand. Someday, when my keepsake box held nothing but air, I would rummage additional gifts to share with Micah. He was ever so easy to please. I dragged in a breath that smelled of the sea and slid my tongue over lips that tasted of salt. I knew not if the flavor came from ocean mist or my tears.

It felt good to acknowledge my little brother's life, to mark his passing in a tangible way. Perhaps this was the first step on my road to healing.

Redness must have rimmed my eyes as I greeted Tate a short time later. He sat with his legs bent and his elbows resting atop the pinnacle of his knees, He stared into the whitecapped ocean as though he'd caught sight of a mysterious sea monster.

"Hi," I said. "Been waiting long?"

Tate raised his head and stared at me. I wondered if my appearance had caught him unaware. "Naw, not long." He patted the sand beside him. "Guess I was off in another world somewhere. Have a seat." Tate studied my face, his brows drawing together as his gaze honed in on my eyes, which still felt puffy and sore. "You been crying?"

I shrugged and then nodded. "Yeah … a little." My cleverness with words astounded me at times.

"Then, I guess we're both a little blue today."

"What's wrong, Tate?" As I sat beside him, I ran my fingers across the paper-wrapped bundle in my jacket pocket. Perhaps a slice of Granny's pound cake would cheer Tate a bit. When he returned his gaze to the sea, my heart kicked into high gear, for I could now view his profile, unimpeded by distance or sparseness of time.

Free of tethers of any sort, his wild curls swished about his head like Old Jack's tail across his rump. I sat unmoving, fascinated by his blacker-than-night curls. Coming from a family of fair-haired people, Tate's darkness intrigued me. He reminded me of heroes I had only read about—sword-bearing swain and knightly lords and princes. Even the brush of whiskers on his chin spoke of strength and masculinity. The wind proved to be my friend as it blew across the dunes with a blustery attitude, for it whipped my hair here and there, concealing the boldness of my stare. I gathered wisps of my curly brown hair, stuffed them behind my ears, and watched Tate. While he kept a steadfast gaze on the sea, I inched a tad closer to him.

"Been thinking about my mother. She died five years ago today … just three days after my eleventh birthday." Tate picked up a clump of hardened soil and whipped it into the ocean without looking my way again.

This was the first time I'd seen Tate in anything but high spirits.

"Tuesday … when we were together, why didn't you tell me it was your sixteenth birthday?" Mildly perturbed, I cruised on, hoping to crash through the barricade of Tate's silence. "I would've baked you a cake or something."

"Maybe that's why I didn't tell you." Though slight, his grin had finally returned. "You know how much I hate your cooking."

I punched Tate's arm, though I was sure he couldn't feel it through the thickness of his jacket sleeve. "I'm sorry about your mother. I know what it's like to lose someone." I felt a swell of tears flood my eyes. Swallowing hard, I blinked back wetness, determined not to submit to another siege of crying. As I fished in my pocket for a hanky, Tate thrust a white, neatly stitched cloth into my hand.

"One of these days you're going to tell me what makes you so sad." Tate's gaze held steady as I honked my nose and wiped spit bubbles from my mouth. "I'd really like to know, Emma. Something really bad has hurt you. If you tell me about it, maybe I can help in some way."

I took over Tate's sea watch, gazing into choppy green waters while I composed my emotions. I desired to tell Tate everything. Get it off my heart, so to speak. But I thought I might die if I read condemnation in his eyes—should I divulge the full truth of my story to him.

"Ma used to say that when you shared your troubles with someone, you divided them in half. You might think some on that."

"Tell me about her." Avoiding the truth had become another bad habit of mine. My hands fidgeted with my skirt as I sat close to Tate, mesmerized by changes taking place on his face. His features shifted and moved about like a bucket of sloshing water, settling, at last, into a far-away smile.

"She was real pretty. Had long curly hair, black and shiny as a crow's wing. I used to like it when people told me I looked like her. And, boy, did she love to laugh. She was always giggling about something. Always happy … always beautiful. Anyway, that's what comes to mind when I think about her now." Tate's smile faded as he chewed on his upper lip and bobbed his head as though in agreement with himself. I knew he was remembering the way his mother's lips curled up … the way her eyes twinkled when she burst into laughter. They were two of the things I most remembered about Micah's laugh.

"'Course … that all changed once she found the bottle."

"Found the bottle?" I didn't mean to sound like a parrot, but Tate's words confused me. I peered into his eyes, which were fixed with a stare into yesteryear.

"My pa was a longshoreman. He left us when I was six. But before he took off, the three of us were a family. A real family. We ate together, laughed together, and on his day off we'd do things … like walk the jetties, or swim in the bay. But the accident changed Pa." Tate sighed and shook his head as he thought back on his childhood. "God help me, I loved that man. Thought there wasn't another person in the world that could measure up to him."

"What happened? I mean … to your pa?"

"Oh, it was a stupid, careless slipup. Pa and some men were hoisting a cargo net, bound for the hull of a ship. One of the metal hooks gave way and the crate crashed onto Pa's foot. Mangled it like squashed tomatoes. The doctor couldn't save his foot. Had to whack it off near the anklebone. After that, Pa turned angry and resentful. He wouldn't smile … or talk to us. Guess he couldn't stand the thought of being a useless cripple. He left after his foot healed. Just … disappeared one night and never came back." Tate jerked his head toward me, aware, evidently, of the impact his words might have on a person who walked with a crutch. "I'm sorry, Emma. I could cut my tongue out for saying such a stupid thing. You gotta know I wouldn't hurt your feelings for the world."

"It's all right. Believe me; you can't say anything I haven't heard a hundred times before. It doesn't bother me most of the time … guess I've sort of grown used to it." My heart thumped as I told my sweet lie to Tate, for careless words had too often wounded my heart and pinched my pride to the point of physical pain. I'd never in my life been complacent about my crippled condition, but the world didn't need to know that. Did it?

"For a while, Ma tried real hard to keep things going for us. Worked as a housekeeper for a time. Took in laundry, too. But it was never enough to support us. Can't tell you how many times we had to move because we couldn't pay the rent. Times went from bad to worse. When I was eight, I quit school and hit the streets, scrapping for money any way I could. Picking pockets, stealing, selling the things I stole. I even worked as an errand boy for a while. I did everything but beg. Something inside me wouldn't let me take charity, though it didn't seem to bother me to rob people blind."

My heart went out to the little boy, Tate, working to help his mother when he should have been attending school and playing with other children. Everyone in my family worked hard, no doubt about it, but survival had never depended upon any of us children the way it had for Tate.

"Ma started drinking a couple of years after Pa left. After that, she couldn't hold down a job for long. She'd spend our money on liquor and smokes. Even with my contribution, there was never enough in the money pot to pay for food and clothes ... and rent." Tate's nostrils flared, and once again, his head shook from side to side. I read disgust and anger in the way he pursed his lips and clenched his jaw.

Papa had warned us about liquor, or the demon's brew, as he called it. We weren't allowed to even consider imbibing strong drink because of the ruination it had dealt so many of our people. Papa claimed the Irish had a propensity for drunkenness. 'Twas the way of it in Ireland, he said, but he'd not be the one to start it up in our new homeland. And that was that. Even Elo obeyed Papa's command.

Tate was quiet. I thought he was through talking. He stretched his long legs to the foot of the dune, and looked up at the sky. I followed his gaze, noting a darkening in the clouds, a tightness in their gathering, as though they had amassed for an assault. I moved not a muscle as Tate sucked in deep breath and released it on a bumpy sigh. He cupped a hand over his mouth and coughed into it, clearing his throat.

"Then she got into some really bad stuff. She'd send me out of the house on bitter cold nights while she entertained one roughneck after another. Many a night I had to huddle in some stink-hole of an alleyway while she ... I don't know what I'm thinking, talking to you this way. It's too sordid a tale for the likes of your ears, Emma. Just trust me when I say it was a hard, hard time for me. If I'd had the sense God gave a turkey, I'd have hightailed it out of there and never looked back. But I couldn't leave her. She was still my ma and I loved her, no matter what. Wasn't long after that she got sick. We didn't have money for a doctor, so we never knew for sure, but I believe she got tuberculosis. Probably got it from one of her ... *friends*. She got weaker and weaker ... coughed all the time."

I reached out my hand and stroked Tate's arm. "What happened to you ... then?"

He turned his head, his eyes penetrating the depths of mine. There could not have been a lovelier sight than the joyous look that emerged on Tate's face in those brief moments. A most exquisite sensation rippled up my spine as his countenance softened, beauty sparking the dark look that had earlier inhabited his eyes. Beneath the sleeves of my jacket, I sensed a ruffling of arm hair; gooseflesh popping up until every hair on my body answered the call to rise up and stand at attention.

"That's the only good part to my story. You see, these two widows from the Methodist church heard about Ma ... how sick she was. A woman Ma used to work for called it to their attention. Anyway, they started coming around, doing things for us, like washing our clothes, bathing Ma and changing her bed ... bringing us food. At first, I wouldn't touch a thing they brought. I was furious they had witnessed our poverty ... furious that they felt sorry for us. I cursed them, told them to leave us alone. Told them I could take care of Ma. Can you imagine a ten-year-old guttersnipe of a boy trying to run off a couple of pillars of the church?" Tate chuckled as though his memories had conjured up a barrelful of fondness.

My spine stiffened like a ramrod at mention of the Methodist church. Tate rambled further, each word spitting a blast of Nordic air across my heart. The miseries of winter settled over my being like a thick coating of ice. Still—I chose to quiet my heart and hear Tate to the end, though I knew his tale would twist my insides like the dough Mama shaped into pretzels.

"There wasn't a thing they wouldn't do for Ma. They loved her, you see. And they loved me. I sold the hand-me-downs they passed my way, and sneered at their kindness. Made fun of them to my street friends, and even mocked them to their faces." Tate lifted his hands, curling his fingers toward his face. "I used these hands to make obscene gestures at them. Called them fat toads and laughed at their portliness. Did every wicked, evil thing I could think of to run them off, though they'd done nothing but make life easier for Ma and me. Know how they repaid my meanness? By praying for me ... and for Ma."

Though I had neither attained great wisdom nor inherited the keenness of a seer, I could have told Tate that was what the ladies would do. It's what my mama did when people needed help. She baked food, cleaned filthy houses, tended sick babies, sewed clothes for children ... and she prayed for them. Too bad my heart wasn't set on Jehovah God, as Mama's was. Perhaps the conclusion of Tate's story would not have upset me as it did. But I knew what was coming, so I began building a wall of defiance between Tate and myself. The more Tate talked, the higher my wall grew, and with its completion came an unyielding hardness in the mortar around my heart.

"They took care of us for almost a year, and when Ma died they took care of that, too. Saw that she had a proper Christian burial, because somewhere along the way, between the kindness and the prayers, Ma gave her heart to Jesus. Mrs. Deardson and Mrs. K came right out and told Ma that God's Son was her only hope, and she'd better do something about him before it was too late. I listened from the hallway—unwilling to show myself, but unable to resist a good story. As they talked about Jesus, I came to believe every word they said. It wasn't just the stories that sold me on the truth; it was their willingness to help a couple of filthy, penniless people like Ma and me. To me, that was true love.

"Things finally started making sense to me. For the first time in a long time, I felt loved. One day, right there behind Ma's bedroom wall, I gave my heart to Jesus too. After Ma died, Mrs. K took me under her wing, gave me a place to live … a place to come home to at night. She caught me up on my lessons and read me so many stories that I fell in love with books and reading, and just about anything that would teach me more about the world. I live with her still, you know. I try to repay her kindness by fetching her groceries and keeping up the yard. She told me how lonely she was before I came to live with her, so maybe God was helping both of us through that really rough time.

"One of the best things about living with Mrs. K is that I have full use of her library. My bedroom shelves are packed with hundreds of books—mine for the reading anytime I want. It's like God replaced all the years I couldn't go to school by giving me every book I'd ever want to read."

"I knew you were a reader, Tate. That's something we have in common."

"Emma—"

Despite my noblest intention to hear Tate out, I lurched for my crutch and rose to my feet, rocking unsteadily on the slope of sinking sand. My mind plowed for an excuse to leave. "I'd better be going. Oh … I almost forgot the cake I brought you." Slipping my hand into my pocket, I rescued the parcel with care, though by its feel the packet contained mostly sweet crumbles. Tate nodded his thanks, our hands touching as I handed him the bundle. I started to turn, but Tate's words stopped me cold.

"Have you tried talking to God, Emma? He can help you with your troubles, you know." Tate smiled as his words tapered off, but it seemed a sad smile, as though he knew something of what I was going through. As though he knew what my answer would be.

I stared at the sea, barely able to breathe for the anger that seethed within me. I knew Tate was sincere, but his message teemed with fraudulent misstatements and counterfeit claims I considered odious. Hateful words sprang to my mouth. I could no more stop their rampage than I could call forth Micah from the dead. "Yes, Tate. I tried talking to your God ... pleading with your God. At one time, I loved and trusted him with every bit of my being." I sobbed. My teeth ground together as words broke loose and hissed from my throat like steam from a teakettle. "Then I found out the truth: It's a pure waste of time to put your faith in someone who'll let you down. You may have found favor with God, Tate, but I didn't, and there's plenty more people just like me. Faith and love—it's all a lot of tommyrot."

With stiff, awkward steps I hurried from the dune, my heart slamming with rage. Feeling as downcast as the day I arrived at Granny's house, I mingled anger and sadness together, stewing up a batch of forbidden words I'd learned from Elo. I spewed them into the salty, windswept air, untroubled by who might hear them. Tate had kidnapped my peace with the sweet mockery of faith. And the thief of broken promises had stolen away my brief spell of contentment. Tate could talk about his God until stars fell from the sky. But I knew the cold reality of it all: The evidence of God's love lay buried on a knoll in Coldwater.

As I trudged the distance to Granny's house, I couldn't banish Tate's vision from my thoughts. My last glimpse of him was unnerving; his mouth gaping like a hingeless oven door, the look in his eyes proof enough that my virulent outburst had shocked his sensibilities. The one person I'd claimed as friend most likely hated me now. Well, good riddance, I thought. In the heat of passion, I was glad to be free of Tate's presence. But as my emotions cooled, I trembled at all I had said and done. Sane enough to understand such moments of anger and rebellion faded with time, I wondered why I'd lambasted Tate the way I had. What would I do if I lost the only friend I had?

# Twenty-seven

For three days I cloistered myself in Granny's house, marking time in the nest of my bedroom. Often my eyes grew soupy, spilling over with yearnings to hear Tate's voice. I missed his stories about working on the docks, and his seafaring tales, chronicling distant times and faraway places. They quickened my pulse as Papa's yarns did. But pigheaded pride wouldn't allow me to seek him out, for he had committed the unpardonable—spoken to me of a loving, merciful God.

Tate thought his words true, but I recognized a fallacy in his considerations. When I pleaded for God to protect and spare my little brothers, I received nothing but misery and heart-clattering pain. Grabbing hold of God's beneficence was as futile as trying to lure a frightened rabbit from his hole. Someday, Tate would learn that God's mercy didn't extend itself to everyone. And when he did, he'd understand what I already knew: The bumpy road of life was a lonely path to travel when you no longer walked it with your Creator.

Curling myself into a shrivel of self-pity, I spent hours reviewing ways the Lord had let me down. Each day I delayed my sojourn to the sea, I grew more resentful of Tate and Granny's faith. What was wrong with them? I wondered. Didn't they recognize God's abandonment for what it was? Hadn't Granny noticed God's absence the day she pleaded for the lives of her children? There were thousands, perhaps millions of angels in heaven. Surely, Almighty God could have charged one of them to keep an eye on her family. And what about the Falin boys? Where was God when I begged him to spare my little brothers? He knew how rambunctious and careless the twins could be.

I tried blocking Tate's words from my mind, but even the walls conspired against me, whispering from the four corners of my room. *Have you tried talking to God, Emma? He can help you ...* The last thing I wanted was to hole up in my room and fan the coals of my resentment to life. But that's exactly what I did.

But after three days of smoldering, I asked myself this question: Who was I hurting by staying cooped up in Granny's house? The answer—only me, for Granny seemed to enjoy having me underfoot, and the boy by the sea ... why, he probably hadn't even realized I'd gone missing.

I returned to the beach that afternoon, wondering if even a widow's mite of my comradeship with Tate was salvageable. For my part, we could resume our friendship ... *if* Tate threw off his preacher's garb and didn't harp on God again.

Keeping my vow to Micah, I knelt in the sand and shoveled grit from his tin. Today's offering was the unmarred sand dollar with its perfect belly star. If only I could place it in Micah's hand and tell him about the animal that once lived in this shell. 'Twas then that one of Granny's feisty sayings came to mind: *If wishes were horses, even beggars would ride.*

I hummed a song as I refilled the hole. It was a song about bright sunbeams and love. The twins used to sing this melody. They'd chirp it out like a couple of mockingbirds at daybreak, their dueling voices fetching laughter to my heart. But now the memory summoned only heartache. I ceased humming when the lyrics registered on my mind: *I'll be a sunbeam for Jesus, to shine for him each day; in every way try to please him, at home, at school, at play.* As I pictured Micah and Caleb, singing their hearts out to Jesus, bitterness flooded my heart like the surge tide that decimated Granny's family. I thought my heart had toughened up a bit, but the only thing it had toughened up against was God.

"Hey, Tadpole. Where've you been hiding? You been sick, or something?"

Tate's silhouette towered on a nearby dune. The sky behind him flared like a prairie fire, but he was just a dark shadow in a bright burst of sunlight.

"What're you doing? Digging for buried treasure?"

Not a hint of retribution or anger tinged Tate's voice. Perhaps he'd forgiven my harsh words of three days earlier. Perhaps he'd forgotten them.

I shook my head and hurried to fill the hole. *This is our secret, Micah. Yours and mine. It's nobody else's business.*

After jamming a stick in the sand, I turned with quickness and walked away from the dunes. Away from the tribute I had created for my brother's eyes alone.

I sighed with contentment when Tate's distinctive height and familiar form overshadowed me. He entwined our fingers together as naturally as two doves in a coo of love. I wondered if he felt the recklessness of my heart as it pumped through my veins.

"I've been worried about you, Emma. Thought maybe you weren't coming back."

I glanced up, seeing nothing in Tate's eyes but concern. "Yeah ... well, I'm fine. Just didn't feel like coming to the beach. That's all." My voice sounded untried and breathless, but I knew it was just mystified by all the raw sensations bumping around my heart.

"I think I know why you didn't feel like coming back. We—didn't exactly part on friendly terms the other day. I really upset you, didn't I?" As Tate tilted his head down and stared into my eyes, I spied a glint of mischief in his. His grin broadened as he tightened his grip and piloted me away from the beach.

"Just what do you think you're doing?" I asked, none too politely. I jerked free of his grasp and hurried toward the sea.

"Are you up to some walking?" Tate shouted at my retreating back. I turned, curiosity halting my tirade. He stood as though carved in stone, nothing astir on his trim body but a batch of loose curls. His broad-legged stance reminded me of a sure-minded hawker at the county fair, sizing up a gullible patsy. I read a dare in his posture and an attitude in his stare. Was my assumption correct? Did Tate think me incapable of enduring long, strenuous walks? If so, he surely misunderstood the gallantry with which we cripples valued our pride—to the point of out-and-out lying when our capabilities came into question.

"And what makes you think I might not be?" My words shot out like silver bullets. As I charged off in the direction to which Tate had been aiming, I squared my shoulders and uptilted my chin to a lofty altitude. The crutch pinched my underarm, but I held my grimace in check, for we'd barely begun our trek. I'd been off the crutch for three days, and I ached from the little bit of walking I'd already done today, but Tate didn't need to know that. Plowing on, I vowed not a whisper of complaint would flow from my lips to his ears.

We opened the wide double doors and proceeded to the center of the old church: Saint Joseph's Church, a high-pinnacled house of worship built by German immigrants in 1859. I'd obtained that bit of information from a plaque near the outside entrance. The church was empty but for Tate and me.

*Is this what we walked miles and miles to see?*

"Have a seat," Tate said, pointing to a high-backed pew. "Let's rest a while." He gazed at the church's interior, his eyes filling with glints of what appeared to be architectural delight. I waddled to a wooden bench, polished to a high sheen. There were twenty or so pews on either side of the aisle, standing as tall and straight as a company of foot soldiers at attention. The pews were dark, like the black loam on our farm when it's ready for the plow.

"Is this what you wanted me to see?" Incredulity dripped from my words like sarcasm from Elo's lips.

"It's just a place to rest, Emma. I'm not gonna try to ram God down your throat, if that's what you're thinking." Tate shook his head in disgust, it seemed, and angled his head upward to gaze at the high-pitched ceiling.

My legs were beyond tired, having exceeded the point of exhaustion during the last half hour of our journey. I leaned my crutch against the front pew and sank to the one behind it. The bench dwarfed me. I craned my neck and head, straining to see over the front pew. As my gaze wandered the sanctuary, it paused on an ornately carved podium and two thronelike chairs atop the dais. Then my eyes roamed to rooftop windows and to a kneeling bench of intricate design. Quiet serenity abode within these walls. I'd sensed it when we stepped from the vestibule into the great room. Now it seemed the walls attempted to transfer that serenity onto me. 'Twas a hopeless cause. Tranquility and I had been strangers far too long: since the winds of death swooped into my world, scattering my lifetime of peace as though it were a sack of confetti.

A cloth-draped table on the altar held a silver chalice and a candlestick at each end. A repository of lighted candles stood to the right of the altar, flames wavering though stillness hung on the air. These prayer candles provided points of light in a room otherwise shrouded by late-afternoon shadows. Scents of burning wicks and melting wax filled my nostrils, dragging into memory a picture of Micah's coffin on our parlor table.

I had stood guard over his casket that night—the longest night of my life—while candles burned at both ends of the burial box. Somehow, the hours passed, my nightmarish ordeal articulating itself in a stream of sobs and noisy bawling. At times, the pain had been too much, and I'd passed into a world of dark oblivion. Only then had the handprint of peace left its mark on my heart. As I held my brother one last time, wax pillars melted to nubs, extinguishing most of the light in the room. Just as Micah's death snuffed the brightness from my life.

*Why did you bring me here, Tate?* A cloudburst of pain rained down on me, flooding my eyes. No hope of squelching the flow this time. The dike had sprung a leak and nothing could hold back the deluge. I laid my head on the pew seat, out of Tate's view, and wept. I'd been practicing the art of crying in silence since the day of Micah's burial. It came in handy now. With my nose stuffed against burnished wood that smelled of beeswax and turpentine, I swallowed my tears and sobbed in silence. The pew carried the same scent as the benches in Christ's Chapel—back home in Coldwater.

As the torrent rolled on relentlessly, with no regard for my shame, I wondered why—at this time and in this place—had my emotions gone haywire? Granny would probably blame the outburst on my monthlies, but their time had come and gone in peaceable fashion and could not be held accountable.

"Emma, what's wrong? Why are you crying, girl?" Tate knelt by the pew, stroking my hair with his dockworker hands. I stole a glance. Through my watery view I observed his dark eyes, narrowing with concern, his lips shifting in wordless motion. As Tate's face drew close to mine, I held the ridiculous fear he was going to kiss me. Instead, he reached out a gentle hand and rounded up my stray wisps of hair, corralling their wildness behind my ears.

I supposed Tate had captured the gist of his mother's wisdom, taking to heart her words about sharing pain and dividing it in half. As he smoothed my hair into place, I knew his goal was to absorb as much of my pain as he could. I felt certain he would remain with me for the duration, whether I wished him to or not. Could I share with him the dark ugliness of my brother's death? I thought not, so I snatched the hem of my skirt and with unladylike comportment dried my eyes with it.

"We're not leaving this church till you tell me what's going on." Tate hefted himself from a kneeling position and sat beside me on the pew, the lines on his face hardening like cooled paraffin. "And don't think you're going to just up and run away this time." A dimple burrowed into his right cheek. I knew it was the closest thing to a smile I would see until I obeyed his command and unloaded my story.

It seemed he waited forever as I gained my composure, sniffles dying down, only to restart like an incurable case of hiccups.

"There was … an accident. My brothers got hurt, and … one of them died."

Tate wrapped his arm around my shoulder, drawing me to him, rocking our joined bodies to a rhythm far slower than my heartbeat. "I'm sorry, Emma. No wonder your heart is broken. I've never had a brother or a sister, but I can imagine the pain of losing one." Tate's grip was tenacious, but a comfort to my aching spirit, for it seemed he might squeeze the pain right out of me.

"How old was your brother?"

I hesitated before answering. Revealing Micah's age meant sharing the entire story, for surely Tate's next words would question how such a young child had died. I wished to share my burden with him, but was I prepared to reveal my guilt, also? I longed to be released from the solitary prison of pain I'd inhabited these last three months, but dare I risk telling Tate the unabridged truth?

"It happened last August. August twenty-fifth." I squirmed on the bench, telling myself I could make it through the tough parts if I just kept talking. "Caleb and Micah ... my brothers ... fell into a well. A stupid old well someone dug up probably fifty or sixty years ago. Micah—he ... he was already dead when we got him above ground. I couldn't save him. It was too late. We thought Caleb had died, too, but he was alive, just barely. He's bad off, Tate. Real bad. I'm afraid he's going to die." Tears welled again, washing Tate's face from my view. I whispered to his shadow, "I don't think I can go on if Caleb dies too." I reached for my skirt hem, but Tate had already retrieved a handkerchief from his jean pocket. I blew my nose, soiling another piece of Tate's clothing. I had developed a bad habit of dirtying up his clothes, one way or another.

I turned my back on Tate, signaling an end to the story.

He'd asked for more than I could deliver. I'd barely survived the tragedy, yet here I sat, talking about the sadness that had almost destroyed my life. I couldn't tell Tate about my neglect or the horrors that had followed that dark August day. He would have to wait for the rest of the story, I decided—if ever I chose to tell it.

I scooted from his closeness and grabbed my crutch, my legs atremble as I stumbled down the carpeted aisle. I knew my quivers were just a prelude to the bad case of nerves that would follow if I didn't get myself out of that church.

I sped past memory-provoking candles. They couldn't have frightened me more had they been a ravenous pack of wolves bent on devouring me. I hurried through the foyer, seeking distance from the church's quietude and my tumbling emotions. Pious icons and religious statues mocked my heretical spirit as I rushed through the heavy oak doors and into the sun's warmth and familiarity. And then, at last, I was outdoors, hobbling about in an abundance of autumn sunlight.

"If the church wasn't our destination, then what is? Where are you taking me now?"

Tate met my sidelong glance with a smile unique to his person: quirky and bulging with mischief. He slipped a hand from his pants pocket and pointed toward the south. I studied the sky, noting with disappointment the lateness of the hour. Granny would surely wear new patches into her floor if I wasn't home by the stroke of twilight.

"I wanted you to see Kempner Park. German immigrants built it as a dance pavilion in the 1800s. Old Man Kempner bought it a few years back and donated the land to the city. Now it's free and open to everyone, and … it's only a block from here." Tate's smile proved a beautiful sight, though it packed a wallop to my insides that made me flinch.

We headed for the park, walking faster than earlier in the day. After viewing the scenery, I had to hurry home. I'd promised Granny I'd be back before dark. I meant to keep my word.

Even the hissing sounds of the word *disobedience* offended my ears, for I had finally come to love and appreciate my grandmother. I'd been blind to her wisdom and guidance before, hearing only the harshness in her voice; seeing only weakness in her rheumy eyes. It took me weeks to comprehend Granny's unimaginable loss; the dreams she'd had for her children, the combustible disintegration of those dreams. But memories and dreams had a bit of forever in them—they never truly died. I pictured Granny—even now—stealing from bed in the dark of night, going in search of her dreams. I imagined her finding them, dusting them off, and holding a candle near so her ancient eyes could take in all their beauty. How difficult it must be at break of day when Granny had to put them away. Lock and bolt them in her trunk of yesterday's memories.

I wagged my head, chagrined by my past behavior, yet hopeful I could be the means of fulfilling at least one of Granny's dreams. Though it would never equal the lost love of her children, I contrived to pour every bit of my unspent love for Micah into Granny's unsuspecting heart.

I wished the afternoon would never end. Despite its disastrous beginning, today's outing might prove the high point of my stay in Galveston. I stole a glance at Tate, wondering if he felt the same as I.

Tate's mouth wore a lazy smile. Below his lower lip rested a nest of black whiskers.

"Did someone steal your razor, Tate?" Artificial innocence resonated in my words as I placed my fingertips on my puckered lips, camouflaging my smile. Tate hastened a hand to his bristly chin, stroking the spiny stubble, sparse though it was. His smile brewed up a storm in my heart, causing it to pitch and yaw like a ship in a tempest.

"Naw, I just overslept this morning. Didn't have time to shave. I'm thinking about growing a beard." It seemed his eyes widened with expectation. Did the handsome Tate think to gain my approval, I wondered, or could he care less what I thought?

I guffawed at his declaration. "With that measly batch of whiskers? Never. It would take you fifty years to grow a decent beard."

My reflexes were fast, but not as quick as Tate's powerful stride. Before I knew what he was about, he clutched me beneath my armpits, spilling my crutch to the ground. Then he lifted me from my feet as though I were a sack of coffee and rested me against his chest. My gaze sank into his eyes like quicksand. What a wicked grin he wore! While my legs dangled the air, Tate leaned in and scraped coarse chin whiskers against my forehead, marking me with his passage into manhood. Though his rub chafed my skin, it seemed unimportant in the moment. Laughter bubbled up from my heart, and for a brief flash of time I knew what it felt like to be in love.

Music drifted on the air as we mounted six stairs and stepped onto the gazebo's planked flooring. As I circled the octagonal structure, I tried to pinpoint the origin of the strain that floated into my ears. Though the slightly off-key tune carried an oompah beat, the melody sounded familiar. I pictured a gathering of mustachioed men wearing felt hats and wide suspenders; their bellies jiggling as they blew into horns and pounded on drums. It seemed to me they pumped out a song from their homeland, wherever that might be.

Someone had grafted a bench onto the gazebo's interior wall. I sank to it, viewing a vista of greenery that stretched beyond my vision. Weeping acacias, swaying palms, willows, and stately oaks dotted the landscape, while a trail of pink-and-white oleander bushes snaked through the park like a river. I sighed at the loveliness, for it possessed the hues and verdancy of a pastoral painting I'd once drooled over in Papa's art book.

"It's pretty, isn't it?" Tate's gaze bored into my eyes. He cocked his head, as though seeking reassurance the trip had been worth the trouble.

"I'm glad we came. It's truly beautiful."

"Speaking of beautiful … you're looking awful pretty today. I like seeing you in skirts rather than those striped things you used to wear. First time I saw you I thought you were a boy." Tate's laugh was a man's laugh, deeply rich and uninhibited. Shoving his hands into pants pockets, he leaned his shoulder against the railing post in a casual slouch. "You were the skinniest little fellow … little gal I'd ever seen." He screwed his face into a quizzical mask, as though stumped by my former appearance.

"Believe me, if I could find my overalls, I'd be wearing them right now." I glared at Tate, daring him to say another word against my beloved garb.

"To each his own." With whipsaw motion, he flung a leg over the railing, straddling it as he would a horse. I caught a look in his eyes. With wariness, I held my breath and my tongue while contemplating his countenance. Tate either wanted to grill me about my former state of being, or worse yet, testify at greater length about his love relationship with the Lord. Choosing not to participate in either discussion, I rose from the bench and stalked to the far side of the gazebo. But as I gazed at the miracle of nature before me, my heart pitter-pattered as though I had sprinted all the way from Coldwater to here.

Lost in thought, I didn't hear Tate's approach. He tapped me on the shoulder. As I turned to him, he bowed, as would a gentleman in the presence of a queen. In total Tate unlikeness, he gestured himself into dance posture.

"Pardon me, miss, but may I have this dance?"

I felt a rush of heat flood my face, my neck, my entire body. *Why are you doing this to me, Tate? Do you think so little of me that you would taunt my lameness?* Mortified by Tate's mocking insensibility, I turned from him and hurried across the stage. A quick glimpse revealed he no longer stood frozen in the mannequin-like position of moments earlier.

"Come on, Emma … it's a slow song. We can do this together. Come dance with me," he coaxed.

I kept my back to Tate. "I've never danced in my life. I don't know how … and frankly, it would be quite an impossible task, bound to this crutch as I am." If a voice could be void of everything but tartness, mine was.

"I've never danced before, either. Who's to see us? Who's to care that we're a couple of first-timers?"

I didn't miss the possibility that Tate's words carried a double meaning. Surely he'd held a girl in his arms before. Unlike me, who'd never known another's embrace, outside the hardy hugs of my family.

"Did you think to make sport of my condition, Tate?" The words wobbled from my mouth as tears pooled in my lower lids. I detested my every show of weakness.

"Heck, no. Look … I've got it all figured out …" Tate slipped his hand beneath my elbow and turned my body to face him. "All you have to do is put your right foot on top of my left shoe, then you'll be on even-keel. Want to give it a try?"

*No, I don't want to give it a try! I'll probably fall flat on my face and prove I'm even more of a bobble-foot than you thought I was.*

Tate relieved me of the opportunity to answer by grasping my crutch and placing it on the bench, even as my feet floundered for purchase. Back into a listing position I sank, my right shoulder tilting starboard. This day seemed one of my worst, if measured against the yardstick of humiliation. First the church scene, in which I had erupted like a geyser, and now—awaiting the comical disclosure of my clumsy gracelessness.

The music flowed into a lovely waltz, though it still leaned heavily upon its oompah heritage. Tate lifted me, my right foot resting atop his left. Then he moved, treading with care as I tried to keep up with the music and him. We took tiny, awkward steps at first. I feared we'd tumble into a leg-sprawling, inglorious heap, but Tate managed to shuffle us around the floor without a single spill. After a time, I forgot to worry about disgracing myself and became entranced with the miracle of the dance.

In my childhood daydreams, I had danced across splendid ballrooms, prancing on light, nimble feet as handsome partners twirled me about the floor. I had concocted spectacular, unbelievable daydreams because I knew they would never come true. But now, as our halting, bumbling motions smoothed into the metered cadence of a lilting melody, I rethought my declarations about dreams. Perhaps—on rare occasions—they came true after all. I lifted my gaze to Tate. His indefatigable smile said it all. *You knew how this would turn out, all along, didn't you? You really are something, Tate.*

I wished we could dance until morning light, but the afternoon melted away, as I had feared it would. The sun sank nearer and nearer to dusk's pealing curfew.

"I've got to go."

A look of disappointment swished across Tate's features, even as a lump of letdown plopped upon my heart. He nodded, his face unsmiling as we walked to the corner of O Street. With a promise to meet at the dunes the next afternoon, we turned onto separate pathways.

I glanced over my shoulder, the distance between us lengthening as I snatched glimpses of my one-and-only dance partner. In the waning daylight I saw his lanky form and his grinning face as he trotted backward in an unorthodox exit. Tate's feat surprised me, his agility smooth and accomplished as he waved a hand each time my gaze turned his way. I couldn't fathom how a person could stay upright and run in reverse at the same time. I laughed at his antics, for surely 'twas only a matter of time before he lost his equilibrium and went sprawling to the ground. But even as I laughed, my heart bucked and gamboled with the thrill of his attention. As Tate drifted from view, I secretly rejoiced in his seeming reluctance to let me out of his sight.

# Twenty-eight

Granny looked me up and down, surveying the length of my legs and the pathway my arms traveled. Her gaze paused overlong on my face. I knew my looks donned a peculiarity of their own, but not enough to warrant the stare that now drilled me to the core. As her eyes squinted to wrinkled slits, she thinned her lips into a wry contortion I'd come to think of as fossilized determination. She had studied me thusly all through the supper hour.

I turned my back on her and dunked my hands into a pan of dirty dishes. Granny's seasoned hands required boiling dishwater, but mine felt relief that the scalding water had cooled a bit. The intensity with which I peered at the dishes might have led one to think they held hypnotic power over me.

A chair scraped the floor. I heard Granny plop herself into it. Then a thump. I turned toward her, noticing the troubled look in her eyes. Though she didn't speak, her silence requested an audience with me. She had something on her mind, and nothing under heaven would forestall her a moment longer from sharing it with me. She pointed to the chair across from her. I dried my hands on a towel, and, with a weary sigh, seated myself in the appointed witness box. *What have I done now?*

"How'd ye say ye got that mark on yer forehead?"

*So, that's why Granny's in such a stew.* I had forgotten all about the whisker scrubbing Tate gave my brow this afternoon. I drew a fathomless breath, readying myself for Granny's inquisition.

"It's a chin-rub, Granny. Tate gave it to me. 'Twas his way of getting back at me for teasing him about his scrawny beard. I told you about Tate, way back ... remember?"

"Of course I remember ye telling me about him. Do ye think I'm already into me senility, child? But I tell ye one thing, lassie. That's not the markings a boy leaves. That's a man's beard for sure, and ye can't be telling me otherwise. How old is this Tate fella, anyways?" Granny's eyes widened a bit as she awaited my answer. Most likely, she thought it would lead to self-incrimination—or perhaps the gallows.

"He turned sixteen a couple of weeks ago. He's nice, Granny. Truth is—he's been a help to me. You know, with me being sad, and all?"

"I'm more than grateful for that blessing, sweet-pie. But I'm thinking it's high time I met the lad. See that he comes for dinner, Sunday next. Then I'll be making up me own mind about yer friend Tate. Tell him to be here at one."

My mind spun a spindle of worrisome thoughts. Would Granny grill Tate, her nosy questions embarrassing both of us? Or would she bore him to death with her never-ending tales? "Tate'll be here, and on time, too. He's not one to turn down good food. By the way, Granny, he loves your cooking."

Tate was coming for dinner! My heart beat with wildness, even as my mind scrambled to compile a spectacular menu for Sunday dinner.

In the quiet hours before bedtime that evening, I shared some of my Tate adventures with Granny. I told her about the turtle clutch he found, and about the reservoir of tenderness concealed within his man-size heart. Though I knew it might open up the forum to questions I'd been avoiding, I spoke of his mother's death, and how Tate had come to love the Lord. I disclosed these things because I knew they'd soften Granny's heart toward Tate.

"Ye don't say," Granny said from time to time, her eyes squinting as though I was a rare moth under her magnifying glass. I understood why she appeared baffled by my verbosity. After nearly two months of head nodding, with sparse words thrown into the kettle at odd intervals, I had suddenly evolved into a jabbering jaybird.

I sifted through my pack of stories, handpicking ones most profitable to my cause. There were tales—unutterable thoughts—that lodged in my throat like fish bones. So I left them unsaid. Sighting Mr. Panduso was one such story; his daily pilgrimages to the dunes inspiring me to build Micah's shrine. But hearing about Mr. Panduso would have resurrected Granny's ancient, pain-filled memories, and my own heart needed no such reminders. Like a web-footed albatross, they clung to my neck, refusing to take flight. I suspected sorrow might pinion itself to me forever, sucking joy from my heart like a hungry leech.

I lay between the bed covers and reflected on my afternoon with Tate. His friendship was the closest I had come to having a boyfriend. Oh, I liked to gawk at good-looking fellows, and dream up fantasies in which they fell at my feet, overcome with longings for me—longings I did not yet understand. However, if a handsome youth had ever dared return a bit of the stardust flowing from my eyes, I did not know of it. Nor did my heart, for long ago I decided that going without love was far more comfortable than experiencing the pain of rejection. Therefore, I simply turned my gaze from a lad's face—before I detected signs of repulsion, or even a spark my presence might have lifted to his eyes.

In the background of reminiscing, I heard Granny's mantle clock, tolling the midnight hour. I first met Tate on a night such as this: soft moonlight shadowing the sand, bright stars flickering in the yawning blackness overhead. I had noticed Tate onshore sometime after the sun breathed its last breath. His untimely appearance had stirred my heart with ireful flames. At the time, I hated the young man. Now I had come to love him.

Had Tate foreknown the journey I intended to take that night? If so, he never mentioned it. Since that lonely night, six weeks earlier, I had come to believe the trite old saying: Life is worth the living. Now Tate's meddling seemed more an act of heroism. Part of me wished he would stick around forever, butting his nose into every jot and tittle of my life. But who knew what the future held? It might find us a world apart. No matter the span of time, or range of separation, Tate would always hold a true measure of my heart.

The later the hour, the more undisciplined my mind became. Tate's last question to me on the beach buoyed to the surface with great fervency. *Have you tried talking to God, Emma?* Though I shoved his words beneath the swells of my restlessness, they repeatedly bobbed to the top with a surfeit of strength. Though my body was weary from a day well spent, his pestering question would not leave me alone. I dared not respond to it without first asking some questions of my own.

What further harm might I endure if I asked God for his help? More disappointments, disillusionments … despair? I had loved God long and hard—the only way my heart knew how to love. Nevertheless, when he slammed my trust back in my face, it left an ugly void in my heart that only fellow heathens could understand.

I considered another horror. What if I sought God, only to have him turn his back on me—because of my disobedience and blasphemy? What if God held grudges against wayward believers and skeptics like me? Jonah's obstinacy led him into the belly of a whale. And Jonah hadn't been nearly as mad at God as I was. I gazed at the ceiling, deliberating over what sort of wrathful recompense God had in store for me. Whatever it was—could it be any worse than the hollow, hurting heart I'd been living with?

Then a more ponderous and aching thought elbowed its way into the shouting match in my head. Had I allowed bitterness to hinder my little brother's recovery? Was my stubborn faithlessness the only thing standing between Caleb's sickness—and his healing? My body shook with the notion. I buried my face in the covers, blotting a river of tears from my eyes.

*God … you're all I have. Please don't let me down. Please don't let little Caleb down.*

Stretching through a fog of sleep, I reached for the haunting melody that drifted just beyond my grasp. As I awakened from a tangle of dreams and sat up in bed, I cocked my head, seeking the refrains I had heard in my slumber. *Singing! Who would be singing this time of night? Where was the music coming from?* Melodious strains toppled over themselves like waves against the shore. Fluid and serene, they lifted my heart on wings of joy. I held my breath, fearing the music would disappear altogether. Was this the song of a make-believe world, or a dream? No—impossible, for never was there born a poet or dreamer who could create the matchless beauty I heard. I found myself floating, if not in body—surely in spirit.

Scrambling from bed, I yanked my robe from a hook and slipped my arms into it. Was the song earthly or ethereal? I wondered. The melody followed me as I hurried down the hall. *Granny will know where the music's coming from.*

"Granny ... Granny." I halted on the threshold of her bedroom, whispering across the way as my eyes adjusted to the dimness. She lay on her back, mouth agape. I thought her dead for a moment, until she gave a snort and blew bumpy snuffles through her lips. I tiptoed to her bed. Granny looked pale in the bundle of bed linens that swaddled her like a newborn. Wrinkles dipped into her cheeks and forehead like creases in a book. A mighty sense of love swept through me as I considered her ancient state—a portent, perhaps, of a time when she would no longer be with us.

Granny was a hunk of woman but appeared small and insignificant in the large four-poster bed. Potent fumes of Vicks VapoRub lifted from her covers, stinging my eyes. From September until May, Granny scrubbed the ointment into her chest at night—whether she needed it or not. Then she pinned a cloth to her nightgown, keeping the vapors tucked in close to her rib cage. She had told me about the outbreak of Spanish influenza ten years earlier that had killed thousands of people. She feared its resurgence. I dared not cough in Granny's presence. Not if I wished to avoid a similar torture as the one she put herself through every night. She turned onto her side, facing me. I nudged her shoulder with gentle hands.

"Wha ... what is it, child? What's wrong? Are ye sick or something?" Granny swung her legs over the side of the bed and reached for her spectacles, all in one motion. When she locked her hands onto my shoulders, I saw the worry in her eyes.

"I'm okay, Granny. Didn't mean to scare you, but I had to know where the singing was coming from." It felt good when Granny loosened her grip on me. She was a true elder, but had strength in her fingers and a grasp that would put a young man to shame.

"What singing? I hear nary a note of singing, child." Granny shook her head and raised her chin, glancing at the ceiling and around the dark room. "The only sound I hear is a bit of wind in the trees."

I drew in a breath and held it, listening for the melody. I feared I had imagined it. Nevertheless, there it was, rolling through the room with all the loveliness of an Easter morn.

"Can't you hear it now, Granny? It sounds like the sea is moaning and singing to me. I don't know … maybe the whole world is joining in. It's the prettiest music I've ever heard." I leaned in close to Granny's face and peered into her wizened eyes. She had wrinkled, shriveled lids, but oh, the warmth that sparked her depths. Granny had to hear the singing. She just *had to.*

She rubbed my arms as she shook her head. "'Tis not a song I can hear, Emma Grace. I'm sorry. Perhaps … you dreamed it up … perhaps not. Ye've been through a lot these last few months, sweet-pie. Why don't you go on back to bed now and get some sleep. Everything will be all right in the morning. Ye'll see."

Again I awakened to singing. Once more I traipsed down the hall, disturbing Granny's sleep. She counseled me, but her words careened into one deaf ear and out the other. I wanted Granny to own up to hearing the music. Otherwise, my next home might be the loony bin.

"What is it, child? Are ye wanting to sleep with me the rest of the night? Don't mind a bit if you do."

"No … no thank you." I thought the beetles in the backyard trees might hear the heavy sound of my sigh. "I'm okay. I think maybe I just fancied up the singing in my head—like you said."

I tossed beneath the covers, weary, yet too excited to sleep. The music was gone. Its vacancy left a hole in my heart. However, the remnants of the song—that melody of perfect creation—tarried in my mind, warming me like a crisp fire on a three-blanket night. I knew I might someday forget some of the strains I heard this night, but the song's magic would stay with me forever.

"Emma Grace?"

I startled at the sound of Granny's voice. My head and shoulders popped above the covers as she neared the side of my bed. *Maybe Granny heard the song, after all.*

"I just remembered something, child. Something very important."

"What, Granny?"

"Many years ago, after I lost my family, I, too, heard singing one night. Just as ye did tonight. Perhaps ... it was the same song ye heard tonight. The world was a black, black place back then. So dark I could hardly see me way from one day to the next. I thought God had let me down. I grew more peeved and resentful at him every day. Oh, child, I turned into a bitter, bitter woman. One day I just upped and told God to go away and leave me alone. Told him I wanted nothing more to do with him." Granny snickered and shook her head as though caught up in the happenings of times gone by.

"Did God leave you alone?"

"Well, it certainly felt like it at the time. Odd, though, how it happened—my family bringing me back to God the way they did. Ye see, one night the truth of my situation hit me smack in the face. I suddenly realized that God was my only choice—my only hope of ever seeing me loved ones again. And I wanted to see my family more than I wanted to live, Emma Grace." Tears rushed to Granny's eyes as she sat down on my bed and took hold of my hand.

"'Twas in the late night hours that I heard the singing. Woke me from troubled sleep, but oh, the joy it brought with it, child. 'Tis hard to describe the warmth ... the love and contentment I felt. As the music washed over me, I sensed the first stirrings of hope, and by the time the music stopped, there was no doubt in me mind that someday I'd be with me husband and young'uns again in heaven.

"Your papa was living with me at the time. He moved back here after the storm to help repair the house, and, most likely, to act as safeguard so I wouldn't let go of life—if ye know what I mean. I hurried down to his bedroom, wanting to know if he had heard the singing too. But I changed me mind and didn't ask him."

"Did Papa hear it?"

"I asked him the next morning if he'd heard any unusual night noises but he said no, he'd heard only the usual creaking of the house. I didn't mention the singing. In fact, I've kept it secret all this time. Hadn't thought of it in years—not until you came to me room the second time tonight."

"It truly was beautiful music, wasn't it, Granny?" My eyes closed as melodic refrains drifted through my memory. I felt I might float away on the clouds of pure pleasure they brought.

"'Twas the most beautiful singing I ever heard. Too lovely to be describing. Who could understand, unless they heard it themselves? 'Tis a relief to be sharing it with you now, sweet-pie. Ye *do* know who sang to me that night—don't ye, Emma Grace?"

My heartbeat pounded against my eardrums as I sucked in a breath and held it. I opened my lips, breathing out an answer.

"No."

"'Twas God, Emma Grace. God. About a month after I heard the music, I was sitting in church, listening to the preacher read Scripture. One of the verses he read said that God quiets us with his love, and he rejoices over us with singing. Oh my, child—ye should have felt the chill that raced up me spine when I heard those words. I knew then that the music had come from God. 'Twas his voice that sang over me that night."

"Are you saying God sang to me tonight?"

"Yes. It had to be him. If it were anybody else, then I would have heard the singing too, wouldn't I?"

My head jerked up, then bent forward repeatedly, like a woodpecker going after a tree worm. A light, giddy sensation spilled through my body, bubbles of joy percolating in my stomach and everywhere else.

"God left a part of himself with me that night, Emma Grace. Not exactly sure what it was. Perhaps—'twas his Spirit. All I know is that I haven't been the same since the hour God sang to me. That's not to say I don't get out of touch with him from time to time. I surely do. But if I go looking for him with all me heart, I always find him."

I recalled earlier in the night, when I talked to God for the first time since Micah died. *God … you're all I have. Please don't let me down.* Had that small plea—those insignificant words—gained God's attention? His affection? Had they pleased him in a way I couldn't understand? Is that why I reaped the gift of his song? Perhaps he had been by my side all along, just waiting for me to come back to him.

"I've been mad at God too, Granny. Guess you and I are alike in a lot of ways." I leaned into Granny's chest and we held onto each other as though we knew this moment would someday prove to be more important—more vitally meaningful—than most of the moments in our lives.

"Are ye blaming God for what happened to Micah? Or are ye mad at yerself?" Though her features were vague against the shadowed light, I thought I glimpsed Granny's lips, curving into a smile.

"Both."

"Well … 'tis honest ye are—now that ye're in a mood to be talking." Granny placed my hand beneath the covers and rose from the bed. She leaned over me, looking her fill before she kissed my brow. "Best we get a little sleep now. Seems ye're well on the road to healing, Emma Grace. Ye know I'll be praying for you."

Granny walked to the doorway, then turned and gazed at me. "Think ye'll be able to get some rest now?"

I took in Granny's flowing gown, stooped shoulders, and tall frame. She reminded me of someone—or something. Ahhh—yes. Her waves of unbraided hair gave her the appearance of a vintage angel who had inhabited heaven for a long, long time. "Yes, Granny. I think I can sleep now."

"Night, child."

"Granny … I love you."

She nodded, signaling another way in which we were similar. Tears clogged her throat as easily as they did mine.

# Twenty-nine

Upon awakening, my bare feet hit the floor and I knelt for the first time in months. It seemed almost hypocritical to pray to someone with whom I had been so grievously angry. Nevertheless, I gave voice to my feelings, toiling for honesty and forthrightness. What sputtered out were sparse, timid utterances. I felt more like a babbling toddler just learning to talk than a young woman who had prayed devotedly since the age of seven. My first sentence was a plea for forgiveness, but every word thereafter centered on Caleb's healing. If sincerity counted as gain, I knew God heard my prayer.

Granny and I smiled often over our cereal bowls that morning. I felt peculiar—different in some exciting yet uncommon way. My heart beat without malice, without bitterness or blame. A person could come to treasure such a feeling.

Guided by habits long instilled, Granny went about her work as though I had not kept her up half the night. We chatted as we did the morning chores, and then Granny left to have coffee at Mrs. Beushaker's house. My face warmed as I considered on whom their conversation would dwell. Most likely Granny and her friend would spend their coffee hour hashing over my business with liberal doses of matronly concern, but no more than any other day of my lengthy stay in Galveston.

I loved to stand facing the sea, finding pleasure when the wind and spray had their way with me. Had I been a boy, I would have chosen the seafaring life, for the ocean now felt like my home. Spirited winds raced across the water, shanghaiing wisps of hair from my French braid, and flapping the hem of my skirt as I turned my back on the sea and walked to Micah's dune.

As my fingers wrapped around the obsidian stone in my pocket, I thought about how the pumiced rock would have captured the twins' excitement. Stunned them—if but for a moment. Ebony, and stretched to the length of a man's knuckle, it had the feel of weighted glass. I'd caressed its smoothness this afternoon, before choosing it for Micah's treasure can.

Papa found the obsidian last fall while tilling our pastureland. Since he knew its origin and composition, he deduced that coastal Indians, such as Tonkawa and Karankawa, had used it as barter. He claimed that at one point in history the stone had been but a speck of rock on a volcanic boulder. After eons of wind and water-flow, the pebble pushed itself free of the great lava chunk—along with a hundred thousand more just like it. How the rock found its way into Coldwater's midnight soil was unclear, but now it had returned full circle, back to the Gulf of Mexico.

I uncovered the biscuit tin and placed my stone among the other treasures I had offered in Micah's memory. After last night's encounter with God, I sensed that today's presentation had to be perfect, for it signified a new beginning with God—and with life.

After walking the beach for an hour or so, I settled myself on the pile of sand Tate and I had dubbed "the dune." I shivered beneath my layer of wool while the wind threw bits of sand in my face and overhead clouds thickened like fat dumplings in a stew pot. *This is just the forefront of another nasty norther.*

Temperatures dropped and gusts strengthened as another hour slipped by. I hoped Tate made haste. It wasn't like him to be late.

Perhaps we could seek shelter and talk a bit before the dreaded curfew hour tolled its appearance. Tate's tardiness concerned me, for he habitually showed up first and took his leave last. Surely, his feelings hadn't jumped track and switched rails during the night. On the other hand, yesterday's intimacy may have conjured up regretful memories for Tate. Memories brimming with repugnant visions of a crippled girl who had danced her heart out. Did Tate treasure the closeness we shared, or did he now see me as a naive youth, plump with immaturity? How would I handle it if Tate considered our time together pure foolishness?

I turned up the collar of my jacket and shifted my face from frontal blasts of frigid wind. Perhaps I didn't suit the seafaring life, after all. Summoning Tate's face to my mind's eye, I imagined his expression when I told him about God singing over me. Even more than the song, I wished to share the baby steps I took this morning when I planted my feet on the straight and narrow path back to God.

I remained at the beach until the sun sat like a burning coal on the water, and splotches of eventide crept onto the sand. I scrunched my shoulders against the wind and rammed my icicle fingers into deep pockets. Lost in a passel of shredded thoughts, I turned and trudged my way back to Granny's house. Today was the first time Tate had not met me at the dune. Dampness gathered in my eyes and followed me all the way home, along with the fine mist covering my hair and clothes. When I came within a stone's throw of Granny's house, I looked up, gazing upon the seemingly impossible sight of Tate's tall form. Rooted atop Granny's porch like the main mast of a sailing ship, he turned and looked my way. I sensed sternness in his countenance though the distance between us proved significant. While Tate remained glued to his position aboard the schooner, I waved and yelled at him like a cavewoman gone mad.

I hurried up the stairs, faster than was customary for my crutch and me. On the top step, I glanced into Tate's face and met the surly eyes of Elo.

"Elo—what are you doing here?"

"Where've you been, Emma Grace?" Elo forced his words through gritted teeth. 'Twas one of his traits for which I had not been lonesome. "Granny said you were at the beach with a *friend*."

My crutch crashed to the porch floor as I rushed to Elo and locked my arms around his neck. After an eternity, he clasped his hands behind my back and squeezed as though he had actually missed me. I yanked the wool cap from his head and ran fingers through his thick blondness, the way I used to tousle the twins' rusty curls. Oh, my. I hadn't realized until now how much I'd missed Elo's contrariness. As I leaned down and grasped my crutch, I lifted my gaze to Elo's face. It seemed as though we had said good-bye a year past, not weeks earlier. Time had nurtured Elo's height and the breadth of his shoulders, but it had also matured him in other ways as well. Somehow, during my absence from home, a sun god had visited the boy who was born handsome and made him more so by composing his own beauty upon Elo's features. I stepped back and stared, surely with mouth agape.

"So—what's this friend's name—the one you slipped off to meet?" Elo's breath sent white clouds into my face as he locked his arms over his chest and cocked his head to a disagreeable angle.

"I was supposed to meet Tate," I said in stammering cadence. "Tate …" I couldn't recall Tate's last name. Had he told me his surname and I'd forgotten it—or had I not listened when he said it? "I met him on the beach a few weeks back. In fact, I thought you were him when I first saw you on the porch."

"What happened? Did he stand you up?"

"Yeah, I guess he did."

"You look different, Emma Grace. Older, maybe. I'm not sure what it is." Through squinted lids, his eyes investigated me for extended moments. He shuffled his feet uncharacteristically and cleared his throat. I heard in his voice none of the scale sliding of two months prior. A no-nonsense man's voice had settled deeply into his throat, suiting him to perfection. With reluctance tingeing his words, Elo continued, "I guess … maybe you're a mite prettier than I remembered. How are you doing, anyway? Are you well—*finally?*"

"I think so. I feel a lot better … and I …" Elo's gaze aimed true as I stuttered along. I couldn't put into words the extent of my improvement or the role Tate had unknowingly played in it. Elo's unstinted observation persevered as I wallowed around in a pile of debris-cluttered words. He wanted the truth. He would accept nothing less. I loved that about my brother, for it spoke of his candor and lack of hypocrisy. Elo didn't believe in lying. He would rather bring a matter to a fistfight than try to wiggle out the back door of untruth.

He took pity on me and finished my sentence. "Yeah—from the looks of things you're doing a lot better."

The front door cracked and Granny poked her head through the opening.

"Get yourselves into the house this instant. 'Tis a gale blowing out there. Ye'll both be icebergs if ye tarry a moment longer."

I grinned at Elo. He rolled his eyes, as if to say how fortunate he was to be living anywhere but at Granny's house.

When we walked into the lighted parlor, I noticed Granny's eyes were red-rimmed and swollen to slits. She appeared to have cried a washtub of tears. Something crinkled at the nape of my neck, causing my hair to rise up like the backbone of a horn-mad bull. I slammed my gaze back on Elo, who wriggled from his jacket with no great urgency.

After slinging his coat over the rack, he turned to me, hands dropping to his sides like a gunfighter. His mouth set itself into a straight, determined line.

"What's wrong? Why are you here, Elo?" As panic filled my heart, blood upped and departed my head. I grabbed the table, steadying myself. 'Twas one time I would have preferred a lie to the painful truth that flashed across Elo's face.

"I've come to take you home, Emma Grace. Mama needs you."

"Is Caleb …? Is he all right? Did he come out of the coma?" My legs trembled beneath my skirt as air in the parlor grew scarce. Either my head—or the room—spun in slow, wobbling circles.

"He's taken a turn." Elo shook his head and switched his focus to Granny's empty hallway. "Doctor said he has pneumonia." His gaze pivoted back to me, and his commander's voice aimed itself straight at my heart. "Mama needs you, Emma Grace. She's worn herself out worrying over Caleb—and you." I noticed Elo's chest rising and falling with swiftness, as though excessive talking used up all the oxygen in his lungs.

I slumped to the floor. No one moved as I sat in a heap of clothes, pain, and fear. I felt my world shrivel to a small circle of words that expressed everything I held dear.

*Please, Father … don't take Caleb, too.*

I stumbled my way to the beach in the darkness of early dawn. The wind became my enemy, driving against me with the force of a thousand bearded pirates. Blinded by a cloud of sand, I struggled onward, praying the path I took would lead me to Micah's dune.

The bus to Coldwater would depart at eight o'clock this morning, and I had much to do before Elo and I began our hour-long walk to the Harbor Street depot.

Granny and Elo would be awake by now, Granny fuming herself into a royal dither when she discovered I had gone missing. However, my trek to the sea was vital—if I ever hoped to see Tate again. I had thought myself clever when I smugly disguised my last name as Grace. I choked on my smugness now, for I had played the dunce, misleading Tate as a common fishmonger might do. Had my secretiveness cost me more than I could measure—the loss of Tate forever? If only I had thought to exchange addresses or last names. I supposed I visualized our friendship as a beginning with no ending of our time together.

Perhaps not all was lost. During a search for clues to my disappearance, Tate might recall the day he spied me digging in the sand. I fingered the missive in my pocket, relieved the wind had not snatched it away. I'd leave the note in Micah's tin and pray that someday Tate's feet would lead him to its location.

I smelled the sea before I saw it. As whiffs of stirred-up ocean poked their way into my nostrils, fragmented light leaked through the mottled sky, lighting up the choppy sea. Steering away from the shore, I hastened to Micah's dune, running my hands along the edge until I found the marker stick. When I found it, I removed the lid, stuffed the note inside, and reburied the can.

I couldn't make myself return to Granny's house. Not yet. As waves lifted frothy whitecaps high in the sea and then tossed them overboard, I sat atop our dune and waited for Tate. Shivers raced through my body, chattering my teeth. I imagined my lips were plum purple from the cold.

Why would Tate come to the beach at five o'clock in the morning? I asked myself.

*Only an idiot would hope for something so ridiculous.*

Elo waited by the front door, his gaze drilling me with trial-lawyer eyes.

"Was he there—looking for you in the dark of night?"

"No. No, I'll probably never see him again."

"Maybe you will—maybe you won't. The only thing you need to concern yourself with right now, little girl, is Caleb and Mama. You got that?"

"I was only trying to let my friend know I wouldn't be coming back." I hitched my shaky hands to my hips, my words flaying the air like a fisherman's fillet knife. "And another thing, Elo—don't you go talking down to me as if I were some snot-nosed young'un. As far as I can tell, you and I are on equal footing."

To catch a glimpse of Elo's smile, one had to be as sly as a fox and quicker than a cottontail. Though I was neither, I did catch sight of the merest twitch of his lips, right before his grin sped into the great beyond. That teensy spasm set loose a spurt of pure joy into my bones. Could it be I had passed muster in his eyes? I doubted any such possibility. As far as I could tell, only three people had made his list of respected individuals. Most likely Elo's own name was at the top of the page, followed, of course, by the names of Mama and Papa.

Telling Granny good-bye proved most difficult. I determined not to cry in her presence, as I had grown weary of weeping, and even wearier of Granny witnessing it. I had done my crying the night before. But when the time came to walk down her treacherous steps, I clouded up again, making the descent doubly dangerous.

Love could creep up and blindside you, I realized. I turned and waved farewell to the crotchety old woman who had captured my admiration and affection. I knew she, too, would feel the hammer blow of loneliness once we parted. An image of Granny, sitting alone in the parlor, her needlework lying untouched in her lap while she trained her gaze on some faraway memory, struck a chord of melancholy in my heart. I missed her already. I decided that during the long bus ride to Brenham, I would concoct a scheme to get Granny to Coldwater for an extended visit. Even though she had declared her journeying days were gone and buried, the idea still heartened me a bit.

Elo carried my bag as we trolled the lengthy maze of blocks leading to Galveston's wharf area. Buffeted by gusts of wintry wind, I found it difficult to place one foot in front of the other. Elo scuttled along with ease, though my suitcase had to be heavier than a well-fed ox. It bulged as never before: Granny's overnight baking spree producing a butter-milk pound cake, two loaves of nut bread, and a huge canister of snickerdoodle cookies. Also in my luggage—three pairs of overalls that had mysteriously disappeared six weeks earlier. Their whereabouts became obvious in the morning light, when I discovered them washed, folded, and neatly pressed in between my packed clothing.

Papa must have thought a tornado struck when I bounded into his arms at the bus station in Brenham. Entangling him in a choke hold that had him siphoning air, I released erstwhile tears and pent-up fear into his welcoming bear hug. I felt a powerful tug to unite with the rest of my family in like manner, but home was still twenty miles away. I had to travel over hillocks and up steep slopes, then down a rough and snaking road before I could be with my family again. But—hadn't I already been doing that, every hour of my life since the day of the tragedy?

Although deeper crevices etched Papa's face than when I last saw him, an undiluted glow of happiness filtered through his eyes. Or so it seemed to me. Why did joy fill him now, when his youngest son abode in the death-grip of pneumonia? Did the luster in Papa's eyes link itself to me—the daughter who had wrapped herself around his neck like a hangman's noose? I tamped down such arrogant thoughts, knowing that boastful pride goeth before the fall. A bit of shame lingered on my conscience, as present circumstances rendered this a most inappropri-ate time for me to be basking in the effulgence of Papa's love.

"Come on, little-bit," Papa said, dropping his arm around my shoulder. "It's past time you were back with your family. Home hasn't been the same without you."

# Thirty

As Mr. Peavy's Buick rolled over our drive, it pulverized caliche gravel into powder, and then sprayed the air with clouds of white dust. I peered over the dashboard, trying to catch a glimpse of my family. Then I spied them in the distance, biding time on the stubbled grass of our autumn lawn. Their faces were distinct now, The Ollys wearing wobbly smiles, while Nathan's poker face masked a thousand unasked questions.

Whom did they expect to greet? I wondered. The waiflike girl who had reluctantly parted company with them weeks earlier? The young woman who could not feed her body for the bounty of guilt in her heart? She no longer existed. I buried her in the past, alongside my unspeakable shame. Moreover—no one was the wiser. Where once my heart labored with empty, hollow beats, it now thumped with freedom. The freedom that came when I decided to hide my guilt from the vision of my family. I harbored no thoughts of uprooting what I had sepulchered away from the world. Why should I—when what it required was my life?

I squared my shoulders and stepped from Mr. Peavy's Buick, delighting in the genuineness of the smile broadening my face.

"Emma Grace, come here, child."

Mama folded me to her chest, a deluge of tears welcoming me home. Her appearance set off warning bells in my head and triggered my heart to pump with fierce exertion. True to form, Elo had not overstated Mama's dissipation. She wore the look of one who had strayed far from the healing light of hope.

*I should have been here to help you, Mama.*

As Mama and I entered Caleb's room, she clasped my hand with firmness. I released myself and moved closer to the bed, my hands shaking as though I had stumbled upon Marley's ghost. *I'm trying hard to believe, God. Please take the doubt from my heart.*

In looks, the twins had favored me from birth, but never had Caleb resembled me more than he did now. That is—when I, too, had existed in a shriveled-up body with nary but a pinch of life left in me. Sickbed pallor had sucked all hint of color from Caleb's usual ruddiness. 'Twas a sad sight to behold. I stroked his overlong curls that fell to shoulder length—but for a bit of shaved hair near his ear where a thatch of fuzz grew in like bristles on a bottlebrush. Grateful I was that the Turkish head bandage had gone missing. If only his scar would show the same courtesy. Like the stitches of my hurried-up sewing, it raggedly pursued Caleb's hairline from forehead to ear.

Lying in the bed before me was the handsomest of lads. Shortsighted folk might concur the wound marred Caleb's good looks—but only those who had never been accused of being overly bright. Still, it was a shame that the brand was permanent. Like the perennial weeds in Mama's garden, it would stick around, reminding us of all we had lost. My family, you see, needed no such reminders.

I knelt by the bed and stroked Caleb's arm, knowing again the wonder of his touch. More than I desired to hold him, I yearned to see a flame rekindled in his eyes—eyes heretofore perceptive and star-bright. I leaned over, my tears splattering his wee fingers as I brushed his scar with a whisper kiss.

Caleb's body convulsed then, a coughing spasm shooting red-flecked spittle across my face and bodice. I leaped from the bed as though a coiled snake had bared its fangs at me. Mama moved in, covering his mouth with a cloth, wiping hawked-up matter from his chin. I huddled on the sidelines and listened to the sound of Caleb's wheezing, the congestion in his lungs thickening by the moment.

"There, there, baby. You're going to be all right, precious boy." Mama's voice hitched a bit as she cleaned Caleb's face with a damp rag. Some of Mama's words winged high, like chaff winnowed from the grain. Others slipped and fell, swallowed up in the tunnels and crevices of her throat.

It seemed that a fire-breathing dragon thrust its cornuted head into my chest, setting my lungs on fire. I thought I might suffocate from the fear that burned within me. My stomach heaved, threatening to spill over Mama and the bed. I slipped to my knees, my eyes smarting and my head throbbing, for I knew the rattle in Caleb's chest meant that he and death walked but steps apart. And I could do nothing to prevent it—other than hold onto the thimbleful of faith from which I had promised never again to part.

"Give me the cloth, Mama." I stood on unstable legs and tugged the sputum-filled rag from Mama's hand. As I doused it in a pan of camphor oil and water, an urgency to pour my strength into Caleb saturated my thinking. "Let me take care of Caleb. I know what to do. Please, go rest for a while." Mama turned a confused stare on me, as though I had ordered her to go into town and rob a bank. "The Ollys have already started supper, Mama. You have plenty of time for a nap." I sped over my points of persuasion, watching her face as seeds took hold and sprouted. Nevertheless, the longer she mulled it over, the more her head wagged. Tempted by the offer—yes—but her need to care for Caleb proved the more overwhelming choice.

"I can't leave him, sweetheart. Besides, you just got home. You're every bit as tired as I am."

I slipped my hand around her waist and lay my head on her shoulder. Without her realizing it, my crutch and I slowly led her to the doorway.

"See that bedroom down the hall?" As I pointed with my left hand, I reclaimed Mama's icy fingers into the folds of my skirt. "The one with the open door? That's your room. You've been sleeping in Caleb's room so long you probably forgot where it was. Do us all a favor and get some rest, Mama. We need you to stay healthy."

Mama smiled as she stepped from the room, but her smile bore such meagerness, one iota more would have cast it into nonexistence. I worried that she had already accepted Caleb's fate as identical to Micah's.

I pushed the chair from my footpath and knelt by his bed. As I talked to Caleb, I pretended his eyes were wide open, ears perked in readiness for his favorite story. I shared my seaside ventures with him and confided secrets about the cache buried in the sand. My words rolled on, despite a throat that gargled tears. I pictured Caleb's face—saw it beam with surprise when I excavated trinkets I'd hidden from the world. I promised my little brother we would take a trip to the ocean. We'd build castles in the sand and frolic in the sea, our hands tightly clasped together as we jumped the highest waves in the world. Of course, we would have to watch out for dangerous jellyfish and stingrays. But, oh, the fun we would have. Afterward, we would play with the treasures in Micah's tin and pretend our brother was there with us.

Micah's freckled face flashed before me. Burying my head into bed coverings, I squeezed my sobs into cotton fabric, lest Caleb detect them through the foggy mist of his coma.

What a weakling I was. So much to do, yet here I wallowed on the floor, blubbering like a baby. Caleb's frailness demanded my stamina, my endurance—not a bucket of cold tears doused upon his tiny flame of life.

The room darkened as though in condolence with Caleb's grave condition. I lit the lantern on the bedside table and returned to his side. Mama delivered a tray of food soon thereafter, but I hungered for little other than Caleb's recovery. It was for that I prayed: *Return Caleb to us, Lord—healthy and exactly the way you created him. As demanding as the day you made him, Lord.*

Did God hear my prayers? I believed he did. Would he grant my heart's desire? Time, alone, would give me the answer.

For three days I lived in Caleb's room, forcing Mama and The Ollys out the doorway when they attempted to relieve me. My illness had separated Caleb from me far too long. I'd not willingly relinquish my post by his side.

I wouldn't look at Doctor Landers. His shaggy Abe Lincoln face, with its abysmal heap of wrinkles, seemed the personification of hope-lessness. When he entered Caleb's room, I skittered out the door like a startled lizard and kept my distance for the duration of the visit. I gleaned more from his worried look than his words could ever express. Caleb was going to die. 'Twas just a matter of time. My faith wanted to take off like a wild Canadian goose in search of warmer climes, but I grabbed onto its scrawny neck and held fast. As I spooned broth between Caleb's chapped lips, washed his shrunken body, and changed soiled pajamas and bed linens, the doctor's gloomy countenance loomed over me like a great gray vulture, circling my scrap of faith, waiting to pick it to pieces.

Then came the moment we prayed would never arrive. Caleb's mild fever took off like a racehorse, combining itself with severe bouts of chills and shakes. The setback called for more than one set of hands. While the fever raged, Mama and I worked together, giving alcohol rubs, urging crushed aspirin into his mouth, ladling broth down his throat—around hacking spells that had weakened in volume, but not in expectoration.

I crumpled to a chair and lay my head against the backrest. "Is he going to make it, Mama?" Words trickled from my mouth like a drought-stricken spring, conversation requiring more energy than I could dredge up.

Mama turned glassy eyes in my direction, seeking eye contact through her haze of tears. She gazed as though she had forgotten my name or thought me a stranger. On the other hand, maybe her fixation focused on my unkempt condition. I was an eyesore no doubt, having gone days without changing my clothes, or running a brush through my hair. Most likely, I had sleepers in my eyes, cobwebs in my hair, and mold growing on my teeth. I brushed loose strands from my face and ran palms down my crumpled skirt, as though a vanishing cream would ooze from my fingers and dissolve the wrinkles.

Mama endeavored to compose herself. She raised fingertips to quivering lips, but since both fingers and lips were atremble, 'twas a hopeless task. She sank to the bedside chair, burying her face in her hands. Her mumble of words proved barely intelligible.

"Yes—he's going to make it, Emma Grace." She swung her gaze toward Caleb's bed, her head shaking as though a neck-hinge had snapped loose. The palsy continued, causing me to regret asking such a stupid question. No one—but the Creator himself—knew whether Caleb would live or die.

We lay beneath a mountain of quilts, Caleb and I—his emaciation wrapped in my arms as I sang to him. Though he burned like an unconsumed fire, he quaked as though he was freezing to death. I knew he couldn't hear me, but still I hummed his favorite songs. While perspiration poured through my pores and drenched the bed linens, Caleb slept. Through blazing fevers, and chills that clacked his teeth together—Caleb slept.

I cried away most of the night, but between the bawling and the dozing, I bartered with God for Caleb's healing. I had to find a way to convince him to spare my brother's life. He could take me in his place, I reasoned. It was true that I now desired life more than ever before, but not more than I wanted Caleb to live. How could my family bear the loss of another son?

Relinquishment came sometime during my chaotic pleas to God. It came, not with glare or fanfare, but with the quietness and peace of a stilled heart that no longer fought God's sovereignty. To this day, I cannot fathom what prompted me to surrender to God's will in the matter of my little brother.

Mama relieved me around midnight, compelling me from the room though I argued to stay. I washed up a bit in the bathroom. As much as I dared without waking the entire household. Cleaned teeth, brushed hair, scrubbed skin—but beyond the surface—sunken eyes ringed with sadness, and a face that had forgotten how to smile.

I assumed my rightful station beside Caleb sometime after first light, relieved that he had held his own throughout the long night. He fought a bitter enemy. How did one wage war against an adversary like pneumonia?

The day passed and then another, Caleb's constitution skinnying-up like the waning crescent before a new moon. Odd—how grief and hopelessness tried to bury their claws into my hide during those worrisome hours. I felt the jabbing and the stabbing as unsheathed talons slashed away at my trust. Nevertheless they drew no blood, for my new-found relationship with God had cast a cloak of protection over me: as impenetrable as young David's when he went up against the Philistine giant. I was like David in one way: Neither of us wore a shield—save the shield of faith.

While Caleb slept, I slipped off to the bathroom, returning minutes later. I was startled to see Elo kneeling beside Caleb's bed. Wary of intruding, I stayed my position in the doorway. But Elo was born with a bevy of antennae in the back of his head, thus he perceived my presence. He stood with quickness and turned his head, staring me down with hard eyes that glazed with a definite sheen.

*Elo—crying?*

With a swift jerk, his head commanded me to Caleb's bedside.

It seemed, along with the nasty bouts of doubt and fear I had fought, that Elo's impertinent glare was all it took to knock me over the edge of good sense. Knowing Elo would not shed a tear unless he believed Caleb's condition was hopeless, I ran to him, attacking him as though I was the youthful warrior, David. My nails became the five smooth stones that felled mighty Goliath. I growled as I pounded Elo's back and dragged my claws down his unprotected arms, knowing all the while that when I scraped away his flesh, I scraped away his pride as well.

"Caleb is not going to die, you witless Philistine," I sputtered into Elo's purple face. "Don't you dare cry for Caleb as though he were already dead. He's going to make it. Can't you understand the King's English, Elo? Caleb is going to live, and you better not think otherwise."

Elo captured my flailing arms with one fist, his eyes as dark as the muddy bottom of our pond. He flung me onto a chair and squatted on his haunches, breathing fire-eating holes into my eyes.

"Don't be telling me what I can and can't do, you mouthy little nit-picker. I'll cry until the Second Coming if I want to." Drops of sweat and spittle clung to his sandy-red mustache as his words hissed out like steam from a radiator. I knew he had turned down his shouting volume for Mama and Papa's sake. He had probably dammed up his flow of foul language for the same reason. "And if you ever come flying at me like a bat out of Hades again, I'll knock you so far into the sunset they'll never find you or your fat mouth. Can a log-headed twerp like you understand *that* part of the King's English?"

In that moment, I didn't know whether I understood the King's English or not. I just barely knew who I was and where I was. Too worn out to even care, I wondered if Elo was about to pinch my head off and eat it on the spot. At least I had stood up to the giant. More importantly, I had stood up for Caleb. That was all that mattered.

The storm of anger vacated my heart as quickly as it had entered. I turned my gaze from Elo's raging eyes and squeezed my little brother's lifeless fingers with my own.

"We have to believe he's going to get well. Don't you understand, Elo? We just have to believe."

# Thirty-one

The family gathered in Caleb's room at dusk. Each of us had said good-bye to him in our own fashion, secluded from other family members. The best I could manage in the way of farewells was to recount one of Caleb's favorite stories, for I could not swallow the horror of telling him good-bye. Papa led us in a short prayer, committing Caleb to God's safekeeping. A forbidden thought raced through my mind: Hadn't Papa prayed the same prayer over Micah?"

*God, please hear our cries. Don't turn your face from us this time. Mama won't make it if she loses another son. Can't you see my mustard seed of faith, Father? Please honor it, small though it is.*

Mama and Papa sent us to our rooms while they huddled in sad vigil beside Caleb's bed. His breathing was a horrible thing to hear. 'Twas like he was drowning inside himself; lungs so thick with mucus they gurgled; chest wheezing as breath rasped wetly from his throat. The worst thing: He hadn't the strength to cough. His strength had ebbed away as silently as life now drained from his body.

I disobeyed my parents, which was more usual than not, now that I think back on it. Grabbing a blanket from my bed, I sat in the hall, my back to Caleb's bedroom as I whimpered my heart out to God. He was, after all, a God of miracles. Drawing from memory, I speculated on happenings that occurred in Bible times. Were we not still susceptible to such miracles? I reminded God that the Falins were in dire need of something in the realm of Jesus raising Lazarus from the dead ... or healing the blind man. In one sense, Caleb was blind. Asleep for long weeks was like being blind. Hadn't Jesus said that we had not because we asked not? Well—I had done my part. I had asked, and asked, and asked. Now it was time for God to follow through and answer my prayers.

With a scratchy wool blanket tucked over my shoulders and my heart beating the slow tom-tom of fear, I kept an ear perked on Caleb's raspy breathing, praying it wouldn't cease. I stood and peeked into his room, seeing the nodding heads of Mama and Papa. Neither had slept much during the last few days. I tiptoed past their chairs and slipped my coldness beneath Caleb's covers, my hand shifting about until it rested on his chest. The better to assure myself that life continued to flow through his veins.

At morning light, I awakened and listened for Caleb's breathing. He was still with us! I sat up in bed and saw Mama and Papa, their faces flat of expression as they gazed at me with red-streaked eyes. I sensed it was love, not displeasure, that stirred Papa to speak.

"Seems you're still having a bit of trouble obeying us, Emma Grace. Guess some things never change."

"I'm sorry, Papa. But you understand that I have to be with Caleb. Don't you?"

"We'll talk about it later. Mama and I are going to get a little rest. You're to wake us if there's any change at all in Caleb's breathing. Even the slightest change—you understand?"

"Yes, sir."

After they left, I got out of bed and tidied the room. As I leaned over Caleb and straightened his covers, I thanked God for one more day ... one more hour with my little brother. As long as there was life, there was hope.

Darkness crept from the room like a slow-chugging train. Chill was in the air. Once again I crawled beneath the covers, keeping my cold feet to myself.

I awakened moments later—or so it seemed at the time. Angry at myself for falling asleep and not keeping stricter vigilance, I hurried my gaze to Caleb's face. Soft brown eyes stared up at me. They blinked with heaviness, as though the coins of death weighted his lids, trying to solder them shut.

'Twas the most beautiful sight in the world: Caleb's sunken eyes, looking at me as though I had two heads and forty-nine noses. I barked a wild, hysterical yelp that made him cry, but I was too excited to stop my nonsense. Trumpeting like a temperamental elephant, my screams summoned the entire family. They raced into the room, Mama bawling for fear her youngest had departed this world.

"Caleb's awake, Mama. Look! Look for yourself." I danced around the room, stumbling on crutchless feet, tilting and lurching as though the floor slanted on unmatched beams. My brother was alive—back from the netherworld of his lengthy habitation. *Like Lazarus coming out of the tomb.* God had heard our cries. *Thank you for our miracle, Father. Thank you …*

Mama clasped Caleb to her breast, her tears bathing his face as she rocked him in her arms.

"My baby's back." Her eyes blazed with rapturous glow as she pressed her palm against his forehead. "The fever's gone. I can't believe it. He's going to live. My boy's going to live."

"Don't squeeze him to death, Annaleen. Give him a little breathing room," Papa admonished gently.

The Ollys clung to each other, tears and laughter colliding in birdlike warble, such a welcome departure from the woefulness of late. Nathan beamed as though the university had just handed him a full scholarship. Though Elo presented his back to the room, I knew he was overcome also. I wished he and I could share this moment together, for I was sinking from the overload of joy that filled my heart. I needed to share it with someone.

In dazelike stupor, I walked to Elo and peered around his shoulder. His glaciated expression couldn't camouflage the entirety of his emotions. As his eyes filled like big fat water pockets, I pressed my chest to his back and slipped my arms around his waist. He made no response. Had I expected any? Somehow, his cold-fish reception mattered not a whit in this moment of monumental delivery. I released my grip on Elo and was about to turn away when a second miracle of the day occurred.

One of his hands squeezed my arm with the grip of Hercules, which set me to giggling like a schoolgirl. I slipped from his grasp, before he could spoil the gift and spout something nasty at me.

Papa sat down beside Mama and gently tugged Caleb from her arms. I watched as he entangled himself in Caleb's savory uniqueness: the way his son fit perfectly in his arms, the sound of his less-cluttered breathing, and his scent—a commingling of medicine, perspiration, and the stench of near death. Papa's breath caught when Caleb shifted his gaze from Mama to him. Papa clamped onto that gaze like a half-starved alligator. As his broad fingers stroked Caleb's matted hair, I gloried in the smile my brother presented him. Tentative and a bit wobbly, it directed itself squarely on Papa's face, rendering his voice box slightly off-kilter.

"Welcome back, Son." Papa wrenched his mouth a bit, fretting his mustache from side to side. From the cut of his jaw, I knew Papa clenched his teeth, staunching his tears before they could spill over. His broad shoulders hovered over Caleb in a silent declaration that he would protect this child with his life. His hands quivered as they slid the length of Caleb's arms and legs, probing, prodding his limbs as though he were a newly purchased heifer. After the examination, Papa's countenance converted from worried frown to the most beautiful smile in God's creation. He cleared his throat and spoke again. "How're you feeling, Son?"

"Wh … wher … where's Micah?" Caleb asked. Unaccustomed as they were to the light, his eyes squinted as the frown on his face deepened. He stretched his hand to the far side of the bed where Micah slept, feeling it with his palm like a person with no sight. When he turned his head to look for Micah, he winced and laid a tiny hand against his brow, as though to still the ache in his head. His countenance appeared troubled, tears slipping past long lashes from which I had often washed morning sleepers. I knew he cried for a loss he did not yet understand. Squiggling deeper into the safety of Papa's arms, he closed his eyes a second time and fell asleep.

The hub of our home was vacant. A rare occurrence, but rarer still was the tranquility of our empty kitchen. I wilted to a kitchen chair and let my mind stew in its boil of exhilaration. The truth of God's miracle took its time sinking in. I hoped I hadn't dreamed it up, as my imagination could be untrustworthy at times, and well I knew it. Hadn't I proved its fickleness that evening in Galveston when I spied Micah's bare feet marking tracks in the sand?

*Don't doubt what you know is true,* I chided myself. Caleb lived. He would thrive. He'd grow strong, and in time his memory would return. That quirky, demanding personality I found irresistible would also reappear.

"God ... thank you for sparing Caleb. I'm so grateful for our miracle. I love you, Lord—and I don't ever want to run away from you again. Not ever."

As I sat in the stillness and wondered about my boldness with God, something moved in the air around me. Not a rush of wind—but perhaps a stirring of breath? *There it is again, whisking against my skin.* I scrubbed my puckered arms and glanced around the room, sensing a presence, knowing I wasn't alone. 'Twas then I felt a whisper of something—tracing my mouth—tingling my lips with cottony fingertips. I closed my eyes and abode in the beauty of the moment, for it seemed as though God had peeled a smile from his face and pressed it into my heart. In those precious, blissful moments, my joy multiplied like the seed of Father Abraham.

# Thirty-two

Odd, how by mid-December I had come to think of Caleb's improvement as a burden as well as a blessing. He longed for freedom. Most likely, the field mice scavenging for food in our far pasture heard about his yearnings, along with the entire household. The sickroom was a jail Caleb wished to escape, as he had quickly tired of bed confinement, quarantine, an overly anxious mama, and an overly strict papa. He sought one thing: freedom to search for his missing brother.

During one of his verbal crusades for release, Caleb ordered me to saddle up Old Jack. He'd fastened his mind on hitting the autumn trails, crested now with treetop plumes of scarlet and gold. He knew, with no little degree of certainty, that Micah hid out among the live oaks and half-shorn trees on our farm. Either there, or in the midst of brush forests that dotted our property.

Doctor Landers put the fear of relapse into our hearts, reiterating that Caleb wasn't out of the woods yet. The raging fever had stirred him from the coma, most likely, but he wouldn't survive another attack. As I recall, he spoke to us with his left brow arched into a tepee and his forehead furrowed to the hilt. I believed he thought my family incapable of resisting Caleb's cogency, and I was out to prove him wrong. So, corral Caleb I did, though it proved a wearisome task.

The family rallied in defense of Caleb's pouting, nagging, temper tantrums, and out-and-out irresistibility that tempted us to give in to his demands. His healing claimed highest priority. Since none of us were immune to his persuasiveness, we linked arms and withstood the onslaught as one.

The doctor chicken-scratched his directives on tablet paper; the dos and don'ts of Caleb's existence, but only Mama could decipher the script. Following his orders judiciously, The Ollys prepared nutritious meals; the boys kept his room toasty warm, and Papa quarantined him from visitors, should nasty germs follow them into the sickroom. The lion's share of keeping him quiet and contented fell upon me. I was the lioness, caring for her young. Though Caleb acted the annoying cub, crawling away from the den and taking swipes with his paw when things didn't go his way, I held my growling at bay. I came to treasure naptimes. They were easy to enforce, as Caleb's eyelids closed at the lowering of a shade, the whispering of a tale, or the humming of a lullaby. He recovered more each day—physically. But his moroseness caused the family untold anguish.

If there was a flaw in Caleb's healing, it stemmed from the intensity with which he missed his brother: his cowpoke companion; his partner in sabotage and demolition. His pining wreaked further damage on our hearts. Fancying Micah's imminent return, Caleb grilled Mama incessantly. Mama withheld the truth, fearing a setback. But she cracked a bit more each day, Caleb's persistent interrogation driving wedges in the gaps of her armor. I watched Mama with care as she daily stepped closer to the line where she would hand over the answers Caleb sought. We dreaded the day, knowing the wall hadn't been built that could protect him from the pain her confession would bring.

Mama requested I remain by her side when she talked to Caleb. Had she asked me to shove the moon to the far side of the sky, I would have rummaged around for a tool and begun the task at once. But to witness Caleb—suffering the most horrendous pain known to mankind—seemed beyond my forbearance. Just thinking about it sent my heart into a tailspin.

'Twas on the seventh day of Caleb's awakening that Mama chose to let fly what she had shuttered behind the sashes of her heart. I cowered on a nearby chair, pondering Mama's power of persuasion, and her taut posture, as she primed herself to answer Caleb's poison-tipped questions. His head rested on bed cushions, an arm latched around the pillow-puppy Mama had stitched during his deep sleep. But his gaze darted between the two of us, his brown eyes carrying a look of fear I'd not spied heretofore.

"Mama ... *where is Micah?*" Caleb asked the question as though he hadn't asked it a hundred times before. He plucked at the bedcovers, his fingers as fidgety as a rooster in the brooding pen.

"Micah went to be with Jesus, sweetie." As Mama gnawed her bottom lip, my heart took off like a wild goose dodging buckshot, my heartbeats tripping over themselves in a scurry to exit hazardous territory. Mama moved to the bed and clasped Caleb to her bosom, swaying him in her arms, humming him a lullaby. Her droning wobbled a bit when her thumb and forefinger kidnapped puddles from her eyes. Caleb tugged free of her tightness, piercing her eyes with a stare.

"Micah's in heaven with Jesus," Mama crooned, her voice as smooth as fresh-churned butter.

"When's he coming back?"

Mama stared straight ahead, seemingly entranced by a speck on the wallpaper. The pulse in Caleb's neck blipped up and down like telegraph keys as he gazed at the one person who could alleviate his fears and abolish his loneliness with just a few words.

Mama tossed a glance my way, seeking help, it seemed. But my gaze strayed to the hands folded in my lap. They held great fascination for my coward's heart.

"Sweetheart ... Micah's not coming back. You see, he lives with Jesus now—in his home."

"I don't want him to live with Jesus! I want him to live with *me*. He's *my* brother." Caleb burst into uncontrollable sobs. As Mama smothered him to her heart and rubbed his back with a velvet hand, our eyes met in shared regret. Oh, that we could shoulder some of Caleb's suffering. 'Twas an impossible hope, for we both knew there is a pain that must be borne alone, with nary a presence to help. Save that from above.

How many times could a heart break and still hold out hope of mending? Mine cracked open anew, fresh pain colliding with old hurt.

Caleb's sobs had awakened my dozing pain. I knew they had stirred Mama's as well.

I thought Caleb's worn-out body incapable of producing so many tears, but I was wrong. He wailed as though a dark hand wrenched sobs from his heart. While the clock ticked off the better part of an hour, Mama rocked little Caleb. Her arms and back afire by now, I was certain. I shook with the need to comfort my brother, but it was Mama's touch he needed. Not mine. The Ollys crept into the room, as did my brothers and Papa. No one attempted to hush Caleb's weeping. We understood the need to cry your heart dry. Now it was Caleb's turn. I knew we all pleaded silently for the same thing: divine help. The kind we couldn't provide the neediest member of our family.

Perhaps God extended his helping hand through the bestowal of sleep. In time, exhaustion had its way and the sobs angled off. Hiccups tagged along for a while, then faded also. Caleb slept, at last.

Nonetheless, I knew questions would arise in the morning; asked through the hiss of missing baby teeth, and the trusting nature of a child for whom death was just a word. Caleb and Micah had been inseparable since conception. Two personalities in identical bodies. God, alone, knew how Caleb would handle his grief; a grief more exacting and burdensome than our own. Perhaps God would heap upon my little brother an extra helping of mercy … and love.

In my daydreams, I envisioned Caleb and Micah awakening together, hopping from bed like a pair of toads, scampering through the naughtiness of the day. I saw them now: running the hills raw; squatting on a ridge to poke sticks in a hole; climbing out on a limb to gawk at a speckled egg. Times they'd never again share. Best I put my daydreams aside and accept reality. 'Twas certain Caleb would be facing it soon enough.

The day waxed adventurous; hearth-warm and as suitable as any for Caleb's maiden voyage outdoors. Accustomed to sickroom darkness, I hooded my eyes and stepped onto the dirt-packed trail. The wind carried whiffs of ripening cedars, Mama's cooking, and the hint of creatures on the prowl. I sniffed the openness, seeking a scent I'd not yet called to mind, but for which I longed. Then I remembered: salt-tainted gusts of wind, spiked with flavors from as far away as the playgrounds of humpbacks and orcas.

Until recent days there'd been no time for me to dwell on Galveston. Now my thoughts roamed like the buffalo, hungry and unhurried as I recalled rolling waves and the sandy beaches where I'd buried a portion of my heart, along with the note I left behind.

I turned my head and glanced at the princely portage trailing behind me. I smiled at Caleb's royal carriage, which much resembled the twins' painted wagon. My heart couldn't help but pitter-patter when I spied the luminance in his eyes.

"Mama sure is silly. Ain't she, Emma Grace?"

I halted the wagon and studied Caleb. He straddled the pile of folded quilts I had carefully tucked into the wagon slats, knowing Mama would peel my skin if her fine stitchery dragged the dirt. A rare smile puffed Caleb's cheeks, reminding me of the clouds that knotted this fine December sky. I felt my knees wobble a bit when Caleb giggled, his laughter melting my bones like heated wax. How I wished I could capture his child's beauty in a photograph or with a charcoal stick and drawing paper.

"Don't say *ain't*, Caleb Roan Falin. Remember? You're supposed to say *isn't*. Why do you think Mama's silly?"

Caleb leaned forward, motioning me close. I sat on dry winter grass, my face inches from his. While I waited for him to confide what had him ever so tickled, I buttoned his jacket and flicked curls from his eyes. I couldn't keep my hands off my little brother. Caleb smelled of good health but also a bit like Vick's VapoRub. I was anxious to discover the mystery behind his smile, since his smiles were as infrequent as Elo's. Caleb's soft words tickled my nose, his breath warm and moist as he whispered into my ear.

"'Cause she don't know that Micah's hiding from us—somewheres out in them bushes." He pointed a pale finger toward a natural growth of thicket off in the distance. "He's coming back ... real soon now. 'Member when we use'ta hide from you, and you couldn't find us?" Caleb giggled at his cleverness. "Me and Micah sure hided good, didn't we, Emma Grace?"

I grinned and gathered Caleb's hands into mine. Perhaps the time had come to help him piece together the puzzle of Micah's disappearance.

"Do you remember Whisper? Our puppy?" I studied Caleb's eyes with care. My family had not yet discovered the extent of his memory loss. I didn't want to probe too deeply, or cut into the slice of peace Caleb now chewed on.

His head bobbed up and down like Mama's sewing machine needle. But soon thereafter his eyes misted over, as recollections skittered to a halt in his heart. A cruel master—remembrance.

"I wish't Whisper didn't fall down and get hurted. I tried to catch him, Emma Grace. But I couldn't." Caleb brushed a cuff across his eyes and looked away. Almost overnight, he had come to disdain tears. I thought him entirely too young to give them up forever. Perhaps he now tracked behind his heroes—Papa, Elo, and Nathan—who would rather give up Mama's cooking than have someone see them with wet eyes.

"Do you remember we told you that we buried Whisper—'cause he died?"

Caleb turned his head toward me, his eyes narrowing as our gazes locked together. I read in his expression a wariness that warned me to tread softly over the pathway of my words.

"He ain't never coming back. Right, Emma Grace?"

I breathed in deeply, releasing a sigh as I shook my head. "No ... he's not coming back." I felt a buildup of moisture in my eyes, but tried to disguise it around a smile.

"Don't cry, Emma Grace. How 'bout you take us over ta Mr. Peavy's house—when Micah gets home. Betcha he'll give us 'nother puppy. It'll be all right." Caleb patted my hand and smiled, his face flushed with excitement.

*How about that? Caleb comforting me.*

"I guess what I'm trying to say, Caleb, is that sometimes a person gets hurt real bad, like Whisper got hurt ... and they ... they ..."

The tears poured; a terrible thing to let flow on a day that had brought laughter to Caleb's heart. What a sad revelation to the brother I had wished to cheer with a bumpy ride on a sunshiny day. I jumped from the ground, latched onto my crutch, and was about to resume our jaunt when Caleb's sweet voice floated into my ears.

"Emma Grace ... me and Micah won't never get hurted like

Whisper did, 'cause you always look out for us. You won't never let nothing bad happen to *us*. 'Member when you told me and Micah that you loved us this much?" Caleb stretched his arms wide, like a bird's wings in flight. He wobbled a bit in the wagon as his left arm tried to outstretch his right. For a moment, I glimpsed Jesus, strung high on a gnarled, wooden cross.

Yes. I loved my brothers. But loving them with every speck of my heart hadn't kept me from failing them.

# Thirty-three

I surged through the rift, rising from yesteryear's memories as from the depths of the sea. As I lifted to the surface, I opened my eyes and looked around. That's when I saw the cave and the quilt, and knew I was at my journey's end. As my breathing quieted and my heartbeat tapered, I wondered if the trip had been worth the struggle. I thought not, for guilt rested as heavily on my heart now as it did before.

I paused, allowing my heart catch-up time. It remained behind, you see, dallying in the open fields of yesterday, rather than returning to the here and now. It tarried there because of Caleb's words: *You won't never let nothing bad happen to us, Emma Grace. You love us too much.* I'd carry Caleb's sweet words of trust with me forever, and remember my unworthiness each time they came to mind. Even now his voice echoed across the mountains of time, making mockery of the forgiveness I sought. Oh, that his childlike prattle would fade and take my bitter-sweet memories with it.

The barren cave appeared inhospitable. Unwonted. Having absorbed my most troubling secrets, did it now wish to expel me from its quarters?

I slipped my shoes on my feet and tied the lacings, shook the quilt, and restrung it. Best I leave the past where it belonged. After all—memories were but shadows of the past. Leaving 1928 behind, I stepped through the cave and entered the autumnal coolness of 1933.

The storm had departed the area, leaving only a soft rustling in the trees and warm sunshine to cover the ground. The rampage was over. Or was it? While I had cast about in my sea of reveries, another tempest blew across my heart. One I hadn't weathered well. Though my journey was supposed to end in peace—peace was still just a wish. A wish I could not yet hold or claim as my own. 'Twas a sad and solitary feeling.

As I walked away from the cave, I felt weary and naked, for the trip had peeled away the layers of my heart like dry onionskin. A few tardy raindrops plopped from the overhang, and the sun peeked between strings of clouds. Two-Toe Creek had settled some, but still bubbled like a kettle of water at full boil.

*Gavin.* My heart stuttered at the thought of my fiancé. Certain now that I loved the youth by the sea, I didn't know what to do about the young man who thought to marry me. Did Gavin pace the floor of my house even now, wondering where his intended had whiled away the afternoon? Or had he already gathered a posse to track down my whereabouts?

I stumbled headfirst into a shaft of sunlight that warmed my chilled body, if not my spirit. Unwilling to trudge home with such a weighty heart, I tracked damp ground, stopping beneath a live oak whose branches still bore the leaves of early fall. I found an arid patch of earth and sat down. I leaned my back against a tree and let my tears flow. I dared not stop them.

After I'd cried myself dry, I closed my eyes, for my excursion had tired me out like an old hound dog after a chase. I forced my eyes open seconds later at the snapping of a twig. Nevertheless, drowsiness and gravity had their way with me. My eyelids drifted closed.

I knew I was but an onlooker in this radiant kingdom: this realm where light existed in its purest form. I found the light incomprehensible, for it moved and changed shapes, glowing in ways I had never imagined. Drawn to its core, the light encompassed my thoughts, my soul, my being. I was part of it, yet separate. A bystander, blessed to enjoy but not partake. I stretched my hand toward the brightness, feeling nothing but air. It mattered not that I could not hold the light. 'Twas enough that I could see it.

A thought came. How had I come to be in this place? Moreover—could I abide in its beauty forever?

It was then I noticed a band of roving lights, halos, really, but of vertical confluence. They bounced and rolled, disappearing altogether. Their overwhelming brilliance claimed my breath. Circles reappeared, shifting constantly, changing forms. My mind could not define the hues that expanded and contracted within the shining abundance.

One bundle of lights snagged my attention and my affection. The assemblage mingled together before popping apart like kernels of corn. Or fireworks, exploding into a dazzle of incandescence. In a breath's time, they rejoined, tangling and disconnecting repeatedly. Poignancy filled my heart, for the lights reminded me of a passel of high-spirited children.

An unknown force compelled me forward, drawing me nearer the circle of lights. 'Twas then I discerned shapes within the halos—humanlike, but not of earthly origin. I gazed at the spectacular sight of young boys, luminous sparks igniting their halos as they frolicked in coltish delight. My heart paused in wonderment, for the children romped and tussled together as in a game. Perhaps it was only child's play, but the winsomeness of it stilled my heart. Once more I moved ahead, closer now to a lad of exceptional beauty. So familiar, yet ... could it possibly be ...? Yes, oh yes. It was Micah. My precious Micah.

His smile beamed as I remembered, yet transcendent in a way I had not witnessed before. I longed to pull him into my arms, but he existed apart from me, in a world quite unlike my own. I knew the two worlds could never meet.

Music surrounded me, exquisite harmony; tones unacquainted with earthly ears. I listened with care as Micah's laughter trilled out a lively melody. I called to him, but he seemed not to notice my presence. Had he heard my cries and listened to my plea for forgiveness, my joy would have been unimaginable. But, as was often the case in life, Micah gave my words no heed at all.

In the midst of these lesser lights, a greater Light appeared, shining as the noonday sun. I watched, spellbound, as the Light accelerated and halted near the children. Micah turned, his eyes feasting on the Light. I, too, turned toward the Light, my heart pounding at the sight of Jesus. He smiled at my brother as though the two shared sacred love. The Savior. I could no more take my gaze from him than I could turn away from Micah. His love spilled over Micah, and dribbled onto me. With unworldly quickness Micah bolted into the Savior's arms, leaned his head against his shoulder, and snuggled in close. What an incredible sight, this binding of the lesser light to the greater Light, the two becoming one. My eyes burned with intensity, for I could not fill them quickly enough with the wondrous sight before me.

Micah giggled at something Jesus said. Then his face sobered as he studied the Savior. My brother leaned in, clasping Jesus' face between his hands, holding it tightly as he talked to his friend. Jesus smiled and nodded. Micah burst into melodious laughter, jumped from the arms that held him, and rejoined the other children.

I saw a light in the distance. It raced toward me, magnifying and multiplying to Morning Star brightness. Then a golden curve yawned across the chasm that separated us, washing me with waves of love and forgiveness. I didn't know how long the cleansing lasted. I knew only that when it was done, my heart was as light and airy as a baby's sigh.

Without benefit of words or signals, Jesus whispered in my heart, revealing what Micah had asked him: My brother wanted the Savior to promise that he could live with Jesus forever—and beyond.

Content to remain on the sidelines, I bowed my knees in adoration and gazed upon the Savior. Celestial beings flowed around his Presence. Perhaps they celebrated the never-ending blessedness of his companionship. I wanted nothing more than to join them.

I startled awake, hearing a lion's heartbeat roaring in my ears. Tears coursed my face, rolling moist and salty against my lips. For once, they flowed from gladness and joy, not from the stockpile of guilt in my heart. In sleep, my knees had shifted to the ground. I changed positions, sitting on a patch of grass as though in a daze.

"Emma Grace? Emma Grace … where are ye, girl?"

I thought I heard someone call my name. Unwilling to release the lingering vision of Micah and Jesus, I ignored the interruption. *But, what if it was the Savior calling me? Or Tate, making his way to my side.* I glanced in the direction of the voice. What I saw sent my heart racing around the track again. A tall form stood at the tree's edge, silhouetted by bright sunbursts.

"Tate … is that you?" My hand trembled as it stretched toward the masculine shadow.

"Emma Grace, where'n the world have ye been?" Gavin stooped, ducking his head beneath low branches. He knelt beside me, his voice tight and scornful. "Did ye think to wait out the storm beneath a tree, ye silly lass? Of all the stupid, foolish … Ye could've been struck by lightning, or scattered to kingdom come by the big blow. What's wrong with ye, girl? Are ye daft, er something?"

I stared at Gavin, disbelieving what my eyes beheld. Reality descended then, landing in my heart, felling me with the blunt edge of a headsman's ax. *Why couldn't you be Tate?*

Gavin lifted me to my feet and smothered me in an embrace. As he rocked the tight knot of our togetherness, he whispered in my ear.

"I thought I'd lost ye, sweet girl. Don't ever scare me like that again. Ye hear what I'm saying?" He stopped the swaying and stared wild-eyed at me. "Why'd ye run off like that, in the middle of a hurricane?"

"Hurricane? Surely it wasn't a hurricane. I've been through storms much worse than this. A hundred times worse." *If you could look in my heart, Gavin, you'd know what I say is true.*

"Sure, and a hurricane it was—down the coastline way. Swept inland, too, all the way to Coldwater and beyond. Radio said a tornado hit over in Fayetteville. That's not so far away, ye ken." Gavin held me at arm's length, studying my face. His eyes narrowed and clouded over like a troubled sea. "Just exactly where were ye durin' the storm? Can ye be answering me that?"

My thoughts whirled, causing my tongue to forget its useful purpose. All I could think about was the hurricane—hitting the Gulf Coast. *Were Granny and Tate safe? Did they make it through the storm all right?*

"Emma Gra—"

"I was in a cave. Well, not a cave, exactly. More like a hollowed-out space in the cliffs. Remember that cave over by the chutes, where the creek makes that little twist and ..." Gavin released my arms, crossing his own as a disgruntled police officer might do. My rambling must have rubbed his patience raw. Giving it no heed, I resumed my long-winded explanation. "Elo and I used to hole up there during thunderstorms. So when the sky turned ugly, I headed for the cave. The wind practically blew me there on its own. But I was never in any danger."

When Gavin flattened me to his chest again, breathing became my highest priority. I pushed free and gathered my jacket from the ground. "Mama's probably worried sick about me. I'm going home ... set her mind at rest."

"Look, sweetheart ..."

I faced Gavin, holding my hand palm-up, halting his attempt to snag me in another love-tangle.

"Best I do a bit of explaining to Mama and Papa. Besides, I want to talk to them about some things. Alone."

Gavin shifted his weight to one leg and recrossed his arms. His eyes held a squint—the sort that crinkled the skin around his eyes when he had an urge to laugh—or spit fire.

"And just what *things* are ye referring to, lass?"

"I'll ... I'll tell you all about it, Gavin. It's just that ... well ... Look—come by this evening and we'll talk. Okay?" I turned my back before Gavin could grill me further, or talk me into walking home with him. I needed to be alone. To think things through. I didn't need him by my side, imposing his persuasive nature upon me. He had filled our courtship with the adroitness of inducement. Things always swung in his direction, and if they didn't, he garnished his words with sufficient fervor to make sure I quietly acquiesced. 'Twas a good feeling to know those days were over.

As I walked the puddled path home, I threw Gavin no glances over my shoulder. I could read his expressive face like the bold type on a newspaper. Right now, it most likely twisted into a fierce scowl, or the snarl of a tiger trapped in a cage.

I glanced around our dinner table. Now that The Ollys were married and gone, it appeared lopsided and lonely. In addition, there was the empty place where Micah sat, which no one could fill.

Supper was almost over. The boys scraped bread crusts against already-spotless plates, and chugged down remaining droplets of milk from their glasses. I hoped my brothers would hear me out before they upped and left the premises. Unclear as to where I should begin, I cleared my throat, snagging the family's attention. I asked the boys to remain a while longer. I needed to tell them something. I read in their uncommon watchfulness this question: What words would make their tarrying worthwhile? One set of eyes seemed particularly disinclined to stick around; Elo's glare warning me to get on with the night's business.

"I wanted to share some things that happened at the creek today." I hesitated, wondering how to bring up old hurts without inflicting new pain. The family stared at me, unblinking eyes urging me to get to the point.

"What happened, Sis? Did the storm blow some sense into your head?" Caleb pumped his arms like a hero from the funny pages and snickered at his sharp-wittedness, then cast a sideways glance at Elo, hoping to find approval in his hero's eyes. At least, that's how it appeared to me.

Mama grinned at Caleb and Papa laughed out loud, our family being quick to hassle each other with the cattle prod of bedevilment.

"Something like that, Caleb." I stared at him, but saw the other brother—laughing and playing, blissfully content in his beautiful home. Caleb was eleven now. I wondered if Micah would gain years in heaven. My heart thumped as I realized I could envision Micah's appearance at every age—by watching Caleb as he grew and matured. I hovered over the images, gritting my teeth against old hurts that would surely stab at my heart, but nothing of the sort occurred. Caleb's face reddened, perhaps because my stare fixed solidly on him. I seemed unable to turn my gaze. The blush heightened the pink of his scar, the jagged reminder of survival that endeared me to him ever more. I returned his grin, appreciating the freedom to tease at will, as I was the sort who gave even better than I received.

Calmed by a steady heartbeat and absence of angst, I poured out my story. It helped—knowing that my family loved me. Despite my failures of the past, they listened as though a queen had requisitioned their attention. I heard my words flow, and wondered how I could so easily uncover deeds buried beneath the years and tears of yesterday's regrets.

"… and I screamed for them to come back, but they didn't hear me. I ran like the wind, but … just couldn't get there in time." Yes, my tears gushed. That horrendous memory would move even a monster to tears. "By the time I reached them, they had already fallen in the well. I tried to bury my guilt, and go on with life, but I just couldn't seem to … to …"

"Sis …"

I turned to Caleb, viewing his interruption as a lifesaver: a pause in which to calm myself during these moments of desperate recall. Moisture in Caleb's eyes tottered on the brink of overflow, sparking them like sunlight on a tin roof.

"We heard you calling us, Emmy." His words crept forth in tones of meek repentance, memories of the tragedy having tamed the tease from his voice. "Me and Micah … we knew we weren't supposed to run off like that. I … I looked back once and saw you. You were gaining on us so I ran harder. I was afraid we'd lose Whisper. We couldn't lose Whisper, Emma Grace." Caleb's voice broke, and to his horror, I'm sure, he wept openly. "I'd take it all back if I could. I'd mind you like you taught us to. Maybe Micah would still be …"

Caleb's sobs tore at my heart. I didn't know what to do with his confession. The last thing I desired was for my admission to shackle him with guilt, such as the burden I had carried for years.

"No, no, Caleb. It wasn't your fault. I was the adult in charge. I should have protected you. You were just a child." Hurrying to his side, I gathered him in my arms and lay my head atop his. A quick glance at Mama assured me she was all right. Papa held her hand, and though it may have been their deepest desire to do so, neither presumed upon the conversation. "Please—please don't take this upon yourself, Caleb. Mama and Papa put me in charge. There's no one at fault but me." I wiped my eyes with Caleb's napkin, leaned over and kissed his cheek. "You were not to blame, little brother." We made eye contact, Caleb and I, my gaze conveying a message of greatest importance: *You were not the cause of Micah's death.* My eyes would whisper that thought to him every day for the rest of his life. I couldn't let life burden Caleb with guilt, as it had me.

As I walked back to my chair, silence hung on the air like shadows on a moonlit headstone. "I wanted to tell you something very special. It's about Micah. He's ... he's wonderfully happy. Not sad, at all. Please ... don't ask me to explain how I know this. Someday—I'll tell you all about it, but I can't right now. Not tonight."

"Emma Grace, if there's something you can tell us that'll ease the hurt, you must share it." Mama held a napkin to her mouth, damming up additional words that might pressure me into saying more than I wanted to say. She didn't like forcing people into things. Knowing me as she did, she knew I'd cave in and spill my heart out if she begged.

"Did you hear a word from God, sweetheart?" I read in Papa's eyes a desperate longing to hear news of his son. He looked straight into my heart, Mama's hand blanching beneath his grip.

"Yes ... in a way, Papa. I saw Micah—in a dream, or maybe it was a vision. You see, God gave me the most incredible gift this afternoon. He knew I'd been bogged down with guilt for a long, long time. Ever since Micah died. I believe he gave me the dream so I could go on with life—joyfully, as he intends us to live. All I really know is that Micah is in the most wonderful place. You can't imagine how beautiful it is. Love flows there like a river. And the light—there's spectacular light everywhere." I wiped my eyes and smiled with all the gladness my dream rekindled. "Someday I'll tell you all about it, and about Micah, too. I promise. But right now, it's too fresh—too intimate to share. I just need to hold onto it for a while longer. You understand?"

Papa nodded. It seemed enough to know his son was happy. Mama broke down, letting flow what she usually reserved for deepest night.

"What's this other thing you had to tell us?" Never one to feel comfortable in the presence of Mama's pain, Elo thrummed the table with his fingertips, awaiting my answer. He didn't fool me. His emotions ran as rampant and unruly as the rest of the family's. His, however, rumbled a mite deeper beneath the surface. Though he hid his feelings from the outside world, he'd never been able to conceal them from me. I saw the sparks now, sizzling in the depths of his eyes—just waiting to pop into flames. But confession and Elo were strangers. To think he would speak from his heart was pure foolishness. I felt great tenderness for my brother in that moment, knowing my divulgence had stirred him to the core.

I turned to Mama and Papa. "I'm sorry for all the work you've done, Mama, but I can't marry Gavin. I'm going to tell him tonight."

"Well, I'll be. So you finally saw the light." Elo's smirk brought a smile to my heart. He had watched over me most of my life. I supposed he still did. "Gonna toss that scum-faced Mick of yours into the manure pile, eh, Emmy G? Guess you were right, Caleb. The wind must've blown some sense into her thick skull, after all."

"You'll not be calling our kin *Mick* as the trash up north do." Papa bared his teeth at Elo, his homeland and his people taking precedence over a rude son.

"Sorry, Papa."

Elo grinned, disproving even a smidgen of repentance on his part. Until now, I hadn't realized how much Elo hated Gavin. Though his prejudice hadn't factored into my decision to end the betrothal, it did my heart good to please Elo. It always had.

"What made you change your mind, Sis?" Nathan's words urged the contemplation right out of me. His face broadened to a smile as he rested elbows on the table and joined his fingertips into a steeple. Tapping his fingers against his upper lip, he reminded me of a judge, or a brilliant professor. I regarded his question, and the weight behind his words. They proved too heavy to lift for viewing before the family this night. The imprint Tate made on my life—his lingering memory in my heart—was a tale for another time and place. Perhaps, I would never disclose my lost love to the family.

I smiled at Nathan, feeling a renewal of oneness with the family. When had the unity begun to unravel? I wondered. Had it started the day I chose Gavin for a husband?

"So—Nathan—you didn't like him either? Et tu, Brute?" Nathan and I laughed together, our contagious mirth lifting similar joyfulness from Mama's lips. "Along with you and Elo, who else knew I was about to make the biggest mistake of my life?"

My family raised their hands like a pack of first-graders who wanted to be first to answer the teacher's question. Of course, Elo wouldn't stoop to such childishness. He simply sat in his chair and stared at me with a villain's smirk on his face. But deep inside—Elo was ecstatic.

"Looks like you'll have me underfoot a while longer." I aimed my words at Mama and Papa, old troubling thoughts filling my head with unease. Suddenly, I was back in spinster-land, not knowing if I would ever marry. Ever bear children. My doubts burgeoned. "I don't know how Gavin will take it tonight. It's a rotten thing to do—breaking up two weeks before the wedding."

My shoulders slumped with regret. I dreaded hurting Gavin. I did love him, though my love lacked the strong foundation upon which to build a lifetime of trust and affection. Dare I throw him away though, when his arms might be the only ones willing to hold me?

# Thirty-four

Tweaker paced the porch floor, her soft purr requesting to join me on the swing. It was a wonder I heard her at all, what with the swing's rusty chains begging for a squirt from Papa's oilcan. I knew Tweaker held me in high regard, but 'twas my lap she liked most—especially when it rocked like a cradle. Lithesome being her middle name, she sprang from the floor and landed atop my muslin skirt, dainty paws denting not a pinch of fabric. I squeezed her to my chest before she could crawl into a tight ball of drowsiness. She didn't seem to mind that I had foiled her plans. Her sandpaper tongue willingly licked my nose while her pale-gray whiskers kissed my cheeks. Poor baby. Had she known that a fast-moving cyclone was about to hit the porch, she would have vaulted from my arms and run for the hills.

It sounded like a good idea to me.

A breeze carried his winsome tune to my ears moments before I spied him sauntering up the road. I had heard this song before, on a night filled with starlight and soft whispers from the man who had encircled me in his arms. The hauntingly beautiful melody stayed with me, humming from my lips at the oddest times: while soaking in the tub, hanging clothes on the line, peeling carrots at the kitchen sink.

Gavin had picked up the tune in County Cork, on the Emerald Isle, and brought it with him to America. Along with his affection for life and love.

As Gavin drew near, a curtain of twilight descended over the hazy glow of evening. Once-green trees now wore swatches of charcoal, as though they'd been singed around the edges. As clouds thinned and blended into the sky, I saw a bit of sparkle and knew I had spied the first star of evening. The wishing star.

*I wish I may, I wish I might, have the wish I wish tonight.* No longer bent toward fairy-tale predilections, I turned my wish into a prayer. While Gavin unhooked the gate, I prayed for words, right and true. Words that didn't drip with apology, as was my nature, but, more importantly, words that wouldn't strip the music from Gavin's heart. This evening's confrontation required I confirm my love and appreciation for him—as a friend. It also dictated I veer far from the path of romantic overtures. Tonight I had to tread the tightrope of communication with honesty and sensitivity.

Gavin waved and grinned, his casual greeting a vast disparity from the seriousness of the evening. Deepening shadows reminded me of all that had to transpire between us. I prayed Gavin's beauty and charm would neither melt the strength of my will, nor erase the good sense God gave me.

Moonlight guided Gavin's steps as he mounted the porch and sat beside me on the swing. He reached out, capturing the hand that stroked Tweaker. My gaze moved from his face, shaved smooth as Mama's plates, and traced the strong lines of his body. The view set loose a bit of carnal longing within me. Chill bumps ruffled my arms and neck, my resolve slipping a notch as I decided to taste Gavin's kiss one last time. I swam in the ocean of his eyes, and within those blue-green depths discovered the passion that had first awakened me to desire. Gavin's eyes held power over me, as they had the first time our eyes bumped gazes. His eyes had robbed me of breath then, as they did now.

"Gavin, I—"

His lips covered mine, recalling to mind the evening of our last embrace. Fearing my own uncertainty, I had pried myself free of Gavin's brawny manacles and wriggled away to safer ground. Now I desired his strength around me again; enfolding me with greater ardency than it had on the moonlit night I ran from his touch.

"Every time I lay eyes on ye, lass, 'tis that much more beautiful ye are to me." Gavin's words rushed out, sounding breathless and smelling sweet. He leaned in, flashing his rascal grin. Diligent fingers combed my hair, lifting a curl, breathing in its fragrance. He peered into my eyes, searching the innermost parts, it seemed, seeking the point of no return. When he merged our mouths together a second time and stamped his seal upon my lips, a shudder of desire skittered down my throat and galloped into my bones.

I closed my eyes, shutting out the firmness of my purpose. His kisses lifted me from the porch swing—into another world: a world that existed behind the shuttered lids of darkness. 'Twas there I chanced upon a memory more real than Gavin's kiss: a time and place from which my heart had never departed.

Lost in thought, I didn't hear Tate's approach. He tapped me on the shoulder. As I turned to him, he bowed, as would a gentleman in the presence of a queen. In total Tate unlikeness, he postured himself into dance position.

"Pardon me, miss, but may I have this dance?"

I felt a rush of heat flood my face, my neck, my limbs. Riled-up and confused, I stared past Tate's shoulder, wanting answers to silent questions my heart was too embarrassed to ask: *Why are you doing this, Tate? Do you think so little of me that you'd taunt my lameness?*

"Come on, Emma … it's a slow song. We can do this together. Come dance with me," he coaxed.

I turned my back on him. "I've never danced in my life. I don't know how … and furthermore, it would be quite an impossible task, bound to this crutch as I am."

"I've never danced before either. Who's to see us, Emma? Who's to care that we're a couple of first-timers?"

"Do you think to make sport of my condition, Tate?"

"Heck, no. Look … I've got it all figured out … all you have to do is put your right foot on top of my left shoe, then you'll be on even-keel. Want to give it a try?"

Oh, how we had danced. The music played on in my heart.

"I can't wait another two weeks, Emma Grace. What do ye say, sweetheart?" Something about Tate's voice bothered me. Rising through a fog of provocative memories, I peeked beyond love-swollen lids, desiring a closer look at the tall, dark youth who had accomplished what no other could: convinced me to dance in the light of day ... in a city park, of all places.

"There's no call to be waiting for our wedding night. I can feel ye're wanting it as much as I am. Oh, sweet girl, ye've never responded like this before."

*Gavin? Why was I locked in Gavin's arms ... his hands touching forbidden places?*

As I jerked his hand from my breast, spurs of guilt dug into my conscience, for I knew I had invited Gavin's touch when I imagined myself in Tate's arms. Oh yes, I'd succumbed to temptations of the flesh—and quite easily, I had to admit. I studied the man who held me, his eyes glazing over with love and desire. Oh, how I wished those eyes belonged to the ebony-haired youth to whom I had given my heart.

"Don't be a tease, Emma Grace. 'Tis not like ye to lead me on, then pretend ye're not after the same thing I'm wanting meself. "

I wriggled from Gavin's arms and walked across the porch. I halted at the railing, presenting him my back as I smoothed my skirt and closed the tortoiseshell buttons of my bodice. Angry fingers fumbling at ordinary tasks. I glanced at the cavernous sky, pinpoints of light tracing patterns on a drapery of darkness. Perhaps I could find my own map in the heavens, and it would lead me away from the mess I had made. I turned, propping my backside against the barrier, staking claim some distance from Gavin. My hands shook with disgust—at myself and at Gavin. I shoved my hands behind my back and grasped onto the banister's stability. As disturbing as Gavin's assessment had been, I knew it was truthful. I *had* responded to him as never before. Even so, he had no cause to take such liberties.

"You had no call to undress me like that, right here on my own front porch."

"Oh, come off it. 'Twas nothing but a touch. Ye were practically begging me to scrabble ye up a bit." Gavin lunged from the swing, grabbing me by the shoulders, holding me prisoner as he hissed out his wrath. "Ye wanted it, Emma Grace. Don't be denying it. And, further-more, 'tis nothing shameful about it. Not a'tall. Ye liked me kisses well enough, didn't ye, girl?"

Yes, I had liked them—too well. But 'twas a deceitful thing I had done to Gavin. The shame of it stuck in the muck and mud of my con-science, and there it set up squatter's rights. I knew it wouldn't budge until I revealed to Gavin what I had rehearsed in my head the entire afternoon.

"Gavin—I need to talk to you about something. Please, let go of my arms and hear me out … before you say anything. And, keep your voice down. Elephant ears are probably pressed to the panes this very minute." I glanced at the parlor window as I walked back to the swing, but if there were any snoopers they were either too quick for my eyes or as hard to spot as wispy haunts on a windy night.

As I gathered my shawl around me, my peripheral vision assured me Gavin remained at the railing. Huffs of air steamed from his nos-trils like irate smoke signals—or were they an invention of my imagination? I sat down, giving the swing a hearty push; a signal, of sorts, for Gavin to stay put. Better I talked to him with a goodly span between us.

"Get it off yer chest, Emma Grace. Whatever 'tis bothering ye … jest spit it out. But if ye're thinking to yank an apology from me for doing what any living, breathing man would be doing …"

Gone, the rascal smile and the charm that effortlessly wrapped dozens of female hearts around its twisted vine. Gavin didn't snarl, exactly, but close enough that I pictured the hair on his back, arching over like a causeway bridge. He jammed his hands into deep pockets and stared me down. I saw his nostrils flare, invisible snorts of air lift-ing sandy locks from his forehead.

"There's no easy way to say this, Gavin. I'd do anything not to hurt you … but …"

"Say what's on yer mind, girl. I've had enough of yer nonsense."

"I've been troubled for some time now—not knowing if I'm really in love with you—or just loving the idea of being married. I don't even know if I'm ready for marriage." I reached for my hanky, but settled for the hem of my shawl, my eyes refilling as quickly as I wiped them dry.

Gavin shook his head and frowned. "Are ye still hung up on Robert's story? I've told ye that I've got no one waiting for me in Ireland. I've not fathered a babe, and there's no lass waiting for me to marry her. Never has been—never will be."

"No, it's got nothing to do with what you did before we met. I loved you, Gavin, and was excited about getting married. I can say that with full truth. I thought God had brought you all the way from Ireland, just for *me.*"

"He did, darlin'. He surely did."

"Please … let me finish. I told you about what happened to my little brother, Micah." Gavin nodded and pedaled his finger in the air, prompting me to get on with my explanation. "What I didn't tell you was that I blamed myself for his death. I never got over the tragedy, you see, because I wouldn't let myself think about it—or face it. The memories hurt too much. The cost of looking back was too high. Oh, I did a good job of pretending, but deep down, I was never at rest—never free of guilt. I knew if I had watched the boys closer—"

"Ye can't be thinking like that, Emma Grace. Nothing good comes from blaming yerself. What's that got to do with the two of us, anyway?"

"I thought guilt was keeping me from loving you with all of my heart. That's what it's got to do with you and me. Something wasn't right inside me. Something wasn't right with *us,* either. I blamed it on guilt and the fact that I hadn't been completely happy or content since Micah died. But all that changed this afternoon. I'm not shackled with guilt anymore. Isn't that wonderful, Gavin?"

"Where's all this leading?"

Gavin's sternness didn't dampen my joy; though it did sober me up a bit. "I see now that guilt wasn't the entire problem. *We're* the problem. I'm not in love with you, Gavin." *We're not evenly yoked … don't you see?* "I can't promise to cherish you and honor you for the rest of my life. But I can certainly promise to love you—as a friend."

"Friend? Ye're wanting me to be yer friend? 'Twas not a *friend* ye were kissing a moment ago, Emma Grace. What's really going on here? Surely ye're not mad because I dared touch yer precious body." Scorn dripped from his words as he leaned back against the railing, crossing his legs and slouching as though my words had not perturbed him. But I knew I had wounded Gavin, wounded him gravely. There was pain in his eyes—as though a thousand deadly needles had pierced his heart.

Then the pained look vanished, and in its place an angry, bitter hardness glared back at me. I tried to ignore the ire that seethed and flared to life behind his wild-eyed stare.

"More than anything else—I'll always treasure our friendship, Gavin. I hope, in time, that you'll …" A veil of tears blurred his image into a ragged, white shape. The shape didn't move, but from the feel of electricity about me, Gavin's anger still crackled in the air. I wiped my eyes and glanced at the window, seeing no movement, hearing no whispers. I prayed my family didn't eavesdrop on this conversation, as it looked to turn ugly. "My feelings have nothing to do with the liberties you took tonight, though I thought them disgraceful. Who gave you permission to grope me and put your hands where you darn well pleased?" Wrath stirred my blood and circulated through my veins with swiftness.

"Are ye saying ye have no feelings for me, Emma Grace? None a'tall?"

"Of course I have feelings for you, Gavin—they're just not the kind you build a marriage on. Can't you see that I'm not the—"

"How could they just up and disappear like that? One day ye love me, the next ye're wantin' me to be your *friend?* Are ye a stinking magician, so's ye can make yer love come and go like a rabbit in a hat?"

"Feelings can change, Gavin. It's best I found out now. Otherwise, I might have made your life miserable somewhere down the road."

Gavin knelt before me and took my hands in his. My whole body shook, for his eyes held dark bleakness within their depths.

"Don't ye know that ye could never make me miserable, sweet girl? No matter how hard ye tried." Gavin swiped at his tears with a shirt-sleeve, his other hand reclaiming mine. His eyes held a pleading look.

*But what about me, Gavin? What if I married you and was miserable my entire life because I married the wrong man? Elo's right. We're unevenly yoked.*

I placed my hands on Gavin's face, leaned over, and kissed his forehead. He locked me to his chest, his ragged sobs buried in my shoulder as he held me in a frenzied, seamless grasp. The kind in which I would have embraced Micah, had I the opportunity.

"I can't let ye go, sweetheart. I love ye more than life."

We cried together, minutes ticking by as my heart ached for the man to whom I had promised my love. I knew not where God would lead me. But this I did know: It wasn't into Gavin O'Donnell's house, or into his bed.

I had to break off with him tonight. My heart told me it was now or never. I slipped my engagement band from my finger and laid it in Gavin's rough palm. 'Twas then I knew my first real moment of peace, although hurting Gavin seared me as though I'd been branded with a red-hot iron.

"Please, Emma Grace. Don't be doin' this to me."

I bawled openly, my heart breaking for Gavin. 'Twas not my nature to hurt people. I felt Gavin's pain as though it were my own. "It'll just be worse if we prolong the inevitable, Gavin. It's best we part tonight … as friends."

Gavin looked at me, suspicion seeming to open up his face and his eyes—and his rage. "There's someone else, isn't there? That's what this is all about. Who is he, Emma Grace?" He squeezed my hands with such strength, I imagined them falling off at the wrists.

I didn't blink a lash. "I've never kissed another man in my life, Gavin. Only you."

His shoulders slumped, but his glare bored on, the drill of inquisition digging for fundamental clues to verify my faithlessness.

"If I find out ye're lying to me, girl, I'll kill him. Ye understand me?"

"Good night, Gavin. Promise me you'll take care of yourself."

Gavin stood, staring down from a kingly realm, pain pinching his face. He walked to the windowsill and placed my ring on the corner ledge. "When ye come to yer senses, this'll be right here, waiting for ye to put it back on—where it belongs."

A curtain of tears fogged my view as I stood and floundered toward the door. I had walked the porch ten thousand times; had known its feel on the darkest nights. Now I reeled and lurched like the town drunk. I flinched as I brushed past Gavin, fearing he might reach out and wrench me from my determination. His labored breathing hurt my ears. His wrath and brokenness hurt my heart.

I aimed my watery gaze forward as my hand twisted the knob that would open the door to the rest of my life. Pausing at the threshold, I stole one last glance at the small silver band I had worn so proudly. It would remain where it was—until a child found it, or the wind blew it away—or until it fell between the cracks of the flooring. The ring no longer belonged to me.

# Thirty-five

The wind blew and the earth trembled, spilling rocks and boulders down the mountainside like loose marbles. They tumbled and crashed together on the valley floor, rendering an awful racket.

I startled awake, the dream fading as I sat up in bed. I cocked my head toward the window and harkened to the sounds that had arrested me from sleep. A downpour pounded our tin roof, and in the distance I heard wooden planks cuffing each other like boxers in a ring. *Another storm ... following so quickly on the heels of the hurricane? It's been a stormy day ... for sure.* I resettled into my pocket of bedcovers, knowing my dream had sprouted from hard-pelting rain and a howling wind that vaulted over field and lawn, shaking shutters and banging the doors of our outbuildings. I lay with my eyes wide open and listened to the clatter.

I studied the room's darkness, seeing nothing amiss, just the everyday props that had long filled the nooks and crannies of my bedroom. As I closed my eyes on blurred objects and shadowed hollows, I heard a different sound. Pebbles—no, stones—hitting the window. I sprang from bed and ran straightway to the casement, leaning my face against the cold glass, fogging it with my breath. As I wiped mist from the window, a bolt of lightning slashed across the sky, flaring the darkness with jagged streaks.

I saw him then, standing on the lawn beneath my second-story window, his hand drawn back to launch the next stone. He spied me and dropped his mischief to the ground. Cupping his hands around his mouth, he hollered into the wind, swaying a bit as he did. He appeared to be weaving at the whim of the wind, but I knew the wind hadn't caused Gavin to totter this way and that. 'Twas something a mite more destructive.

I rammed my palm against the jam, loosening the tired old window from its autumn nest. As I lifted the sash, rain swept through the opening, dousing me from top to bottom.

"Emma Grace ... I need to talk wi'ye. Ye can't be leaving me out here ... in the storm ... and the ... 'Tis a coldhearted woman who'd be doin' ... doin' that to her man."

Slurred words. Yet I understood them with freshwater clearness. 'Twas a fact that Gavin's thick head had not received or accepted the truth of my message this evening.

I grabbed my robe, taking time to don my socks and shoes, for I knew I couldn't manage Gavin's brawn and a crutch at the same time. I robed myself in record time, praying as I tied my sash that Gavin's braying wouldn't awaken the household. Perhaps the storm's uproar would pillow his drunken hullabaloo. If not—Elo would have his gun cocked and the trigger pulled before I had a chance to right things between us.

As I pushed my way through the front door, the wind slammed it shut behind me.

"Get onto this porch, you crazy man." An icy wind shoved my words right back down my throat. I waved my arms and motioned Gavin to the porch, but he seemed planted in the yard. With my temper scaling the walls of ire, I ran into the yard and right into the face of a wet blue norther. Rain soaked my hair, and everything between it and the nubbins of my toes.

Gavin's head lolled against his chest, stuporlike; groggy. My anger sloshed onto him, drenching him with buckets of cold disgust, but it did little to wash away his drunkenness. While rain rolled across the yard in waves, I shoved on him and guided him toward the porch. A gust slapped us from behind, billowing Gavin's hair into the wings of a peregrine and almost toppling me over. I jerked his coat sleeve and dragged his sogginess as best I could while the Irish in me flared again. I had a good mind to collect Papa's bullwhip from the barn. Best I let that idea fly, for I would surely wrap the tip of it around Gavin's throat. We plodded across the yard, his arm around my shoulder as we trudged the meandering path his legs chanced upon. It took some time, for his legs flopped and crumpled like a headless chicken, and, at times, I wilted beneath his weight. Those strong legs of his were all but useless now. Perhaps his bones had soaked up too much whiskey.

From the corner of my eye, I spied a flash of pants and flapping suspenders. The image streaked past Mama's dried-up flowerbed, into a thickness of trees and shadows. I knew it was either Geronimo or Elo. Another streak—dashing around the far side of the house. *Nathan?*

Gavin and I mounted the porch. His shoe caught on the crest of the top stair, sending both of us sprawling. He nose-dived into a slick slide, his head splitting one of Mama's clay pots. Dirt and geraniums flew across the porch, mixing with the muck on our shoes, and rain blowing in beneath the covering. I debated on leaving Gavin where he lay, in his soupy gumbo mess. Or, should I pray for high waters to wash him downriver?

I rose on all fours, then to my knees, swiping ooze and mud from my face. My nose rubbed against the cold steel of a double-barreled shotgun, which had aimed itself at Gavin's backside. I screamed, but a moment only, for Elo clamped his hand over my mouth, squelching further outbursts. He raised a finger to his lips, signaling me to cease my noise. What did he think? That he was on a hunting raid this horrid night, and Gavin was the wild game?

"Put your stupid gun away, molasses-head!" I yelled.

Nathan stepped atop the porch, as soundlessly as had Elo.

"Did Gavin hurt you, Sis?"

Nathan's concern angered me even more. "No one is hurt, except you two if you don't get out of here and let me handle this on my own. The last thing I want is for Papa to come down and get into the fracas."

"It's too late for that, Emma Grace." Papa stood in the doorway; bat in hand, and fierceness etched on his face. "What's that drunken cur doing out here in the middle of night?"

"He's out to kidnap Emma Grace."

I shook my head, Elo's bankrupt reasoning skills sealing my lips with disbelief. I stared at his naked chest and wide expanse of shoulders, mere inches from my face. They bore no visible signs of the frigid night air that clouded our breaths when we spoke. It proved true my theory about Elo: He had been born into a tribe of blond warrior-natives—natives who were immune to cold, heat, and pain. Perhaps Mama and Papa had found Elo out in the woods when he was just a babe, and ...

"Of all the idiotic conclusions you've come to in your life, Elo, this is truly the most pitiful one of all." Having rediscovered my tongue, I plowed my words and my fist into Elo's midriff, barely causing him to draw breath. But I did shake loose a passel of raindrops that had wrapped themselves around his golden chest-curls. "Now—I want all of you out of here. Don't you see I have to do this on my own? I made the mess—I'll clean it up."

Looking skeptical, Papa didn't budge from the wide-legged stance he had assumed. Nathan and Elo stood on either side of Gavin; rock pillars to block his getaway. Two bare-chested monoliths of equal stature, one wearing glasses, the other a frown carved in granite.

Gavin mumbled incoherently, capturing my attention. He sat up, rubbing his head, shaking muck from the bed of his scalp. He looked like a shaggy, mud-wallowing golden retriever.

"Wha ... happen't to me?" He tried to rise, but his feet slipped from beneath him. Sitting spread-eagle on a soggy dirt cushion, he glanced at the circle of ire surrounding him, his gaze halting on the spit-and-polished shotgun pointed at his head. "Did I hurt ye, Emma Grace? 'Tis a sorry lot I am. I meant ye no harm, darlin'." Bubbles foamed from Gavin's mouth—alcohol dulling his swallowing reflexes, I assumed. I could almost feel empathy for him.

"You're sorry, all right. 'Bout the sorriest example of humanity I've seen in all my fifty-five years. What's wrong with you, boy? How'd you get caught up in the Devil's clutches so early in life?" Papa shook his head, lips pursing to a thin line. I remembered the firmness of that line—had seen it often in my naughty misbehaving days of childhood. 'Twas a dreadful look to behold.

"I've a mind to swab his throat with turpentine, Papa. That'll burn off the alcohol in no time. What'd you say?"

I gasped aloud, quirking Elo's face into a slanted smile. Of course, I had played right into his hands.

"You'll do no such thing. In fact, I want the lot of you to leave. Gavin and I need to talk … in private." When no one budged, my tongue rolled on. "Give me a little credit, will you? I know how to handle Gavin." I tapped my foot, feeling exasperated and probably a bit angrier than the occasion called for. "Leave! Do you hear what I'm saying? I want you all to leave—now!"

They took their own dear time, but finally sauntered from the porch. Nathan shoved his rifle into my shaking hands. "All you have to do is holler, Emma Grace. We'll take care of him for you."

"Thanks, Nathan."

I watched until they had disappeared into the house, noisily wiping their feet before shutting the door. Glancing at Gavin and noticing no improvement in his condition, I gritted my teeth, then snapped them open and spewed out my first command. "Get up, Gavin. I'll fix a place for you out in the barn so you can sleep off your drunkenness. But, come morning, I want you out of here. Do you understand me?"

I huffed down the stairs without a backward glance, not knowing if Gavin followed, or if he had slunk back to the groggy land of inebriation. Nathan's .22 rifle rested in the cradle of my arm, and over my head was a jacket from the parlor coatrack. Papa had pitched it to me before he closed the door. I aimed for the barn, sidestepping puddles and bare patches of earth, now mud-caked and slippery. Water sloshed inside my shoes, rain barreled down my neck. I slipped my arms into Papa's coat; my head bared to the driving torrent, and crossed my arms. I tried to shake off my anger, but it was as stubborn as an old ewe that won't be budged from the sheepfold. It dug its hooves firmly in the ground, showing not a notion of departure.

In the barn, I lit a kerosene lantern and waited for Gavin. When he sidled through the door, I thought I'd never seen a more wretched sight. He appeared the captured convict: beaten, trapped, and at the end of his tether. I watched from a distance, his filth-caked stance steadying as he turned his gaze on me. I laid Nathan's gun on the workbench and removed Papa's coat.

Familiar barn scents clung to the air; leather and hay, horse and cow dung; smells that seemed a calming tonic to my nerves. They also covered a portion of Gavin's whiskey stench that had fermented like old sweat.

I grabbed the hayfork and pointed it at the watering trough. "You can wash up there." Gavin glanced at his surroundings as though he'd not seen the inside of a barn before. "There's a chamois to dry off with." I nodded my head toward a piece of hide, hanging from a nail above the enamel basin. "Mama makes the boys clean up here before she allows them in the house."

Gavin nodded and peeled himself out of his waterlogged jacket.

"Best you get out of those wet clothes. Papa keeps a pair of overalls in the tack room. You can sleep in them tonight. Hang your clothes where they'll dry, 'cause you'll be wearing them home in the morning, soaking or not."

I lifted the pitchfork, sending hay flying into a corner of the barn. When the pile peaked like a softly rounded knoll, I looked at Gavin and pointed my fork at the straw mound. "There's enough hay for you to crawl into if you get cold."

I rammed the hayfork into a stack of fodder and gathered my long, sodden braid in my hands, squishing water from its heaviness. I dared not look down the mess of me, knowing my appearance was only a mite better than the stoop-shouldered man who still clutched his dripping jacket. He hardly resembled the man I had thought to marry. Having moved but a few feet from the barn door, he stared at me with mouth ajar, seeming not to know which of my bossy orders to follow first. Up to this point in our relationship, Gavin O'Donnell had not gorged on a bellyful of my ire. Did he perceive me now as one whose fangs were bared and oozing venom? Did he wait for the next strike?

My wrath flittered a bit, and then faltered altogether, slipping away into the shadows of forgiveness. In that moment, I knew I still loved Gavin. But 'twas a different love than before; as vastly different as winter winds and summer breezes.

"One more thing, Gavin." His gaze shot up, as though he expected to see the pitchfork come flying at his middle. "You'll be owing my family an apology—once you've gone home and cleaned up a bit, and thought this night through."

"Emma Gra—"

"As for me—I meant what I said earlier. I'll always treasure our friendship. You can guzzle a thousand jugs of moonshine and it won't keep me from being your friend."

"I don't deserve yer friendship, girl. No' after the way I've acted today."

I wanted to take his hand, run my fingers down the fun-loving face that now brimmed with anguish. I had hurt him dreadfully, and for that I suffered true regret. "Gavin—I'm so sorry I hurt you today. Can you find it in your heart to forgive … a friend?"

I noticed Gavin's mouth, tightening at the corners. He clamped his jaws together, forcing a knot of muscles along the ridge. My words had reopened wounds and reawakened his wrath.

"I don't think I can ever forgive ye for what ye've put me through today."

I lowered my head, knowing Gavin's pain ran like deep waters; as deep as the sureness in my heart that our joining was not meant to be.

"I understand. Maybe—maybe someday you can forgive me." Tears welled in my eyes, making double of everything I viewed. I turned to leave, but a sudden motion jerked me around, smashing me against Gavin's chest. Blinking away my wetness, I found myself staring into the eyes of a wounded lion. Anger and vengeance leaped in the depths of his eyes, flames that seemed out of control.

Gavin's drunkenness cost him nothing in the way of strength. He slammed his mouth to mine, grinding my lips and breathing the stink of soured whiskey down my throat. Waves of nausea and revulsion rolled through my stomach as he probed my tongue with his, tangling the two in a catfight. I tried to jerk free, but was imprisoned by his overwhelming power. He pushed me to the floor, my back in the dirt as he fell atop me. While his weight pinioned me to the ground, his mouth and hands did their damage elsewhere. Somehow—his lips never left mine. And somehow—he never stopped shoving his suffocating kisses down my throat. He braced his left arm against my collarbone, his right hand roving my body, touching everything it desired to touch. And there was no one to stop him.

It seemed I viewed the scene from a dreamworld, seeing the struggling girl on the floor, but not knowing how to help her. My senses returned soon enough, my make-believe world vanishing when Gavin raised the hem of my gown and ran his hand between my thighs … and higher.

He lifted the lower part of his body and fumbled with his trouser opening; lifted it high enough for me to yank my knee upward, striking him between the legs. He bellowed and rolled free; doubled over in pain, grunting, cursing, and hissing out words I'd not heard … even from Elo's lips. It bothered me not at all—the pain I had inflicted upon Gavin. For no matter how much he hurt, it could not compare to the pain his betrayal had cost me this night.

I stumbled to the workbench and grabbed the rifle, pumping a bullet into the chamber as I whirled around and aimed the barrel at Gavin. My hands shook as never before, for in that instant I was ready to kill the man I had once loved.

"Get out … of here … now! Before I blow your head off!" I whipped my head about, wrangling hair from my eyes as I kept Gavin in the target area of my rifle.

He rose to his knees, shaking and glaring at me, bright eyes filled with torment. The sight of his drooling lust offended me, for it drew me into a realm of evil I'd heard about only in whispered secrets.

"Ye … ye belong t'me … I'll … not be lettin' another have ye …" Gavin gasped and wheezed, his eyes streaming water; tears of pure, stabbing possessiveness. "… as long as I draw breath …"

"That won't be long if you don't leave—now! Don't *ever* come back, Gavin. I was wrong about you. I thought we could be friends, but you just killed everything in my heart that once loved you."

Bent over and clutching himself, Gavin opened the door and pushed himself through. I walked behind, my rifle unsteady as it pointed at his back. A swarm of Eveready flashlight beams flooded the entrance, aiming at Gavin's heart like arrows in the night. We walked out the door into the storm, and into the angry presence of Papa and my brothers.

They rushed to my side like fierce, victorious warriors; tall, blond Vikings who couldn't wait to get their hands on the miscreant of my humiliation. Elo and Nathan dragged Gavin through the mud, and then lifted him as though his weight was of little consequence. His feet cycled the air as they carried him past the reach of light—and out of my life. Elo would pound his own wrathful retribution into Gavin, along with the fear of eternal damnation. 'Twas a fact. Gavin would not dare come near me again, the little that was left of him after Elo's powerful paws proved who was king of the jungle. Elo had not uttered an idle threat in his life. Most of the 535 people in Coldwater could attest to this truth firsthand—or knew someone who could.

Odd how my mind heeded unspectacular occurrences during those moments of angry relief: Papa's flashlight shining through a sheet of rain, magnifying each drop as it traveled a slow-motion path to earth; the way Papa directed my brothers with mute signals; the way they obeyed his silent commands.

"We heard you scream, Emma Grace. Did the filthy rotter hurt you, sweetheart?"

Papa's rough tenderness snapped me out of my brave posturing. He caught the rifle as it fell from my hands, the shakes coming in waves now. I vaulted into his arms. He carried the rifle and me up to the porch, out of the storm's bluster.

"Did he hurt you, Emma Grace? You've got to tell me the truth. If that skunk laid one finger on—"

"No, Papa. I'm okay … truly, I'm all right." The last thing I wanted Papa to do was call the constable, who would blab the news all over our township. "Why did you think I screamed, Papa? I never hollered once. Maybe you heard the wind, or …"

"Yeah, you did, honey. You just don't remember."

*No, Papa. I didn't scream. But maybe one of God's angels did.*

# Thirty-six

Though I hadn't confessed the truth of Gavin's savagery to anyone, Mama hovered over me like a mother bird, cooing and soothing my ruffled feathers with hugs and promises that everything would be all right. She would spend the night worrying over me. I knew she would.

After a hot bath and hair scrub, I climbed wearily into bed and waited for the sandman to come calling. But he never showed up. Memories of the near rape and Gavin's treachery combined with my wistful thoughts about Tate and the love I had lost years back. They consumed every remaining moment of the dark, unsettling night. Though I knew relief at having severed the cord between Gavin and myself, 'twas not relief I felt when I thought about living the single life; a lifetime of unfulfilled plans and dreams. As I contemplated the future, I saw only emptiness before me.

We Falins were a visionary family whose dreams waxed abundant. Elo had his heart set on being the best farmer, hunter, angler, and horseman in Texas. Actually, he expected to be best at whatever he attempted to do. Nathan's dreams included college, where he planned to earn degrees in a wide range of academia, including agriculture, for his heart held special feelings for the land. He thought to prosper our farm, and had recorded his strategies to do so in stacks of thin-lined notebooks from which he never ventured far. My dream was simple. I had latched onto it at an early age, and I clutched it to my bosom even now for the beauty and joy it pumped into my heart. I wanted to be a wife and mother. Now that dream seemed as far removed as the plans Gavin and I once made to get married on October 27, 1933.

It's not that I disliked the eligible men in Coldwater. I had known most of them since grade school and we got along fine. But not one made my heart putter like a trawling engine the way it had when Gavin first arrived from Ireland, eight months earlier. And, to my knowledge, I had not caused accelerated heart rates among the small, select group of bachelors we maidens referred to as stags. As Papa would say, "The pickings are mighty slim around Coldwater."

The emptiness loomed before me, but I would fill it. With Sundays full of the old hymns and heartfelt worship. With family get-togethers, babies bouncing atop my knee while nephews tormented my braid. Only—it wouldn't be my babes who cuddled to sleep in the hollow of my shoulder or my toddler whose toothless gums teethed my little finger raw. And when the cars pulled from our driveway at eventide, my arms would be just as empty as when my sisters first arrived. Oh, there'd be summers of canning, where my busy hands joined those of The Ollys and Mama; pickling cucumbers and beets, boiling fruit we'd later spread over the bread we baked. There'd be cows to milk and new colts to adore. Still, my arms would be void and unadorned of the one thing I desired above all others.

At dawn's light, I slipped from bed and changed into traveling clothes. In the bathroom, I washed my face, brushed my teeth and hair, and tidied up the sink. I tiptoed down the hallway, lifting the old cardboard suitcase from the top shelf of the closet. I carried it to my room and packed it with sufficient clothing and necessities to last a few weeks.

"What in the world are you doing Emma Grace?"

I hadn't heard Mama's soft approach. Nor had I detected her morning humming that signaled the household awake. Mama had sneaked up on me.

"I'm going to Granny's for a while. I've thought it through, Mama. You can't shake me from my plans." I watched her eyes—the window to her soul. She smiled and walked to the bed, refolding one of the skirts I had thrown into the case. Her smile confused me a bit, being that I thought she would try to dissuade me.

"What a good idea, sweetie. I'll help you pack."

"But—what about Polly? I'll miss seeing the baby … and her." The thought of not holding Polly's nine-month-old baby boy had ushered the only real doubt to my mind. Our family hadn't seen Polly since she moved to Arkansas with her husband, Hank. I sat down on the bed, heavyhearted.

"I called them yesterday, sweetheart. Told them the wedding was off. They've already made plans to come at Christmas instead of now." Mama tilted her head, a half-smile cambering the curves of her cheeks. She knew me so well.

"Thanks, Mama."

Mama's eyes held me with a steady stare. I wondered if she could see my heart pumping with the sadness of lost hopes and dreams. She smiled and stretched her hand to my head, stroking the fullness of my hair. "What's wrong, dear? Are you thinking you'll never find another man to love? A husband to build a home and life with?"

"More like I'll never find a man who'll love *me*. I do come with a few warts, you know."

"Whatever are you talking about, sweet girl? Surely not your leg. It's totally unnoticeable, unless someone happens to be studying your shoes. Don't you still beat Caleb every time the two of you race?"

I giggled, for I truly was a thorn in Caleb's side when it came to footraces. I knew Mama was right. I no longer thought of myself as an oddity, as I had earlier in my life. Still—after eighteen and a half years of being different from everyone else, I still felt like an outsider at times.

"You have the most beautiful heart of all my children, Emma Grace. It has always spilled over with love—for babies and children, and every one of God's creatures you could get your hands on. You don't think God will let all that love go to waste, do you?"

Mama sat on the bed beside me and pulled me close. I guessed I needed a good cry, for the next thing I knew, I was bawling into her shoulder like a two-year-old.

"You know I love all of my children equally, but you have been spe-cial to your papa and me since the day we first held you—out in that itchy old cotton field. God spared you for a purpose, Emma Grace, and that purpose wasn't to grow old in this house alongside your papa and me.

"What we need to do is thank the good Lord you found out in time that you and Gavin don't belong together. Thank goodness, you *didn't* get married." Mama pulled us apart and brushed her hand over my brow, smoothing pesky curls from my face as she'd done a thousand times before. "There's a man out there, somewhere, just waiting for you to show up. And a mighty fortunate fellow he is." She cupped my chin with her fingers and turned my head, persuading me to meet her gaze. "He'll come along, sweetheart. You'll see. One day you'll open your eyes, and there he'll be."

The day was brisk, with sassy winds making a pigeon-nest of my hair as I stepped from the train in Galveston. I set my suitcase on the platform and looked around. Red-capped porters and blue-coated baggage men bustled down the walkway, transporting luggage and assisting travelers in one way or another.

I glanced at the sky. Cloudbanks brooded overhead, gathering, it seemed, for a squalling downpour. The scent of sea brine had me wishing my toes were wriggling through slippery gray sand right now. From behind my closed lids, I pictured murky-green seawater, distant whitecaps rolling toward shore, foamy curls being swallowed up by choppy breakers.

"Hey, lady. You sick or somethin'?"

I opened my eyes to a scruffy-haired boy of eight or nine who stud-ied my face with intensity. His hand clutched the handle of a dusty wagon, and his baggy breeches were so long they cuffed his ankles instead of his knees. I smiled inwardly at smudges of brown that streaked his hands and face. He pinched the bill of his cap, doffed it, and bowed to me.

*Someone must have trained you well.*

"I'll tote your suitcase for a nickel, ma'am. Whadda'ya say?" He shifted his weight from one foot to the other, as the twins used to do when they were in need of bathroom facilities.

"What's your name, kind sir?" My greeting seemed to catch him off guard. His brows closed together and he puckered his lips as though he'd been sucking on a green persimmon. His griminess didn't bother me a bit, for I'd already spotted a noble knight behind that ruffled frown of his.

"Nobie."

The child's gaze was steadfast, his eyes narrowing with suspicion, it seemed to me. Did he think I made sport of him? Because of his shabbiness? I prayed not.

"Nobie …?"

"Nobie Percher." He slid a hand beneath his nose as though he were playing a harmonica. Without thinking, I handed him my handkerchief.

"Nobie … Per …?"

"Percher—like the fish. Ain't you never heard of a perch before?" He blew into my hanky several times, wiping his nose with hardy strokes. When he rammed the cloth into my hand, I dropped its wetness into my skirt pocket and smiled broadly. The lad had knowing gray eyes. I'd not reveal a speck of distaste to Master Percher.

"Of course I've heard of perch. In fact, I've caught more perch than there are stars in the sky."

Nobie narrowed his eyes again, studying me as if I were a prized tiger-eye marble. Then he grinned, satisfied my teasing was harmless. At least, I hoped that was the reason for his wide-gapped smile, from which several baby teeth had gone missing.

"How far're you going?"

"I'm afraid it's a very long walk, Nobie. All the way to the east end of Winnie Street."

"Never heard of it." He stared at me, unsmiling, as though anxious to get this transaction settled so he could move on to more pleasant adventures.

"It's about twenty-five blocks from here." I could almost see his head calculating the fifty blocks it would take him to go to Granny's house and return.

"What say I cart your suitcase a nickel's worth, then you can carry it the rest of the way?"

"Fair enough, Nobie."

He tossed my suitcase into his rickety wagon, and down the road he flew. I galloped behind.

"Nobie!" I hollered. He turned, tapering his stride, allowing me to catch up. "Slow down a bit, okay? Hey, why aren't you in school today? Is this a holiday or something?"

"No ma'am. Needed the money." He looked straight ahead, reminding me of a proud Elo who despised charity above all else.

"Well—you just let me know when my nickel is up. I'm used to hard work, Nobie. I can carry it just …" I looked at Nobie's proud face, hoping I had caught my blunder in time. "I'm more than grateful that a strong lad, such as you, turned up at just the right time. It surely would have tuckered me out to carry my suitcase all the way to Granny's house." For dramatic effect, I ran a hand across my brow, wiping away imaginary sweat.

"Glad I happen't along. Girls ain't known much for their strength, you know."

Right then, I knew that Nobie and I could be great friends, if happenstance allowed such a bizarre pairing. He sounded and even acted a bit like Falin boys. In my heart, I started thinking of him as another little brother.

I dug as much information out of Nobie as was possible in ten blocks' time. He lived with his mother and five siblings near the wharf area. His papa had died two years earlier: killed aboard an oil derrick when a boom broke loose and crushed him to death. Or, as Nobie so ably put it—"got kill't deader'n a turkey with his head blown off."

"Does your mama work too?"

Nobie seemed pleased that I counted him as one of the main providers for his family. "No, ma'am. She's got them babies to tend."

*Babies? What's this? Oh, Father—help me not jump ahead—but are you about to guide my feet to a path I never dreamed I'd be taking?*

"How many babies, Nobie?" My heart beat with wildness as I awaited his answer.

"Hannah and Rosalie had their first birthday, oh … I dunno … maybe two or three months back. Mama was carrying 'em in her pouch when Pa got kill't."

"Do you think I might meet your family some day? You and I have a lot in common, you know. I have a lot of brothers and sisters too."

Nobie shrugged. Most likely he knew not to invite near strangers to his house without getting permission first.

"I tell you what—if you give me your address, Granny and I will stop by some day and see if your ma's up to visiting. How's that sound?"

He shrugged again, but shared his home address with me. He lived on Avenue C. I rummaged in my purse, locating one of the few dollar bills I had in my collection of egg money. Mostly, I had coins. Mostly, I had pennies. "Here are your wages, kind sir, and a mighty fine job you did." I winked at him as I handed him the dollar. "And—if you're ever in need of a referral, just let me know. I'll be glad to recommend you."

Nobie's eyes popped wide when he saw the bill. He shook his head with vigor. "Can't take this money, ma'am. Didn't tote your bag but a nickel's worth. A nickel's all I have coming."

"Of course, it's all you can charge. But what about the next time I need you to carry my luggage, or take a sack of groceries home for me? What if I have no money and can't pay you? This dollar is an investment in the future." Nobie twisted his mouth to the side. I knew my words were as unclear to him as a coin in a mud puddle. "I'm asking you to take the money, and when I need you again, you will have already been paid."

Nobie's keen mind snapped to attention. His eyes squinted as he asked, "What if you use up your dollar's worth, and still want me to help you? Then how will I get what's coming to me?"

"Well—I guess at such time, I'll just have to fork over another dollar. Sound fair, Mr. Percher?" Nobie thought a moment, then gave his head a tentative nod. "But, Nobie, before we become business partners, I have a favor to ask of you."

He looked at me long and hard, cold suspicion crinkling the corners of his eyes. "Just what kind of favor're you needing?"

"I'd like you to call me Emma Grace. That's my name, and since you'll have to keep up with all our money transactions, we should be on a first-name basis, don't you think? You'll be our bookkeeper, and I'll depend on you to let me know when I owe you more money. Does that seem fair?"

It must have sounded all right to Nobie. He turned around and headed toward the train station without saying another word. I thought I heard him whistling a clever tune, but perhaps it was just the wind.

# Thirty-seven

Across the space of time it took to cart my luggage in his rackety old wagon, Nobie Percher stole my heart like a runner sliding into second base.

"He was so cute, Granny, doffing his cap and bowing like I was royalty or something." Fondness rippled my words into weak, breathless giggles. As I expounded on his gravelly voice and trunk-hard demeanor, Granny's shoulders bounced a bit. She lifted her spectacles, swiping wetness from her jolly eyes. A vision of Nobie's lean shabbiness tiptoed across my memories, sobering me a bit. "You think we could do something for Nobie's family? Maybe take them some food or help out with the babies? I could do their washing for them."

Granny's coffee cup halted midway to her mouth. Then came the look—the one I'd come to dread during my residency in Galveston years earlier. That look that made me question if I'd put my clothes on backward or spoke the Portuguese tongue and Granny couldn't understand me.

"Ye can't jest barge into a person's home like that and take over. Ye have to be invited. People have their pride, ye know. Nobie's mother appears to have taught her young'uns about honesty and hard work. Ye don't want to be upsetting the apple cart, Emma Grace, or doing some-thin' that would embarrass them."

After Granny retired for the night, I stood at the kitchen window, pondering her words. Best I tread lightly with the Percher family. Find a way to help them without denting their dignity. *Will you show me how, Lord?*

The excitement of my first train ride, my first glimpse of the wind-scoured sea as we crossed over the bay today, and meeting Nobie had me keyed up and unable to sleep. I leaned against the sill, viewing the night curtain that had dropped earlier in the evening. The outside of the window was warty as a tree toad; weathered to gray and peeling patches of paint. Yet the inside frame bore shellac that rivaled the smoothness of Olly hair. 'Twas a picture of my life after God sanded guilt from my heart and coated it with a velvet glaze. Was it any wonder that I had found my way to Granny's porch steps after Gavin's attack? 'Twas in the place that I had come home to God.

The wild wind blew, howling between frame dwellings and whin-ing down the parlor stovepipe. While the trades raged, layers of crushed-shell lifted from the pavement and swirled in clouds of pallid dust. I prayed for calmer breezes, knowing I would have to postpone my venture to the beach until they abated. I yearned for the sea: its stiff blow of wind; the kelp floes that bobbed between the breakers; and my feathery friends that found nourishment on its doorstep. I conceded that an even greater obsession tugged me to the sea: the tin in which I had buried Tate's note. I had to know if he'd discovered it, and if so, why had five years passed without a word from him?

A thought came: Perhaps I should visit the ship docks and inquire of Tate's employment. I thought it futile since he was probably on the far side of the sea, fulfilling his dream to sail its perimeters and view its enchantment. Had he found true love … somewhere on a tropical isle? My heart thrummed a frantic drumbeat as I imagined Tate with his woman, lying on the beach; arms entwined as they shared love beneath the moonlight. Had she borne Tate a child? I turned from the window and shook my head, as though I could dislodge the troubling pictures from my mind.

After visiting with Granny the next morning, I ambled to the kitchen and packed a lunch while she watched me from the parlor.

"Where ye off to, sweet-pie?"

"I don't want to wait until afternoon to go to the beach. I promise I'll be home before dark, but don't worry if I don't get back until late afternoon. Okay?"

"Tell ye what … I'll make us some dumplings for supper. How's that sound?"

"Sounds wonderful. Love you, Granny."

With quickened heartbeat and anticipation pulsing through my veins I raced down the steps and aimed my excited feet toward the ocean.

Maybe I'd not lost Tate, after all.

Sea breezes wallowed beneath my petticoat and would have hoisted it over my head had I not pressed my skirt with a firm hand. As sunshine melted into my scalp, it spread a toasty sense of well-being over my body. Today was a mild, sit-down-in-the-sand kind of day. If I were in Coldwater, I would have completed my chores by now, and would be riding Old Jack to Holly's house, six miles down the road. After Karen and Kade smothered me in hugs, we'd play together until one, or all of us, collapsed in an exhausted heap.

As I crossed an expanse of deep, loose sand, I played tug-of-war with the sea: drawn to its embrace, yet pulling back from its allure. My first priority was to locate Micah's dune. Afterward, I would bask in the ocean's soft green mysteries. The sea and I would become one again, even if its wetness covered but the tips of my toes.

Would I spy Tate on the beach? I wondered. Would his tallness face the water as it had in years past? Would his gaze be latched to the horizon where golden sun mated with glimmering sea? Or might I spy him near the water's edge, his eyes searching for the girl with whom he had danced the dance of love?

I tracked through hillocks of grit and granule, most unfamiliar, for they were not the drifts of my brother's treasures. My head was full of fanciful dreams as I poked and prodded, discovering all too soon that the sand dunes of my memories no longer existed. Five years of tides and rain, storms and windfalls had reshaped the terrain, sculpting it into unknown valleys and flattened ridges. Micah's baby elephant dune—once protected by taller, mightier peaks—had disappeared. I spent hours among the pallets, scratching and digging with my hands, but to no avail. The altered landscape was as foreign to me as the thought of giving up.

As the sun scuttled lower in the flushed sky, my gaze turned to the sea more often. The barren shoreline appeared a lonely place. There were no couples strolling hand in hand. And nowhere did I see a lanky giant, staring at the far side of the sea. There were only terns and waddling gulls on the rummage for scraps of leftovers. 'Twas disheartening to know that if I returned to the beach every day for the rest of my life, I might never spy the ebony-haired youth of my dreams.

Muscles in my back and limbs flared with rekindled flames. I had strained in a bent-over position far too long. Gathering my lunch pail and jacket from the ground, I set out for Granny's house, determined to return on the morrow and accomplish my goal. As I walked the outlying dunes, I recalled the first time I saw Mr. Panduso, plodding a slow path of certainty, his hands clutching a bouquet of flowers. He had removed his hat and bowed his head, and then placed the flowers on a peak of sand. Tate said he did this daily.

A clump of dunes near the seawall bore a familiarity the others lacked. Fearing another letdown, I entered the remaining congregation with but a smidgen of hope. Wind blew through the dunes on warm rushes as I plowed my toes through a hundred more piles of grit. Having become more deeply discouraged, I aimed my feet toward Granny's house. 'Twas then my foot nudged a stone or possibly a shell. I thought to kick it from sight, but stopped and inspected it instead. The tip of a broken twig—just a speck of brown in an ocean of gray sand—stood upright in the ground. I dropped to my knees and dug with passion, my hand grazing a tin that rested twice as deeply as it did the day I planted it.

I pried the can from its burrow and wrestled with the lid, my gaze spying the note exactly where I placed it five years earlier. Though I had memorized every word, I read and reread the missive, feeling disappointment, frustration, and relief—all in the same moment. *So—Tate didn't have a way to contact me, after all.*

How, then, would I ever find *him?* I whispered the question over and over, but no one heard me save a complaining seagull on a nearby clump of grass. While the bird trooped his territory like a sentry on guard duty, I lay my head in my hands and cried at the sad ending to my love story. *I don't know how to find him, Father. I don't even know if you want me to find him.*

Time sauntered by and dusk now whispered over the narrow brim of day, telling me it was time to leave this place. But my hollow heart wouldn't depart until I had appeased its hunger for answers. And so I fed it the only food I had: the vacant, barren years that lay before me, and the dreams I'd only just begun to believe in again. I could think of nothing else to stuff into its yawning, empty mouth.

The true answer came as I walked the path to Granny's house. It traveled first to my heart, calming its hectic beat. Then it settled in my mind like a roosting hen, calling a halt to all my fretting. 'Twas the greatest pleasure of all when it plugged into my soul like a finger in the dike, stopping my flow of fear and disappointment. The answer brought peace and deep assurance with it, for I now believed that if Tate and I ever found each other again, it would be at the doing of my heavenly Father.

Granny poured herself a cup of breakfast coffee and a cup of tea for me. The winds slumbered quietly now and sunshine warmed the kitchen, cozying up an intimate warren in which to breed our morning chitchat.

Granny had visited Coldwater twice in the last five years. I thought her more lovely every time I saw her. Her hair was snow white now, the color of rainless clouds on a summer day. She was still a mountain of a woman. Perhaps an old mountain that stooped a bit near the crest. A mountain that had added girth with the seasons, explaining the reason Granny's knees crackled and popped like the bark of a thawing cottonwood whenever she eased herself from a chair.

"Do you recall my friend Tate?" I asked her. "You never met him, but right before Elo came to fetch me home, you told me to invite him over for Sunday dinner. Remember?" I nibbled on a flaky biscuit, though I had already gorged myself to puffiness on eggs, bacon, grits, and country-fried potatoes.

Granny cupped her chin and tapped her nose with her pointer finger.

She appeared stumped for a moment, but then the puzzle pieces fell into place and she smiled, her memory proving true once again.

"Yes'm, I do. He was to come for Sunday dinner but you and Elo had to go home. Ye never did get to offer that invite, did ye?"

"No—and I never heard from him again. Not after the day he and I went to Kempner Park. I really liked him. Wish we could have exchanged addresses, or at least told each other our last names." I could hear Granny's thoughts as though she spoke them aloud: *If wishes were horses ...*

"'Tis a pity, Emma Grace. Perhaps it just wasn't meant to be." Granny blew into her cup and sipped gingerly on her coffee. "What did yer young man look like, sweet-pie?"

My face must have lit up. I felt warmth spread across my cheeks, down my neck. Granny noticed as well, her eyes widening behind her thick spectacles and a sly smile smoothing wrinkles from her puckered lips. But, for once, she let the moment pass without uttering a single naughty word.

"He's real tall—like Elo. And his hair is blacker than midnight. Tate's probably the most handsome boy I've ever met."

"What about Gavin? Didn't I hear ye say the same thing 'bout him?"

"Granny ...!" My voice warned her not to speak of the man I hoped to forget. "Yes ... he was handsome too. I've sort of come to believe that it's my right to be surrounded by attractive men, what with Elo and Nathan ... and Papa."

Granny chortled and leaned her head back, resting it against the spindle-backed chair. She closed her eyes, as though investing a little time in her memories. "Emma Grace—for some honey-sweet reason I've never rightly understood, the men in our family are just too blasted good-looking for their own good. No two ways 'bout it. Don't seem fair that our family got so much beauty, when other families have to go without." Granny lowered her head and peered through slatted lids, waiting for me to either chastise her or compliment her flair for bragging.

She got the laugh she was looking for. I giggled at her boasting, knowing she spoke more truth than exaggeration.

"Ye know, your description brings to mind a *good-looking fella* that happen't along, oh, I don't know, maybe three or four years back. A good bit after you and Elo left for Coldwater. He was tall, dark, and handsome,

as they say. Anyways—he was asking after a family by the name of …
umm … Grace. Yep, that was the name. Said he'd been walking the neigh-
borhoods, asking if anyone knew them. Told him I'd lived in Galveston
for near fifty years, and I'd never heard of a family by that name. Told him
he was sure enough welcome to come inside and have a cup of coffee with
me, if he'd like." Granny turned a naughty grin upon me and winked with
wickedness. "He was mighty handsome, Emma Grace. Too bad ye weren't
around to get a peek at him."

"Granny … that had to be Tate! Don't you see? I never told him my
last name. He thought it was Grace. Oh—I can't believe it. He did come
looking for me, after all. Did he ever come back? Have you seen him again
… anywhere?"

"Whoa … slow down, child." Granny shook her head. "No, I'm
sorry, I never saw him but that one time. It never occurred to me that he
was yer young fella, sweet-pie. I surely would've told you straight out if
I'd known this guy was yer Tate. Fact is, I don't even recall him telling me
his name."

*Tate had come looking for me!* As I rocked on the verge of tears and
laughter, I struggled for calm so I could grill Granny for more information.

"'Twasn't a man, exactly … but near enough. Don't recall word for
word what he said, just that he'd been looking for the Grace family a
long time. Ye see … he was a hollering up from the street, and I was
yelling back to him from the porch, so we never got introduced proper-
like. I do remember him saying that he'd searched the county registers
and all the phone directories in the area, but hadn't found the folks he
was looking fer."

I nodded my head, too excited to carry on intelligible conversation.
After exhausting Granny's recollections, I stole away to be with my
thoughts. My warm, happy thoughts that chased each other by the tail as
I hurried to my bedroom.

*But … he came looking for me years ago. No telling where he is now—
or who he's with.* I wanted to clap a hand over my errant thoughts and tell
them to be quiet. Later—I would think about Tate and with whom he
might be sharing his time. But right now, all I wanted rolling around my
head was the precious news that Tate had come looking for me. He hadn't
forgotten me, after all.

# Thirty-eight

As the train rolled to a screeching halt, it hissed between the wheels and spit clouds of steam onto the tracks. Gray smoke panted out the tall smokestack and would have rained soot and smut upon all who milled about the station but for a breeze that whisked it to the heights. I wished the winds would stretch down and kidnap that strong stench of creosote that had harassed my nose all afternoon. While the armor-plated locomotive huffed and puffed like an irritated dragon, I returned my gaze to the long walkabout.

I'd spent the afternoon frisking the station with my eyes, foraging for a glimpse of my new friend. Did his tardiness mean he'd returned to school? Or was he sick? I removed my basket from the bench and set it on the concrete walkway, making room for other visitors who might want a seat. I had occupied this wooden pew for hours.

I spied him at last, meandering down the sidewalk, dragging his empty wagon and looking as healthy and fit as a youngster had the right to be. He stopped and tilted his head, studying passengers with what seemed a speculative eye. He cast his gleam upon a hearty fellow in fashionable suit and tie, carrying one small overnighter. Nobie sidled up and tugged the man's coat sleeve. Did he think this fine specimen of manliness needed his assistance? The man gave him a brief glance before waving him away. Though Nobie appeared unperturbed, my heart sank. He looked around, spying a frail, elderly lady who presented an aura of class. Nobie doffed his cap and bowed, as he had to me a week earlier. She shook her head with vehemence at whatever he said, then withdrew a handkerchief from her reticule and covered her nose. No doubt, to ward off the smoke—and Nobie's distinctive aroma.

I had had enough. I marched up to Nobie, positioning myself so the scornful-looking woman could hear every word.

"There you are, kind sir. I've awaited your arrival for hours." My napkin-covered basket rode my hip as I curtsied to Nobie and snatched a peek at the woman. She had perched spectacles atop her nose, and now peered at us with sharpness. Was her mouth-droop a permanent affliction, I wondered, or caused by our unsavory presence? As I stared her down, she retreated in a glare of snobbishness, which I found exceptionally predictable.

"You needin' my business again so soon?" Nobie screwed up his face, a habit that I now understood spoke both the language of favor and displeasure. 'Twas difficult to distinguish between the two.

"Nope. Not today, Nobie." As we set off in the direction of his house, which was located a few blocks from the station, I felt a twinge of concern about visiting his mother, uninvited.

"Ma won't take badly to you, Miss Emma Grace. She likes visiting with people. She can talk up a storm."

"I want your ma to know that this basket is an appreciation gift—not charity."

"Whadda' ya mean—appreciation?" Nobie stopped the wagon and stared at the basket. "Appreciation for what?" He stuffed his hands in his pockets and squished his face into a scowl.

"For carrying my luggage—and … for … for being my friend. I don't have any friends in Galveston, you know." I turned my gaze from him and his all-seeing eyes. Tall buildings surrounded us: The Ice and Cold Storage Building, catty-corner from our spot on Strand Street. And the McDonough Ironworks Building, directly across the street. I gazed at the tall brick structure, so unlike the frame buildings in Coldwater, of which not one was over two stories high. I noticed movement behind a smoked-over window on the second floor of the

ironworks building. A man stared at Nobie and me. I had to admit—
we did look the odd couple. I returned his stare as though I could see
his face.

We continued up the street, Nobie by my side as we rounded the
corner and stepped onto Avenue C. There, the street bore no pavement,
just dustiness and rows of small dwellings along either side. I spent the
next minutes praying I wouldn't cause Mrs. Percher's pride even a pinch
of pain.

"That's my house." Nobie pointed to a small, weathered house that
some might call a shanty. I smiled broadly, for the house stood straight
on its foundation, and in no way resembled the dilapidated hovel of my
imagination. Colorful autumn chrysanthemums bordered the house on
either side of the stoop. Throughout the sparse yard, I spied not a speck
of litter.

Nobie barged through the front door, but I hung back, hesitant
about my reception. He disappeared for a moment, reappearing with
his hand in motion, signaling me to come inside the house. Quite a surprise awaited me there.

I stepped through the door and stood beside Nobie while he untied
his footwear and dumped them onto a pallet of newspapers. I glanced
around, expecting the worst, but seeing an orderly, well-kept home. A
woman held out her arms in welcome, and waddled toward me. 'Twas
the best she could do, for a youngster had wrapped himself around one
of her legs and seemed oh so disinclined to let go of her.

"I'm Sadie Percher, and these are my children. We're honored that
you've come calling on us." She swept her arm in a graceful half-circle,
indicating two babies, a reed-thin lad of about twelve, and a beautiful
girl, perhaps seven or eight years old. Sadie scooped the clinging child
into her arms. "And this is Frank. He's three—soon to be four." Frank
lowered his head, burrowing it into the hollow of Sadie's shoulder. The
other children stood like statues, wide, unblinking eyes staring as
though I were Santa Claus, himself. One would surmise I was the first
outsider ever to cross their threshold. "You must be Miss Emma Grace.
Nobie talks about you nonstop. I'm afraid he's quite taken with you."

I grinned at Nobie, who made a grunting noise and ducked his
head. Sadie Percher lowered Frank to the floor, and wrapped me in a
sturdy hug. My mind twirled in circles, for Nobie's appearance and the

house's appearance were as different from each other as lush forest and desert sand.

I smiled at each member of the Percher family. "I'm Emma Grace Falin—and Nobie is my newest friend. He helped me out when I first arrived in Galveston. I'm staying with my granny for a while—Granny Falin. She lives over on Winnie Street." I wondered if the little ones in my audience understood a single word of my hurried-up speech.

I knew in an instant that the towheaded babes were identical twins, which, of course, reminded me of Caleb and Micah. I yearned to cuddle them in my arms, but they stared at me with wary, uncomfortable eyes. I knew it might be some time before they allowed such familiarity as the kind I desired.

"Have a sit-down, Miss Falin." Sadie pointed to a wine-colored divan, old and wearing at the seams, but appearing freshly brushed. She wore her thick hair in a loose bun at the back of her neck. Her hair was auburn and reminded me of finely polished mahogany, with a few wiry strands of gray thrown into the midst. *Like icicles on the redwoods in Papa's nature book.* My imagination was at work again.

"Please—call me Emma Grace. Everyone does." I sat down, Nobie, the young girl, and the older boy joining me on the sofa. I couldn't have been happier.

The moon was coming up full over the rooftops when I departed the Percher home several hours later. At Sadie's insistence, I stayed for supper, which consisted mainly of food from my basket: canned peas, yams, Granny's oatmeal bread, sliced ham, potato soup, and apricot preserves for dessert.

I had learned much about the Percher family during my brief stay in their home. Intimate secrets I sealed in my heart: the near poverty in which they existed, saved only by Sadie's occasional day jobs as a cleaning lady, Nobie's contributions, which he took as seriously as an elder took his high position in the church, and the older boy's paper route. Now that the depression was beginning a decline, Sadie hoped to obtain more work. "But who watches the babies?" I had asked. "Why, Brenda Gayle, of course," Sadie had replied. "She's only eight, but she tends them as well as I do, and she's far more patient," Sadie had shared with a laugh. Her eyes shone with love when she spoke of Nobie, for he, of all her children, had taken upon himself the job of replacing her husband. He seemed to miss his pa more than the other children. Nevertheless, Nobie could be a real hard pebble in the shoe, she had confessed. He constantly ignored her strict code of orderliness and cleanliness, managing to scruff himself up, no matter the consequences. He also ditched school whenever the wind blew in a different direction. He preferred wearing his older brother's clothes, thinking they aged him, believing more customers would hire him and his portage carrier if he wore Thomas Henry's attire, and if he appeared a bit scuffed. Her Nobie was of a strong will, Sadie explained, and he had more determination than all her other children, combined. "In that way, he's most like his pa," she had beamed.

My steps were light as I hurried back to Granny's house in the near blackness of night. I couldn't wait to tell Granny about Sadie and the children. Together we would formulate a plan, discreet though it must be, of how to share our abundance with the Percher family.

# Thirty-nine

The ironworks building was three stories high, vacant of flooring, and so cavernous it echoed. Thick, hand-fashioned bricks constituted the walls, making it nearly fireproof. As Tate mounted the stairs to his cubbyhole, he glanced below at his hardworking men. The foreman's office—if an open-air stage could be called by that name—commenced where the stairs left off: a one-story platform that hugged the brick enclosure. Three sides were open to the great room, but hemmed in by railing like a horse corral. The floor of his workspace also served as a ceiling to the storage unit below. The building had no other floors, save a cement base at ground level that opened onto Strand Street. Five forges, strategically anchored to the concrete expanse below had smokestack horns growing out of their bellies: tin tubing that stretched to the ceiling and beyond, dispatching cindery smoke above the roofline.

For as long as Tate could remember, he'd loved creating designs and working with his hands. Now he exercised his talent daily, crafting iron and steel into fleurs-de-lis, rosettes, spears, collars, pickets, and vines. He also molded iron into candlesticks, gates, fences, sconces, balusters, railings, weather vanes, urns, baskets, window bars, and any other item the customer requested. The ability to craft designs from raw substances seeped from Tate's essence like life-fluid from a wound. Tate's creations had not gone unnoticed. Word of his skill had multiplied like the orders piled atop his desk.

When paperwork called him away from the forge and up the stairs to his office, he was seldom alone, for the water barrel and two windows also occupied his floor and wall space. Four fellow ironworkers and their apprentices traipsed the stairs with consistency, drawing drafts of cool air through the windows, and guzzling water down thirsty throats.

Tate's buddy Fritz Stouser, deliveryman at the icehouse across the street, had transported the second twenty-pound block of ice to the water barrel at midafternoon. The iceberg was now the size of a dime. And no wonder, Tate thought, with forges belching out firestorms from five o'clock in the morning until late afternoon; spitting flames hot enough to melt steel. Since melting steel was what ironworkers did— ten hours a day—six days a week—heat was a necessity they'd learned to live with.

Tate walked to the window and glanced at the street below, as was his habit when taking a breather. Opening on a slant, the window granted few inches of view, so Tate leaned his height over, resting his arms on the sill. A boy and young woman on the street corner came into sight, snagging his interest. Something about the woman yanked a knot in his breath. He narrowed his eyes, his feet shifting as he slammed the window shut and grabbed a bandana from his back pocket. He scrubbed at the scrim of smoke and smut on the window, and then peered through the clear circle of glass. His gaze latched onto the woman who had tipped her face and was looking at him. There, for all the world to see, stood a girl who looked so much like his Emma that it made him want to yell for her to stay put. He could be by her side in three seconds flat.

Tate raked his hair, his fingers shaking as he rolled his shoulders and pinched his eyes closed. He was losing it, he thought. Yes—the girl had dun-colored hair like Emma's. Yes—her pert features held the same beauty. But this girl didn't walk with a crutch, nor did she appear to have the unsure flightiness of Emma. They were look-alikes, nothing more. After giving himself a good talking-to, he turned from the window and walked to his desk. He'd gotten his hopes up too many times to allow late-day mirages to fluster him anew.

He jerked the ladle from a nail, filled it to sloshing over, and gulped water by the mouthfuls. The cottony dryness quit his throat, but the image of boy and woman would not leave so easily. He flung the ladle aside and hurried back to the window, staring through the porthole like a starving prisoner looking for food. As he scrubbed at the glass like a man gone berserk, he peered at the street corner below. Hair lifted on his nape like the scut of a startled deer, for the boy and woman were gone. Tate wagged his head, throwing glances up and down the street. The couple was nowhere in sight.

His hands shook as he rethreaded the ladle onto the nail. In the five years since Emma's disappearance, he'd spied many girls who resembled her, but none so much as the young lady today. He returned to the window a second time and gawked at the corner where he'd spied her and the youngster. Arguments raged inside his head as the long moments passed. *The girl didn't have a crutch … it couldn't be Emma. But the hair—no one has hair like Emma's.* Tate stood transfixed, eyes focused on the spot where one glimpse of the petite beauty had caused his heart to flop about like a beached redfish.

Tate remained at the window, though his coal-fired forge was set and primed to melt the hardest steel. He gazed at the street as though a pot of gold awaited him. What he searched for was far more valuable than gold. With reluctance, he turned and walked down the stairs, retracing his steps to the workbench. He'd probably never see the young woman again.

Tate tied and adjusted his headscarf, located his glove on the anvil where he'd tossed it earlier, and slipped it on his hand. Wedging a helmet on his head, he walked to the channel-iron table, selected an angled length of cold-rolled steel, and grasped it with tongs. Carrying the weight aloft and with ease, he dropped the viewfinder over his eyes and stepped up to the forge. He knew he had to work with unusual care today, the forge spitting tongues of flame that could lick fabric from the arms of an absentminded ironworker. But as he studied the fire, other flames came into view. Flames that had erupted the night he met Emma.

The fire had raged for a time, devouring all the driftwood, flotsam, and seaweed he'd scrounged from shore while the girl slept. He'd finally coaxed her to the flames, encouraged she would come so near. Then he'd talked himself blue, trying to engage her in conversation, but it had all been one-sided. Sometime during his ramblings, she'd slipped away … without a word.

He'd stomped live embers with his boots and buried them in the sandy depths. Then he'd kicked fresh grains over the black hole, covering the blister with a bandage of sand. He'd sat on the beach for hours, wondering why the youngster had tried to end her life. Wondering what would become of her. Would he read about her in the paper?

GIRL'S BODY FOUND IN PORT BOLIVAR BAY.

Days later, beach chatter had claimed his attention as he rested among the dunes. He'd spied her in the water, frolicking and tussling with a passel of children. That was the day he realized she wasn't a child, at all, but a young lady. Had he given her his heart that day? Or at a later time?

Weeks after that, he'd sat on the beach and asked God what to do about the needy girl he'd come to love. He'd sat for hours, viewing the nightly changing of the guards: brightly-studded star warriors replacing weary sunbeam soldiers. Ancient constellations had risen up in twinkling star-shine, but still no answer had come from their Creator. He'd wondered when his feelings had taken a detour. Was it the day he placed his hand on Emma's shoulder and peered into her eyes, viewing not an adolescent girl with wounded heart, but the beautiful woman she would become? She'd reminded him of the priceless conch he'd found on the beach. After taking it home, he'd cleaned and polished it and placed it on his bookshelf: a treasure to admire and protect forever.

All the confusion in his heart had been God's fault. He'd pleaded with him for answers. "Didn't you know I'd come to love the girl you sent me to save? Come on, Lord … I need some help here." He'd closed his eyes, waiting for the still, small voice to speak. He'd been listening to that voice for almost five years. But the night stumbled along in silence.

Sometime later, he'd looked to the heavens again, and smiled, the scales peeled from his eyes. Emma was his—a gift to love and cherish forever. He was terribly happy, but bewildered still. She was only thirteen years old. His own manliness—along with all its rampaging, heart-thumping desires—had grown like thistles in a valley. How would he wait until Emma grew to maturity? His willpower wasn't that strong. Perhaps it would have been better to remain blind to the truth. Life would be a lot more tolerable. Even so—he'd bowed his head in gratefulness, his heart at rest. He would trust God to work it all out. "Thank you, Lord. I know you won't let me down."

Tate's gaze fused on the fire. "But you did let me down, Lord. You let me believe that Emma would come to love me—that she'd be mine someday, but she left without a word, and my heart hasn't been the same since."

Tate cleaned and sorted his tools, hanging tongs on hammered hooks, scraping the fabrication table clean, and sweeping around the forge and anvil. He laid the collection of hammers in their individual compartments, hung his leather apron over the hook, and placed the marking pencils and soapstone in a drawer.

He considered staying at the factory all night, working until dawn. He preferred a night in the old brick building to spending an evening in the Caldwells' stuffy, overdone mansion. Besides, he wouldn't be good company tonight, not with these heart-pinching pictures of Emma roaming around his head. He wished he could phone Miriam and call off the dinner engagement with her parents. Anyway—the whole arrangement seemed too intimate for Tate's peace of mind; too presumptuous on his plans for the future. A tight knot squeezed his chest, constricting and breath-draining. Miriam and her mother may have made wedding plans, but he hadn't. Sometimes Miriam pushed him too far. She was like a headstrong horse, determined to run ahead of the team, no matter who controlled the bit and bridle.

The only thing he wished for this night, other than seeing Emma again, was a long stroll on the beach. And to sit on their dune. It seemed the only fitting place for him to think back in time; back to the happiest two months of his life.

Tate went to the back room, converted now into a changing room complete with toilet, sink, and shower. After a shave and shower, Tate stepped into pressed trousers and slipped his arms into a freshly ironed shirt. He tucked in the shirttail and buttoned the high shirt collar. He twisted his neck, loosening the tightness that suddenly felt like a hangman's noose. He gathered his pocket change, knife, and wallet from the shelf and stuffed them in his pants pocket. As he lifted the heart-shaped locket he'd been carrying for five years, he studied it with care. He didn't know if it was Emma's, or not. He'd found it in the sand sometime after she disappeared. His heart told him it belonged to the girl he loved. He'd never stopped hoping that one day he would slip it around her beautiful neck. For that reason—he never let the necklace out of his sight.

When he glanced in the tarnished mirror, he viewed spiked hair, pitch-black and glistening with water. He ran a hand through its thickness, not caring if it lay flat or stood out like porcupine quills.

"Tate? Where are you, darling?"

Tate cringed, Miriam's falsetto voice grating on his nerves like an osprey screeching in the wind. Why was she at the factory? He had explained he would meet her at her parents' house at seven o'clock. Had she come to make sure he didn't back out? He felt like a child whose mother came to fetch him home from school. Leave it to Miriam to change their plans to suit her own needs. She might be Galveston's most beautiful debutante, but her smothering ardor made him want to hop a freighter to the Orient.

"Be right out." Tate sat on a stool, pondering his predicament. Why couldn't he respond to Miriam as he had to the beauty of his youth? The girl with seventeen freckles sprinkled across her face? Perhaps it would be best for everyone if he stopped thinking about Emma altogether and accepted Miriam's all-but-spoken-aloud marriage proposal. But how could he? He'd given his heart two long years to fall in love with the dark-haired girl whose beauty was legendary. It hadn't happened. He doubted it ever would. Perhaps he'd never find the right woman. Maybe he was one of those fellows who could give his heart away only once in a lifetime.

Tate raised his head toward the ceiling. *What do you say, Lord? Do you plan for me to remain a bachelor all my life … like old Paul in the Bible suggested we do? Since you've not seen fit to bring Emma back into my life, you must think I should die an old man—without ever knowing the love of a woman. Or the joy of holding a child of my own making. Well, you know what? I'm not like old Paul. I need a woman's love, and a passel of kids to go along with it. What are you trying to tell me, Lord? That you want Miriam to be the mother of my children?*

Tate peered through the window—again. He'd frequented the loft with such regularity, his workers now made daily wages on how many times he'd visit the water bucket in a day.

"Hey, Tate—you been eatin' them red chili peppers again?" Smokey looked at his apprentice and winked. "Or have you got some hot mama getting you all steamed up?"

The men howled like a pack of deranged hyenas, Tate being an easy mark to tease. He couldn't blame them. As for his emotions, they were as riotous as bells on a horse collar. Tate felt as though he were swimming against the tide. Every time he picked up a hammer, or tried to design a pattern, his mind turned to mush. It was hard to focus with a putty-soft brain. Or when your thoughts were adrift like a lifeboat in a raging sea.

Tate ignored Smokey's gibes, knowing he deserved every pestering bit of torment the crew shoveled his way. He couldn't get the woman and boy off his mind; couldn't concentrate on his work, or the men who called him boss; couldn't remember what he ate for lunch, or if he'd made plans for the evening. He dangled, it seemed, somewhere between Miriam's skilled flirtatiousness and the shy Emma, whose face had flamed when she spied the warmth in his eyes that he couldn't hide.

In late afternoon, Tate ambled to the window, perhaps for the twentieth time that day. He no longer expected the vision in his head to reappear on the street below. He had wasted too many hours, too many days, hoping for something that would never happen. He walked to the window because he had nowhere else to go, nothing better to do. His men had left for the day, and he'd broken his date with Miriam. The house Mrs. K bequeathed him at her death a year earlier was too empty without her in it: too cold and shadowed for Tate's comfort. Most nights, he slept on the back-room cot and avoided the lonely house altogether. He missed Mrs. K more than he'd thought possible.

Tate's gaze fell on the street. He watched as it filled with an influx of trucks, cars, horse-driven wagons, and pedestrians. Workers going home; businessmen calling it quits for the day. From his second-story view, his gaze roved over the busiest street in Galveston: Strand Street, and the side street adjacent to it. The dwindling image of a small boy and wagon captured Tate's attention. He stood immobile, unable to react as he watched the wagon's back wheels turn the corner and disappear. He blinked his eyes, questioning if he had imagined the scene, or if it was real. It had to be real, for the boy looked exactly like the lad he'd spied a few weeks earlier.

By the time Tate had ripped the leather apron from his neck and cleared the building, dusk had fallen over Galveston. Incandescent light beamed from Strand's streetlights, revealing fewer vehicles and pedestrians on the red-tinged cobblestones. He rushed up Twenty-Fourth Street and onto Avenue C, his eyes adjusting to twilight as he searched for signs of the boy and his wagon. The street was vacant, deserted of people and cars. By the looks of the houses, it seemed that the residents on this street would probably never know the luxury of owning an automobile.

He turned and walked back to the factory, his heart lighter than it had been in days. He would spend every spare moment—from daylight to dusk, if necessary—looking for the boy with the wagon. The quiet desperation of searching for someone was nothing new to Tate. He'd been through it before: when Emma vanished without a word of goodbye or a thought as to what her disappearance would cost him. If he had to, he would begin his search all over again.

# Forty

Nobie's day had been anything but good. His teacher sat him in the corner; even put that stupid dunce cap on his head, just because he had filled his slate with drawings of soldiers instead of arithmetic problems. Nobie hated ciphering more than he hated most anything else. During recess, the oldest O'Grady kid had called him a snot-nosed ba ... that word Ma said he'd better never say unless he was itching for a whupping. Nobie had plowed his head into Tim O'Grady's breadbasket, even though he was half the bully's size. He grinned, remembering how the kids had cheered him on. Only trouble was, all the noise had rallied ol' Mr. Harper to the playground, and Nobie had ended up with a sore bottom after all.

After school, Nobie trudged home, harboring no intentions of telling his ma about his day at school. She'd hear about it soon enough from that ugly old baldheaded principal who liked to carry his paddle everywhere he went. Nobie sneaked behind the house, collected his wagon, and headed for the train station.

Traffic at the station was pitiful today. Nobie glanced around, looking for a paying customer amongst the meager pickings. He sidled up to a man and woman. Gushers he called them, because of the lovey-dovey look in their eyes and the way they gushed all over each other.

They couldn't keep their hands to themselves. If he hadn't needed the money so much, he would have beaten a wide path around their mushy goings-on.

"Hey, mister. Need some help with them bags? I'll tote 'em for you for just a ni ... a dime."

The man glanced down at Nobie. "Beat it, kid. I believe I'm strong enough to carry our luggage. What'da'ya think, sugar? Think I'll have any trouble handling our suitcases?" He smiled and winked at the woman, who held onto his arm like little Frank clung onto Ma's skirt.

The woman had a silly, sappy look on her face as she snuggled close to the man, giggling and pressing her fingers against his arms. "Oh, baby, I think these arms could carry just about any ol' thing they wanted to." She giggled again, which made Nobie want to run to the bushes for a good puke.

He ambled down the walk, hating weekdays, not just because of school, but also because they were slack days at the station. Rare was the weekday he found more than a handful of passengers departing the train. Weekends were best, though Ma wouldn't allow him to hustle up business on the good Lord's day.

Nobie sat in his wagon, waiting for a customer to happen by. His eyes widened at the sight of a giant fellow, walking straight at him. Nobie pondered hard. Had he broken some law about pestering passengers, some law he'd never heard of? He kept his gaze on the sidewalk as two huge feet planted themselves in front of him. He raised his head, his gaze traveling up a mountainous length of man. At first, the man's face appeared stern, but then relaxed into a smile. At least Nobie thought it was a smile. His mouth went up a ways, and his cheeks had dents in them, so he guessed it was a smile. Now—the man looked more worried than angry. He squatted on his haunches and placed his broad hands atop Nobie's shoulders, forcing him to look in his eyes.

"I'm wondering if you could help me, son."

*Son? I ain't your son, you no-count mister. My pa's a lot tougher'n you. He could take you out in no time. Whup ya so hard you'd never walk straight again ...*

"I'm looking for someone ... a young lady. I believe I saw you with her a few weeks back. The two of you were at the corner of Strand and

Twenty-Fourth, down by the ironworks factory. Do you know the lady I'm talking about? She has long brown hair, with these … gold streaks … sort of like there's sunshine running through her hair. Know what I mean?"

"What's the matter, did something go missing? I ain't no thief, mister, if that's what you're accusing me of."

"No—no, nothing like that. You're not in any kind of trouble, son. I just need to find the woman you were with that day. I've been looking for the two of you for some time now."

"I ain't your son, mister, and I'd 'preciate it if you don't call me that." Nobie studied the man's eyes. It appeared he spoke the truth, but a fella couldn't be too careful these days. If someone was out to hurt Miss Emma Grace, they'd have to go through him to do it. "I don't know what you're talking about, mister. I ain't been around no women, and sure enough not on Strand Street. Your eyes must've gone wacky on you or somethin'. I gotta get back to work." Nobie tried to get up, but the big hands held him fast to the wagon seat.

"Look, maybe I'm going about this all wrong. I mean the lady no harm. I think I might have known her—years back. I'm just trying to find an old friend."

"I told you I don't know who you're talking about." Nobie jerked himself from the wagon and took off at breakneck speed. He heard the man, close behind.

"If you see Emma, tell her Tate is looking for her. Did you hear me, son? Tell her Tate wants to talk to her." The man's voice was further away now.

Nobie stopped and turned to him. "How'd you know where to find me, mister?" he called out.

The man's face took on a whopper grin. "I pondered it long and hard, young fella. Tried to think of why you toted that wagon around the way you do. Then I remembered—the train station. You see, I used to work the station too—when I was about your age. Rounded up every penny I could, carrying folks' luggage home, and showing them around Galveston. I took a wild guess and decided that an enterprising youngster, such as you, might find work here too."

Nobie shuffled down the sidewalk. He thought his head might blow off from all the anger that boiled inside it. If that Tate man thought he was going to tell Miss Emma Grace about their conversation, he was dumber than he looked. *I ain't never gonna tell her about you ... mister. She's ours now—not yours. Even if you're a po-leece man, I'm never gonna tell her.*

# Forty-one

I snuggled in a chair at Sadie's table, drinking a cup of tea and enjoying the quiet. I'd prepared a pot of stew earlier. It simmered now on the two-burner hotplate Sadie called a stove. She had no workable oven, nor money to get hers repaired. I felt good about my day's work, knowing that I'd helped make life a little easier for Sadie and the children. Her wash hung on the line. The babies and I had scoured it to death at midmorning, the three of us getting a good soaking beneath the sun's cordial rays.

I had volunteered to stay with Sadie's children for the day, as she had found work cleaning a mansion at the corner of Rosenberg and Broadway. She wrote the address on a bit of paper and tucked it into my apron pocket before departing in early morn, Frank riding her hip like a pony. 'Twas good to greet the children home from school this afternoon, albeit Nobie wasn't in their midst. And though it felt good to help a friend, 'twas I who reaped the gain, for I'd spent the entire day with Hannah and Rosalie, in a wonderland just south of paradise. The babies had let me hold them, and had, in fact, spent a good part of the day climbing up and over me as though I were a heavily branched tree.

Thomas Henry left around three-thirty to join a companion in delivering the evening newspaper. Hannah and Rosalie slept on a pallet, lips puckered and cheeks flushed to coral, like the labyrinth coils of a seashell. Brenda Gayle had quilt-swaddled herself into a ball on the divan, and now read the tattered remains of an old comic book. I made a mental note to bring some of my books over for the children to read and to buy some new comic books for them as well.

The front door burst open and Nobie sprinted into the kitchen, looking a bit shaken and more than a tad angry.

"Are you in trouble, Miss Emma Grace? Did'ya break the law?" Nobie's chest heaved in and out like a hand accordion, his eyes wild and fierce. I wrapped him in my arms, trying to calm him as he sucked in air and spewed more questions. "You got the po-leece looking for ya? Whad'ya do?"

'Twas then I caught onto Nobie's scheme. He was baiting me for some unknown reason, playing out a child's game I didn't yet grasp. I had fallen for such acts before when my brothers cast a lure that I quickly snagged onto. But after I'd nibbled on it a while, they yanked me out of the water like a striped bass. So, I followed along with Nobie's gag—like a pen swan treading the wake of her cob. I hoped to one-up him—eventually. You had to stay on your toes around Nobie Percher.

"Well—I did hold up that filling station a few days back—the one down on Market Street." I bit my lips, cracking not a smile as Nobie's eyes swelled to harvest moons. "But the owner said I had such a nice smile that he wasn't going to call the cops. Told me to come in any time, borrow whatever I needed from the cash register. He even invited me over for supper, said he wanted the little missus to meet me." I grinned at last, thinking Nobie would get a hoot out of my perjurious jabbering.

His face startled, his shoulders slumping as he edged from my presence. I drew in a breath, flabbergasted by his troubled countenance. What was wrong with Nobie? I had expected a sharp-witted retort, his capable mind having flung more than one comeuppance in my face since first we met. Surely the little squirt didn't believe my confession. He was out the door before I could relay the truth. Before I could assuage any hurt rendered by my foolishness.

Brenda Gayle jumped from the sofa and joined me at the table.

"Did you really ... really rob a filling station?" She looked as fearful as Nobie's fake ... No—the look on Nobie's face wasn't one of pretense. He truly believed I'd committed a felony. He thought me a common criminal, just as Brenda Gayle did. My vision clouded as I recoiled from the pain I saw in the little girl's eyes. She had thought of me as a friend. Now she looked at me as though I were a stranger—someone she couldn't trust. How little the children knew me.

"Darling, I was just teasing with Nobie," I said as I tugged Brenda Gayle's reluctant body onto my lap. "I realize now that he believed my tall tale, didn't he? I'm not a thief. Never stolen a thing in my life that I recall. When I find a penny on the street, I look around to see who dropped it so I can give it back to them." I squeezed Brenda Gayle with reassurance, crooning as I rocked her in my arms. I hoped she would absorb the love I felt for her and all of Sadie's children.

When Sadie returned in late afternoon, with Frank asleep on her shoulder, I told her about the misunderstanding.

"It's not like Nobie to show fear—not for himself or anyone else. He'd rather eat a live bullfrog than have someone think he was afraid." Sadie shook her head as she laid Frank on the pallet and sank into a chair. I poured her a cup of tea, and together we brooded over Nobie.

"I'm not going home until I set things right between us—and find out who gave him such a fright." I worried with my hair while fear curled around my heart. Sorry I was that I'd made Sadie's eyes fill with tears.

"Yes—yes ... We'd love to have you stay the night. He'll come home 'fore long and then we'll hash it all out." We sat together, forgetting our hunger; forgetting the stew, our eyes trained on the door.

The babies and Frank roused from sleep, and Thomas Henry's lankiness ambled through the rear door a short span later. We ate the stew and chatted with the children. It seemed that hours passed while we waited for Nobie's breathlessness to barge through the front door.

'Twas past twilight when he stepped over the threshold, his eyes finding mine at once. He looked at me with surprise, and perhaps a bit of dismay.

"Come here, Nobie." He shuffled to Sadie's side, his head a-droop and his eyes averted from my felonious self. "Miss Emma Grace has something to say to you. Want you to hear her out with both ears wide open."

I reached for Nobie, knowing he was a spooked horse that needed a gentle hand. My heart cantered about as he ambled to me on sluggish feet. I expected him to wince when first my arm wrapped his shoulder, but he settled against me without complaint, his warmth a satisfying compress on my wounded nerves.

"Sweetheart, I made that up about robbing the filling station. I thought we were playing a game. You came in here all excited about the police being after me, so I went along, saying silly things I knew you'd never believe. But you did believe them, didn't you, Nobie?" I peered into his gray-cloud eyes, spying a swirl of conflicting emotions.

"But there *is* a man looking for you, Miss Emma Grace. He didn't wear no police clothes, but he couldn't fool me. He was a cop, all right—tall-up, like a building, with mean-looking eyes and huge feet … big as my pa's."

My first thought was that Elo had come to fetch me home … again. My heart raced, for when Elo came looking for me, trouble always waited at the other end.

"Did he have blond hair and blue eyes, and—?"

"No way. This fella's hair was blacker'n a skunk's tail, and his eyes were real, real dark … and mean as the Devil's."

I squeezed Nobie's arms and planted my face close enough to count his eyelashes. Despite the confusion I saw in his eyes, I grilled on, for my heart had already jumped the corral and was now galloping out of control.

"Did the man tell you his name, Nobie? This is extremely important. Try to remember his name." I relaxed my grip and lowered my voice, knowing Nobie couldn't think straight if I screamed at him like a banshee. His gaze roved upward, his brain searching for a name on the ceiling, it seemed.

"Yeah, I think he said to tell you that Nate was looking for you. Think it was Nate."

"Sweetie—I used to know a boy … a tall, dark-haired boy named Tate. Could the man have said Tate?"

"Yeah—that was it. Said to tell the young lady that Tate was look-ing for her." Nobie grinned and puffed himself up a bit. "But I didn't tell him a thing, Miss Emma Grace. Not one thing about you. I'll pro-tect you from him—I promise."

I hugged Nobie and kissed his cheek, his hand wiping it away more quickly than I had planted it. Though his words of protection pleased the heck out of me, he had no way of knowing that my greatest pleas-ure sprang from the knowledge that Tate was looking for me. How did he know I was back in Galveston? I wondered. Why did he connect Nobie with me? My head whirled in bewildered bliss, a thousand ques-tions scrambling for answers while my heart harvested the bounty in Nobie's words.

"Where did you see him, Nobie? Were you at the train station?"

"Yep—but business was mighty poor today. Didn't hire on to one cust'mer all afternoon." He shuffled his foot and looked at the floor. I had the notion that Nobie felt he had let me down because he hadn't found work today.

"There's always tomorrow, Nobie. Bet a hundred people will be begging you to cart their luggage home tomorrow." His reaction to my whopper was the biggest smile I'd ever seen on his gap-toothed mouth.

I dug in my purse, retrieving pencil and paper. My heart twitched like bunny whiskers as I scribbled words on the page, folded the note, and handed it to Nobie. "When the man asks after me again—the *next* time you see him—give him this note. Please, Nobie. It's very impor-tant. Tate is a good man, understand?" I searched his eyes; eyes that shielded an emotion I couldn't comprehend. "What wrong, Nobie? What is it?"

He shrugged and kept his gaze fastened on the floor. "What if that ugly old man wants to take you away from us? Then we won't never see you again."

Nobie's eyes wouldn't meet mine, though I tried to force them to. I knelt on the floor, tilted his head with my fingers, and waited until his gaze touched mine. His eyes held a sad, troubled look.

"Don't you know that I will never let that happen, sweetie? I love you and the babies ... all of you ... so much. Nothing can keep me away from you."

# Forty-two

With his nerves chafing together like new shoes on sore feet, Nobie steered away from the train station, and searched for work elsewhere. Though the station was where he most needed to be, he couldn't go near it because of that man Tate. So he and his wagon wandered further south, drumming up business on the inland streets south of Strand—after Nobie had scouted them for the dark, dangerous stranger of his nightmares.

But prospects were scarce. The drugstore man hired him to deliver medicine to a woman on Church Street, and he earned two more pennies by taking the same lady's dog for his poopy walk. But after three days of dragging his wagon around downtown Galveston, the collection in Nobie's pockets added up to a pauper's mite: four pennies and one nickel. And the ragged scrap of paper Miss Emma Grace had given him.

On the fourth day, with much reluctance in his heart, Nobie returned to the station. There wasn't much money in the tin can at home; barely enough coins to cover the bottom, and Ma hadn't had a cleaning job since the day Miss Emma Grace watched the babies for her.

Nobie stole into the train yard, keeping a close watch on the men who wandered about, looking for friends or family most likely. The tall man wasn't in sight. Nobie melted into a shaded, shadowed area on the ticket platform, and tucked his booted feet away from the sunlight. But his heart shot into his mouth every time he spied a pair of long legs. And every time he thought about that man Tate, it felt like vermin were crawling all over his skin.

The porter helped an elderly woman from the train. As he held her elbow, he glanced around the station, spying Nobie atop his wagon near the ticket office.

"Hey, Nobie. Can you give us a little help here? Mrs. Crendle needs you to carry her bag home." The porter, whom Nobie knew only as Mose, motioned to him with his long, uniformed arm. "You hear me now, son? Let's have a hurry with it."

Nobie carted Mrs. Crendle's case to her apartment on Twenty-Fourth Street. He liked the old lady, partly because she tipped good, but also because she never asked him a hatful of nosy questions. However, he could have made two deliveries in the time it took him to get her home, for she had the rheumatism real bad.

Nobie closed a tight fist around the silver quarter in his pocket. It was worth the risk, he figured. He and his wagon turned off Twenty-Fourth Street, onto Mechanic, just one block from Strand. He scuttled back to the station, hovering mostly in the shadows, reappearing only when a likely patron debarked. He waited a couple of hours, near-dark folding into dusk as passengers arrived and detrained. But nary a one needed his assistance.

"Hi, Nobie."

The deep voice behind him sounded too familiar. Nobie dug in his right toe, ready to make a dash for the woods, but a monstrous hand clasped his shoulder like a steel claw. He couldn't have moved if his pants were afire. He turned his head, heart a-thunder at the sight of the man called Tate.

"Been looking for you, son. You're a hard one to find."

The man smiled, friendly enough. Too friendly for Nobie's comfort. He squatted beside Nobie's wagon, his hand resting on the wagon handle as though he'd not let it fly away this time. Nobie felt trapped and frightened, like the baby monkey he'd seen in a cage at McRamey's Feed Store. Anger fired his heart. Somehow, he and his wagon would escape the giant's clutches.

"You have a good job, Nobie. Helping people the way you do. My hat's off to you."

"How do you know my name?" Nobie glared at the man, hating him for his hound-dogging ways, his nosiness, his easy smile, and his eyes that pretended to be kind. Hated him, too, for making Miss Emma Grace's heart beat like a baby bird's. He had felt it all aflutter when she hugged him to her chest and kissed his cheek a few days back. Most of all—he hated the man because the man thought Miss Emma Grace belonged to him. *You're dead wrong, mister. She belongs to us.*

"Did you tell Emma about me, son?" The man stared into the depths of Nobie's eyes, as though he could untangle a truth from a lie with just a look.

"I asked you how you knew my name." Nobie gritted his teeth, determined not to answer. He felt flames shoot across his face. Even worse, he felt the sting of tears behind his lids. But he wouldn't cry. No matter what the man did to him. One thing was for sure: He wouldn't let the ugly old man steal Miss Emma Grace away.

"I've known old Mose most of my life," the man said. "He told me your name. Remember—I told you I worked here when I was a lad? Had a job similar to yours, right here at the station. Only—sometimes I didn't earn my money quite so respectably as you do."

"I told you I don't know the lady you're talking about."

"I think you do. What did she say when you told her I was looking for her? You did tell her about me, didn't you?" The man held a steady gaze, which made Nobie squirm. He turned his eyes from the stranger, studying the train as though he'd later have to draw it from memory.

"Guess you could say I've been looking for Emma my whole life. I'll find her, you know—one way or the other. Just wish you'd tell me where she is. I really need to talk to her, Nobie. I won't insult you by offering you money. That's not the way friendship works. Please—just help me find her."

"I don't know any Emma." Nobie stood up, his hand itching to grab the handle that the man cupped with a big-knuckled fist. "And … another thing—I don't want you following me no more. Ain't there a law against following after kids?"

The man turned his sad-looking eyes away. He shook his head and pinched the bridge of his nose. "If Emma asked you to tell me where to find her, and you don't do it—well, I just don't think real friends treat each other that way."

It seemed to Nobie that the man stood there for an hour or more. Finally, he turned and walked from the station.

As Nobie struck out for home, he jammed his hand into his pants pocket, fingering Miss Emma Grace's note. He walked west on Strand, following a roundabout route, trudging home in the opposite direction of the man. But as he walked, his legs waxed heavy and his feet bogged down, as though he waded through a river of thick molasses. The man's words tugged on Nobie's conscience; stinging his eyes, hacking at his heart with a dull knife. He felt ashamed. What would Miss Emma Grace think if she knew he had not done the one thing she asked him to do? *I don't think real friends treat each other that way.* Nobie walked on, but the going was slow and worrisome.

He halted at the corner and plopped down in his wagon. His heart hurt, for he'd let Miss Emma Grace down. He didn't like letting his friend down. As he sat with his elbows on his knees and his head in his hands, he pondered the lie he'd have to come up with when she asked him about the man and the note. Nobie didn't know if he could tell Miss Emma Grace a lie.

Nobie jerked the wagon about-face and sped down the blocks that led to Strand Street. He ran all the way to the ironworks building. He stopped and looked around. The man was nowhere in sight. Nobie spied the front door, and a side door. He calculated that the front door was locked for the night. He dropped the wagon handle and sprinted to the side door. It was closed, but not locked.

He entered the narrow hallway and flew through the dark interior as though goblins were after him. As he called out the man's name, it echoed back to him from the narrow passageway.

"Mr. Tate! Mr. Tate!" Nobie slowed his gait and looked hard at the end of the hallway. When the man suddenly bolted through a side door and almost slammed himself into the wall, Nobie jumped so high he thought he'd left his skin behind on the floor. A truckload of grin spread across the man's face. Nobie could see his white teeth all the way from where he stood. He supposed it was a nice-enough looking face, after all.

"I got this note to give you—from Miss Emma Grace. She said to be sure you got it."

# Forty-three

Even with the wind blowing from the south, the breeze carried a snitch of autumn in it. I snuggled deeper into Granny's porch rocker and tucked the blanket beneath my legs. The road was vacant and quiet. Not one long-legged, dark-haired man strode its dustiness, looking for a girl he once knew. I thought I would surely spy Tate on the street this day, waving to me from a distance, his legs awhirl as he bounded up the steps and into my embrace. But Nobie's hand had received my note four days earlier, and still Tate hadn't come calling.

The sun swagged low in the sky, neighbors' rooftops blocking all but an upper rim of the amber fireball. 'Twas the time of day when the sun relinquished its right to rule over our part of the world. The wind brought the subtle scents of surf and tide with it, and all things coupled to the sea. I believed that ocean scent was the fragrance of life, for in what other depths did such a bounty of creation exist and thrive—from eons past until today?

As twilight hastened to nightfall, I maintained my vigil, though the view grew blurry and dim.

I had used up four days walking these planks, morning till night, save for snatched moments of eating and tending to life's necessities. I felt as though I had joined forces with women of old: gentle ladies who had stretched their gazes beyond unplowed fields, looking for husbands not yet returned from war; seamen's wives who had climbed the widow's walk, searching for ships lost at sea.

"Come in, child. 'Tis too late for yer young man to come calling tonight. He'd be in a terrible fix to find an address on this dark street. Maybe he'll show up tomorrow."

I glanced at the doorway, Granny's white hair poking a halo into the night's dimness. I didn't have to see her faded eyes to know that empathy crowded all other emotion from their depths. Deep silence tagged behind her words.

"I'll leave the lantern so's ye won't be tripping yer way into the house."

"I'll be in soon. Just want to watch the moon come up." In truth, I wanted to give Tate five more minutes to prove Granny wrong.

An hour or so later I folded the blanket, abandoning my post, relenting to the thickening cold. I heard a car and wondered if it was Mr. Pehacek's Packard or Mr. Herndon's pickup. I turned, seeing an auto roll to a stop in front of Granny's house. I stood with lantern in hand, mesmerized by head beams that spun tunnels of light into the darkness. Then I heard the metal click of a door unlatching. An alpine of a man unfolded his body and stood behind the car door without speaking. His hair blended with the night, even as his persistent gaze discharged an arrow straight into my heart.

"Emma?" he called.

I set the lantern on the floor, my mute self gaping at the vision before me. It was as though a seizure struck, enfeebling me from head to foot. My mouth wouldn't spout its multitude of words, my hand wouldn't wave, my nailed-down feet wouldn't budge. The only working part of my body was a heart that sputtered and stalled, threatening to quit altogether.

"It's Tate, Emma. May I come up? I need to talk to you."

My head must have bobbed, for he slammed the door and bounded up the stairs as though there were two steps, not ten. He stopped just short of bowling me over.

What happened next was a blur. Somehow, we were in each other's arms, his mouth covering mine as it had in my dreams of years past.

When we parted at last, my lips pulsed tender and swollen, yet I wanted more. More time in his embrace, more pressing our bodies together; more shared breaths and pounding heartbeats. I knew a lifetime in Tate's arms wouldn't satisfy my hunger.

I gripped his arms, my legs too unstable to stand on their own. Rock-hard muscles burgeoned with inflexibility. *He must still be working at the docks.* Tate's voice was shaky, but oh, the smile I heard in its deepness.

"Oh, Emma—you're even more beautiful than I dreamed you'd be."

I released my grip and finger-combed long straggles of hair that had wrapped my face and neck. I knew I composed a frightful sight.

"It's time you knew my name, Tate. It's Emma Grace Falin, but you can call me Emma if you want to. I'm sorry I never told you my last name, back when we were—"

"I've been thinking about us a lot, Emma, and I don't want to waste a minute on apologies. We're together again. That's all that matters to me."

I thought my heart would crack open from all the happiness his smile shoveled into it.

"Let's go inside, Tate. Out of the cold." I wanted him in the light where I could view him until I was filled to the top and overflowing.

"Cold? What cold? There's not an inch of me that's cold right now, sweetheart. I've been on fire since the day I saw you on the street corner."

"Wha—"

"I'll tell you all about it later. Right now, we have a lot of catching up to do." He smiled again, lifting my heart on eagle wings. It seemed my flight might take me straight to the portals of paradise.

We sat on the parlor sofa until well past midnight. I supposed we could have stayed there for a year or more and never tired of each other's company.

As Tate's gaze flowed over me, I studied him as well. His was a striking face—a truly breath-snatching face. Perhaps more handsome than any I had gazed upon. It had an openness that invited me to share its secrets; an appeal that hastened a caress from my fingertips. I moved my hand from his cheek to his shadowed jaw, feeling the stubble of new growth. While I traced my finger over his brow, my gaze fixed on Tate's chocolate eyes. The union of our gazes stilled my heart, for it seemed as though we were one.

"You've got eleven freckles. Did you know that, beautiful?"

Tate's words jarred me. "You've been numbering my freckles?"

"You used to have seventeen. I counted them one day at the beach, when you weren't looking."

I giggled and leaned into Tate, our foreheads melding together like blown glass. It felt good to laugh with the man I feared I had lost forever.

He took my hands in his, surprising me when he lifted my fingertips and covered them with butterfly kisses. His gaze poured over my hand, which appeared half the size of his own. "No rings. Good. I was afraid if I ever found you again, it would be too late—you'd be married, or engaged, or something." As we looked into each other's eyes, I knew I had to tell Tate about Gavin.

"There was a man. We had set our wedding date and everything. But I knew something was wrong with our relationship. When I realized I wasn't in love with Gavin, I broke up with him. Guess I never got over you, Tate. Perhaps that's the reason God led me back to Galveston."

"But why did you leave in the first place? Why did you disappear like that, Emma? I didn't know what to think. Didn't know how to find you. I searched for you like a crazy man—walking the streets—going to our dune every day. Waiting there till late at night."

"Elo came and took me back to Coldwater. My little brother was deathly ill, and my folks wanted me home. I left a note for you in Micah's tin. Had my name and address on it. I hoped you had seen me digging there and you'd remember it later. I couldn't think of any other way to get hold of you, Tate."

Tate shook his head. "It never occurred to me to look for a note. I saw you digging one time, but thought it was just another secret you were keeping from me."

"There were so many things I couldn't share with you back then. But that's all in the past." My hands cupped his face as I gazed into his eyes. He had to know the truth behind my next words. "I came back to God, Tate, and it was just as you said it would be—only better. I've even forgiven myself for Micah's death. I'm happier now than I've ever been."

Tate ducked his head, it seemed in prayer. When he raised his eyes, I saw a glint of tears, but mostly I saw the love in his eyes. "Beyond telling me that you love me—there's nothing on this earth I'd rather hear. Somehow … I knew you'd give God another chance. But—where's home?" he asked. "You mentioned Coldwater. I've never heard of it."

"It's a small town near Brenham, a community of farmers for the most part. I have a big family: Mama and Papa, three married sisters, Elo, my older brother, and my younger brothers, Nathan and Caleb. I told you about Micah—Caleb's twin. He died five years ago."

Tate nodded his head in recollection. Then he straight-eyed me, his face serious and troubled. "So—this Gavin fella—what happened between the two of you? There's something you're not telling me."

I didn't want to spoil the night, this magical night, with thoughts of Gavin; with remembrances of what he had done. Anymore, I tried not to think about Gavin at all.

"Later on I'll tell you everything you want to know, but not tonight."

"Promise? Just know that when you're ready … I'll be here." Tate tasted my lips again, his warm breath sliding moist whispers into my mouth. "I'm just glad he's out of the picture." He leaned back, studying my face. Perhaps my recollections had penned a bit of sadness upon my features. "I don't need to worry about him, do I, Emma?"

"No, you don't. He's not part of my life anymore—and never will be again. What about you? Are you involved with anyone?" My heart ticked off a thousand beats while I waited for his answer.

Tate sucked in a breath, his eyes narrowing as he shook his head and sighed with heaviness. "Wish I could tell you there's no one in my life." He seemed to take pity on me, seeing the spurt of tears in my eyes and the slump of disappointment in my shoulders. "I don't love her, Emma. Never have, though I've tried to talk myself into it many times. I just never could give her my heart." He smiled and leaned over, kissing my nose. "It's you I love, Emma Grace Falin." His finger thumped a place on his chest. "There's no one who can fill the spot right here—but you."

"Know when I first fell in love with you?" Tate asked. I shook my head, joy bells clanging such a noise in my head I feared I'd miss Tate's words. "I fell in love with you shortly after we met that first night. I knew when it happened. I just didn't know what to do about it. I had never been in love before. I prayed about it. I mean, gosh, you were just a kid, and I was barely a man. Know what God told me to do?" My head shook as though swinging on loose hinges. "He told me he would take care of everything, and for me not to worry about it. 'Just give her your true love.' That's all I had to do, he said." Tate laughed and shook his head. "Boy—he sure took his sweet time making it right between us, didn't he?" I bit my lower lip and smiled. I was too happy to talk. "I was scared, Emma." Tate's brows knitted together and his smile disappeared. "I was sixteen, you were only thirteen. I was confused and afraid I'd do something wrong. Then you upped and went away. Guess I thought my falling in love with you had somehow caused your disappearance. My life really went into a tailspin then, but after three or four years of not hearing from you, I started trying to make a life without you. That's when I began dating Miriam. Miriam Caldwell."

"Who is she?" I didn't want to know, yet I had to know.

"She's the owner's niece."

"The dock owner? His niece?"

"No ... no. I forgot—you don't know I'm an ironworker now. Remember the day I didn't make it to the beach?"

"How could I ever forget? I waited for you till daylight was gone, praying you'd show up. I had to leave early the next morning."

"I'm sorry. I did show up, but not until about seven thirty or eight that night. On the way home from work I passed a man, all dressed up in fancy duds. His car had a flat tire, so I offered to change it for him. I was already filthy from the docks. Anyway, guess he took a liking to me. Asked me to come over to his house. Told me he wanted to talk to me about becoming an apprentice at the ironworks factory. I didn't know I was talking to Mr. McDonough himself—owner of The McDonough Ironworks Company—until we introduced ourselves a while later. I jumped at the chance. I've always liked working with my hands."

"I've still got the crane you carved me." I felt shy mentioning it to Tate, though I didn't know why.

"I'd forgotten the crane. I'll carve some more things for you. Anything you want. Oh, by the way ... is this your necklace?" Tate smiled as he dug into his pocket and pulled out Mama's locket. I gasped aloud and started bawling uncontrollably. "I found it a few weeks after you left and it's never been out of my sight since then. Somehow—I knew it belonged to you."

Finding Tate and getting Mama's locket back all in the same night. I couldn't fathom so many blessings at one time.

After my emotions settled a bit, I said, "I searched for Mama's locket every time I went to the beach. I can't believe you found it, Tate. Thank you … thank you so much."

"I'm sure I had some help." Tate pulled me to him and slipped the necklace around my neck. "I've been waiting five years to do this. Glad it's back where it belongs."

Tate lifted me onto his lap and curled his arm around my shoulder. We fit together with perfection, our heads touching as we whispered our words of love to each other.

"So—you've been working as an ironworker all this time?"

"Yep. Get to draw designs and craft them into iron and steel. Made shop foreman last year. There's eight men working under me now, but there's so much work, we could easily hire three or four more workers."

"It broke my heart when I couldn't tell you good-bye, Tate. But there was no way to write or call you. I didn't know your last name."

Tate slipped his arm around my shoulder and drew me close. "I think maybe God wanted me to give you a little time to grow up, darling. He didn't want me robbing the cradle, you know."

As Tate looked into my eyes, his gaze stretched its sizzling fingers across my heart, warming me against the chill in Granny's parlor. His eyes sparked a memory: the black stone I'd placed in Micah's tin, but which now lay inside my suitcase, along with his other treasures. Tate's eyes made me think of the obsidian stone, for his eyes were dark now— midnight-black with passion, and they glistened with an aura of love.

"I want you to marry me, Emma. Soon. Very soon. Then we'll share the same last name."

Unable to answer Tate with words, I nodded my head and swallowed back a trickle of tears. After clearing my throat, I said, "And what name will we share, Tate?"

"Fletcher, darling. You'll be Mrs. Tate Fletcher."

By the time Tate left that night, he knew why I no longer walked with a crutch, and why I had been so secretive when first we met. He knew about my nieces and nephews, Caleb's love for baseball, and Elo's skill at hunting, farming, fishing, and working horses. He also heard about Nathan's passion for learning, about my three beautiful sisters and their husbands, and all about Mama and Papa. In turn, he told me about the death of his beloved Mrs. K, and the house she had willed him, about his crew at work and his friends at church, and about the girl he would break up with tomorrow.

Tate insisted we petition Papa for his blessing and his permission to marry, but neither of us wanted to ask him by way of a long-distance phone call. So we made plans to drive to Coldwater during the Thanksgiving holidays two weeks from now. On the Sunday after Thanksgiving, Tate would return to Galveston and work until the Christmas respite. And then—we would get married on Christmas Eve.

I had wished to say my vows in Christ's Chapel as The Ollys had, but with the buzz about Gavin and me still fresh in the minds of Coldwater residents, I decided the wedding should take place in our home.

Neither of us wanted to say good-bye on the first night of our togetherness. Perhaps we held the fear that something might happen as before; something that would keep us apart.

As I stood in the doorway and watched Tate drive away, tears spilled from my eyes. But they were joy tears: for finding him again; for loving him with every parcel of my being.

After he left, I climbed into bed, too excited to sleep. I said my prayers, wondering all the while how a person could properly thank the good Lord for such a bountiful gift as Tate Fletcher. As I lay there, waiting for sleep to overtake me, I weighed the name Emma Grace Fletcher against other names I'd heard, and judged it the prettiest of all. But the name Mrs. Tate Fletcher was even a mite more beautiful.

# Forty-four

"But—it's beautiful, Tate. I can't believe you don't want to keep it."

Tate glanced around the room, studying the same images I viewed: dark walls, curving staircase, dully-lit chandelier, and heavy window hangings.

"It's just too dark and dreary. Maybe we should sell it and find a smaller place; something that's not so hard to keep up."

I snickered at the expression on Tate's face, which was somewhat like the look of a child who had wandered too near a soiled diaper. I stretched on tiptoes and received his kiss. "What's the real reason, Tate? Why don't you want to live here?"

"You know … I came to love Mrs. K like she was my real mother. I just don't want to be reminded of her all the time. Know what I mean?"

"I have a thought: We could brighten up the house with a little paint, maybe change out the rugs and put in lighter carpet. And get new drapes. Definitely get some new drapes. It would look like an entirely different house." I peered at dark brown paneling, walnut, most likely, envisioning the walls with a swash of sunlight streaming through. "I've got it—we could tear out this wall and install French doors, strip off that old wallpaper on the ceiling, and maybe—"

"Hold on a minute. This house is just too big, Emma. I don't want you spending every spare minute cleaning this monstrosity."

When the thought came, it struck like a bolt of lightning. I could almost smell the singe of electricity; hear the unnatural sizzle as flames licked the heavy drapes into melted puddles of velvet.

"Tate—will we be poor? I mean, will we need to be careful with our money, or—"

"Money's one thing we don't have to worry about, sweetheart. I've been saving and investing my income for years now. Besides, when we sell the house, we'll have quite a nest egg."

"I don't want to sell the house, Tate. I think it's lovely. But, you're right, it is too much for me to take care of … by myself." I grinned at Tate—like the proverbial Cheshire cat, I'm afraid.

"What're you cooking up in that beautiful head of yours? Huh?" Tate crossed his arms, his scowl so pathetically artificial, I burst out laughing.

"Why—to hire Sadie, of course. She and the children could come over every day and help with the cleaning. We could even turn one of the bedrooms into a playroom for the children. You'll love her kids, Tate."

"If they're anything like Nobie, I think we may have a problem."

"Oh, Tate—Nobie's the dearest of them all. You'll see, darling. You'll see."

Our last two weeks together in Galveston winged by like a hungry bat chasing a mosquito. We packed our afternoons, evenings, and weekends full, not caring what we did, so long as we did it together.

We returned to Kempner Park and danced atop the gazebo, though no music accompanied us this time. We walked to our dune and admired the sea, dreaming of the day we'd travel to faraway ports. Tate took me to my first moving picture show: *A Farewell to Arms.* We snuggled our heads together, sharing a box of popcorn and whispering secrets of love. Viewing the movie was like reading my favorite book, only with living, moving pictures to better describe the scenes. I couldn't wait to tell my family about the movie, as none of them had been to a theater.

The Saturday before Thanksgiving was an Indian summer sort of day, spilling over with fiery sunshine and breezes that had lost their bite. Tate and I drove across the causeway to Pelican Island, where we fished from a pier, picnicked on the beach, and waded in the bay.

'Twas not the first time Tate had seen my leg in its undressed state, but that sighting had been five years earlier. I felt unashamed as I held onto his arm, water covering my bareness to the knees. Afterward, Tate dried my legs with a cloth napkin, and surely took his own sweet time doing it. I wondered what he thought when he stroked my shorter leg, gentleness ill-disguising the tremble in his hands. I knew not what I'd do if pity fueled his shakes, for pity was as unacceptable to me as the thought of losing Tate's love. I held my breath, waiting for him to speak.

"Does your leg ever trouble you, sweetheart?"

"No, never. Well—maybe if I've been walking on it all day."

"It would be my greatest pleasure to massage it for you—every night for the rest of our lives."

"I love you, Tate."

"I love you more."

Tate took me to a fancy restaurant where I had my first taste of boiled shrimp. I decided I much preferred Mama's fried chicken. At the end of each lovely day, we sat in Granny's parlor and dreamed our dreams together. Perhaps it is true that you can unveil a man's true character in the dark of night. It was in the darkened parlor, during a beautiful, passionate kiss, that I discovered Tate's moral constitution, as well as his fortitude.

"Sugar—we can't do this anymore. We can't ... well, we can't keep kissing and holding each other like this. It's getting harder and harder to stop ... with just ..."

I supposed I wore a dumbfounded look as Tate further explained our situation. "The good Lord gave you back to me, Emma. The best way I can show my thanks is by keeping my hands off of you until we're married."

Tate stood and walked to the stove. He bent over; lifting a chunk of wood from the firebox, shoving it into the iron belly, clunking the door shut. He dusted his hands on his denims and turned to me. "The one thing I'm not going to do is bring shame on you or myself. I can't rightly ask your papa to give us his blessings if I'm not deserving of his trust. Do you understand what I'm saying, Emma?" I nodded, certain I did know of what he spoke.

"You're saying that we love God and each other too much to go against his teachings. Right?"

Tate nodded. "You hit the nail right on the head, sweetheart. Do you know how much I love you?"

"Yes … I think I really am beginning to understand how much you love me."

# Forty-five

A miracle happened during the Thanksgiving holidays. Elo bonded with Tate as he had never bonded with anyone—except Papa, of course. The two grew so close, I found myself chasing after them like a new puppy, barking up a storm, but capturing only enough attention to garner a glance or pat on the head. Oh, Tate threw me a bone from time to time: a wink, a secret smile, or a quick smooch behind the porch. But prefer my company over Elo's, he did not. I thought about buying a roll of Tanglefoot Fly Paper to spread over Tate's pathway. I was that desperate to snare his attention and spend more time with him. After all, he would be returning to Galveston in two days. We'd not see each other again until Christmas. Oh well, at least I had Tweaker to love on.

"I'll say one thing, Emma Grace. He sure brings out the stars in your eyes." Mama laughed as she pulled an embroidery needle through the pillow covering.

The back door slammed. I glanced up as two giants strode into the parlor, the blond one leading the way. Elo halted a few feet from the arched entrance.

Tate marched up to me, stooped over, and sowed a kiss upon my cheek. He squatted; his eyes filled with mischief, as if he had sneaked a piece of Mama's custard pie and swallowed it whole. The effect of his pocket-size smile stretched to the pit of my stomach, drawing up a hunger for our wedding night, when the two of us would become one flesh. I pretended his presence didn't buoy me to euphoric heights, and kept my eyes on the dress I hemmed. But I had never been successful at holding back my gaze when it wished to rove elsewhere. I looked into Tate's beautiful eyes and melted.

"Let me guess … You're going to buy a pickup like Elo's, right?"

"Close enough. Elo and I are going to the auction over in Burton, and afterward, if there's enough daylight left, we're going to stop by Lake Somerville and do a little fishing. Don't look for us till late." Another quick peck on the cheek and off the two went, wide-straddled paces leading them to the doorway before I could gather my wits to speak.

"What are you going to buy at the auction, Elo?" Elo stopped, turned, and stared at me as though I had called him a bad name.

"Elo's going to help me select a thoroughbred stallion; one that's willful and high-strung, like Samson. I figure if I get a horse that's every bit as headstrong as you are, I can teach both of you to behave at the same time." Tate chuckled and walked away, while I sputtered and fumed, racking my brain for a good retort. The giants' laughter trailed after them—much as I had scampered behind them earlier in the day.

I caught a glimpse of movement in the corner of my eye, turned, and saw Mama's shoulders in a feverish quake. Her embroidery hoop concealed her face, but I knew she was having quite a laugh behind that cloth.

"What's so funny, Mama?"

She coughed out the loud chortle she'd been holding back. "You've got your work cut out for you, dear. You're marrying quite a handful—which will make it a very even match, indeed."

Wasn't Mama always right? I grinned, knowing I wouldn't have it any other way.

The next month dragged by. I spent my days sewing, reading Tate's letters, packing my belongings, cooking, and working with the animals.

Holly and Molly came over and baked Christmas goodies, and for reasons unknown to me, asked if I would watch the kids while they helped Mama clean the house from attic to porch. I couldn't believe my good fortune.

On the days I didn't receive a phone call or letter from Tate, I was snappish and unpleasant to be around. At such times, I would ride Tate's horse, Pocahontas, whom he called Poco. He fell in love with the chestnut mare the moment he spied her at the auction in Burton. Overnight, Tate and Elo became partners in the horse business. The first colt resulting from the pairing of Samson and Poco would be Elo's, and a fair trade it would be for all the feeding, grooming, and training he would give the colt. After the first foal, the men would jointly own all offspring, and try to build up the herd by buying new stock. Tate's main contribution was in financing the partnership.

On my better days I treated the family like royalty, knowing time and distance would soon separate us. The newly installed phone in the kitchen eased my mind a bit, but still, I dreaded the parting and gave way to tears more often than I should.

Three events shaped our December: Polly's first visit home in two years, the wedding, and Christmas.

Tate's arrival, late in the evening of December 22, both thrilled and shocked me, for he wasn't scheduled to arrive until the next night. He brought Granny with him. After helping her into the house, and after being introduced to the rest of the family, he grabbed my hand and jacket, and off we raced to his car.

He drove to a far pasture and parked on the fence line road. For a few moments, we just stared at one another. As we settled into each other's arms, I discovered we could express our happiness without words.

On Christmas Eve morning, I awakened with a start. At ten o'clock Tate and I would join our lives together. I slipped to my knees beside the bed, greeting my heavenly Father with thanksgiving; for this day, this season of his Son's birth, and for the Falin flock gathered within these walls, among whom Granny was numbered. I thanked him for my plenteous life, and for the young man he had sent five years earlier to help turn my feet from the path of destruction. My grateful heart could have remained in praise all day, for untold blessings that had reordered my dark nights into glorious morns.

*Joy really does come in the morning.*

Too nervous to eat breakfast, I bathed and slipped into Holly's wedding gown. It fit me to perfection, thanks to Mama's skill with a needle and thread. She had sewn a row of fine lace along the scooped neckline, and around the white pique hem. Each of The Ollys had trimmed Holly's dress to suit their own tastes. I chose only one additional adornment: a lace bow attached to the waist at the back of the dress. The long ties widened at the hem, and would form a decorative train when I walked to Tate and became his wife.

Having washed my hair the night before, I placed a wreath of flowers on my head and adjusted it so that the red poinsettia petals were centered precisely. Polly had weaved some of Mama's potted greenery into strips of dried vine, and then tied the vines into a garland of exceptional beauty. I turned my back to the dresser and looked in the hand mirror. Waves of light-brown hair flowed to my waist. I giggled, recalling the young girl who had bemoaned her brown curliness; the girl who hated Mama's scissors because they cropped her hair to look like lamb's wool, or worse, like a boy's hair.

*Tate loves my hair.*

I stopped midway down the stairs and looked for Tate. Pastor Emery stood in the parlor archway with his back to me. Other guests, and my family, of course, talked together in small groups while they awaited the bride's appearance. Nathan talked with Josephine Emery, the preacher's daughter, and Caleb looked to be trading whoppers with the rowdy

Aarsgard offspring. As I observed my sisters and their husbands, huddling and laughing together, it struck me that The Ollys grew more beautiful with each passing year. I noticed Elo then, standing with our newest neighbors, the Farleys. I pursed my lips and hoped I wouldn't laugh aloud. I should have known that Ellabeth Farley, their beautiful eighteen-year-old daughter, would catch Elo's eye. My oldest brother looked thunderstruck.

*Elo? Thunderstruck?*

Papa had cleared the room, save for a few chairs for the older guests. Ours was a stand-up wedding, and afterward we would serve a buffet lunch. I envisioned it now: people spilling into the yard, onto the porch, filling the kitchen, living room, and the area beneath the stairwell, most likely. 'Twas good that the day had dawned with a feeling of mildness about it: the sun shining its most spectacular best, and the wind too lazy to be a nuisance.

I slipped the whooping crane Tate carved for me into my bouquet of flowers: *Something old.*

A brand-new penny rubbed the sole of my foot—for good luck, everyone said. But I knew that luck was just a word. God was the Father of all blessings; all good things came from him: *Something new.*

I fingered the locket Tate gave me on the night of our reunion. He'd found it on the shore—something I had been unable to do, though I'd searched for it every time I went to the beach. Tate told me he'd not been without it since the day he spied its shininess in the sand. Neither of us could understand how he'd known the locket was mine. But it hadn't been mine to keep, just as it had never been Mama's to keep. Someday I would unlatch the necklace and place it around my daughter's neck and the circle would continue. *Something borrowed.*

High on my thighs, The Ollys' blue satin garters held my stockings secure: *Something blue.*

I stepped into the parlor. Tate spied me first, and we smiled at each other. Two long strides brought him to my side. I hoped my mouth didn't gape, for he'd never looked more handsome. His looks were those of a fashion model: navy suit, white shirt, and pinstriped tie—a complement to his dark hair and powerful physique. I wondered if he bought the suit for our wedding, or if looking like the King of England was a common habit of his. His hair carried a sheen, slicked back as it was, most likely to control those pesky curls that had a habit of riding his forehead. A subtle scent of pomade lingered in the air, masculine and tempting. I glanced around, wondering if our guests recognized the glow of love and tell-tale look of longing that had to be evident on my face. I felt it now, flooding my cheeks and filling my heart with warmth.

Tate looked at me as though I was the fairest damsel in the land. I supposed, to him, I was. He whispered in my ear, "What do you think, sweetheart? Does the most beautiful girl in the world still want to marry me? There's time to back out, you know." Tate's long fingers slid down my cheek and tilted my head to receive his kiss. The room seemed to spin, voices receding to faint murmurs as our lips joined. For that moment, it was just the two of us, sealing our hearts and our love for eternity.

Life with Tate Fletcher was surely going to be an exciting, unforgettable journey.

"Have you said your good-byes, Emma? The car's packed and ready to go. So am I." Tate's gaze slid into mine, a long, slow plunge that melted my toenails. "Are you hating to leave, sweet girl? You look a little … perturbed."

"I just have one more person to say good-bye to, Tate." Though his eyes asked a question, he nodded his head and smiled a smile that revved my heart into a hard, fast beat.

"Take your time, beautiful. We'll spend the night in Brenham. Just twenty miles down the road … and then you'll truly be mine."

Should Tate live to be a hundred, I doubted he would ever understand the thrill I knew when he spoke those words of ownership to me. It's what I had been secretly dreaming of since the day we danced in the gazebo.

# Forty-six

I had not walked the solitary trail in five years. Shame had kept me from it.

I spied it now, beyond the field—the hill of our loved ones' rest. I turned my feet from the cow path and headed for the knoll, leaving my four-legged companions behind. The old bossy lumbered on down the trail, her young'un close behind. As the mama cow swatted flies with her straw-stiff tail, her enormous eyes focused on the clearing up ahead where a scattering of hay awaited her and her baby.

The sun dangled low over the horizon, hanging by a thread, it seemed. Sunlight spread a blanket over the land, lighting up the far side of the knoll, but casting the near side in shadows. Dying sunbeams outlined the markers that sat atop our grassy dome. I saw their shapes from afar: rectangular gravestones, two-armed wooden crosses, and square slabs of granite.

Winter's stubbled grass crackled beneath my shoes as I mounted the hill. On the way to Micah's gravesite, I passed weathered monuments, aged to gray by years of crosscurrents and seasons of rain. Some of the engravings were unreadable, for they'd been too oft traced by the windy finger of time.

Micah's cross stood straight and tall, an etching of dark wood against a pale orange sky. His marker did not list, as other markers did. Nor did his mound have the haphazard look of a blue jay's nest, as some did. Micah's place was free of weeds and unruly stubble, cleaned and picked over like pecan meat stripped from the shell.

*Mama's still taking care of her baby.*

As I circled the site, I spied a rolled-up rug that Mama must have tucked behind Micah's marker. *For her knees, when she weeds his bed.* I unrolled the rug, laid it near the cross, and sat down. Leaning over, I rested my head against the wooden beams and whispered words of love to my brother.

"Hi, sweet Micah. I brought you some treasures. Been saving them for you a long time."

My fingers trembled as I opened Micah's tin and removed his possessions: the black obsidian stone, Papa's pocketwatch, bits of eggshell from the turtle clutch, the perfect sand dollar, an eagle feather, five sparkly creek stones, and the arrowhead Elo had polished to glass. There were other things as well. I carefully lifted Tate's whooping crane from my pocket and added it to the pile.

"I think Tate would want you to have this, Micah. It's the beautiful bird my … husband carved for me. He's wonderful, sweetie. You'd really like him."

I hummed some of Micah's favorite tunes as I dug a trench in the grass and loam. Then I placed his belongings in the ground and buried them at the foot of his headstone. The cross would protect them.

"We miss you so much, little brother. Caleb doesn't know it, but sometimes I see him tapping out messages to you with his fingers. I've even spied him talking to you as though you were right by his side. I know he tells you things he won't tell the rest of us. But I want you to know that we're all doing fine. Mama and Papa aren't so sad now. I think it helped when I told them about seeing you in heaven. It did their hearts good to hear how happy you are … and to know how much you love Jesus."

As I talked to Micah, I plucked marbles of dirt and stray twigs from his gravesite, swept there by an afternoon wind. I swiped away my tears and kissed my fingertips. Then I pressed them against the name on the cross.

*Micah Roan Falin.*

"In the twinkling of an eye I'll be with you again, sweet Micah. I'll wrap you in my arms as I do in my dreams at night. Just a while longer and we'll all be together in your beautiful home." As I blotted my tears with the hem of my petticoat, I felt a shaky smile spread across my face.

"But until then, little brother—I've got a lot of living to do."

# Readers' Guide

*for Personal Reflection or*
*Group Discussion*

# Readers' Guide

Emma Grace Falin, like many of us, is trying to find her way in an imperfect world. In deciding to face her past and the guilt she still feels, she actually finds that God is at work in her life "for the good." We all have past situations and broken relationships we must face in our walk with God. He wants to bring us revival and renew our understanding of his love and hope for our lives. As you answer the following questions, think about areas in your own life that can be healed through the power of God's revival in your life.

1. With every good book, there is a good title. What is the significance of *Coldwater Revival* in the context of the book? Who finds revival? What impact does this revival have on the lives of the Falin family?

2. Guilt can keep us from enjoying our present lives. What were the effects of guilt on Emma Grace? How did it shape her perspective on her relationships and circumstances? What effects has guilt had on your life? How have you dealt with guilt?

3. We long to find peace in the deepest places of our souls, but sometimes it can be a most difficult road to go down. What leads Emma Grace to search out peace in her life? What does she have to do to find her place of peace? Where do you need peace in your life? How can you follow Emma Grace's example of seeking out peace?

4. "Life was a sea of tangled memories—both good and bad. Barren was the possibility of unraveling one from the other." How were Emma Grace's good and bad memories entwined in her day-to-day life? How did untangling them help her appreciate and enjoy her life more?

5. The Falins, like most families, told stories over and over again about their children growing up. What is a story that your family tells about you growing up? How does it make you feel when they tell the story again? What significance does it have for you and your family?

6. It seems Emma Grace was never confident about who she was. What are some examples of how she struggled with who she was and her place in her family? How did her family try to make her feel confident and secure? How have you dealt with insecurity about who you are?

7. Sometimes, as with the Falin family in chapter 5, we can see how a good thing went wrong when we look back on a time in our lives. Think about a time in your life when a situation that seemed best for you, a friend, or family, resulted in a tragedy. How did God work on both sides of the experience to turn tragedy into good?

8. It's hard to be younger and see your older siblings grow up and move on. Emma Grace always seemed to want to be like The Ollys. What memories do you have of growing up? What was the hardest "grown up" event or thing to wait for? How did waiting affect your relationship with your older siblings and family?

9. Children have vivid imaginations. In this book we witness this when the twins pretend they are going to the North Pole in the middle of summer. What games of imagination do you remember playing as a child? What props were used? Where did you go to play the game?

10. God often uses the people we're closest to for communicating his will for us. How did God use Emma Grace's family to lead her in her relationship with Gavin? Has God used your family in a similar way? If so, how did he lead you to his will through them?

11. Emma Grace had to make hard decisions to find healing in her life. Why is seeking healing so difficult? Think of some characters in the Bible who found healing. What did they have to face? What have you had to face to receive healing in your life?

12. Everyone in the Falin family had his or her own way of dealing with grief. How did each family member deal with loss? What is healthy and not so healthy about the ways he or she chose to grieve?

13. Looking back on childhood mistakes, we sometimes apply adult perspective in judging how a situation could have been different. How does Emma Grace do this to herself? What did she hear her family say to her about the accident? How did this impact her and her future?

14. Emma Grace has doubts about Gavin and whether she should marry him. What do you see in Gavin that seems suspicious? What did Emma Grace initially see in Gavin? Do you think her fears are justified?

15. Elo seems, at times, to be unemotional and uncaring, yet he is always there for Emma Grace as a playmate, defender, and brother. What does he do or say that shows how much he loves Emma Grace and his family? Who in your life has "looked out" for you?

16. Mama and Papa Falin seem to be wise, caring parents. What are some examples of their parenting skills? How do they take into

consideration the different personalities of each of their children? What lessons can you learn about parenting from them?

17. "Know this, little one. You hold a place in my heart that no one else can fill. You always have … always will. It's tearing me apart to go off and leave you like this, but for now, it's the only way I know to help you. Your family loves you, Emma Grace. I love you. Don't ever forget that. Just try to get well … for all of us." What do you think was going through Papa's mind as he said good-bye to Emma Grace? What does this scene show about Papa and his love for his family, especially Emma Grace?

18. The necessity of leaving Emma Grace with someone else to get well was hard for the Falins. Yet they knew that if anyone could relate to the loss that Emma Grace felt, it was Granny. How are Granny's and Emma Grace's grief alike? How are they different? Compare and contrast how they deal with their losses. Why is Granny's house the best place for Emma Grace? How does each come to respect the other?

19. Though Tate knew that he loved Emma Grace long before she knew that she loved him, he was willing to wait for God's timing. Which of his actions show his willingness to wait for her to discover her love for him? How is Tate different from Gavin?

20. Love always finds a way. How does love find Emma Grace in the midst of tragedy and hurt? What are the circumstances that God uses to bring Tate and Emma Grace together? God is making a way for his love in your life too. What have you seen him do in your life that affirms his love for you? How can you be more open to him working in your life through circumstances and relationships?

# The Word at Work Around the World

A vital part of Cook Communications Ministries is our international outreach, Cook Communications Ministries International (CCMI). Your purchase of this book, and of other books and Christian-growth products from Cook, enables CCMI to provide Bibles and Christian literature to people in more than 150 languages in 65 countries.

Cook Communications Ministries is a not-for-profit, self-supporting organization. Revenues from sales of our books, Bible curricula, and other church and home products not only fund our U.S. ministry, but also fund our CCMI ministry around the world. One hundred percent of donations to CCMI go to our international literature programs.

CCMI reaches out internationally in three ways:

· Our premier International Christian Publishing Institute (ICPI) trains leaders from nationally led publishing houses around the world.

· We provide literature for pastors, evangelists, and Christian workers in their national language.

· We reach people at risk—refugees, AIDS victims, street children, and famine victims—with God's Word.

## Word Power, God's Power

Faith Kidz, RiverOak, Honor, Life Journey, Victor, NexGen — every time you purchase a book produced by Cook Communications Ministries, you not only meet a vital personal need in your life or in the life of someone you love, but you're also a part of ministering to José in Colombia, Humberto in Chile, Gousa in India, or Lidiane in Brazil. You help make it possible for a pastor in China, a child in Peru, or a mother in West Africa to enjoy a life-changing book. And because you helped, children and adults around the world are learning God's Word and walking in his ways.

Thank you for your partnership in helping to disciple the world. May God bless you with the power of his Word in your life.

*For more information about our international ministries, visit www.ccmi.org.*

Additional copies of *Coldwater Revival*
and other RiverOak titles are available
wherever good books are sold.

If you have enjoyed this book,
or if it has had an impact on your life,
we would like to hear from you.

Please contact us at:

RiverOak Books
Cook Communications Ministries, Dept. 201
4050 Lee Vance View
Colorado Springs, CO 80918

Or visit our Web site:
www.cookministries.com